# A Wolf in Hindelheim

JENNY MAYHEW

 WINDMILL BOOKS

Published by Windmill Books 2014

2 4 6 8 10 9 7 5 3 1

First published in Great Britain in 2013 by Hutchinson

Windmill Books
The Random House Group Limited
20 Vauxhall Bridge Road, London SW1V 2SA

Addresses for companies within The Random House Group Limited can be found at:
www.randomhouse.co.uk/offices.htm

The Random House Group Limited Reg. No. 954009

www.randomhouse.co.uk

A CIP catalogue record for this book
is available from the British Library

ISBN 9780099558972

The Random House Group Limited supports the Forest Stewardship
Council® (FSC®), the leading international forest-certification organisation.
Our books carrying the FSC label are printed on FSC®-certified paper. FSC is
the only forest-certification scheme supported by the leading environmental
organisations, including Greenpeace. Our paper procurement policy
can be found at: www.randomhouse.co.uk/environment

Printed and bound by CPI Group (UK) Ltd, Croydon, CR0 4YY

# A Wolf in Hindelheim

Jenny Mayhew has worked as a television documentary researcher, a film screenwriter and a university lecturer. She has a doctorate in English literature, and lives in Edinburgh. *A Wolf in Hindelheim* is her first novel.

*A Wolf in Hindelheim*

*Hindelheim, South-West Germany.*
*October, 1926.*

# 1.

Something was happening in this place where nothing happened. From a field on the eastern edge of the Pohlmann farm, two herdsmen watched in silence as the vehicle came into view. They had seen the motorcycle and its adjoining sidecar buzzing around the village of Mittelbach and along the lanes down there in the valley – but up here in Hindelheim? That was new. The herders would need to consult their memories, and each other, and maybe even their wives, later on, about when – if ever – a police vehicle had last come clattering up the old track, all the way out here.

It was a fine, dry morning, but patches of recent rain still stood in the track's deeper grooves, spilling watery mud as the wheels of the motorcycle sliced through it. The rider, a young deputy constable, was struggling with tensed arms to steer past the farm entrance when a shout from his passenger, accompanied by a gloved slap on the door of the sidecar, brought them to a jerking halt. An older man's head leaned out from the sidecar. Holding his cap in place with one hand, he vomited into the mud.

A mild wind was blowing in the direction of the dairy yard,

from which a dog trotted out, nostrils twitching, to investigate. It was joined a few moments later by Matthias Pohlmann, a buck-toothed rake of a man with a wild, infant smile. As the motorcycle spluttered onwards, Matthias and his dog examined what the policeman had left behind. 'Hey, look at this,' Matthias called over his shoulder to his niece, as she turned out of the milking parlour. 'Guess what the constable had for breakfast?'

Gretchen Pohlmann came to the gate and stared over it with her cool green eyes as the motorcycle climbed another incline and passed out of sight behind a hedgerow. She was fifteen, and magnificent in the pregnancy which everyone could see and no one could fathom. Several farm hands eyed her as she turned back into the yard, each of them suspecting the next man of having planted the seed in her belly.

✠

Half an hour later, in a cloakroom under the staircase of the Koenigs' house, Constable Theodore Hildebrandt of the Mittelbach rural police substation washed the bitter taste from his mouth using a cake of oily soap which seemed to have been made, to judge from the look and taste of it, from lard boiled up with herbs and the ends of old candles. He noticed, without surprise, that the drying cloth had been trimmed at the edges; that the wallpaper was mildewed; and that what natural light might otherwise have entered the cloakroom was obscured by ivy growing over the window. Gone were the days when households like this one would have had new towels or shop-bought soap.

He did not want to look in the mirror – but nor did he want to follow the public, noisy retching that had accompanied his arrival in Hindelheim with the further humiliation of a stained collar; so he looked. Staring back at him was a bilious face, almost skeletal at the cheekbones, with a scar running downwards from the corner of one eye and disappearing under his collar. The eyes, which had seen four decades and a carnival of suffering, looked startled and somewhat amused to find themselves peering out of their over-emphatic sockets into the world of the living.

'You don't scare me,' Theodore told his reflection. He was lying.

Using his good arm to open the cloakroom door, the constable stepped into the gloom of the hall and heard a woman's voice call out.

'Here! Come here!'

Shuffling forward until he could see down the length of the corridor, Theodore Hildebrandt caught sight of a woman's figure silhouetted against what must be the back door. The door was open, and the daylight beyond obscured the details of her face – but he could see that she was young, or at least short, and seemed to be wearing flannel trousers above boots with rounded, almost clownish ends. She looked at him.

He was still wondering what she wanted, when she called again. 'Here, come on!'

A clattering sound surprised him from the other direction, and he turned to see a dog running down the stairs – a dull brown, skinny thing. It hurtled past the constable's legs, down the corridor towards its owner. A moment later, the woman and her dog disappeared outside, leaving Theodore feeling dim and frustrated, as if she had thrown a ball at him, and he had failed to catch it.

His duty lay in the other direction, where he had left his deputy in the parlour, taking details from one Johanna Koenig-Müller. It was Johanna's husband, Heinrich Müller, who had summoned them by telephone early this morning. It was their baby who was missing. Constable Theodore Hildebrandt should be listening to the fears, pleas and suspicions of the infant's anxious parents.

3

But at the threshold of the parlour, the constable paused and looked back down the corridor, past the carved wooden stair-rail and the faded green wallpaper, towards the back door, where the woman with the dog had appeared and then disappeared. By holding the door open for a moment, she had let in a dose of autumn: the air, now tinged with woodsmoke, promised invigorating skies beyond. In this dark house with its stifling atmosphere of loss, the young woman seemed to have found a means of escape. She was living and moving while the rest of the household seemed to stand still, worn down, waiting. Theodore did not know the young woman's name, but he knew that he must find out where she had gone.

Hovering in the parlour doorway, where he was hidden from view by a thick oak door that stood ajar, the constable could hear his deputy, Klaus, asking the obvious questions: *Was this where the baby was last seen? Where exactly . . . ? What time was her cot found to be . . . ? And you've asked your neighbours . . . ?* 'Of course we have,' the woman's voice cut in, sharp with anxiety. Johanna Müller was evidently a force to be reckoned with, in her moment of crisis, and Theodore guessed that Klaus would be daunted by the interview. Good. Let him manage it. The deputy had recently asked for more substantial duties than driving and note-taking. Here was his chance.

A rattle of china on the other side of the door suggested the arrival of coffee, which made the constable linger for another moment. He had emptied his stomach on the way into Hindelheim, and could not be sure of filling it again before the evening, as they had several more visits to make before returning to Mittelbach. As the smell hit his nostrils, Theodore Hildebrandt felt his stomach lurch with hunger. But he ought to resist. Pouring bitter coffee into his empty, spasming guts would be a mistake with certain consequences. And besides, other appetites were now awakened. Hungering for fresh air and new company, he turned on slow, uneven feet, and started for the back door.

A trail of smoke rose on the far side of the kitchen garden. It beckoned Theodore past thinning herbs and yellowed rhubarb, down a path between lichen-covered outhouses of various sizes. The fringes of the path smelled of rotting vegetation. A few more, limping paces took the constable to a cleared area on the edge of an orchard, where the crackling smoke sent up from a bonfire slowed as it drifted away through the branches of apple trees and over the fence into the encircling wood.

She had her back to him, dragging a long, spindly branch onto the burning pile. Pausing to pick up a fallen apple, she inspected it for damage, took two large bites and then hurled the core away from her. As the dog pelted after it, barking, she caught sight of the constable and stood still, watching him approach. Her cheeks bulged with half-chewed apple flesh. As he got nearer, Theodore could see that the smoke, or perhaps the brisk autumnal air, had reddened the tip of her nose.

Despite a plain, rather sombre face, something about the young woman was not quite docile. She put Theodore in mind of his first horse, which could kick out or bolt for no apparent reason. He stepped carefully towards the fire, into her conjuring circle. Her eyes were fixed on him, deciding whether to allow the intrusion.

The dog bolted towards him from the apple trees. It was the same lank creature that had passed him indoors – a mongrel of medium size, with a short coat stretched over its hungry frame. Removing his cap, Constable Hildebrandt held it ready to whip the animal's nose if need be. 'Nasty-looking dog you've got there,' he said.

It gave a shrill, three-note whine. The woman lowered her hand to soothe the dog, while keeping her eyes on the constable. She replied, 'He's not used to praise.'

Although there was no smile to indicate it, the woman had found the playfulness in Theodore Hildebrandt's remark. He took it as a good sign, even an invitation. 'You're assuming I meant it as a compliment,' he said. Now that he was close to her, the constable decided he had been wrong about her face. It was not plain but still – a different thing. Behind the pale, unmoving surface, a rapid assessment was taking place. Theodore hoped he would pass the test.

'It makes no difference how you meant it,' she said. 'The Kaiser decides for himself how to interpret what humans say.' She scratched at the dog's meagre fur. 'He thinks you took off your cap as a mark of respect to him.'

'*The Kaiser*?' It was a perverse name for this scrawny mutt.

'He was the emperor of the litter,' she countered.

'Well there's a coincidence. So was I.' Theodore risked a smile. He knew what his smile looked like – not pretty. 'And what's your name?'

'Ute,' she replied. A coil of smoke from the bonfire rose up beside them, catching her in the eye. She passed a hand quickly across her face, transferring a smudge of dirt from her fingers to the otherwise milk-white skin. The speed of the movement, con-strasting with her still expression, held the constable's attention. 'I'm married to Peter Koenig,' she explained, blinking to clear her eyes. 'Johanna's brother. If you'd like to speak to him, I expect he's in his study, by the front door.' She nodded past him, towards the house. 'We call it the surgery. Shall I show you?'

'No,' he said, too quickly. 'Not yet. I'll find my way there once I've . . .' he gestured, 'seen the extent of the property, and the entrances to it.' He turned to look away from the bonfire, across to the edges of the garden and the surrounding wood.

The Koenig house occupied a lonely spot, to Theodore's eyes, even by the standards of this small village. Only one neighbouring house – belonging to the Gröhlicks, Ute explained – could be glimpsed at a distance, beyond a boundary wall. There was no outlook as such; no distant view giving a sense of elevation or of their position relative to other houses and farms in the area. The lane which Klaus had driven up ran past the front door, on the other side of the house, now out of sight.

From where Theodore stood, his view beyond the garden was almost wholly of trees. Great crowds of spruce trees loomed beyond the fence, standing solid as a legion of ancient soldiers. The nearest fringe of the wood had been depleted in patches by people taking trees for timber or firewood over the decades, and in these parts new stems pushed up amid profuse undergrowth. A path of sorts ran behind the fence, but Theodore would not have noticed the gate that opened onto it, at the far end of the orchard, if Ute had not pointed it out. Trailing, knotty brambles had taken possession of the Koenigs' fencing, almost burying the rotting gatepost, while the branches of a young fir pushed through from the other side.

There was a battle in process, the constable noted, between wild and cultivated land. The Koenigs' vegetable plots, thick with weeds, seemed likely to slip out of human control.

'It's been hard for the family to manage it since the war,' Ute said, apparently reading the constable's thoughts. 'And during it too, I suppose. But when Peter's father died, and then Johanna and Heinrich had their first child, this became a fight too many.' She pushed a strand of hair behind her ear. Again Theodore noted the quick movement of her small, muddied fingers. As if in doubt about whether she had made herself clear, she added, 'Keeping the garden in order, I mean.'

Theodore nodded. It was not only a question of lost manpower, he knew. In the worst years, when the harvests failed on top of everything else, people raided one another's gardens for whatever they could find, even in places like this. He said, 'Is it a battle you fight alone, Frau Koenig?'

Ute shrugged, lifting her shoulders with an ease that reminded him suddenly – sharply – of how it is to be young and agile. 'I like it out here,' she said. Scooping a few stray sticks from the edge of the fire, she threw them into the centre, to feed the hungry blaze.

Theodore could understand her preference to be outdoors on a day like this one. The clouds moved swiftly above them, allowing periodic bursts of golden light to fall on Ute's face. It was the best season because the shortest, in the constable's view; a last dance before the certainty of winter. Watching Ute, he asked: 'Have you been married long?'

Ute straightened to look at him, blinking as she registered that this was an interview and that she was under scrutiny, perhaps under suspicion. 'A few months,' she replied. Her manner was wholly serious now, the earlier playfulness gone. She answered carefully, as if any vagueness or mistake would bring a reprimand. 'Peter completed his medical training in June. When he got back from the university, or shortly afterwards, I moved out of my aunt's cottage.' She pointed past the roof of the neighbouring house, to a gash of clear sky. 'Down by the school field, next to the Frankel store. It's where I've always lived,' she explained. 'Until now.'

The constable swept a glance over her figure, to confirm his initial assessment that she did not appear to be pregnant. If anything, the flannel trousers were too big for her, pinched together at her tiny waist with an old, frayed belt. He wondered if they belonged to someone else. 'What was your name before?' he asked, for no particular reason beyond an urge to collect whatever she was willing to give him.

'Prinz,' she answered, in the same serious tone. 'Before, I was Ute Prinz.'

# 2.

It was quiet in the parlour, where Deputy Constable Klaus Hildebrandt found himself, after an age of waiting, still alone in the presence of Johanna Koenig Müller, distraught mother of a missing baby. She stood now at the window with her back to him, a broad-shouldered, upright woman of around thirty, with a head of buoyant brown curls. Her coffee cup lay untouched on the tray. Since giving her account of the previous day, by way of half a dozen terse answers, the woman had fallen silent. Klaus Hildebrandt could not blame her for this; the prospect of losing a newborn baby, even if it were to be for only a few hours or days, struck him as the very worst thing that could happen to a mother. He did not want to imagine how his own wife, now expecting for the first time, would react in such circumstances.

A carriage clock on the mantelpiece chimed once, marking the loss of another quarter of an hour. The next time it struck would be eleven o'clock. They had been here for almost an hour already, and had other visits to make. Where was the constable? Should Klaus look for him? Undecided, he picked up his cup and, though he had drunk the contents long ago, dragged a last, cold drop of moisture between his lips. He tried, and failed, to return the cup to its saucer without making a noise.

The near silence of the room was broken, every few minutes,

by the creaking of a wooden rocking horse in the adjoining nursery. It was an alcove, rather than a separate room, leading off the parlour through an archway. Johanna had gestured towards it at the start of the interview, but had not invited the deputy constable to go in. From his chair by the fireplace, Klaus could see the rocking horse and some other nursery toys, and caught glimpses of Johanna's elder child as he played with them. The boy looked, from these brief sightings, to be too big for such childish toys and too old to be playing alone in a nursery on a school day. The sounds he made were wordless grunts and wails, together with the occasional smack of a hand against the wooden furniture. He was doubtless mentally deficient, Klaus thought.

'What is the constable looking for in the garden?' Johanna Koenig asked suddenly, without turning from the window.

Klaus followed her gaze outside, but while he was seated, he could not see much beyond the dead rose bushes on the other side of the glass. There was a trail of grey smoke rising, he assumed, from a bonfire in the garden beyond. To see what Johanna saw, the deputy would have to cross the room to join her, which seemed presumptuous. Fumbling for a reply, he said, 'I expect . . . he's checking to see which other buildings overlook this one, and whether any of your neighbours might have—'

'They didn't,' Johanna cut in. 'I've already told you.' She turned to face him. Her neck was taut, and the eyes that fixed on Klaus Hildebrandt were large and wild, their pale blue irises surrounded by a dark outer ring. Then the question he dreaded: 'What will you *do*, Deputy?'

Klaus had no answer to this, and he did not share the constable's sangfroid when faced with awkward questions. Theodore Hildebrandt, his father and supervisor, would probably sidestep the question, or return it boldly, with: 'What would you like us to do?' But Klaus was more sensitive, as he saw it, to the decorum of a situation. He respected the uniform they both wore, and the unstated message that adhered to it; that policemen should enforce, not debate, the law. In this case, though, how could they enforce anything? Until the baby was found or returned, one way or another, there was no certainty to the crime, and no culprit to charge. Everyone in the house, the village, and indeed the region, might be considered a potential child thief – just as every nook and cranny, every barn and bed between here and Angenberg was a potential hideout. And there were just two of them, constable and deputy, to conduct such a search – even supposing they had the time and means.

'Well, the first thing . . .' he replied, putting his notebook on his knee, where Johanna Koenig could see it. 'The first thing,' he repeated, 'is to send a report down to regional headquarters.' It would be the last thing too, he guessed.

Johanna exhaled sharply through her nose, and gave him an odd, searching look. Klaus could not tell whether she meant to rebuke or plead with him, or something else. 'A report,' she said. 'Yes, I suppose you would.'

The Koenigs' housekeeper, who had showed them in, entered the room to clear away the coffee cups. She was an elderly woman, with a lined face, but she moved with stealthy precision, heaping china onto the tray with minimal noise. Klaus wondered if the constable had spoken to her on his way to the garden. He opened his notebook to check her name, among a list which Johanna had dictated to him.

The list began with *HEINRICH MÜLLER*, who had made the telephone call to Mittelbach at eight o'clock this morning. Klaus had initially written *JOHANNA MÜLLER* next to Heinrich, but then Johanna said that she went by her father's name of Koenig, and so he had scratched through the surname, regretting the untidiness this caused. The other members of the household were: *FRAU WILHEMINA KOENIG (SNR), DR PETER KOENIG & UTE KOENIG (WIFE), HELGA STRAUSS (HOUSEKEEPER), DIRK KOENIG MÜLLER*

*(CHILD)* and – with an asterisk to mark her indefinite status – the absent: *MARIA-THERESA KOENIG MÜLLER (INFANT)*.

'I'd appreciate it,' Klaus said, looking up from his notes, 'if you could confirm that there were no visitors to the house yesterday. Before the incident occurred?'

Johanna crossed her arms in front of her, and relayed the question. 'Did Peter have any patients on Sunday, Helga? Or did Ute have a visitor?'

The housekeeper answered without changing expression or lifting her gaze from the tray. 'Not as far as I know.'

'Helga would know, you see,' Johanna said, looking at Klaus and through him. 'She answers the front door, which most visitors use.' With a quick intake of breath, she seemed to rein in her wandering thoughts. 'Wait a minute, Helga,' she said. 'What about the back door? Didn't you say something about a delivery, while I was sleeping?'

Helga did not answer immediately. Klaus straightened in his chair, alert to the possible significance of this newly remembered detail. He thought he saw the housekeeper shift her hands on the tray, although she might be merely trying to get a better grip. She replied, 'Only Elias Frankel, from the store. He came to deliver a packet and then left again. That was about three in the afternoon,' she said, looking not at the deputy but at Johanna Koenig. 'Perhaps a little earlier.'

Johanna acknowledged this with a nod, and Helga turned away. Jotting the new information in his notebook, Klaus Hildebrandt felt fortified. He could manage this interview alone, after all. 'If you don't mind,' he said, snapping the notebook shut, 'I'd like to see the baby's crib.'

Meeting his glance with another look that confused him, Johanna Koenig dropped into a chair opposite his. 'He doesn't speak,' she said.

'I'm sorry?'

'*The child,*' she answered, with an emphasis that rang out in the silence of the room.

The deputy constable waited to see if Johanna would say anything more, but she only waved her fingers in the air, giving him permission – or dismissing him. Klaus stepped past her into the nursery, a tiny box of a room filled with warm, sad smells. The boy, Dirk Koenig Müller, stood beside the head of his rocking horse, conducting a silent conversation with the creature. An outsized six-year-old, Klaus guessed, or some years older but stunted. His eyes were set too close together. Paying no attention to the stranger in the doorway, Dirk poked the horse's eye.

There was one piece of ordinary, adult furniture in the room: an armchair upholstered in threadbare fabric, with a cushion lodged in one corner, flattened by regular use. Grandma Koenig's dozing chair, Klaus guessed. Johanna had told him that her mother, Frau Wilhemina Koenig, had sat here with the baby yesterday after lunch, while she herself, still wearied by the birth of Maria-Theresa five weeks earlier, had retired to her room with Dirk, to rest for an hour or two. She had slept for longer than intended, and it was her husband, Heinrich Müller, who had come to the nursery after returning from walking his dogs, at around four-thirty, to check on the baby. He had found Johanna's mother asleep in her chair – this chair – and the cot beside it empty.

The cot was, of course, still empty. A blanket lay furled at the base where it had been pushed away or dropped. Klaus, staring at it, could hardly breathe. He now understood why the baby's father, Heinrich Müller, was not here – why, unable to stay and wait for news that might never come, Heinrich had left the house at dawn this morning, taking his dogs into the wood to mount a solitary, impossible search.

If it had been Klaus's child that was taken, then he too . . . But he stopped himself from pursuing this line of thought, and turned out of the nursery with a straight back, clutching his notebook tightly against his police uniform.

⁜

'Do you have children, Frau Koenig?'

'No.' Brushing mud and char from her hands, she looked at the constable, waiting.

He said, 'I have to ask you . . .'

Ute nodded. 'I know. But I don't know who took the baby or what,' she drew in a breath, 'what could have happened.' Her eyes landed on his face and stayed there, at once grave and quizzical. 'I was out with the dog yesterday afternoon, from before two, until soon after five. You'd like to know where, I suppose.'

Theodore said he would. From the fire beside them, gusts of smoke moved one way and the other, changing direction with the wind. The smell of burning leaves and wood was strong in his nose and lungs, but he had no desire to move out of the way.

'I walked down to my aunt's cottage,' Ute explained, pointing in that direction with another of those quick movements that surprised him. 'I go there most days, to sweep it out and check that nothing's amiss. Not that there's anything there to speak of,' she added. 'Aunt Ernesta died there years ago, and by the end she had nothing.'

Theodore wondered about this: an empty cottage.

'Peter thinks there will be a use for the place when the new road comes up here,' Ute continued. The Kaiser, having noticed her hand move, barked twice, sensing a game. She bent for a stick and threw it. 'He says there'll be people from town motoring into the hills to hunt, or to improve their health. We could offer Aunt's cottage to paying lodgers, he thinks, to bring in a little income?' Here she straightened to look at him, evidently hoping that the constable would agree with this assessment.

14

Theodore made a noise which could sound like agreement, to optimistic ears. People were expecting a lot of things, good and bad, from the new road; and whenever feelings ran high on any local topic, he knew that the consequences would land at his door. Disappointment could take many forms, and Constable Hildebrandt had seen most of them. Brawls and bruised eyes. Surly accusations. Barns that burned down overnight. Whatever the new road brought with it, the constable would be clearing up the mess, one way or the other.

He said, 'Did you stay at your aunt's cottage all afternoon?'

Ute watched the dog run back to her with the stick. She took it from his jaw and then, to the animal's surprise, threw it on the fire. 'No,' she replied. 'I went to the schoolhouse to collect some notes I'd left there. It was Sunday, so there were no lessons—'

'The schoolhouse?' Theodore interrupted.

'Oh.' She frowned in apology. 'I taught there for the last three years, until this summer. It was a temporary post,' she added, anticipating his next question. 'The new schoolmaster arrived in August, and since then I've been trying to avoid him.' There was a pause while she looked at Theodore, wondering, as it seemed to him, whether she ought to make this admission. 'But in fact he was in the schoolroom,' she went on, 'so I had no choice but to stay and talk to him. He was alone there, clearing out all the . . . the rubbish, I suppose you'd call it, from the shelves. Things the children had made or found, over the years – or pulled apart and pickled. Dead beetles. Dried-up frogs.'

Theodore heard and sensed the effort she was making to control her feelings about the place. Resentment, he guessed, or even grief. The world of the schoolroom had absorbed this young woman intensely for a while, and now – at the age of twenty, or twenty-two at most, he guessed, she was shut out of it. Grieving.

'In any case, I exchanged a few words with the man,' Ute continued, 'and it kept me out longer than usual. When I got back here, it was getting dark.'

The constable looked back up the path that had led him here, across the kitchen garden, to the back door of the house. His eyes moved across the building.

None of the windows stood open, and most of the glass panes on this side of the building were in shadow, reflecting only the dense woodland that surrounded the house on three sides. Dead rose bushes in front of the parlour added to the wintry impression. All the colours in the garden were concentrated in the area where Theodore stood; in the orange–brown leaves of the orchard, and the red glow of the bonfire, and the shafts of sunlight warming Ute's face and his own.

'You use this entrance, by the kitchen?' he asked, pointing at the back door.

'Usually,' Ute agreed. 'But yesterday, because I was late returning, I came up the lane and through the front door, to find Peter in the hall. I thought for a moment he was waiting for me.' She paused. 'But then he told me.'

'Told you?' Theodore prompted. He wanted to hear her say it.

She searched his gaze, and answered, 'That Johanna's baby was gone.'

✠

The constable was silent for a moment. He knew that Klaus, in the parlour, would be wondering where he was, impatient to complete the next task on the day's list. But Theodore had a strong sense that this woman standing near him at the bonfire held the clue to what had happened here yesterday. Or perhaps he was just giving himself an excuse to linger beside her, for his own private satisfaction.

He looked again at Ute's face, bent over the fire. Was it the heat, or something else, that had brought a new flush to her cheeks? Her hands, the only part of her body not buried under heavy woollen clothing, were criss-crossed with small scars and scratches, he noticed, presumably from the brambles.

He said, 'Your husband is a doctor, Frau Koenig?'

Ute looked up and nodded. 'But it's hard to make a living here. He edits a medical journal, with a friend of his in Angenberg. That's something regular.'

'I suppose he sees some patients, though, from time to time? You implied that his study serves as a surgery.'

Instead of answering this, the woman frowned at him. She said, 'Do you think that someone came and snatched Maria-Theresa, Constable? Is that what happened?'

*You tell me*, thought Theodore. He said, 'The alternative would be that she disappeared.'

Ute, still frowning, pursued her question. 'Why would anyone do such a thing?'

'To ease some heartache, I presume.' He thought, as he said it, that the notion ought to be foreign to her; incomprehensible to someone at her optimistic stage of life. But it did not seem that way. He sensed that Ute Koenig's young heart had already known sharp discomfort. A sense of sorrow was perceptible in her watchful eyes, but it was a disciplined sadness, Theodore thought; held at bay by a strong will. He recognised, with a stab of guilt, that the combination thrilled him.

He ought to leave now, before he lost all ability to regard Ute Koenig with an objective, neutral eye. That was what he ought to do.

He said, 'Tell me something about the mood in the household yesterday, Frau Koenig, or in recent days. You're a relative newcomer here. Did anything strike you?'

Ute gave him a searching look, as if trying to locate the intention behind Theodore's question. Eventually she replied, 'There was nothing out of the ordinary yesterday morning, if that's what you mean. It was quiet, before I went out. Peter was in his study. I cooked lunch with Helga in the kitchen. Johanna and Heinrich were in their room with their children, as far as I know. Since they came back from Angen with the new baby, a few weeks ago, I haven't . . .' she hesitated, 'haven't had many opportunities to talk to them.' After another pause, she went on, 'Their boy is quite a handful, and I think Johanna is still tired with this – with the new baby.'

The dog brushed between them, looked up with a plea, and made the same move in reverse, making a figure of eight between their legs. Normally the constable would move away from such contact, muttering expletives; but in the presence of this woman, Theodore barely even noticed the dog.

'Though there was something,' Ute added suddenly. 'Do you know the children's tale about a group of elves who cut leather for a shoemaker in the night-time, and lay it out for him to work into shoes the next morning?'

Theodore looked at her in surprise, and nodded.

Ute hesitated, as if finding herself on the edge of a confession. The smudge of mud or wood lichen on her cheek drew Theodore's gaze again. 'Over lunch yesterday,' she continued, 'Peter said something to Heinrich about clearing weeds in the garden before winter arrives. He has sudden bursts of enthusiasm for outdoor schemes, but they usually vanish after a few minutes, and he goes back inside to work on his journal. And Heinrich, well.' Her face contracted with slight, fleeting amusement. 'He has little inclination for hard work, especially at Peter's behest. They have never, as far as I know, seen eye to eye.'

She stopped, as if expecting Theodore to ask a question. Realising that she had mistaken the focus of his attention, he said briskly, 'Go on.'

'I'm only saying this because you asked about the mood in the house,' Ute continued, with a quick shake of the head. He could not tell whether it was a gesture of frustration or apology. 'And I can only answer for myself. It feels to me as if someone or something wicked is playing a game on everyone here. This morning, when I drew back the curtains in our bedroom . . .' She

18

motioned towards an upstairs window, but the constable, hearing *our bedroom*, could not bring himself to look. ' . . . I looked out and saw this pile of dead leaves and twigs and brambles,' she continued, 'ready to set alight. It took me a moment to realise what had happened. They must have raked the path and cleared some of the beds, or Peter did, intending to burn the debris – but then Heinrich discovered that the baby was missing, and this –' she indicated the fire – 'was forgotten.'

Theodore watched her. 'And you were reminded of the shoemaker?' he prompted.

'Or his elves,' Ute agreed. She smiled for the first time in their conversation, but it seemed to spring from a sense of puzzlement rather than joy. 'I thought, when I opened the curtains: "All the work has been done. I only need to set it alight."'

Theodore was still wondering what to make of this – was it a hint, a challenge, or an admission of some kind? – when the bonfire spat out a fleck of burning matter. He heard the *crack*, and saw the tiny red-hot speck land on what he had learned to think of as his 'good' left arm. Forgetting for an instant that his other arm was not merely worse, but attached to his shoulder by coils of twisted and sometimes painful scar tissue, he struck out with his right hand, trying to smack at the burning particle before it could singe the sleeve of his coat. Turning too sharply, he stumbled.

'Agh!' The pain of the sudden movement forced out a groan, but before he knew that he was tipping forward, Ute Koenig had caught him and was steering him out of the smoke with a firm, steadying hold. Regaining his balance, Theodore found himself in the young woman's grasp. The scratched and muddied fingers of Ute's right hand curled around his singed left sleeve, while her other hand held his. Any more pressure and the grip would have hurt. Any less, and he might have fallen.

'Be careful,' Ute said. She meant the fire, he supposed.

Theodore's racing pulse reinforced the message, flooding him with the thrill of danger as he looked into her face. Now that he was steady on his feet again, he could withdraw his forearm from Ute's grip. But he kept hold of her right hand. Turning it over to check for a burn-mark on her palm, he stared down at the soft, pink flesh.

Ute Koenig stood, astonished, as Constable Hildebrandt eventually relinquished her hand and looked at her. Then, in silence, he turned away.

# 3.

Establishing that the baby's father, Heinrich Müller, had not yet returned; that Doctor Peter Koenig was visiting a sick neighbour; and that the elder Frau Koenig was in her room, indisposed, the constable and his deputy took their leave. The two men met at the front of the house and answered each other's questions briskly, each of them hearing more than was spoken, and sensing a shift of attitude or attention in the other. Three hours ago, when the telephone rang in the station office and Herr Müller made his curt but urgent request, the summons to Hindelheim had seemed to both Theodore and Klaus Hildebrandt an inconvenient chore; but now they moved to the vehicle in separate, pensive silence.

Klaus helped his father into the motorcycle sidecar without saying that they had spent too much of their Monday morning here, or that the constable might have warned him before wandering off into the Koenigs' garden, leaving his deputy alone with the baby's strange and anguished mother. None of this needed to be said, because Constable Theodore Hildebrandt could read the accusations on his son's face – and behind them, he could see a gathering cloud of other, persistent concerns. Duty or freedom. Virtue or joy. Even as a boy, Klaus had been a worrier, too solemn for his own good. The war had not helped, of course. The war had not helped anyone, with anything, Theodore thought.

As the motorcycle engine started up, he looked at the front door and the window next to it, which must be Peter Koenig's study. Curtains were drawn inside it, and the darkness of the room conspired with the spruce trees opposite, so that Theodore could only see the outline of his own head and shoulders, protruding from the vehicle, reflected in the glass. He drew up his collar, preparing for a breezy homeward ride along the bumpy, unpaved old hill road.

In addition to the usual, anticipatory tightening of his stomach before a journey which was likely, if not bound, to make him sick, the constable felt seized by a less familiar excitement. He had an absurd desire to leap out of the wretched sidecar and bound across the hillside – this part would require a supernatural power to come to his aid – where he would find and fight whatever brute had snatched the infant from the Koenig household. Returning to Hindelheim with the monster's bloody head, Theodore would fling it down at Ute Koenig's feet, and she would grasp his warrior hand in wonder and admiration – not in order to keep him from stumbling.

As they pulled away from the Koenig house and sputtered onto the lane, the constable took a last look back. Above and beyond the sloping roof, a column of smoke rose from the bonfire and dispersed among wispy clouds. Not once during the visit had Theodore heard a baby's cry, he mused; although he had been listening for it. A light but restless autumn wind had swirled about while he was in the garden, carrying other sounds – dogs, hens, a herder's whistle – into earshot, from various directions. Why, then, was he convinced that the Koenig-Müller baby was still close by the house, or even in it?

Should he have gone to see Ute's aunt's cottage, standing empty, recently vacated? And if, just supposing, they found it there – a swaddled, secreted bundle?

22

He shut his eyes for a moment, to banish the idea of snapping handcuffs onto the small, pale wrists of Ute Koenig.

✠

The forest stayed with them for part of the ride, a dark mass clinging to one side of the path as the motorcycle rumbled downhill, past grazing pastures and the occasional farmstead. Theodore took in the view, knowing that it would soon be disrupted. The dirt track beneath them was due to be paved all the way from the valley junction to Hindelheim and beyond, through these gently curving, wooded hills, to join a lumber road on the other side. What had started, centuries ago, as a cattle path trailing uphill from Mittelbach to nowhere in particular, was now fated to become a significant thoroughfare. It had a destiny, a projected future.

Work on the new road had begun six weeks ago at the valley junction, half a mile below Mittelbach, and would soon bring men with axes and shovels – or worse – up past the farms that had stood in isolation for many decades, through communities that had so far resisted the age of the automobile with vigorous disdain.

When the first truck unloaded its crew of road diggers at the valley junction in September, the innkeeper of the tavern that stood between the village of Mittelbach and the valley road decided – without consulting his wife, a mistake he would soon regret – to replace the old roadside sign with a large, painted advertisement for *The Valley Junction Inn: Lodgers and Visitors Welcome*. Within hours, the signwriter at Mittelbach was spotted at work on the new board; and as a result, the innkeeper was showered with mockery by his wife and customers for his Promethean ambition. Did he think the world was going to change, just because the old hill road was to be raked over? Would a constant succession of hooting motorists transform the fortunes of the lonely inn?

'Change is coming,' the innkeeper insisted to his critics. 'You'll see.'

And so they did. Solitary farmers and old-time sceptics,

pushing handcarts laden with cabbages into Mittelbach on a market day, looked on as the diggers and rollers and foul-smelling mixing machines crawled through the village, widening the road. At night, with their eyes shut, these individuals saw the disasters that lay ahead: felled trees crashing through the roofs of their houses; cattle driven mad by the buzzing of a thousand chainsaws. God save us, they prayed, from the schemes of machine-crazed men.

✠

Soon after the constable had left, Heinrich Müller emerged from the wood with his dogs and exchanged a few words with Ute Koenig in the garden. They both went indoors, where a midday meal was laid out on the kitchen table. Only the elder Frau Koenig and her grandson Dirk sat down to eat, however, Grandma's gaze moving absently over the table while the boy chased steam from his bowl and made wordless mewing noises. The others moved in and out of the kitchen, pacing from window to window, too restless to settle.

They stood close to the glass panes and looked out, then turned to each other, looking for signs of strain or clues as to what might happen next.

Ute gave a summary of her conversation with the constable to Johanna, when asked, and again to her husband Peter. Afterwards, when by silent agreement the members of the household dispersed to watch and wait, Ute headed for the trees, followed by the Kaiser. The bonfire was burning low as she passed it, a smouldering heap of charred wood and ash.

She lingered there for a moment, and looked down at her hands. The afternoon air, no longer warmed by this morning's splashes of sunshine, was cold enough for gloves; but Ute had chosen not to wear them, preferring to retain by sight and feel the startling sensastion of Constable Hildebrandt's touch on her palm. Had she invited it? she wondered. No. He lost his

24

balance; that was all. She had grabbed the man without thinking, only to stop him from falling into the flames.

Looking back across the kitchen garden, she saw Peter's ginger head at the kitchen window, next to the back door. She raised her hand to wave, but changed her mind. It did not seem right to make such a gesture, at such a time, when the household was . . . not quite in mourning, but in suspension.

From the gate at the bottom of the Koenigs' orchard, a path skirted the edge of the wood and led down into the village, emerging near the schoolhouse. Ute often took that route to the store, or to her aunt's cottage – but not today. Seeking to extend her time away from the house, she continued further into the wood, where the spruce trees were taller and the sounds of human activity disappeared. Crows called high above her, and fir cones crunched underfoot. The Kaiser ran ahead, exploring the undergrowth, and then stopped and barked.

Drawing level with the dog, Ute found herself looking down at what seemed to be the head and back legs of a hind, connected by an indistinct bloodied mass. She bent over it, and a fly buzzed up and hit her face. As she shook it off, the creature's flyblown eye seemed to blink. Ute recoiled, and the dog echoed her surprise, jumping to one side. She waited for the deer to move again. She kept watching, waiting. To be safe, she tore a branch from a fallen log, disturbing a tribe of woodlice beneath.

*One strike*, an inner voice warned. The ghost of Aunt Ernesta was never far away. *Fast and hard*, it urged. *Nothing likes to be killed twice.*

She brought the branch down and felt a soft snap under her knuckles. The stench was fierce. 'Oh, no,' she said aloud, regretting her panicked response. Of course the deer would not move! It had not been trying to blink at her – the thing had been dead for long enough to collect flies on its eyeball and to be disembowelled by birds, maggots, rats. The movement of its eyelashes was a stupid, nervous illusion.

Ute was still berating herself forty minutes later, when she opened the door of her aunt's cottage. With a broom she swept the floor, from front to back, taking care under the two beds. The routine soothed her, and she remembered how Aunt Ernesta had soothed herself with a daily ritual in this room. At five o'clock every evening, whatever the season, Aunt would light a fire and send a whispered greeting up the chimney with the smoke, to her dead son Jurgen. 'In case his spirit is passing over,' she would say. 'He needs to know that he's welcome.' Now the hearth was cold, and Ute paused before it, wondering whether Cousin Jurgen was up there somewhere, feeling abandoned. There was no particular need to clean the tiny outdoor washhouse, now that she had moved out, so she replaced the broom in its corner and sat on the front step for a while with the door and shutters open, to air the place.

A squirrel ran on bowed legs across the lane towards a scattering of acorns. Hoarding time, Ute thought. She turned to look at the cupboard that held Aunt Ernesta's meagre hoard of trinkets – most of them momentos of Jurgen. It would have to be cleared out one day, when Ute could find the necessary stamina to contend with the dead woman's recriminations. Not today, though. There was too much else to think about.

Young voices, released at the end of the school day, drifted over from the school field. It was strange to be listening to them on this side of the field, when a few months ago she would have been inside the schoolroom, cleaning slates, pushing benches under the three long tables, preparing the next day's lessons.

Talking to the new teacher yesterday, Ute had learned that his lodging allowance, a modest sum paid by the School Board, had been snapped up by Frau Gröhlick even before the man arrived. As soon as he was appointed, so he had told Ute, he received a letter of congratulation from Frau Gröhlick, in which she offered him her spare room until he found somewhere better – while hinting that he would not, in fact, find better lodgings in Hindelheim. Ute wondered now if the lure of collecting rent from an outsider was one reason why Frau Gröhlick refused to recommend her for the post, after three years of training.

No, she decided. The reason went further back. Ute Prinz had only ever been considered a temporary presence in the schoolroom by the likes of Frau Gröhlick. She had not been training for anything, only filling in, at low cost to the Board. It was because of that early black mark against her character – an invisible but lingering stain. Even now, after marrying the new Doctor Koenig, Ute had not managed to erase it.

What would Constable Hildebrandt make of all this neighbourly suspicion, Ute wondered, if she were free to explain it to him? What had he concluded from this morning's unsettling, unexpected interview? That look on his face when she held his arm! Of consternation, and something else – something wild.

From the steps of the Frankel store, which neighboured the cottage, came the indistinct murmuring of two women. Customers or passers-by, exchanging the news, she guessed. *A police constable came to Hindelheim, to see about Johanna Koenig's child* . . .

Ute found that she was shivering, and wondered how long she had been sitting on the doorstep – two hours? Two minutes? A new sharpness had crept into the air, numbing her mind and fingers. Not many days left for loitering outdoors, she realised. Hauling her stiff body upright, she called the dog, and closed the window.

✠

The police substation at Mittelbach had three rooms for the constable's personal use: a kitchen on the ground floor, with a place to sit by the stove, and two small bedrooms above the office. When Theodore Hildebrandt had taken up residence there four years ago, Klaus had been nineteen – independent as measured in years, though not always so in disposition. The constable suggested to his superiors in Angenberg that his son would make a conscientious deputy; and somewhat to his surprise, perhaps for reasons of economy, they agreed. Klaus at first accepted the job as his lot, and had subsequently come to regard it, under Francesca's influence, as his due.

Francesca was Klaus Hildebrandt's wife. She had moved into the second bedroom with Klaus about a year ago, and Theodore initially expected that the cramped accommodation would drive the couple out as soon as they could save enough to rent a place of their own. But the constable had underestimated the girl's ambition. Francesca grew up in wartime, fighting for every scrap of food, forever hunting and hoarding against the next hungry winter. She had worked on the land by day, and in factories or workshops at night, managing, from a young age, a workload that would daunt many men. To Francesca, the little kitchen beside the station office was a prize seized, and she had no intention of relinquishing it. Her plan, which the constable now understood clearly, was to drive him out, one way or another, and install Klaus Hildebrandt as constable, in his place.

Theodore did not resent the girl's ambition; in fact he secretly admired it, and wished that Klaus had more of her resilience. But Francesca's influence on her young husband seemed, to the constable's eyes, to bring out the righteous streak in Klaus. Theodore blamed himself for this. Bereft of his own gentle wife some years before the war, he had left their son of eleven with neighbours when he himself went off to fight. No one had expected the fighting to last so long; and on the rare nights when, in a tunnel or a ditch or the wagon of a military train, waiting for the world to explode around him, Theodore considered how Klaus's life was progressing – even then, while so much else was ending – he assumed that the boy would teach himself how to become a man.

Not so. As Theodore was to discover at the war's end, Klaus

had fallen prey to a circle of godly, censoring women who took it upon themselves to steer the boy towards his own – meaning their own – best interests, and to protect and guard him from whatever they, in their pious timidity, knew to be wicked. The experience had left Klaus with a fear of disorderliness which worried Theodore. One day, he suspected, that fear might somehow prove to be dangerous.

☩

Francesca Hildebrandt filled the bathtub every Tuesday morning at six, carrying pans of hot water from the kitchen into the washroom behind it. Each step was accompanied by a protest. She had enough to do with a husband to cook and clean for, and a baby on the way, without stooping down to fill Theodore's tub. She was first downstairs in the morning and the last up at night, and no one seemed to mind that she was expecting a child: such was the punishment women took for being women.

Behind Francesca's back, as she stood with crossed arms waiting for him, Theodore Hildebrandt lowered himself the last few inches into the water. Covering his genitals as best he could, in case she broke the routine they had established, he said, 'I'm in. You can go. Shut the door behind you.'

It was the request he always made – to be left entirely alone for these ten precious minutes, once a week – and it was, as always, refused. 'You might fall getting out, and no one would know,' Francesca said, positioning the doorstop so as to hold the door ajar. That way, she could listen to Theodore's splashing, and he would have to listen to her shuffle about and cough and grumble as she boiled up a stink of chicken bones. 'You ought to find a woman to take care of you,' she added, 'before you get so stubborn that no one will put up with you.'

At this, the pensive, quizzical face of Ute Koenig loomed in the constable's mind. He saw her dusty crop of hair, and the smudges of earth or ash on her cheek and hands. He heard her say, 'Be careful,' and felt a thrill run up his spine at the prospect of risking something with her, for her. She meant, of course: be careful of standing too near the flames. But just supposing she meant also: be careful of my world, of me?

He soaped the too-taut skin around his neck, which leaned perpetually forward like a tortoise peeping from its shell. When in the spring of 1918, the right side of Theodore Hildebrandt's body was shredded by exploding shrapnel, he was taken to a field hospital to have what remained of his insides stuffed back into what was left of his skin. The resulting patchwork gave him the appearance of a rag doll, with rough stitching under the right ear, and an imbalance in the limbs.

But this motley casing was nothing compared to the chaos beneath. Prone to vomiting and knotted bowels, Theodore often felt that his body was inhabited by infernal shades who were trying to punch a way out through his gullet. According to his private theory, when he had lain open in the field tent, being patched up with borrowed or mistaken fragments of other men's flesh, the spirits of several dead soldiers had crawled inside him to find a new home. Now he carried these can-tankerous ghosts about with him in the world of the living, where they did not let him forget that he – all things considered – was the lucky one. He was alive.

The water in the bathtub had cooled, and the chill of the early morning air raked up goose pimples on the constable's exposed skin. He could see his breath in the room, competing with the draughts that whistled across the bare floor from an ill-fitting window frame. But despite the cold, Theodore did not call Francesca to help him out – not yet. He did not know when he would have another chance to be alone with the thoughts, vision, and touch – yes, he could still feel her hand on his arm – of Ute Koenig.

# 4.

In the office later that morning, he received a telephone call from Angenberg. Chief Inspector Lorentz Streicher.

'Theodore?'

'Yes, sir.' As younger men, they had been friends, but Theodore knew better than to risk a comradely tone.

'Is that you?'

He raised his voice to confirm, 'I'm listening.' Their voices seemed to crawl towards each other across the distance, never quite meeting, but overlapping for a second each time.

'The mayor's coming . . . Ah, Theo. Good. I say, the mayor is coming your way on Friday, with a visitor . . . What's that?'

'This week, sir? Do you know what time—'

'This week. Friday the twenty-ninth. Three days' time. He'll have a visitor with him, name of Herr Dammertz. An industry man. You got that?'

'Herr Damm—'

'Repeat the name, Constable.'

He was evidently growing anxious, so Theodore shouted. 'DAMMERTZ.'

'An industry man,' the chief inspector's voice continued. 'He recently bought a claim for several tracts of fruit-growing land to the west of the Angenberg highway. Wife's what they call a Riesling heiress. Papa exported wine. Now there's talk of building a bottling and canning operation on your side of the highway, perhaps further up . . . Are you still there?'

Theodore stretched out the cramped arm that was holding the receiver, and replied into the mouthpiece, 'I'm listening. That's . . . interesting to know, sir.'

There was a pause before the distant voice resumed. 'I'm telling you this so that you will understand the importance of the mayor's visit, Theodore. They may stop at Mittelbach, so make sure everything's in good order, will you?'

Theodore replied at a pitch that was just a little too quiet for the chief inspector to hear, 'Our doorknobs will gleam like the morning star herself, sir.'

Klaus Hildebrandt heard this at his desk on the other side of the room, and shot a castigating look over the row of empty chairs that stood between them. The chairs constituted a waiting room, of sorts, while the deputy constable's desk served as a public reception area. Constable Hildebrandt presided over the telephone, a wall map, and a cupboard containing guns, keys, a snuff tin and various items which Theodore had received as gifts, and which Klaus denounced as bribes. To prove that he was willing to compromise, the constable had suggested that they categorise these small indulgences as 'appurtenances of office'. His son was resolutely unamused.

'I can't hear you,' the chief inspector said, raising his voice. 'Just make sure you and Klaus are ready for the visitors, buttons gleaming. The mayor has an eye for these things, Theo.'

'Yes, sir—'

'And if you want to know their itinerary, contact Officer Zelinsky. Zelinsky,' he repeated, unnecessarily. Theodore would have heard the name if it had been whispered through a keyhole. 'He's coordinating with the mayor's office for the Transport Division.'

'Officer Zelinsky,' Theodore repeated, drawing another look from Klaus – this time one of incipient concern.

'Oh, one more thing,' the chief inspector added, with new energy. 'Those horse thieves. The gypsies who were making a pest of themselves by the quarry a month or two back: you got rid of them, didn't you?'

Theodore paused to select his answer. 'Would you like me to check?'

'Do that,' Chief Inspector Lorentz Streicher urged. 'Do it today, and make a thorough job of it. The last thing we want is for the mayor and his visitor to run into a gypsy caravan.'

There was no opportunity, or need, for Theodore to mention to his chief the suspected abduction of a baby in Hindelheim: it was a minor incident, in the regional scale, of a type that was probably not uncommon in Angenberg. Out here, the constable usually dealt with stolen livestock rather than lost children, but his colleagues in town would, he guessed, deal sometimes with snatchings and killings. Yesterday's daily report from the Mittelbach substation, which logged the telephone call from Heinrich, and the Hildebrandts' visit to the Koenig-Müller household, among other items, had been sent to regional head-quarters as normal; and Theodore was not surprised that he had received neither a response nor any particular instructions. What kind of miracle would prompt his superiors in Angen to send a dozen men to the hills to look for a missing, weeks-old baby?

On their own, the constable and his deputy could not do much more than they had done yesterday by showing their faces in Hindelheim, and hoping that the sight of their uniforms would be enough to make the culprit hesitate, if he were watching. *Or she*, Theodore forced himself to add. Though he hated to admit it, the culprit could be a woman with a still face and ill-fitting clothes and miraculous, grubby fingers.

✠

Returning the telephone receiver to its cradle, Constable Theodore Hildebrandt looked at his deputy, who was waiting. 'The new world is on its way to Mittelbach,' he said. 'Our friend Zelinsky is arranging a tour for the mayor, and we're to have our best smiles ready to greet him. Time to tell Pavel the good news. Come on.'

'Now?' Klaus threw a look of concern at the door which led through the kitchen. The smell of boiling chicken fat had been seeping through it all morning. 'I think Francesca is preparing lunch.'

Theodore wiped a handkerchief across his face to muffle a cough. The chicken had been, at best, a scrawny and bloodless creature when alive. In death, served up in increasingly mean doses over six consecutive midday meals, the miserable thing had begun to take its revenge on human society and on Theo's digestive system in particular. He calculated what was left to eat – the bird's feet and slippery, twice-cooked skin; perhaps a hairy wing, between the three of them. 'A pity,' he said. 'But I'm afraid this can't wait.'

Picking up his cap, he added with a sly glance, 'If we hurry, we should be there in time for some of that good gypsy stew.'

Within an hour, the motorcycle and sidecar were rattling over loose stones towards the disused quarry, past small valley farms interspersed with oak and birch trees. It was a bright, cloudless day, and the golds and reds of broadleaf trees were reflected in the still surface of a pond. Three ducks took off from the water, one of them catching gunshot as it passed the bank, and falling into the path of a pursuing dog. Lunch, Theodore hoped. His hunger sharpened as they reached the encampment and were greeted with the smell of roasting meat.

There were more dogs in the camp than gypsies, and the constable readied his cap to flick at any bared teeth. In the first year of his post at Mittelbach, four years ago, Theodore Hildebrandt had received complaints of a Rottweiler that was

34

causing alarm in the village. As he approached the dog, it attacked and knocked him over, taking full advantage of the constable's lameness; and so Theodore, struggling on the ground and unable to right himself, had reached for his belt and used his gun. Chief Inspector Lorentz Streicher afterwards reprimanded him for misuse of his police pistol; and so he now looked around for sticks, or armed himself with other, subtler weapons that might achieve some deterrence.

'Theodore, is it? My friend?'

Pavel broke through a line of drying clothes, his hair wild, his smile missing several teeth. He was of indeterminate age, and everything about him, from the protruding eyebrows to the forearms which were bare throughout the year, seemed to be made of unbreakable, sinewy wire. Hooking one arm around Theodore's neck, he called, 'Natascha! See who's come!'

When they had found places to sit, Natascha brought bowls of steaming rabbit and beans and chestnuts from the fire. Deputy Constable Klaus Hildebrandt hesitated over his bowl, and then used his spoon to divide the stew, as if it were a divining rod seeking out signs of corruption. Between mouthfuls, his eyes darted towards a shallow pit near the camp, which held all kinds of waste.

'Tell your boy,' Pavel observed to Theodore, 'that the beans were dead when we put them in his bowl. They won't leap out at him.'

Natascha raised a hand to the deputy constable's face and gave his cheek a pinch. 'Leave the young man alone,' she said, with a smile that reached all the way to her loosely coiled hair. 'It must be hard for him, living in the shadow of his father.'

'Oh yes,' Theodore agreed, catching his deputy's eye. 'He prays every day for my good looks. I tell him: wait, the day will come. Put up with your youthful energy for just a few years, and then you too will reap the rewards of old age.'

Klaus did not join in the laughter, and Theodore felt his son's indignation as a low, massing cloud that had begun to gather speed and roll towards him. The storm would break one day soon – but not now. The constable was not ready for it.

When they had eaten, Pavel threw down his empty bowl and picked up a rifle, which he started to clean with an oiled rag. Theodore said what he had come to say, giving a summary of the police chief's warning. 'The mayor wants to show his investor a promised land. Everything settled and tidy. No transient life. Nothing that would make an outsider uneasy.'

'We're not highway robbers,' Pavel protested.

'I know it,' Theodore agreed. 'You're horse thieves. Big difference.'

Pavel opened a tobacco tin and offered, 'Smoke?' He held it open towards the constable, hiding its contents from the zealous young deputy, Klaus Hildebrandt.

Theodore looked at the banknotes stuffed into the tin, and then lifted his eyes. 'Not this time, Pavel,' he said. 'You need to move on, out of the valley. Out of the district, if you want to be left alone for the winter. There are changes coming.'

'But we can come back, once the mayor's cleared off back to Angen?'

Theodore did not answer this. He stood and walked, slowly, one hip moving higher than the other, towards a clearing where the horses were kept. There were sturdy horses for the wagons, others for riding, and ponies for the children. The face of the old quarry curved away behind them, a ragged bite taken out of the hillside; and stretching behind that was a series of hills, rising green and grey into the sky. Among them, not visible from here, was Hindelheim.

As Pavel moved up beside him, the constable said, 'They'll start with lumber roads and small factories. Repair shops to serve the motorists. Stores and inns for the houses that will follow the roads. The starting gun has fired, and the mayor is waving his handkerchief to get the race moving.'

They both took a moment to consider this. Then Pavel replied, 'I thought we'd tucked ourselves away here, found a nice little belly spot on Mother Nature in a part where no one else was looking. But she's everybody's whore, it seems. No special favours.' With a nod of resignation, he said, 'We'll move on. You know where.'

Acknowledging this, Theodore turned to ask the question that kept pushing to the front of his mind, demanding attention above everything else. 'I don't suppose you've heard anything about a missing baby, from further up in the hills?' He pointed. 'Place called Hindelheim?'

'No,' Pavel answered, and nodded towards the caravans, 'but you can count the young 'uns we've got here. If one takes your fancy, talk to Natascha – maybe she'll make you a deal.'

✛

The drive back from Pavel's camp to Mittelbach took them past the Valley Inn, near the turning from the Angenberg highway. Theodore shouted from the sidecar, and Klaus, in ominous silence, obeyed the signal and stopped the motorcycle to let him out.

It was well known to those who frequented the Valley Inn that Constable Theodore Hildebrandt visited one of two local women there every week, on his bath day. As he passed through the salon and up the narrow staircase at six o'clock on Tuesday evening, a group of regular drinkers, and another individual sitting alone in his favoured corner, returned the constable's nod of greeting, before returning to their thoughts.

Sabina was waiting in the first room off the landing, warming her socked feet by rubbing them between her hands. 'I'd almost given up on you, Comrade,' she said as he came in. It was a term that both of the women used for him, apparently by mutual agreement, though Theodore had never asked why. He supposed that it was a way to make light of their encounters; to modify their repulsion by mocking and indulging his needs. Perhaps it gave them a sense of patriotism as they laboured over the patchwork of his body. Riding the Comrade to orgasm was like tilling the fatherland, striving for the greater good.

He never spoke to either woman about the other. It was simply known that a certain amount of money would be on the bedside table every Tuesday afternoon, and that in winter Theodore would pay the innkeeper something extra to have a fire in the tiny grate.

'What's on the agenda today, Comrade?' Sabina asked, working at his buttons with unhurried speed. 'Any salacious crimes to report to your fellow citizen?' She was a big woman with improbably pale skin, the near-blue pallor of which fascinated Theodore. Something with that colour should be cold to the touch; but when he pressed a hand over one veined, heavy breast, it gave out a surprising heat.

'A missing baby,' he said. 'In Hindelheim. Do you know anything?'

She did not, but agreed to tell him if any information came her way.

Sometimes they toyed with each other's flesh, twisting the bedclothes off and on, adjusting the hard pillow. Today, Theodore lay quiet and still. On the ceiling above him, the lamplight began to throw up the shadow of a bonfire. He shut his eyes, and the image imposed itself on his eyelids: a young woman with a fearless gaze and reddened ears, making witchery with twigs and fire.

# 5.

Wednesday began with a low mist hanging in the air. Constable Theodore Hildebrandt took a walking stick into the station yard and made a slow, hobbling tour of the premises that were to be graced with a mayoral visit on Friday. Plenty to do before then. The sign above the station door was weathered, and the electric bulb broken. The wood pile, stored at one end of what had once been a stable block, held only the scrappy remnants of last winter's fuel – a single fire's worth, saved for an emergency. Would the mayor expect to be greeted with a smoky salute, Theodore wondered; a fire burning in the office hearth? He decided to call on the woodcutter and request an early delivery of firewood, on credit, to be settled at the next pay day. It had not occurred to the inspector, of course, to offer a supplement to the constable's regular budget on this occasion.

Was Theodore supposed to offer his visitors refreshment? And if so – how to prepare Francesca for that possibility? He cast a nervous glance at the building, and decided to delegate the task to his deputy. It was time for Klaus to take more responsibility, in any case – starting on the home front, with his formidable young wife.

Beech leaves lay scattered across the yard, along with dried and browning husks of chestnuts and beechnuts. Swapping his walking stick for a broom retrieved from the stable, the constable started to sweep. It would take him three times as long as a fit man to clear the yard, but he enjoyed the movement – dragging the brush behind him with his left arm, or pushing it in front of him, little by little. The left sleeve of his coat bore a tiny hole in the woollen weave, near the cuff, as a memento of Monday's encounter – but was it merely an encounter, and nothing more? – with Ute Koenig.

He paused for breath, adjusting the weight over his hips. How long had it been since they'd had a bonfire of fallen leaves here in the yard? High time for one, Theodore decided. There were more than enough wood chippings and broken or rotting scraps around the place to make a clearance worthwhile.

But as he was choosing a site for the fire, the constable was interrupted by a group of visitors. The four of them emerged quite suddenly, and quietly, out of the mist that lingered over the station entrance, where the yard met the road through Mittelbach village. There were three childen, led by a woman whose name Theodore had forgotten, though he recognised her instantly as Rudi Hoffmann's housekeeper.

Leaning on the broom handle, Theodore listened with feigned surprise to the woman's account of the miscreants' behaviour – the latest, she told him, of a number of troublesome recent episodes. She had brought the culprits up to the station so that Constable Hildebrandt might give them a lesson in discipline. 'Leave it to me,' he said, with a conspiratorial smile. Experience had taught him that it was the quickest way to get rid of her.

The housekeeper turned away, leaving the three children standing in a solemn row facing Theodore. Two girls and a younger boy. 'So,' he said. 'You are accused of pelting Doctor Hoffmann with his own apples.'

'We deny the charge,' replied the elder girl.

'You may deny it now,' the constable said, 'but once you've

spent a night in the cell here, you might change your plea. Come.'

He led them to the furthest of the old stables, which had been converted some years ago into the Mittelbach prison, a holding cell with a narrow horsehair bed, designed to house one man for a night or two, until he was either released or transported to Angenberg. Opening the door with a struggle, as it was stiff from lack of use, Theodore herded the children inside. 'In you go. All of you. Don't mind rats, do you?'

With a wary tread, the three children entered the damp little box of a room. To their novelty-starved eyes, it was a haunted mansion, marvellous as a cathedral. The boy tilted his head to look at a series of cobwebs strung between the high corners of the room, while the girls dared each other in whispers to look under the bed.

Klaus Hildebrandt approached from the station office, with a letter in his hand. Joining the constable at the doorway of the holding cell, he looked inside with alarm. 'For God's sake,' he protested. 'They're children. You'll scare them.'

'I hope so,' Theodore replied. 'Help me with this door.'

'You're not going to lock them in?'

'Not while the hinge is in this state,' the constable agreed, frowning at the rust that had gathered there. 'We should fix it before the mayor comes. And let's find some penitent wretch to lock up tomorrow night, to convince the dignitaries that we know our business.'

Klaus stared at him for a moment, and then held out the letter. 'It's from Hindelheim,' he said. 'They found the baby.'

From the cell, the girls called out, 'Herr Constable, for how long are we to be kept prisoners here?' and 'Herr Constable, will you feed us?'

But Theodore no longer noticed them. His head was bent over the letter, absorbed. Klaus yanked the cell door open, and told the three young prisoners they were free to leave. They

41

emerged with sullen looks, shuffling into the yard with disconsolate murmurs. There weren't any rats in there. Not even a locked door – some prison! Now what were they supposed to do for the rest of the lousy day?

⁜

*Herr Constable Hildebrandt,*

    *Enclosed for your attention is a death certificate for Maria-Theresa Koenig Müller, daughter of Frau Johanna Beatrice Koenig Müller and Herr Heinrich Ebner Müller, residing at this address. Cause of death is infant pneumonia. Age of the deceased at the time of death is estimated at five weeks and six days, the corpse having been discovered late yesterday, 26th October, in a shed at this property. While death may have occurred at any point between the child's disappearance, discovered at 4.50 p.m. on Sunday 24th, and the recovery of the corpse at 9.35 pm on Tuesday 26th, it is my considered opinion that death occurred in the first few hours of the given time period; hence the absence of noise from the aforementioned shed. Signs of inflammation of the nasal passages, together with other physiological evidence of a fever leading to—*

'Death,' Theodore muttered, skipping ahead to the signature at the bottom of the letter. *Dr Peter Koenig, Hindelheim.* The letter and the accompanying death certificate, which Klaus held in his hand, had been written last night, just as the constable was leaving the Valley Inn.

'Get the motorcycle,' he said, folding the letter.

Klaus looked at him as if fearing that this madness of Theodore's might be contagious, passed down the bloodline from father to son. 'But it was an accidental death,' he protested. 'There's nothing more to investigate. This is a legitimate certificate, made out by an authorised physician.'

Theodore took a breath to argue, and then stopped himself.

'You're right,' he reasoned. 'This explains it. I'd just like to meet the baby's father. For the sake of formality, if nothing else. It was Herr Müller who called us up there, remember. Don't you think we should offer our sympathies?'

✠

They were let in as before by the Koenigs' housekeeper, Helga. And as before, the woman's closed, worn face showed almost no reaction to the constable's greeting. Doctor Koenig was occupied at the moment, she told him, without waiting to be asked. Theodore noted the assumption; that they were here to see Peter Koenig.

'You could wait,' Helga offered, leading them into the dim space of the hall, where a bench occupied one wall, presumably provided for patients.

But Theodore was not in the mood for waiting, least of all in the gloom outside Peter Koenig's study – when Ute Koenig might be in the garden. He glanced down the corridor ahead of him, and up the carved staircase leading from the hall; but there was no sign yet of the woman or her dog.

'We'll take a look at the shed,' he said, 'where the child was found.'

Helga saw that she could not refuse this request, and so she turned in front of them down the corridor. Theodore continued, to the back of her head, 'We had a cold evening in Mittelbach last night. It was worse up here, I suppose?'

'Cold enough,' came the reply.

'Cold enough for a fire?' Theodore asked, glancing into the parlour as they passed. He could not quite see the fireplace. 'The doctor's note said that the baby was found around nine-thirty,' he went on, 'by whoever went outside to fill the log basket, I suppose?'

'That would be Heinrich Müller,' Helga replied. 'The child's father.'

'Is he in?'

'This way,' Helga said, turning out of the back door and down three steps into the kitchen garden.

The woodshed stood between two other ramshackle outhouses. Theodore realised that he must have walked near it on Monday morning, when he followed the smoke of the bonfire down this path. Was the baby inside the shed then, dead or sleeping or too numb with cold to make itself heard?

Helga opened the shed door, which Theodore judged to be just thick enough to obscure some degree of sound. He removed his cap, to prevent it catching on the angled roof, and stepped in. The logs, stacked in three large piles, filled the shed with the sweet smell of sap. Straightening as far as he could, Theodore found himself looking down at a box that occupied a clearing on the floor between the wood piles. The lid lay over it, at an angle, not yet hammered down.

Klaus looked in from the doorway, remarking over his shoulder, 'They've not buried it yet?'

'Lift the lid, would you?' Theodore asked.

'What?'

'Never mind.' He could tell that Klaus had heard him. The 'what?' was an outburst of shocked trepidation, not a question. Theodore knew that his son's world contained certain sacred, untouchable things; among them, coffins and babies.

Gripping the end of a protruding log, Theodore tried to lower himself to the little box, but struggled, causing the stack of logs to shift.

Eventually Klaus stepped in to help. Dropping onto his haunches, the deputy constable took a deep breath, and lifted the lid.

Shrouded in a blanket, the baby's face was mottled and swollen. It looked preposterous, Theodore thought, like one of the undeveloped chicks that fall out of their nests sometimes in the springtime; all bulging skull and unfinished pinkness. He nodded at Klaus, who put the lid back in place and swung back outside into the fresh air.

As Theodore turned out of the shed, he heard barking. With greater enthusiasm than he normally felt for this noise, he turned towards it, expecting to see Ute Koenig and her mongrel. Instead he saw four large hunting dogs being led up from the orchard through the mist. Their master, plump, with a bloated, greying face, guided the dogs into a large enclosure, surrounded by wire, with kennels at one end and gnawed bones at the other. Some kind of leash or chain dangled from his hand.

# 6.

Once he had shut the dogs in their enclosure, Heinrich Müller turned towards the constable. 'Thought you might come back,' he said, approaching Theodore with an unhurried stride and a glance from hooded eyes. 'I told Peter to expect you, but he could not entertain that idea that a *police constable* – excuse the emphasis, I merely imitate his snobbery – would question the almighty power of his signature on a certificate. Arrogant shit, our dear Herr Doctor Koenig.' He stopped and offered his hand, 'I'm Heinrich Müller, father of the poor mite you've just inspected.'

'Constable Hildebrandt,' Theodore replied, trying not to wince as the man crushed his hand. 'You dislike your wife's brother, Herr Müller?'

Heinrich produced a pipe from his jacket and proceeded to fill it with tobacco, working it down with a fat but agile thumb. 'We are six adults living under one roof,' he replied, leaving the constable to draw his own conclusions. From the balding hairline, and sacks of skin beneath his eyes, it seemed possible that Heinrich was around Theodore's age. He was certainly older than his wife, Johanna. Bringing the pipe to his lips, he said, 'So, ask away.'

Theodore had the impression that Heinrich was taking some

pleasure in this encounter, if only because it provided the chance of conversation with an outsider. Three adults under one roof was a burden, in Theodore's experience; he could not but sympathise with a man who endured double that number. 'You called us on Monday to report the child as missing,' he said. 'Now that it's been found, I'm wondering how to complete that report, before we send it to Angen.'

Heinrich gave him a shrewd look. 'You mean, you are wondering how she got from there,' he gestured towards the house, 'to here?'

Theodore nodded. 'And when. And why.'

'Ah,' Heinrich said, removing his pipe. 'Why – the saddest piece of the puzzle. For no damned reason at all. And I mean, *no reason.*' He pointed the stem of the pipe towards his head in emphasis. 'None at all. Do you understand me? The opposite of reason. Sheer bloody lunacy.'

He turned to Helga the housekeeper, who had been standing on the path with her back to the house while the constable made his morbid inspection of the wood pile. 'Do you want to tell him?' Heinrich prompted.

Theodore watched Helga's weathered face absorb this question without leaving a mark, other than a slight tensing of the lips as she said, 'No.'

This seemed to be as Heinrich expected, and the black beads of his eyes gleamed with a kind of bitter amusement. 'Have you met my wife's mother, Constable?' he asked.

Theodore had not.

'She's out of her mind,' Heinrich replied.

'Not all of the time,' Helga interrupted, with a slight frown. 'She forgets things.'

'That's right,' Heinrich agreed. 'She forgets things. Little things, like whether her husband is alive or dead. Whether her children are infants or adults. Details. Right, Helga? Happens to us all sooner or later, so I've heard. Isn't life entertaining?'

Theodore, watching him, said, 'You think the baby's grand-mother moved it?'

In reply, Heinrich stuck the pipe between his teeth and pulled on it. Theodore turned back to Helga, noticing as he did that Klaus had moved some way off and was standing in the mist outside the dogs' enclosure. Sickened by the sight of a dead infant, the deputy was perhaps seeking a kind of refuge in the wholesome simplicity of barking animals.

With evident reluctance, Helga took the invitation to speak. She said, 'It used to be Wilhemina's job to fetch the wood inside, when Doctor Koenig – Peter's father, I mean – was alive. We think,' she glanced at Heinrich and continued, 'if the baby cried on Sunday afternoon when she was in the chair beside it, she might have picked it up, and then forgotten what she was doing. She suffers from confusion, like Heinrich says. If she carried the baby down the corridor, I should have seen her from the kitchen. But Dirk was with me . . . That's Johanna's and Heinrich's little boy.' She looked at Heinrich, as if urging him to relieve her of the burden of talking. He did not.

'So she could have passed the kitchen and come out here through the back door without you noticing,' Theodore said. 'And by the time she got to the log pile, she was distracted?'

'That's right,' Helga agreed. 'We think she put the infant down on the logs there, and maybe stood for a while and tried to remember what she was doing there.'

Theodore watched the housekeeper's face as she spoke, surprised as much by the sorrow it failed to hide as by the scenario she described. 'You've asked her?'

After a pause, Helga answered, 'She can't remember.'

'Cannot remember,' Heinrich Müller echoed, his voice resonant with irony. 'I hope you can find a way to phrase that in your report, Constable. Peter could supply you with some technical terms for the old bat's madness, I daresay.'

Theodore glanced again at Klaus, who now turned back to

48

join him. There was a look of disapproval, verging on disgust, inscribed on the deputy's furrowed brow. *This is an unauthorised inquiry*, the expression said. *And you tricked me into it.*

Perhaps it was true that Theodore had lied to Klaus about his reason – *reasons* – for returning to Hindelheim. But now that he was here, the constable felt that this was the start of a search, not the end of it. Heinrich's baby had been found, but now the truth – or at least some pieces of it – had gone missing.

Theodore looked again at the row of outhouses, each a different size and age from the others, but all in a state of rusty disrepair. Moss and nettles had settled into gaps in the timber. 'Did no one look in these on Sunday evening,' he asked, 'when you realised the child was missing?'

Heinrich gave a nod, and scowled at the sheds. 'Took a lamp into every one of them myself,' he said. 'But I must have missed her, somehow. I was calling to my child, and . . . it sounds idiotic now . . . I thought she would hear me and call back.'

Moved in spite of his reservations, the constable felt the first hint of misgiving about his decision to intrude on the grieving household. He looked over at a charred patch of ground where Monday's bonfire had burned, and past it into the misty orchard and woodland beyond. Still no sign of Ute Koenig. Could he ask to see her?

'Will you and your wife be,' Theodore said, pausing to select a word, 'satisfied if the report describes the child's loss as an accident, Herr Müller?'

'I don't see what else it could be. You can talk to Johanna again if you want, when she's done with giving our boy his bath.' Heinrich checked his watch, and added, 'I'll be in trouble for walking the dogs beyond the allotted hour. I'm meant to dig a hole, so we can get the box buried before dark. Will you let us bury her now?'

Before the constable could answer, Klaus said, 'I'll help you.'

In surprise, Theodore turned to look at his deputy, who

stood, pale-faced, at his elbow. They exchanged a look, the younger Hildebrandt daring the elder to refuse an act of kindness to this suffering family.

Theodore did not comment. He had no objection to the burial. There was no likelihood of the coronor deciding to order an autopsy on a newborn infant, miles from Angenberg, whatever the constable said in his report.

Leaving Klaus to salve his conscience, or whatever it was, by digging a grave, Theodore nodded at Heinrich, and went in search of Ute.

✠

The gloomy corridor led him from the back door past the kitchen and two other, closed doors, which probably belonged to Johanna Koenig and to her mother – so Theodore surmised. Behind one of the doors he could hear a childish sound, midway between humming and keening. That would be Dirk, the mute boy, he assumed.

Some houses, built to the same design as this one, have a cosy kind of darkness, the constable thought – the kind that captivates children on winter holidays, as they play in candlelight with costumes improvised from old curtains. Perhaps at some earlier stage of its life, the same had been true of this house. When Peter and Johanna Koenig brought back their first, adolescent lovers, perhaps, for snatched moments of sexual ecstasy, the dark rooms took on an appealing, seductive intimacy.

Now, though, it was hard to imagine a couple taking breathless, abandoned pleasure between these walls. An invisible curtain seemed to have fallen over the Koenig household, blocking out the horizon and the possibility of unconstrained joy. Entering the parlour and finding it empty, Theodore paused to think. Why had Ute Prinz turned into Ute Koenig, and imprisoned herself here?

50

Jealous nonsense, he countered silently, recognising the familiar turn of his own thinking. Self-justification was his mind's favourite trick. He could perform it so deftly that he couldn't always see where he had hidden the ace. Watch out, Theo, he told himself. There may be another explanation. You may not like it. *Be careful.*

He stepped from the parlour rug into the adjoining nursery. This small, musty alcove was as Klaus had described it to him, with one addition. Sitting alone in an armchair among a scattering of wooden toys was a woman of perhaps sixty, blotting her nose with a handkerchief. Her skin was smooth enough to belong to someone half that age, but framing it was a cloud of wire-grey hair. Theodore greeted her. 'Good afternoon, Frau Koenig.'

She looked up with watery blue eyes and smiled. 'A policeman.'

'Constable Hildebrandt,' Theodore specified, correcting the overstatement, 'from the substation down at Mittelbach.'

This was registered with a nod of one who had lived far longer in the area than Theodore. Frau Koenig had seen other constables come and go. She said, 'You're waiting to see Doctor Koenig, I suppose?'

Theodore looked around for a seat that would bring him to her level, but could find only a child's rocking horse. Clutching the fibrous mane, he lowered himself by awkward stages onto its too-small saddle. Before the war, he had been an excellent rider, the best of the young troopers recruited in his region. Now the best he could do was to sit on a painted miniature – and even that took some effort. Life, as Heinrich said, was entertaining. Once he was sure that the rocking horse would not break beneath him, he returned his gaze to Frau Koenig.

She was staring in his direction, without focus – or perhaps, without interest. Nothing moved in the room; there was no one to overhear his confession.

'I wonder if you know where I could find Ute,' he said. 'The doctor's wife.'

'*I'm* the doctor's wife!' Frau Koenig exclaimed, with a blaze of sudden good humour.

Theodore found himself smiling with her, and as the cheerfulness started to fade from the woman's face, he said, 'Your daughter Johanna has lost her baby daughter, I understand. Did you know that, Frau Koenig?'

The eyes, no longer cheerful, looked at him in undefined anxiety.

'It was sleeping here, on Sunday afternoon,' Theodore said. He looked around for the cot that Klaus had described to him, but could not see it. Perhaps Johanna had moved it. Through the wall came a muffled, yelping sound: her other child again, Dirk, resisting his bath. 'I suppose the baby's crying woke you, did it?' he continued. 'So you picked the child up to comfort it. Do you remember that?'

'I'm not sure.' Her mind seemed to grasp at something out of reach.

'Do you remember going outside, to fetch new wood for the fire?'

Frau Koenig said nothing. Theodore considered releasing her, but did not. 'They tell me you've lost your mind, Frau Koenig. What do you say to that?'

'She has nothing to say to that,' a voice said from the doorway, 'because it is an impertinent question.' Theodore turned to meet the wire-rimmed, disapproving gaze of Peter Koenig, who continued, 'I can spare a few minutes now if you wish, Constable.'

# 7.

Outside, mist continued to roll across the Koenigs' garden, blanketing the patch of land which Heinrich Muller had chosen as a burial spot for his infant daughter. His dogs prowled nearby in their enclosure, from time to time snapping their jaws at one another, or crunching on a bone. A sweet, wet smell of rotting apples hung in the air.

Heinrich watched as Deputy Constable Klaus Hildebrandt thrust the spade again and again into the earth to make a small, deep hole. 'You've done enough, Deputy,' he remarked. 'I'll finish here.'

'Almost done,' Klaus replied, and kept digging. If the man had asked him why he was lending his efforts in this way, Klaus would have struggled to know the answer. It was not a policeman's duty, and it was not quite a moral one. There might be some connection with his father, but he was not sure what, and was grateful that Heinrich did not ask. Grateful, too, that with the exertion, air was returning to his lungs.

'Children yourself?' asked Heinrich.

Klaus glanced up. 'One on the way.' Soon, he almost added. Francesca had warned him at four o'clock this morning, and every few minutes afterwards until he got up, that it would not be long now. She had been experiencing new pains and symptoms for the past week or so, and Klaus had his own, private set of concerns about the child's arrival. But he could hardly share this worry with someone whose senile mother-in-law had just killed his baby. The awfulness of it stopped his arm in mid-air, as he was digging.

He leaned on the spade and looked up. Heinrich Müller stood staring away from him, gazing into the mist with a stillness that could be resignation. 'It's a peaceful spot,' Klaus said.

'Hmm? Yes, that's one way of putting it,' Heinrich answered, making a shuffling half-turn. He was plump, despite the regular dog walks that took him away from the house each afternoon. When he breathed through his mouth, instead of dragging air through the pipe or up his nostrils, he had a tendency to cough and wheeze. 'Different when I met her, though. Johanna.'

Klaus nodded.

'Lot of bustle in those days,' Heinrich continued, gesturing at the house with his pipe. 'Back and forth to town, with her father and whatnot. She could make me laugh, you know.' The memory seemed to surprise him, and he paused. 'Did a fair bit of laughing herself, back then.'

Before the child arrived, Klaus thought. Before Johanna gave birth to a mute and somehow retarded son. He searched for something to say. 'Have you always lived in Hindelheim?'

'Me?' The man's thick eyebrows shot up. 'God help me, no. Angen boy, born and bred. Good with numbers. Made it to Inspector of Taxes at the Municipality and then . . .' He drew circles in the air, the smoke from his pipe blending with the mist. 'Johanna said if I was still alive after the war – said it with a smile, mind. We thought everyone would be. Germans, anyway. If I survived, she would marry me.'

He shot Klaus a look of bright amusement, confiding, 'She terrified people even then, my wife, but for the right reasons. You could see their eyes following her. They'd turn to their

54

friends and repeat something Johanna had said. Couldn't believe her nerve. Yes, she was a bold little hussy.' He chuckled then coughed.

Clearing his throat noisily, he went on. 'As you can see, I survived. Administrative duties, thanks to. Finance division. Counting the cost of war – that's quite a thing. But. But!' He wagged a finger at Klaus. 'It turns out that my survival was no great consolation. Their darling father, you see. Devoted to him, those two.'

Klaus frowned, trying to keep up. 'Peter Koenig? And . . .?'

'Peter and Johanna.' Heinrich nodded, and then repeated the names slowly, binding them together with a suggestiveness which Klaus chose not to hear. '*Peter. And. Johanna.* Adored the old croak, even though he barely noticed them. Too busy paying court to his floozy, down in the . . .' He broke off, as if changing his mind. 'But I'm getting off the point,' he said. 'You asked me a question, Deputy?'

Klaus could not remember how the conversation, if that was what it was, had started. He demurred quietly, and after a moment, lifted the spade again and shovelled. Heinrich wandered towards the enclosure, to talk to his dogs.

✠

When the grave was ready, Klaus left the spade lying beside the pile of loose earth, and went to retrieve his coat. He had left it at the dogs' enclosure, slung over a wooden post that held up the fencing. Heinrich was still there. They shook hands.

The older man ran a hand along the back of his head, as if to coax some disordered thought into logical order. He said, 'Mind if I tell you something?'

Klaus invited him with a glance to go on.

'Our son, Dirk – I think you've seen him. He's a difficult child. Won't speak. Must do certain things in a certain way, or else all hell breaks loose. That's why we're still here, by the way.'

He turned his fleshy, greying face towards the deputy. 'I remember your question now. I never intended us to live out here, of course. Came up on Sundays, during the war, when I could. The plan was to put some money by, and have Johanna join me in town. But then she had the boy, and there was no going anywhere. Screams blue murder if we bring him into the garden without his special hat!'

Heinrich stopped to suck on his pipe. Scowling at the house, he continued. 'She thought it would be different this time. The good doctor buzzing about to supervise, ensure a healthy crop and all that. But it was not quite . . . There was something wrong with this one too.' He paused to cough.

Klaus, buttoning his coat, looked at the ground.

'I took Johanna to Angen for the birth,' Heinrich resumed, with a wheezy intake of breath. 'Decided we were owed some privacy for that, at least. But word gets around of course – look at this place.' He pointed towards the roof of the neighbouring house which stood some distance away, only partially visible in the mist. 'Our country neighbours have nothing else to do but poke around in other people's affairs and fumble with their—' He stopped himself abruptly, drew on his pipe and then grunted, finding it had gone out.

Klaus watched as he refilled the pipe from a tin, using a broad thumb to tamp the tobacco down.

'We came back,' Heinrich continued, 'a few weeks ago. There was a rat's head outside our bedroom window, on the ledge. A little homecoming gift.'

Struggling to see the significance, Klaus said, 'It could be a cat . . .?'

'Skewered,' Heinrich cut in, 'on the end of a stick.' He held his index finger up, vertically. 'Local kids, probably. Time to time, they come and stare at Dirk. My wife wanted me to *do* something, Christ knows what. We argued in the usual fashion, and I suppose she left me with some kind of guilt simmering away in the old guts – you know how women can do that. I started to think about Elias Frankel.'

The name struck Klaus as familiar. He repeated it silently.

'Neighbour of ours, runs the Frankel store. Handsome young devil, so the women seem to think. He earns a bit on the side by setting traps, selling skins, that sort of thing. From time to time he supplies the children around here with wild pets. He bagged a squirrel for one of them, alive, and put a kind of collar on the creature. I thought I might ask Elias if he knew about anyone catching rats and cutting their heads off.'

Pausing to savour a fresh puff of smoke, Heinrich went on. 'Never got round to it, somehow. Then here I am on Sunday afternoon, putting the dogs away after their walk, and who should I see up there at the back door.' He pointed up the path, which led into the kitchen garden, now veiled in mist. In the hour or so since Klaus had followed the constable out here, the back door had disappeared from view.

'Elias Frankel, no less,' continued Heinrich. A new tone, of curiosity mixed with something sharper, entered his voice as he said the name. 'I called out and went over to speak to him. Forget what I said now, something about Johanna being pestered. Elias took it the wrong way. He turned and stared at me with those slow-blinking eyes of his, and for some reason I was – incensed. I told him to get out, get away from her. He called me a useless cretin and I – drove him off with the back of my hand. May have touched his leg with my boot too, to give him the message. That's not something I'm proud of – it's just what happened. Primitive instincts, I suppose. Keeping strangers away from the cave.'

'What time was this?'

Heinrich made a dismissive gesture. 'Three, four maybe. It was still light.'

'Before you discovered—?'

'Hmm? Oh, yes. Before I went in to wake Johanna and check

on the baby. But there's no connection, Deputy.' He turned to face Klaus, speaking with an earnest frown. 'I don't want you to think I'm trying to confuse the – the explanation. It's not something for your report. Been on my mind, that's all. You understand?'

Klaus nodded slowly. 'Yes,' he said. 'I think so.'

✠

Leaving Heinrich alone to bury the child, Klaus went inside to look for Theodore. He found the housekeeper dusting the stair-rail in the hall. Constable Hildebrandt was in the surgery, she said, with the doctor. She pointed again at the wooden bench.

Sitting down on the hard, creaking bench, Klaus was reminded of being in church as a child – shivering on the pew in the cold, and straining to be humble before God the Father. He remembered the school bench too, rocking beneath him as the class rose to chant, in unison, '*Salvete, Magister*.'

Changing his mind, he stood up again, and asked Helga for directions to the Frankel store.

# 8.

Peter Koenig's study was no brighter than the rest of the house. Curtained and carpeted in the dark shades beloved by moths, and dominated by a desk and oak cabinets, it smelt faintly of iodine and misery. In another kind of place, the constable thought, this would be a dining room, with gilt candlesticks and a table for entertaining visitors. But the rooms in farm country like this were not arranged for idle talk. A man did not return from the grazing fields to sit on his neighbour's chair and eat his neighbour's food. If he came to visit, it was for a purpose.

'Will you take a seat?' the young doctor offered, indicating the chair opposite his desk. Removing his glasses, he continued, 'I shouldn't have used such a brisk tone with you, Constable. If I was rude, I apologise. My patience has been somewhat strained by these events in the family. To learn that my mother was responsible . . . or rather irresponsible . . . for what happened to Maria-Theresa is quite a shock to the system. As a result, when I heard you ask her—'

'I had no reason to speak to Frau Koenig as I did,' Theodore interrupted, with a glance of conciliation. 'As you say, the household has a heavy enough burden.'

Peter nodded in acknowledgement.

Theodore noticed a journal on the desk between them, and leaned forward to read the cover: *The Foundations of National Health: Issue III, Autumn 1926, edited by Prof. S. von Brodnitz [D. Phys, Stuttgart, M.D. Berlin, Surg. Heidelberg], W. von Brodnitz [D. Phys, Stuttgart], & P. Koenig [M.D. Heidelberg].* He returned to the first name, *von Brodnitz,* and decided to look it up on his return to the station.

'I received your letter,' he said. 'And the certificate.'

'All in order, I hope?'

The constable nodded. 'Though it's not for me to judge.'

'Hmm,' Peter agreed.

'The coroner . . .' Theodore paused, and saw the doctor's eyebrows lift. 'The coroner will refer any questions to you directly, if necessary. Out of curiosity, though, if you don't mind? I noticed that your sister's child was born in Angenberg, not here.'

'That's correct,' Peter replied, leaning back in his chair – in his father's chair, Theodore guessed. Everything in this room would be inherited from the elder Doctor Koenig. The books, medical instruments, jars on the shelves: these were saint's relics, of a kind. 'They went to the Hospice of Mary Magdalen,' Peter continued. 'I won't pretend that the decision passed without debate, but I understand it. Johanna's waited many years for another child, and she wanted to be sure of having the midwife constantly at hand.'

Theodore wondered what had been left out of that explanation. He noticed that the young doctor's eyes were pale blue like his mother's, and perhaps like his sister's, though the constable had only met Johanna Koenig briefly. Their colouring was different – Johanna's hair, as he recalled, was brown with bouncy curls, whereas Peter's was lighter, almost ginger. But they shared an expression, he thought: direct, demanding.

He said, 'I realise how this might sound, coming from one with my looks, but that little corpse in the box out there did not seem to me . . . well formed.'

Peter's expression stiffened as he replied, 'She was born with a larger forehead than average, and certain other idiosyncrasies. Though what you would conclude from that, I do not wish to imagine.'

Suspecting that Peter had, in fact, imagined it quite clearly, Theodore said, 'Influenza, was it?'

'She had a head cold for several days,' the doctor replied. 'I expect it developed into pneumonia in the shed, though as you might imagine, it is hard to be sure of every detail at this stage, without taking measures which – I hope – none of us would consider necessary. But do you have an alternative diagnosis, Constable?'

He was tempted – *infanticide* – but resisted. 'No.'

'Then . . .?' He gestured, inviting the constable to make his point, or leave. Theodore did neither.

'It must be hard,' the constable said, looking up from the desk at the shelves that surrounded it, 'for you to establish a practice and reputation out here, so far from your fellow professionals.'

Peter Koenig responded with a mild smile. 'I edit a journal, in collaboration with a friend. A respected practitioner in the field—'

'What field?'

'—whose expertise,' Peter continued, ignoring the question, 'I value highly, not least because it keeps me up to date with the latest lines of inquiry.'

Theodore frowned, and looked down again at the journal – *The Foundations of National Health*. 'Is that what this is?' he asked, tapping a finger on the title. 'An inquiry . . . into the nation's health?'

'If you like.'

Theodore sat back to consider. 'What are the "foundations", Doctor?'

Peter Koenig smiled again, this time with more amusement.

Sliding a pen back and forth between his fingertips, he said, 'Are you a medical man, Constable Hildebrandt?'

'In a sense,' Theodore replied. 'Medical men stitched me back together in the field. I'm their monster.'

'I meant—'

'I know what you meant.' He held the man's gaze. 'Am I capable of understanding your answer? Probably not, but oblige me.'

Peter ran a hand over his moustache. Theodore noted a fine scattering of freckles on the doctor's cheeks. 'Very well,' he said. 'In layman's terms, one wants to make sure that the fit and healthy are helped to stay that way. Those best suited to having children should be encouraged to do so, for the sake of preserving and improving upon that good health in successive generations. Sometimes,' he added, putting the pen down with a small sigh, 'it seems that our public officials are trying to build on sand, resting all their hopes on the rescue of the weak.'

'Ah,' Theodore said. 'So if an individual were to be born weak—'

'You're assuming infirmity is determined at birth,' Peter interrupted, glancing at him. 'There's a great deal of debate over the matter.'

'I understand. But let's suppose that a child, a baby,' he said, catching the gleam of anticipation in Peter's eyes, 'is in such a poor state of health, for whatever reason, that it will not ever lead a strong, active life – would there be any justification in, let's say, putting it to sleep?'

The doctor was watching him intently. 'I don't know of any law that would justify it.'

'Natural law?'

Peter fired back, with smiling enthusiasm: 'What do you mean by that?' He seemed to be relishing the debate.

'I don't know,' Theodore admitted. 'To be honest, I've never understood the term. My son's wife uses it sometimes, to explain how the world should be. She would like to sweep me out of the house, along with all the other unnatural things.'

The doctor was on his feet, apparently too invigorated or impatient to remain at the desk. He paced around it for a moment, allowing Theodore to assess him in profile, from the patient's chair. To judge from his smooth forehead, and the healthy gloss of his hair and moustache, Peter Koenig was no more than twenty-five years of age, and could be younger. A suitable match for Ute, the constable had to admit. Strong foundations the two of them would make . . . But what was he doing thinking about that?

'I sense, Constable Hildebrandt,' Peter said, 'that for reasons I have yet to fathom, you are looking for a fault in my practice or person. You would like to challenge Maria-Theresa's death certificate, or the sad business with my mother, but have so far been unsuccesful. Failing in that first line of attack, you've turned to medical ethics, seeking to cast doubt on my integrity, trying to rummage around in my, ah, ah, philosophy for something—'

'Is your philosophy a secret?' Theodore put in. He heard the note of petulance in his voice, and realised that Peter's accusation was justified. The boy in him was trying to snare young Doctor Koenig and pull him down to Theo's own level – God knew it was low enough – so that he could get in an envious blow or two. Pathetic, really. He crossed his left arm against his body, where the the fingers of his right hand found the singed hole in his sleeve. *Where was she?*

'Have we met before, Constable?'

The question took Theodore by surprise. He looked up to meet Peter's searching gaze, and calculated. He had come to Mittelbach from another small town in the district four years ago, which would be roughly when Peter Koenig started his medical studies. It was unlikely that their paths had crossed during one of his trips back from the university . . . But Ute, Ute

63

Prinz as she would then have been: she had been here all along, just a few miles from Mittelbach, and no doubt passing through it sometimes, without Theodore being aware of her existence! The idea filled him with strange urgency. 'I don't remember,' he said, looking at the clock, and then the door.

'As I thought,' Peter agreed. 'Which is why I'm puzzled by the personal nature of your hostility towards this family, Constable. First you interrogate my wife, then my mother, and now—'

'Where is your wife?' Theodore interrupted, rocking out of his chair.

'What?'

'Your wife,' he repeated. 'Frau Ute Koenig.' Gripping the back of the chair to steady himself, he said, 'She went out to light the bonfire on Monday morning. I'd like to ask her if she heard a noise from the wood pile as she passed it.'

Peter picked up the glasses, which he had laid on his blotting pad, and returned them to his face. 'My wife is in town for a few days,' he said, tilting his chin up to look at Theodore through the lenses. 'I don't believe I need to tell you where or why, unless you have a legitimate reason for asking?'

Theodore said nothing.

With a glimmer of amusement, the doctor added, 'My diagnosis is an over-active imagination, Constable Hildebrandt, for which I prescribe a diet of plain bread and water. Stay away from stimulants, man. And for God's sake, find something else to occupy you.'

✠

The front room of the Frankel house, which served as Hindelheim's general store, was kept shuttered to protect the boxes, tins and jars stacked on the shelves. A serving counter had been built across the room to divide the shop, accessed from the front steps, from the small kitchen area behind. Deputy

Constable Klaus Hildebrandt stood at this counter, in the cluttered semi-darkness, with his notebook open in front of him.

Staring down at him from an impressive height on the other side of the counter was the long, angular face of Elias Frankel. The man was his junior by a few years, but taller by several inches. If Klaus looked straight at him, his gaze met Elias Frankel's throat, where a pronounced Adam's apple, amid a haze of dark stubble, emerged from a frayed collar. The 'Frankel eyes', as Klaus would later hear them described, were dark and still, though one eyelid closed further than the other.

On stepping into the store, Klaus had thought it resembled a cave, with objects crowded onto every surface and hanging from the beams like stalactites. And here, guarding the hoard, regarding him with the gaze of a sleepy lizard, was the proprietor.

'What were you doing at the Koenig house on Sunday afternoon?' Klaus asked. He had already introduced himself.

'Delivering a package.'

'For Johanna Koenig?' He waited for a reply, but none came. Holding the storekeeper's gaze was awkward, and not only because of the height difference. Somehow, Klaus felt as if he was caught in one of the animal traps Heinrich had mentioned. He glanced down and picked up his pencil, arming himself. 'I need to know what was in that package, Herr Frankel.'

Putting both hands down flat on the counter – long, pale hands, with prominent knuckles – Elias brought his face close to the deputy's and replied, 'Lll. . .ace.' He drew out the 'l', showing his tongue. 'I took her a piece of lace she'd ordered,' he said. 'You'll have to ask Johanna what she did with it.' A smile tugged the edges of his wide, bristling mouth, sharpening his cheekbones.

Klaus Hildebrandt, reddening, wrote: *Lace*. 'What time was this?'

'Why does it matter?' Elias Frankel countered. 'Are you going to arrest me for working on a Sunday?'

To give himself time, Klaus underlined one or two words in

his notebook, and went over the full stops until they looked like squashed gnats. 'I'll say you arrived between three and four in the afternoon, and left ten minutes later. That sound right?'

Elias Frankel shrugged, and shifted weight from one leg to the other. The action caused him to surge high above the counter before he came down again, almost to the deputy constable's height. He wore the customary white shirt and black waistcoat favoured by merchants and tradesmen in the area, though both had been dulled to differing shades of grey. His long chin was framed by an even longer tangle of hair, which fell around his pale face. He said, 'Dead, is it? The infant.'

'I'm not at liberty to discuss that. Is there something wrong with your leg?'

No reply.

Klaus looked along the shelf behind the counter, which held a number of apparently useless items alongside the normal grocery goods. There were pine cones, various broken eggshells, a bowl of small brown – walnuts? He could not see clearly. Something dried and translucent, possibly a snake's cast-off skin. On the end wall, several rows of butterflies had been pinned to a board. 'Are these for sale?'

The other man, watching him, replied, 'Not normally.'

Baulking at the hint of a bribe, Klaus said, 'I understand that the baby's father got into an argument with you. Heinrich Müller asked you to leave, and when you resisted, he used physical force. What do you want to say about that?'

With a half-smile, Elias Frankel answered, 'I'm not at liberty to discuss it.'

Klaus felt his cheeks colouring at the provocation. 'I don't suppose you know anything about a rat either,' he said carefully, keeping his voice even.

'I know a fair bit. Any rat in particular?'

'The one that was left at the Koenig house a few weeks back, to scare the mute boy.'

Again, no reply.

Klaus closed his notebook. 'Are you sure there's nothing else you want to say now, Herr Frankel, before we hear it from another source?'

The storekeeper studied him for a moment, and then turned away from the counter. Stooping under a bunch of dried herbs that hung from the beam, he shuffled into the furthest part of the room, which Klaus could not see clearly. It was a dimly lit space, with a stove and cooking pots and a square table. A fly curtain hung over the back door, letting in shards of light as it moved in the breeze.

Klaus watched him lean over the table and pluck a piece of paper from the clutter of objects. A document of some kind. He waited for Elias to return to the counter with it, but instead the man took a stool, sat down, and started to read. The silence was broken only by the cracking of the storekeeper's jaw as he pushed the remnants of a meal into his mouth. Bread. What looked like half a boiled egg. A swig of something from a mug.

The deputy constable saw that he had been dismissed. With rising indignation, he turned out of the front door and down the three steps.

✠

His motorcycle was parked on cleared ground outside the store, among a scattering of acorns. There was no street as such running through the tiny heart of Hindelheim – only a continuation of the unpaved lane which Klaus had turned off, twice in one week, to reach the Koenig house. A schoolhouse neighboured the Frankel store, with a playing field stretching out behind it, white in the mist. Several smaller houses stood on the edges of the field, including a row of timber-framed cottages. At one of these, a woman pegging clothes on a line paused to scowl at the young policeman. It was not a day for drying laundry, and Klaus wondered if she had come out only to look at him.

As Klaus stepped up to the vehicle, a man appeared behind it, stepping out of the mist and taking him by surprise. He was a broad-shouldered bull of a man with small eyes staring from a large, flat face. Klaus had the impression that he had been standing there for some time, perhaps inspecting the motorcycle. There would not be many motorised vehicles of any sort in Hindelheim, he guessed – at least, not yet.

Surprising Klaus a second time, the man snapped his heels together and brought a hand to his forehead in a salute.

*A taunt*, Klaus thought, glancing back up the steps at the Frankel store. *They are mocking me.* He suspected that Elias Frankel had signalled out of the window, inciting his friend to make this excessive gesture of respect. If Klaus were to respond with a nod, tacitly accepting the salute as an appropriate greeting to one of his rank – a deputy constable of a minor rural substation! – the man would doubtless burst into gleeful laughter, and Elias Frankel with him. That was what they wanted him to do.

He got onto the motorcycle without acknowledging the man, and started the engine. Glancing in his mirror as he pulled off, Klaus saw the man's hand drop to his side, and began to think he might have been mistaken about the gesture. He thought he caught a look of disappointment on the man's face – and then it vanished into low cloud, as the motorcycle picked up speed and moved away.

# 9.

That night, in his bed above the station office, Theodore wondered if he was going mad. He felt that he had left something behind at the Koenig house, and feared that it was his mind. While his body lay here, his mind was still lost in gloomy corridors, peering into gloomier sheds. Looking for Ute Koenig. *Gone to town.* Why?

Her husband had caught him, dissecting his yearnings with a shrewd professional eye. *I'm puzzled by the personal nature of your hostility towards this family, Constable.* In reply, the constable could only squirm on the wrong side of the desk, unable to supply a reasoned defence. It was the same way with Klaus sometimes. How did these young men become so sensible, Theodore wondered, while he in his maturity could be overturned by the sight of a woman's red-tipped nose?

Lowered voices and creaking floorboards in the next room indicated that Francesca was pacing again, detailing the movements of her unborn child while Klaus appeased her with replies of just sufficient length to draw her back to bed. Theodore thought of his own wife. Her sweetness, long gone now. Sugar for worms.

Eventually silence fell, but still the constable could not sleep. After some more hours of wakefulness, he dressed in the half-light and left the house. With the village of Mittelbach asleep behind him, he stood at the bank of the river that flowed down to Angenberg, fed by tributaries from the hills. It was reassuring to watch the water always moving, always in the same direction – and it heartened him to see the occasional fish turn against the flow.

On the opposite bank was a derelict mill. Theodore did not know how or when it had fallen into ruin, sometime before his arrival here, but he guessed there had been several years when there was no grain to mill – or at least, not enough to sustain such a building. Weeds sprouted from the rotten window frames, from which the glass had been removed, along with every scrap of metal and piece of useful timber. The last people to make use of the place were two thieves on the run from Angenberg, who had taken shelter for a few nights under what was left of the roof. They had stolen a bicycle from outside a bank, and given its owner a bloody nose. For that crime, the savants at police headquarters had declared the couple to be 'violent reprobates of the first order', and issued orders to all substations to find and arrest them as a matter of urgency. Theodore suspected that a bank manager in Angen, robbed of the bicycle that normally took him to his home in the suburbs, had put in a call to the chief of police.

The thieves had made a fire in the derelict building one evening, out of rotting boards, and sat by it with their arms around each other. Theodore had stood here on the bank, watching them. He had walked away without disturbing the pair, and never told anyone; not even Klaus. There were many things the constable could not tell his deputy.

Ute, though. He could tell Ute Koenig about the thieves. She would—

'Stop,' Theodore told himself, aloud. He was at it again; letting his lonely hopes get ahead of him. He did not, in fact, know what she would think or say or do, about anything.

Eventually, a bell in the village chimed six. Theodore made his way to a fork in the road where several labourers were assembling to start the day's work of clearing, widening and flattening the old path to create the new road. Tomorrow the mayor would bring his guests to see the progress and the possibilities afforded by it; and despite his wariness of officialdom, Constable Hildebrandt knew that the tour was important. Many of his neighbours still struggled against hunger and were scarred by losses of one sort or another. Even a small change, such as the renovation of the derelict millhouse into a factory building, would provide a few more precious opportunites for work and trade.

So, he would be ready to greet the mayor tomorrow. But first, there was something he needed to do. It was a clear, cool morning, with none of yesterday's mist. As the sun rose, the colourful leaves of the beech trees on the lower slopes brightened in contrast to the dark evergreens further up. Every day now, the view changed, with shades of orange, purple and green merging and replacing one another, racing towards a uniform, lifeless brown. Theodore waited by the roadside until a farm wagon appeared in the distance, rising and falling over the ruts of the old track. It was the Pohlmanns' wagon, making its regular trip down from Hindelheim into the valley. The driver was a heavily pregnant young girl with startling green eyes. One of the Pohlmanns. The constable had seen her in Mittelbach making deliveries.

He asked if Ute Koenig had taken a lift in the last couple of days, and whether she had mentioned whereabouts in Angen she would be staying. The girl made a sullen reply, offering up the information without any sign that she cared about it, one way or another.

✠

In the Central Pharmacy in Angenberg, Ute waited for the pharmacist to finish packing her supplies. She took yesterday's

71

telegram from her pocket. When it had arrived, taking her by surprise, Ute had thought that Peter must have remembered another item to add to the order – but no, the message was quite different. She read it again.

*M-T found in shed. Painless death most likely Sun night. J & H showing fortitude. Mother confused. See you as planned. P.*

Folding it carefully, she put the telegram back into the pocket of her coat, and buttoned the pocket. It was not the kind of note to leave lying around. Imagine a stranger finding it. Imagine the pharmacist picking it up!

'If you would sign here, Frau Koenig,' the man instructed, turning a receipt towards her on the counter. Ute did as asked, and took the package in both hands.

The Kaiser followed her onto the street. At the tram stop, a woman in the waiting crowd trod on the dog's paw, causing a whimper and an exchange of glances. There was no space on the first tramcar that stopped, and Ute decided not to wait for the next. Holding the bulging bag, she walked past office buildings and shops in the paved part of town, thereafter turning down narrower alleys, some of them thick with grime.

Once she reached the rooming house, she planned to take out each bottle or sachet of powder and look up the name in Peter's pharmacology manual, to teach herself its properties. Book medicine, as Aunt Ernesta used to call it, seemed to Ute a wondrous new world. As with Aunt's rituals and potions, the medicines she carried now could ease or cause a troubled night, depending on how they were used. There was something paradoxical in it, she thought. Was science so far from magic? Peter said so. When Ute, watching him at work on his journal one day – admiring the concentration in his face, the precise movements of his pen – compared him to a sorcerer, he rejected the notion with a vehemence that startled her. She had decided from then on to avoid certain subjects, including her aunt's superstitions, and her own.

Ammonia fumes greeted her as she entered Angenberg's factory district. Thick air and narrow streets conspired to block out the light. Overhead, clothes dried on lines strung between apartment buildings. Finally, Ute turned past a hardware store into the dark staircase of an apartment building, and climbed to the third floor.

The apartment was shared by up to a dozen tenants at any one time; most of them shift workers, unknown to one another. Ute's friend Marlyse Pohlmann was the most recent newcomer, having moved in a few weeks ago, after securing work in town as a kitchen assistant. There was a common room where the curtains were kept permanently closed – presumably, Ute thought, to provide a constant, artificial twilight for tenants who had to sleep during the day. She followed a man into the apartment, neither of them acknowledging the other. He shuffled wearily across the common area and disappeared into a room off it, shutting the door. The Kaiser, obeying Ute's hushed commands to stay by her side and make no noise, sniffed the floor until they reached the kitchen stove, where his tongue came out to mop up spilled crumbs.

Marlyse Pohlmann stood under a light bulb suspended from the ceiling, boiling a saucepan of water. The shelf above her was crammed with a motley assortment of crockery, each stack of plates belonging to a different resident. She was Ute's own age, but almost her opposite in physical appearance, with rich, dark hair cascading over a fleshy neck. Like her cousin Gretchen Pohlmann, Marlyse had striking green eyes and a sensuous, lethargic beauty.

She returned Ute's greeting with a familiar nod. They were old friends, who did not need to bother each other with questions. 'You've got a visitor,' was all Marlyse said, her eyebrows lifting slightly at the news. 'Been waiting a while. Says he doesn't want coffee.'

Ute was puzzled. How could she have a visitor when she herself was the visitor here, sharing Marlyse's narrow bed for a few days while the dog slept beneath them, on the floorboards? Following Marlyse's glance, she turned to look back across the room.

Constable Hildebrandt was sitting at the end of a table – the only table, in fact – which was pushed against the wall, between the door and the curtained window. Ute had been so preoccupied with keeping the dog under control that she had failed to notice him as she came in.

'I was in the area, Frau Koenig,' he said, pulling himself up from his chair with an obvious effort. His peaked cap lay on the table beside him. 'I hope you don't mind?'

For a moment Ute was too stunned to speak. When had she last had a visitor, even in her own home? But no – it was the telegram, she realised. That was why. The constable had come because of the telegram in her pocket. *Painless death . . . showing fortitude*.

Approaching the table, she placed her brown bag of medicines carefully on it, replying, 'It's good to see you again, Herr Constable.'

He held her gaze for a moment without speaking. Ute found it hard to interpret his expression in the dim, artificial light. His green uniform seemed, here in this room, more official than before; almost alarming. 'I'm Marlyse's guest here,' she said, breaking the silence. 'But I'm sure you're welcome to sit wherever you'd be most comfortable, Constable.' She gestured at the rooming-house furniture: an old, stained couch and two or three armchairs, some covered, some not.

'No. I've been sitting long enough,' he replied, and looked over her shoulder.

Ute could hear a slurping sound behind her, and the slow

chiming of a spoon in Marlyse's hot drink. She guessed that her friend would be watching them, and listening, with mild but unconcealed curiosity.

Clearing his throat, the constable continued. 'You've heard the news from Hindelheim, I suppose?'

Ute nodded. 'Yes. Peter sent a telegram.'

'You were already here in town on Tuesday night, I think, when the child was found? Found on the wood pile,' he added, pausing as if to impress the image on her.

Ute glanced down to pull off her gloves. 'I don't know what to say,' she replied. 'Is there a problem, Constable? I thought, when Peter's telegram arrived, that the matter must now be settled. Not happily, of course, but – resolved?'

'You're right.' He nodded. 'The danger, if there was a danger, has passed. No more harm can come to the child now. It's in the ground.' There was another pause, while the man seemed to decide what to say. 'I'm . . . told I have a tendency to pick at scabs, Frau Koenig. An ugly habit. I must learn to leave scars to heal of their own accord. That's what your husband would advise, I expect.'

Ute searched his face, surprised by this reference to Peter, and by the tone of it. 'I'm not sure I understand,' she said.

The constable, hesitating again, glanced past her. Then he picked up his cap, saying, 'My deputy is expecting to meet me shortly at the corner of the street. I must wait for him there, but . . . perhaps you might spare a few minutes to accompany me, Frau Koenig?'

At this she stood still, watching him for a clue. Was it a device, a standard procedure, to extract someone for questioning? Would there be a police vehicle on the street, with another officer waiting to drive her to an interview room? Or was he . . .? She glanced down at Constable Hildebrandt's arm, finding the sleeve of his coat where she had held onto him, steering him away from the fire.

Back up to his eyes, which looked at her now with that unexpected concentration Ute had seen, and felt, before. She asked, 'Does Peter know you're here?'

'I saw him,' he confirmed, raising his cap to his head, 'and he told me that you were in town. However, I'm sure Doctor Koenig would not want me to disturb you without your willing compliance.' No, Ute thought, catching something harder in his expression: this is an accusation, not an invitation. 'So I'll wish you a good evening,' the constable concluded, 'and leave you alone. Pardon me for the interruption.'

✠

Ute watched in confusion, holding her gloves in her hand, as Constable Hildebrandt turned out of the room. She could hear him starting, with difficulty, down the stairs.

Turning, she found Marlyse leaning against the kitchen drawers, drinking from a mug. 'Will you watch the dog?' she asked.

Marlyse looked at her, frowned, and looked up at the clock. As Ute knew, her evening duties at the Bridge Street Beer Hall would start soon.

She begged. 'Just a few minutes?'

With a shrug, Marlyse conceded. 'Long as you tell me what it's all about.'

'I will,' Ute promised, sensing as she said it that she would not, in fact, tell all – even to Marlyse. Something had shifted in recent months which neither of the friends had remarked on openly. Decisions, alliances, dependencies: all the small struggles of their lives had begun to draw them very gradually, almost imperceptibly, apart. As young girls, sharing a slate in the Hindelheim schoolhouse, they kept few secrets from each other. These days, little by little, they were becoming strangers.

She caught up with the constable at the bottom of the stairwell, where he was catching his breath. He nodded, to

76

acknowledge her change of mind, and they stepped out together onto the street, where Constable Hildebrandt led the way, slowly but with an air of purpose. There was a butcher's shop on the first corner, which had closed at noon having run out of meat. Ute could not see the constable's deputy, or any other figure in uniform, waiting on the pavement; and nor was there a police vehicle in sight. When the constable crossed the road junction and continued down the next street, she concluded that he must have been referring to a different corner.

At the next junction, they paused while a lorry turned past them into a yard full of scrap metal and old tyres. Then the constable, looking about, swung suddenly to the left, and started down another street . . .

'Herr Constable,' she said, drawing level with him. 'I thought you were going to wait for your deputy on the corner?'

Theodore Hildebrandt raised his left arm and pointed. 'In there,' he said. There was a café diagonally across from them – in the middle of a row, Ute noted, not on a corner. 'He's meeting me there,' the constable said, setting off towards it.

# 10.

Klaus Hildebrandt was oiling the hinge of the cell door when a motorcar pulled into the station yard, swinging past the beech tree that stood next to the gatepost, and forcing an elderly woman to step out of the way. Klaus watched the vehicle's approach with some alarm. Had the mayor come a day earlier than planned? Had Theodore been mistaken or lied about the timing of the visit? The deputy constable straightened, hastening to brush down his uniform as the passenger door opened.

A police officer stepped out with an expression suggesting that he enjoyed the reaction his appearance had caused. Officer Zelinsky was around thirty years of age, with eyes the colour of a summer thunderstorm. 'Deputy,' he said, with a brief nod. 'Is the constable in?'

Klaus felt the colour rise in his cheeks as he invented, 'He's gone into the village, I think, to investigate a complaint from one of the residents.'

Officer Zelinsky smiled. 'Covering up for the old man. I like your loyalty, Hildebrandt. We'll take care of the problem between us.'

'Problem, sir?'

'You drove the constable out to Hindelheim on Monday, I

believe, at the request of a Doctor Koenig. A family matter. Did you take notes?'

'Yes . . .'

'Show me.'

Klaus turned into the station office to fetch his notebook. There he hesitated, thinking. Should he try to delay the officer somehow, until his father got back? Officer Zelinsky seemed to be in a hurry to discuss or do something – perhaps the burial was unlawful, after all? Klaus kicked himself for failing to check the regulations before helping Heinrich Müller dig the infant's grave. A rush of unexpected emotion had galvanised him into action yesterday, after seeing the tiny corpse surrounded by sawn logs. Now he regretted his spontaneity. It was out of character, a mistake. If his father were here, Klaus would have some protection. The constable would defend him, if only out of stubbornness.

Where was the old man, damn it? Why had he chosen today to play truant, when – for once – he was wanted here?

Theodore was bound to resent the interference of an officer from headquarters, Klaus knew – especially when that officer was Zelinsky. The two men had crossed swords on several occasions, each rising to the other's provocation. Officer Zelinsky sneered at the constable's lax manners and morals, while Theodore despised Zelinsky's ambition. Among his many claims to success, the officer had once been responsible for swooping on a derelict building near here, by the river, where he captured two violent thieves who were wanted in Angenberg. By Mittelbach standards, it was a thrilling raid, from which Constable Theodore Hildebrandt, stationed less than a mile away, had been excluded.

A wasp crawled slowly across the windowpane, refusing to accept the season's signals that it was time to die. Looking past it, Klaus saw Officer Zelinsky pacing across the yard, frowning towards the station office. Cool blue eyes. Pressed uniform. Hair combed to perfection. A man who did not like to be kept waiting. If Theodore returned now, or if Klaus were able to delay things until he did come back, what would happen? An argument, no doubt – in which the constable had what chance of claiming the high ground? None, of course. It was almost bound to end in disaster, with Theodore Hildebrandt insulting Zelinsky, and damaging his own cause.

As Klaus thought about this, he decided that it would be better to obey the officer in order to protect his father, rather than wait for his father to protect him.

•I•

Zelinsky had returned to the motor car, and was in the front passenger seat, drumming his hand on the open window. A junior police adjunct waited behind the wheel.

Klaus gave him the notebook and stood uncertainly beside the car door while the officer flicked through it.

'Full marks for record keeping, Deputy.' He ran his finger down a list then turned the page, and repeated the motion. 'From this I wouldn't guess you were Theodore Hildebrandt's son. This is the hand of a man of conscience. Of unfulfilled promise, I daresay.'

Klaus met his glance and hesitated. 'May I know what the problem is, sir?'

'You conducted these interviews with Theo, did you?'

Klaus answered carefully. 'We met the bereaved mother together, on our first visit to the Koenigs' house. In order to save time, we spoke separately to—'

'Did you see him bully the old woman?' Zelinsky looked up, and without waiting for an answer, continued, 'The chief inspector received a complaint yesterday about Constable Hildebrandt's abrasive and accusatory conduct with members of the grieving family. He's sent me to make amends. I plan to make a *courteous* visit to the household,' he leaned on the word, holding the deputy's gaze, 'and I'd like you to accompany me, so that you can learn from it. Follow us in your vehicle, Deputy.'

'Now?' he asked, growing uneasy.

Officer Zelinsky's head re-emerged in the window. With a smile, he said, 'Do you hear that sound, Hildebrandt?'

Klaus listened. He could hear birds. Hammering, perhaps from the blacksmith's shop. The distant mechanical churning of a mixing or digging machine. 'The roadworks?'

Zelinsky nodded. 'It won't be the route to El Dorado, except in the mayor's dreams, but when it can bring lumber from that side of the hills onto the Angen highway without making a thirty-mile detour, then you'll see six times the volume of motor traffic passing by this little outpost. Passport checks, weighing and taxing of goods, transport-related crimes: those will all need dedicated, efficient police officers.'

He paused, and then continued, 'I know the chief inspector is already considering how to expand the capacity of this place. If you want to take a role in that new world, Deputy – and I think you should – then here's the choice you need to make. Follow the contrary path of your father, deciding who to believe and who not to believe, in matters that are far beyond your rank and remit – and so ensure that you will never wear a better uniform than that one. Or, apply some discipline to that healthy mind of yours, show the proper respect for divisions of authority, and allow yourself to reach your potential. Do you see what I am saying?'

Klaus found that his mouth was too dry to speak, and so he made an equivocal noise in his throat, which Zelinsky seemed to understand. Slapping the notebook back into his hand, the officer said, 'Are you for the new world or the old, my friend? That's what you need to ask yourself. Something to think about as we go, hmm?'

✠

They sat at opposite sides of a narrow table, with a bowl of sugar between them.

Theodore turned a spoon slowly in his coffee, wondering which of them was more nervous than the other. He guessed that Ute Koenig had rarely, if ever, visited a café with a man she did not know, in a town that was not her home. Equally, he wondered when – if ever – he had last sat in a place like this, with a young woman?

'What brings you to Angen, Frau Koenig?' He raised his cup and lowered his head to meet it. The coffee was hot, and it scalded his mouth.

Ute, who had not yet touched her drink, explained that Peter needed some supplies for the surgery. He had given her a list, which she had deposited with the pharmacist, returning today to collect the medicines.

'Huh,' Theodore said, as if impressed with Doctor Koenig's ingenuity. 'Running errands for the doctor. Quite a change from your previous duties, at the school?'

She lifted her cup then and took a sip, but did not answer him – reasonably enough, the constable thought. They both knew it was not a question. He saw that her hands were scrubbed clean of Monday's garden dirt. No muddy remnants of the bonfire – *our* bonfire, he thought – lingering under her nails. Pity.

Having told him as they entered the café that she could not stay long, Ute had sat down in her coat to emphasise the point. An ivory shirt collar was visible above it, slightly frayed, and the hem of a skirt below the coat, at her knees. Theodore would have to imagine the in-between. He challenged himself to a private game: could he rouse her to such a heat of passion – ha! – that she would become uncomfortable, and choose to remove the coat?

'Forgive me, Ute, but—'

Her eyes flicked up at this use of her first name.

'I thought the war had changed that tradition,' he said, 'of women relinquishing all power and prospects to their husbands.

My mother did it, of course, as hers did. But you . . . are . . .' He took a breath, finding that he was short of it; that he, not Ute, was the one in danger of burning up with embarrassment. *Good God, Theo, what is happening to you?* 'You are living in that house,' he continued, 'and – and parcelling up your freedom. Making a gift of it, to Peter Koenig. I wonder if any man could deserve that.'

Ute swallowed her mouthful of coffee, pressed her lips together and wiped them swiftly, with a napkin. 'Peter asked me,' she said. 'No one else would.'

'No one else?' Theodore repeated. It was unthinkable. 'I'd guess that every young man within—'

'No one,' she repeated.

Her eyes were bright with private determination or discipline, and she sat on the edge of her seat, holding the cup in both hands as if fearing that the constable might snatch it from her. Theodore was ashamed that just a moment ago, he had sought to amuse himself by stirring up this woman's emotions. He did not yet understand them, but there was no mistaking their force.

After a silence, Ute said, 'You wanted to ask me something. About Johanna's baby?'

At the neighbouring table, a couple laughed as they divided a slice of cake. Theodore nodded. 'Yes,' he replied, though it was not quite true. His conversation with Peter Koenig had provided at least a partial explanation for the baby's death. The constable thought he knew the 'why', if not all of the 'how' and 'who'.

The question that remained in his mind, and under his skin, was one that Ute Koenig would not answer, and he could not ask: *How can I take hold of you?*

✠

Elias Frankel had been living alone at the back of the Hindelheim General Store for four months now, since his young half-brother, Otto, went off to school. Otto's father had died within days of Otto's departure – from loneliness, some people said. Some people said otherwise. The double loss left Elias as the only remaining Frankel in what everyone in Hindelheim still called 'the Frankel store' or 'the Frankel place' or even, though she had now been dead for eight years, 'Ida Frankel's'.

Ida Frankel had built the store. Ida Frankel ran the store. As Ida Frankel's elder son, Elias was expected to do as she would have done, and keep the store open day and night, welcoming neighbours at all hours into the shop that was also a home, for talking, drinking, sometimes dancing.

But Elias was not like his mother, except in the sharp angles of his cheeks and chin, which to some eyes gave him a strange beauty. He rose late, rarely before ten in the morning and often much later, and opened the store – the front room – when it suited him. Sometimes it suited him not to open the store at all, but to go into the wood instead, and watch whatever was feeding or fighting or mating or dying there. He would become absorbed in the watching, and forget to go home; or remember, and choose not to.

Today Elias Frankel cooked a breakfast of soup shortly after midday, and was still eating it two hours later. The kitchen table was covered with objects of fascination, pieces of bark and rock, and the sketches he'd made of them. There were half a dozen incomplete drawings of a spider's web; one particular web which he had almost walked into at dawn this morning, returning from a nocturnal walk. It was hanging between two trees at head-height, six feet off the ground. Elias had stood and studied it in the early light, as the rising sun gradually clarified its threads. Then he hurried back, loping from one long leg to the other, in order to get the web down onto paper while he still remembered it. None of the drawings was right, but he propped up the least bad one in front of him and considered it, while spooning lukewarm soup from the pot in which he had cooked it.

Also on the table was a book of anatomy, illustrated with

dissections of men and animals. Elias had commissioned Otto
to steal it from the Angenberg Library one day, being too
conspicuously tall to make an effective thief himself. He liked to
know how things looked, inside and out; living creatures
especially. How they moved, and which muscles worked in
which direction. Women would sometimes tell Elias, as they lay
curled or slumped on the sheets of his or some other bed, that
he treated their bodies as if they were athletes training for a
race, or ponies up for sale in a horse fair; always pushing them
on, faster and further, to see how they would respond. They
complained of aches and bad treatment – and more often than
not, came back for more. Elias did not ask them to come or go.
He enjoyed women too much to want to keep one.

Scraping his spoon along the bottom of the pan, Elias
noticed a letter half buried among other papers. He had read
the first page yesterday, and put it down somewhere. Here was
the second, penned in large, slanting handwriting:

*The supervisor kept me back after class and said that I would
have to share slates and books with the other boy who doesn't
pay his bills and that if it goes on like this I will be sharing shoes
and trousers too. He told me to stop grinning and did he look
like a music-hall comedian because he wasn't joking. Another
boy heard him talking and followed me and knocked the books
out of my hand saying they weren't mine. When I bent to pick
them up he took hold of my belt and tried to—*

A noise at the front door drew his gaze up momentarily. Shut
and bolted from the inside, the door rattled as someone outside
tried to open it. A man's voice called out, 'Anyone home?' Elias
returned his attention to the letter.

*This is the same boy who stole my boxing glove that you gave me
as I told you last time. He won't admit it but I know. I'm not*

85

*scared of him only biding my time until the right moment comes when I will knock his jaw together and watch all the teeth come jangling out. Then I will hit him again down to the floor.*

Another noise, at the back this time. Footsteps in the yard.

*Remember I told you that I thought a man was watching me? Well yesterday he called through the gates to say that he worked for some people at the market who—*

From the yard came a soft whistle, and a patter of steps. Elias got up and limped to the back door, which stood open with a fly curtain hanging across it. He parted the threads of the curtain with a long finger, to see out.

A wooden staircase with two broken steps led from where he stood down into the back yard, which was lower than the front of the store, being built on a slope that continued into the paddock beyond. From an outhouse came a rustling sound. As Elias watched, a young boy stepped out of the shed and brushed flour from his arms and shorts. The boy seemed to assume that the door of the shed, which stood open, hid him from the storekeeper's view. A girl followed with more circumspection, arms crossed over the bulge in her clothing which contained whatever she had stolen.

Snatching up a shotgun which stood ready beside him, Elias pushed out onto the steps, calling, 'I see you, devil-spawn. Don't you know I'm always watching?'

The two broken steps gaped beneath him, requiring an awkward, sideways stretch that jolted his injured ankle and slowed his descent. As the children scuttled to the gate, he yelled after them, 'Thieving rats! I hope you choke on the poison!' Reaching the bottom of the steps as they disappeared through the gate into the school field, he thrust the gun into the air, where they could see it if they looked back.

'Don't move,' said a man behind him.

The storekeeper heard him, but turned anyway. He found himself looking into the blue eyes of a police officer. Close behind him was the deputy constable from Mittelbach, who had come asking questions yesterday afternoon.

'I asked you not to move, Herr Frankel,' the officer said. 'If you hadn't been threatening the lives of your neighbours with that gun, perhaps you'd have heard me. Now lower the weapon.'

Elias Frankel's gaze moved from the officer to the deputy constable. He lowered the shotgun, which the police officer snatched from him.

'What do you say, Deputy: reckon our boy here has a licence for this?' Keeping his eyes on the storekeeper, the officer went on. 'Let's take him to Mittelbach, ask him a few questions. Put him in the sidecar. I'll follow, keep an eye on him.'

Elias Frankel continued to watch as Deputy Constable Klaus Hildebrandt stepped towards him, jaw clenched tight.

'Better put the handcuffs on him,' the officer added, causing Klaus Hildebrandt to blink before he took hold of the storekeeper's arm.

✠

Led around the side of the building to the lane at the front, Elias saw with some surprise that there were two police vehicles parked there: the motorcycle from Mittelbach, which had come yesterday, and a black motor car. The car's driver was kneeling in the dust to inspect its exhaust pipe, evidently worried – as well he might be – by the effects of the drive up here, on the old hill road. Staring open-mouthed at the car was the boy with flour on his clothes. The girl-thief, standing beside her fellow conspirator, glanced up as Elias Frankel was led out, but then returned her attention to the greater spectacle of a motor convoy in Hindelheim.

Ordered into the motorcycle sidecar, Elias glared at it in disbelief. How was he supposed to fit inside that thing, all six foot of him? It looked like a bucket, not a road vehicle. The deputy constable, not content with hounding him yesterday, had obviously returned to humiliate him. Elias felt a hand grip his shoulder to reinforce the command. There was no choice. He climbed in, flinching from the effort of folding up his knees. As expected, the sidecar could barely contain him.

Klaus Hildebrandt leaned down to cuff his wrists together, and Elias tried to catch the man's eye. The deputy, refusing to look at him, put the key to the handcuffs in his top pocket, and fastened the pocket.

With a shout from the police officer – 'On! You go ahead!' – the engines started, shocking Elias into the realisation that this was happening, they were moving. He turned his head to look back at the building. The front door was bolted. But the back? The hen huts? How long would this take?

The two vehicles moved off slowly, the motorcycle leading. They turned past the thieving children, who had now been joined by several other observers – neighbours who had heard or seen something from their cottages. Running from the school field to join the small crowd was the soldier, Elias noticed: Eckhardt Gröhlick. Eckhardt's great moon of a face was red with exertion and with the anxiety of missing out on some action.

'Eckhardt!' Elias shouted. He made an exaggerated motion with his head to catch the man's attention. 'Eckhardt Gröhlick!'

Lumbering forward, Eckhardt Gröhlick caught up with the motorcycle as it slowed to round a bend in the lane, by the old water pump. Centuries of use and leakage had softened the ground around the pump, causing both vehicles to crawl, snail-like, through a ditch.

Eckhardt leaned into the sidecar, gripping it with both hands, his tiny eyes squinting at Elias in earnest bewilderment.

There was no time for a greeting. Elias shouted. 'Look after the place, will you?'

# 11.

'Something has happened to Frau Koenig's memory,' Ute said. She leaned forward over her cup; talking more freely, it seemed to Theodore, now that she was no longer talking about herself. 'It seems almost . . . as if she's living at another time, when her husband was alive. Doctor Koenig died at the end of the war, did I say that?'

'They're connected?' the constable asked. 'His death and her – absence of mind?'

Ute paused, as she always did, before answering. 'There was a good deal of sickness in that last year. Influenza. My aunt caught it but recovered, with the help of Ida Frankel's tonic – but that doesn't matter.' She picked at an invisible splinter on the surface of the table. 'Doctor Koenig was still in Hindelheim then,' she went on, drawing herself back to the point. 'He was occupied with his patients, and when Ida herself contracted it—'

'Herself?' Theo interrupted. 'What do you mean?'

Ute looked at him, her eyes moving across his face as if assessing what he knew, or how much she should tell. 'Ida Frankel ran the store. Everyone went there, of course – where else would we buy anything in Hindelheim? She was always welcoming, so the place was busy – as busy as it could be, anyway. If Ida got sick, I suppose there was a greater chance of the contagion spreading.'

Theodore nodded, though as ever he had the impression that Ute was telling him something else, in parallel, which he was failing to pick up.

With a frown, she continued, 'And her little boy, Otto, was just a baby. But he was not able to save her – the doctor, I mean. He suffered when she died, and I think his family . . . Everyone could see it. Then he went off to the Front. It was the very last month of the war, I think.'

Theodore felt his own memories battering at the door. He drained his cup, seeking to rouse himself with the last of the coffee, and then returned it with an effort to the table, using his left hand to support the weak right elbow. 'You believe that Frau Koenig's mind was elsewhere,' he said, 'as she moved the child?'

Ute answered carefully, in a quiet voice. 'From what I've seen of her, it seems possible.'

A sudden scraping of chairs at the next table interrupted, as the couple who had shared a cake got up to leave. Talking to her companion, the woman unwittingly let her skirted backside brush against the edge of the neighbouring table, causing Theodore to pull his fingers back to avoid contact. When he looked up, Ute was watching him, and he felt that she could see his awkwardness.

She took a breath. 'I ought to get back.'

'Will you be staying in town for long?' He followed this question with a look of disapproval and suspicion. It was not engineered. The constable suspected that he might not see Ute Koenig again, and he sincerely disapproved of that prospect.

'Until Sunday,' Ute answered. 'Peter is coming tomorrow. We're to have dinner here with a friend of his.'

'Would that be von Brodnitz?' Theodore hazarded. 'The eugenics man?'

Momentarily surprised, Ute said, 'Oh, I see. Peter told you.'

Theodore did not tell her that on returning to Mittelbach yesterday evening, he had visited his physician friend, Rudi

Hoffmann, to ask if he had heard of a von Brodnitz, the leading author of Peter Koenig's medical journal. Instead the constable asked, 'And when will you next stay here again, with Marlyse Pohlmann?'

Ute picked up her gloves and put them down again. 'I'm not sure,' she said. 'We . . . She has her own life now.'

'Only now?'

Ute acknowledged the implication with a quick, amused smile. 'No, of course. Marlyse has always been her own person. It's just that we've been living together in the cottage since my aunt died, so it's become a habit with me to – to think of her that way, as always being there.' After a pause, she went on, 'I don't know how it happened, exactly. There was no discussion, as far as I remember. They carried Aunt Ernesta out in a box three years ago, and the same day, Marlyse moved in.'

It had grown darker in the café as they were talking, and a waitress, newly arrived for the evening shift, drew the curtains in order to conserve a smudge of orange heat given out by the gas fire.

'And now your friend has left Hindelheim,' Theodore said. 'Because you moved to live with Peter Koenig?'

Ute gave a hesitant nod. 'And because she fell out of love with someone. Or the other way round.' She paused. 'A disappointment, either way. I think Marlyse hopes to make a success of herself here, and get her revenge on the man that way.'

Theodore was about to pick up on that word, revenge, when Ute spoke again.

'Constable?'

She looked at him with a still intensity that caused him to hold his breath.

'Do you think there are wolves around here?'

'Wolves?' He rocked forward in suprise. It was the abrupt leap from Marlyse Pohlmann that most surprised him. 'I don't – I don't know. Why?'

Ute frowned, explaining, 'There was some talk in the summer, about a wolf. Elias Frankel, the storekeeper, thought he saw it in the hills, towards the quarry. The younger boys wanted to believe it, of course. They're forever trying to tame rats and squirrels, so the idea of a creature like that roaming nearby . . . you can imagine. It must have been something else, though – a wild dog or fox, because there are no longer any wolves here, are there?'

Theodore made an inconclusive gesture. A new customer entered the café, bringing a gust of cold air with him, which drew Ute's gaze towards the door. She turned back with a new thought. 'Won't your deputy be waiting?'

'Why do you ask?'

'Because you said—'

'About the wolf,' he said. 'Why does it matter?'

'Oh.' She brought a hand to her cheek, running her finger over it distractedly, just below the eye. The constable had seen Peter Koenig do the same thing the day before. Perhaps it was catching. Over time, people who live in close proximity adopt the same words and facial expressions, Theodore found, the same way as neighbours in remote places smell like one another, their clothes and skin scrubbed with the same soap. Soldiers, too, he thought, all stink alike; leaking blood and fear.

'It doesn't matter,' Ute continued. 'It's only that I found myself thinking about it again, on Monday, after – after you left.'

At the reminder, Theodore caught and held her gaze. *Woman of fire*, he thought.

The waitress interrupted to clear their cups. Would they have anything else?

Ute shook her head and Theodore, to keep her from leaving, urged, 'You were saying. On Monday.'

Reaching once more for her gloves, Ute held onto them this time. She said, 'I found the corpse of a deer, in the wood. It was rotten, crawling with flies. Dead, without a doubt. Partly eaten by something . . . But it's strange,' she added in a confessional tone, looking at him. 'We see dead foxes and other things all the time, and yet this one . . . just for a moment, it seemed alive.'

'Alive,' he repeated.

'But it only seemed so,' Ute said, 'and only for a moment. It was dead flesh. Carrion. There's no mystery to it, really. I know that. You must think I'm mad.'

Theodore began to form a reply, but did not say it.

'My aunt saw everything as a sign of good or bad luck, Constable. I'm afraid I've developed her habit. It seems that we've had a run of it lately – bad luck, I mean. If it was a wolf, though, a real wolf in Hindelheim . . .' Her eyes shone at him, urging his agreement. 'That would be a good omen, wouldn't it? A sign that everything will be all right?'

✠

Leading the two-vehicle convoy out of Hindelheim, Deputy Constable Klaus Hildebrandt recognised features that had become familiar to him over the last few days. The pig sheds here. The barn over there. The angle of the slope past the Pohlmann farm. Leaving the hamlet behind, they followed the edge of the wood.

Glancing for the umpteenth time into the sidecar, Klaus saw his passenger's face in profile, and wondered whether cold or fear or something else was causing the clenching of the man's jaw, and the rigidity of his gaze. Elias Frankel had no coat or gloves or riding helmet to protect him from the wind, he realised. Back at the store, Klaus had almost said to Officer Zelinsky: 'Wouldn't it be better, sir, for you to take the prisoner to Mittelbach, in the motor car?'

But he had not. For some reason, Klaus had gone ahead and shoved this giant of a man into the sidecar and clamped his wrists together.

Long shadows stretched across the track in the last of the day's sunshine. It was coldest in the straight parts of the road, where they drove fast and the air whistled around them, finding exposed patches of skin, turning the spine to ice. Cold, too, in the densely forested stretches, where spruce and then fir, and finally beech trees overshadowed the road. With sudden urgency, Klaus took advantage of a relatively smooth part of the track to gain speed. Cows looked up at the buzz of the motorcycle, and with a glance behind him, Klaus pulled sharply round a bend. When he turned to look again, the officer's car had fallen some way behind and was moving slowly, navigating a watery dip. Veering to one side of the track, Klaus stopped. Trees occupied the slope to one side of them, dense enough to provide some cover from the following vehicle.

The engine clicked shut, creating a sudden silence. Klaus walked briskly around the front wheel, and felt the passenger's eyes follow him.

'What happens here?' Elias Frankel called after him.

'Nothing.' He stood with his back to the sidecar to urinate, praying that Zelinsky's car would not turn the corner in time to see him. For the moment, there was no sign of it, and no sound except for the splatter of liquid on fallen leaves. Brown fungi sprouted from a tree trunk, and other, paler varieties stood in the ground by the deputy constable's feet.

'Don't want the officer to know you have a weak bladder?' mocked the voice behind him. 'I'm surprised you held it in this long. I could see back there you were pissing yourself. Never arrested anyone before, I bet?'

Fastening his trousers, Klaus heard the clink of a chain, and swung round. In the sidecar, the prisoner held up his wrists and shook them again, jangling the chain between the handcuffs and evidently enjoying the reaction it had caused.

'Clever boy,' Elias continued, as Klaus turned back towards the vehicle. 'Taking a piss all by yourself. Showing Papa you can operate restraints. This is a big day for you, Deputy. You've almost convinced me you're a full grown police—'

The deputy's hand flew out and caught him on the nose, knocking his face sideways for an instant. He brought his chained hands up to shield himself from a second blow, and Klaus hesitated. A look of surprise passed between them. Now that he was standing over the passenger, Klaus could see that the man was shivering.

From behind them came the noise of the car. On impulse, Klaus tugged a scarf loose from his neck, and dropped it onto the man's lap, where it was seized by blue-white fingers. Elias looked up with a silent question, but Klaus did not answer.

With Officer Zelinsky's car now closing in behind, the motorcycle moved on. They followed a stream down through lower, patchier woodland with frequent open clearings. Klaus drove as fast as the mud and loose stones would allow, his forearms tensing with each vibration. He was shivering now, like his passenger. There was no cause for alarm, he told himself. Whatever had caused him to strike the man was a momentary, fleeting thing. No one else saw it. It would have no consequence. Beside him the trees thinned out altogether, giving way to open pasture. They were on the lower slopes, nearing Mittelbach, where the hills began to flatten towards the valley bottom. The sky was hazy, with a low, distant strip of red where the sun was about to disappear.

Ahead, half a dozen men were at work on the new road, labouring with rakes and machines and what looked like a giant cauldron, pushing out a broad, smooth surface of finely ground stones. Klaus slowed to greet the diggers, who had made way for him some hours before, and on two other occasions in the week. This time the men had made some progress, and it was obvious from their faces that they were reluctant to have the two police vehicles drive through the newly completed stretch of road.

A man whose relatively clean overalls declared him to be the chief of the crew asked Klaus to loop around the works over the verge, assuring him that the ground adjacent to the road was firm and well drained. As he spoke, the crew chief looked several times at the sidecar. Over a purple nose, his eyes bulged with curiosity.

With an imperious beep of the horn, Officer Zelinsky leaned out of the car behind to demand an explanation for the delay. Before the crew boss could repeat his request, the officer motioned with a flick of the wrist. 'Follow us, Deputy!'

The car pulled out, sweeping past the motorcycle onto the grass bank, to make the detour and to demonstrate how it should be done.

As commanded, Klaus turned his vehicle after the car, driving off the road and down a slight incline. Though not severe, the grass slope was steep enough to throw his passenger to one side, drawing a shout of protest. With a sideways glance, Klaus drew to a halt. He looked at the scattering of road workers, who had gathered in a loose semicircle to watch. Zelinsky's car rumbled ahead.

'Get out,' he said. 'Walk to where the officer's car is now.'

With some difficulty, Elias Frankel levered himself out of the sidecar. None of the spectators moved to help, which did not surprise Klaus. The deputy constable knew that he could rely on the natural wariness of the crowd to provide a guard for his prisoner. He heard a jeering voice call out.

'How did you earn those, boy?'

Another man broke in. 'Been in a fight? Want us to give you another one?'

As Elias struggled out, Klaus warned, 'If you try anything . . .'

'You have the key, Deputy,' Elias replied, standing. He rattled his manacled wrists with a look of disdain. 'It's in your top pocket. What could I do?'

'I have a pistol too,' Klaus said. He saw Elias blink, taken aback. With a nod of the head, the deputy constable indicated a box strapped behind his seat. Then he pulled off, leaving Elias Frankel to fend for himself among the taunting road workers.

He edged forward over the rough ground. Zelinsky's car had left tyre tracks which he could follow, though these became deeper where the ground was wet. Looking at two such grooves running through a patch of mud ahead, Klaus experienced a jolt of foreboding, and saw himself getting stuck, wheels spinning in the mud while the road crew watched. It would not do to show ineptitude here. Positioning his front wheel beside the outer groove took him closer to a ditch on that side, but meant that he was riding on firm ground, while the sidecar passed neatly between the two car tracks.

A good decision, he thought, as he started to skirt the mud. Being lighter than the car, his motorcycle was unlikely to sink into unbroken ground. He was moving, keeping the sidecar in the grooves while arcing alongside the tracks with the poise of an acroboat. Almost there. Just get past this cleft in the wet ground. The ditch was close to his wheel, but there was no need to fear the proximity, because he had found just the right line of movement, the right position for his vehicle.

But what was happening to the front wheel? He gave it more throttle, and found his back wheel tipping . . . . tried to brake, and felt the motorcycle lean out further over the ditch . . . still moving, but the movement was wrong. The motorcycle's weight beneath him pulled the sidecar up, and then it was flipping with him and over him as he smacked down into the ditch and for a space of time saw nothing.

Then he saw, felt, heard, everything all at once, as pain and noise coursed over him. Earth in his mouth. Blood in his throat. A great pressure on his chest. Roaring in his ears, and shouting, and up above him, against the sky, the wheels of the sidecar still turning.

They got the overturned vehicle off him and came down to his level, three or four of them, with cracked hands and faces, smelling of oil and sweat. A hand pawed his head, while another patted his chest and arms. One man shouted at another to help him remove the deputy's coat to check for broken ribs. 'Are you with us?' they asked him. 'Come on, now. Wake up. Best you stand up now. It's only grazes.'

Klaus let them lift his shoulders, but then waved them off and sat for a minute trying to clear his head. Blood trickled down his forehead and he blinked it away, looking first at the ground right in front of him, and then at the motorcycle being manoeuvred out of the ditch, along with the dented sidecar. His eyes moved in and out of focus, following the trail of his catastrophe back up onto the higher ground and back to the start of the road works. While everything hurt, nothing was so bad that it buckled under his weight. He moved onto his knees and leaned over, planting his hands in the grass for balance. He spat mud. 'Where is he?' he tried to say, but the words tumbled together indistinctly, so he said it again. 'Where. Is. He?'

'Officer's gone ahead,' the crew chief answered. 'I've sent one of the boys after him. He'll bring the car back shortly, don't you worry.'

This was not what Klaus meant. Struggling to his feet, he looked for the place where Elias Frankel had got out of the sidecar. There, two road workers were gathering up tools, having apparently taken the accident as a signal that work was over for the day. An older, thinner man stood on his own, apart from the others, looking towards Klaus, arms hanging limp at his sides. Klaus wiped his eyes and scanned the wooded banks behind the old man, but from this angle, he could not see far.

Turning away from the road to search in the other direction, he groaned. There in the distance ran a tall figure, lurching from weak to strong leg, head angled forward, through grass and mud and onwards, towards a cluster of orange-brown oak trees.

'We've got to stop him,' Klaus said, turning to the crew chief. 'Tell your men to run. To get my prisoner. He's— We're taking him to the station for questioning.'

The crew chief scowled into the distance, and shook his head.

'Not today, you're not. He's forded the stream, look. I send my men over there and they're going to come back with boots ripped apart. Some of them aren't in the best of health either. If I get them chasing your criminal till they're gasping, who's going to make up for the weak ones tomorrow? There's half an hour lost already from righting your vehicle – not that I'm complaining, you understand. We help a fallen man, that's as it should be. But I'm the one that has to get this road built in time, with a handful of misfits and no funds to get them reshod. No offence, Deputy, but you've got your job to do, and I've got mine.' He turned away, to order his team back to work.

Klaus glared at the horizon, where Elias Frankel had now disappeared, and let out a long, painful breath from his bruised lungs.

# 12.

Constable Theodore Hildebrandt moved slowly along the darkening street once Ute Koenig had left him. He could still see the taut hope in her eyes and hear the note of foreboding in her appeal: . . . *would be . . . wouldn't it, a sign that everything will be all right?* Had his murmured agreement convinced her? It was tempting to think that, by following him to the café and talking to him as she had done, Ute was signalling a wish for freedom – throwing a rope out of the castle window in the hope of being rescued. But even Theodore could not persuade himself that that was the case.

On the edge of the road that led north out of Angenberg, he accepted a lift in a horse-drawn buggy. While he struggled to mount the step, the elderly driver climbed down and came to Theodore's aid, though bent almost double himself. Dismissing the constable's injuries with a wave of his hand, the man said, 'I know plenty of old dogs in worse shape than you. Neighbour of mine had his legs blown right off.'

The horse set off with a slow, measured, muscular action. 'She won't be winning any chariot races,' the driver warned, 'so I hope we're not chasing thieves.'

As they passed beyond the street lights into darkness, Theodore listened to the rhythm of hooves change from asphalt to stone, and smelled the transition from coal smoke to rotting matter in the waste-pits on the edge of town. Further along the highway, the smells changed again, to woodsmoke and live-stock. Two trucks passed in one direction, and a bat flew past from the other. It was a cold, clear night, with an eyewatering breeze, but there was a rug to cover the constable's knees, and his mind was too busy with new questions to dwell on the usual discomforts.

He said, 'Have you heard of a wolf roaming hereabouts?'

'Wolf?' the driver echoed. 'No, sir. Uh-uh. Not in these parts.' After a pause he added, 'Where exactly do you mean?'

Theodore indicated that he had no particular place in mind. 'Further up in the hills maybe, where the new road's headed.'

'Oh, the hills,' replied the man, as if to a different question. 'No, no. A wolf favours marshland. Open spaces.' Then he began to describe how his wife had called him out of the house one evening to see a pack of wolves passing along the edge of a lake.

'When was that?' Theodore asked.

'A couple of years ago,' he said. 'Maybe ten.'

Or maybe not at all, Theodore thought. Maybe the old man heard about the incident from someone else long ago, and misremembered it as his own experience.

As they approached the valley junction, the glow from half a mile to the east suggested that several households in Mittelbach were still awake and occupied with the last chores of the day. Turning into the station yard, the constable was surprised to see a light on in the garage area of the old stable block, next to the holding cell. He found Klaus inside, hammering the frame of a cot together. It had taken shape since Theodore saw it last.

'Fit for a prince,' he remarked, stopping in the doorway to watch. The light seemed inadequate, because Klaus leaned in close and then paused to touch his eye. When he started again, the movement of the hammer was so brisk that Theodore could feel the anger flying off it. 'I left you for a day without warning,' he acknowledged. 'A bad time to choose, right before the mayor's—' He stopped abruptly, frowning. 'What happened?'

Klaus straightened to look at him, revealing a swelling high on the left cheekbone, under his eye. The right eye glared. 'Elias Frankel escaped.'

Theodore searched his expression, his bruise, for an explanation.

'Officer Zelinsky and I,' Klaus began, pausing to fill his lungs, 'arrested him in Hindelheim for disorderly conduct and were bringing him back here to answer further questions. At the road works I slid into a ditch, and the motorcycle went over. While the workmen were helping me, the prisoner ran off across the fields.'

'What are you talking about?'

'Which part don't you—'

'All of it!' Theodore bellowed, before catching himself. Chastened by the sight of his son's swollen red eye, he began again in a lower voice. 'Elias Frankel? That's – the man you spoke to in Hindelheim? I barely know the name . . .'

'Exactly,' Klaus said, throwing down the hammer. His hands were shaking, and he gripped the workbench to steady them. 'You don't know, so don't judge until you've heard all the facts. Elias Frankel is the storekeeper. He may or may not be responsible for harassing the mute boy, Dirk Müller, some weeks ago. He visited the Koenigs on Sunday – their only visitor – and insulted Heinrich Müller enough to earn himself a lashing. When I questioned him about it yesterday, he offered no defence whatsoever. In fact, he was aggressive and rude.'

'Is that an offence now?' Theodore exclaimed. 'Did you and Zelinsky agree to arrest this person because he got up your nose?'

'I'm trying. To tell you—'

'All right.' He threw up his hands. 'I'm sorry. I won't interrupt.'

Klaus took a breath and continued. 'Zelinsky turned up here, with a driver, saying the chief inspector had asked him to smoothe things out in Hindelheim after our last visit there. Apparently Doctor Koenig made a complaint about you.'

'Huh.'

After a pause, Klaus admitted, 'I had the impression Officer Zelinsky only stopped here to let you know that. He seemed ready to pick a fight. Maybe it was lucky you weren't here? If you'd argued with him, on top of everything else . . .'

Seeing the implication, Theodore nodded. 'So he asked you to go up there with him. Which you did.'

'What else could I do?' His face, under the bruising, was wild with alarm.

'Go on,' Theodore prompted.

'We went to see the Koenigs, and Zelinsky told the doctor that we weren't trying to dispute his account of the accident. He said that you'd misunderstood your orders—'

'Orders? God in heaven.'

'—from Angen,' Klaus went on, 'to make a full report of the incident. That seemed to satisfy Peter Koenig, and I thought we were done there. I was expecting to turn around and come back. But Zelinsky wanted to "redress the balance", is how he put it. He said we must do something about Elias Frankel, to show Johanna Koenig and Heinrich that we were taking their concerns seriously.'

'Idiot!'

Klaus flared. 'How was I to know—?'

'Not you,' Theodore cut in, attempting to soothe him. But Klaus heard the harshness in his voice and raised his own in response, almost shouting.

'I obeyed him. Yes. I obeyed a senior officer and I will not apologise to you for that! It was a legitimate visit to a man who had given us grounds for suspicion. Just because you hate Zelinsky, it doesn't mean that his judgement is wrong. And in this case – are you listening? – he was right. How do I know? Because when we got to the store, there was Elias Frankel on the back steps, pointing a gun – listen, will you – pointing a gun, at two children! Now you tell me that's an innocent man!'

Theodore shut his eyes for a moment, hoping that when he opened them again, it would prove to be a bad dream.

·✠·

It was not a dream. Returning his gaze to Klaus, Theodore found the man's swollen eye and desperate alarm hard to bear. He looked down into his cap. 'Let's suppose Zelinsky was right,' he said. 'This Elias Frankel is no good. He deserves to get his knuckles rapped – but for what? What's his crime?'

Klaus frowned. 'I told you—'

'He bullies children, right, and he's not filled with brotherly love for his neighbour Heinrich Müller. What else? Did he put Heinrich's baby on the log pile?'

'I don't know. No, I don't suppose so,' Klaus admitted.

'Did you suggest it to Zelinsky?'

'No!' Their eyes met. Klaus seemed uneasy, confusion mixing with his indignation. He said, 'But why would he run, unless he's got something to hide?'

Theodore decided not to answer this. If he made any assumptions, he would be no better than Zelinsky – and if he were no better than Zelinsky . . .

'I think he was helped,' Klaus said quietly, interrupting his thoughts. 'To escape, I mean. I think one of the road workers may have given him the key to the handcuffs. It was here in my pocket when the motorcycle tipped . . .'

Theodore looked up with a frown. 'You had him in handcuffs?'

'That's what they're for, isn't it?'

Another silence opened between them. With weariness creeping over him, the constable looked once more at his son's bruised face. He asked, 'Been to see Rudi?'

'No need,' Klaus mumbled. 'Nothing's broken.'

'Even so.'

'Where were you today?'

'Angen,' Theodore equivocated. 'I'm sorry . . .'

'With a woman, I presume?'

Theodore felt his gaze, but avoided it. 'It was a conversation,' he replied, 'nothing more. She's married.'

'That doesn't usually stop you,' Klaus observed. He started tidying away the woodworking tools. 'Francesca and I plan to raise our child in a good house,' he went on. 'A law-abiding house, if you can imagine such a thing. Have you considered what kind of example you are going to set for my son?'

Raising his eyebrows at this question, Theodore replied, 'I may have some despicable habits, Klaus, but trying to set an example to other people is not one of them. What kind of self-righteous prig would live his life with that aim?' He watched his son's back, and continued in a quieter tone. 'Don't suffocate your child at the cradle. He'll grow up with a cord around his neck, and to free himself, he'll do something that pains you. And what then – will you leap in to take the blame, and so exacerbate his fury? Or else, suppose he does everything by the book and to his Mama's wishes – will you try to make yourself responsible for his actions then too? If he wins a prize, will you claim it?'

'I'm going inside,' Klaus decided.

Theodore stopped him in the door, and said, 'No one wants you to walk in my shadow, Klaus. But if you do nothing but fight it, where will that get you?'

❖

At a table in the centre of the Rose Gardens the next day, Ute slipped her apple strudel to the Kaiser in surreptitious stages, under the tablecloth, while Peter, opposite, ate his with enthusiasm. On the bandstand, a brass ensemble blew a marching tune over the few tables that were occupied at this late point in the year. Shafts of sunlight, interrupted by the movement of small, busy clouds, fell on the horn and trumpet, accentuating their gleam.

The outing was meant to please her, and it should have been – was – a treat. But the unexpected extravagance of it took away Ute's appetite. Why was Peter pretending that they could afford to come to a place like this and eat pastries, on a whim? She watched the rapid clicking of his jaw, and the neat way he brushed flakes from his moustache. There was a strange energy in him today, she thought. He tapped his foot to the music, and when he looked at her, his eyes were bright.

'Another cake, darling?'

'No . . .'

'Quite right. Mustn't spoil ourselves before this evening and offend Wilma.' He cleared his throat with water, and said, 'A piece of news from home. It seems that Elias Frankel has got himself into trouble.'

Ute stared. 'Elias? What kind of trouble?'

Peter lifted his hands and shoulders in an expansive shrug. 'Whatever it was, he exacerbated it by running off when the police tried to take him down to Mittelbach yesterday. Apparently the constable's motorcycle tipped over, and Elias took the opportunity to escape.'

'But—' She shook her head, struggling to understand. 'But the constable was in town yesterday. He can't have been—'

'Hildebrandt?' Peter interrupted, with a sharp glance. 'You saw him?'

Deciding to give an abbreviated account of the meeting, Ute replied, 'He was at Marlyse's apartment, when I got back there. But only for a minute or two. He asked if I'd heard about Johanna's baby, and then he left.' Peter's frown mirrored Ute's own puzzlement. 'I wonder if it had to do with Elias?' she continued. 'Perhaps he wanted to know something . . .'

'Constable Hildebrandt wants to know everything that is none of his business,' Peter put in. 'I can't imagine what state the police station is in, when he spends his days gallivanting around, nosing into other people's private affairs. You know I found him in the nursery on Wednesday, questioning Mother as if she were the suspect in a murder investigation! Some ambition the man has.'

Ute felt the colour rise to her cheeks. She wanted to protest that Peter had misunderstood him; that the constable was neither a busybody nor ambitious. The man was alive to every fault in himself, forever biting his tongue. After yesterday's second, surprising encounter, Ute had reached the conclusion that Theodore Hildebrandt was the most unexpected person she had ever met. He was bold and at the same time, hesitant. He was sad, yet he gave her hope. There was no way she could share this insight with Peter, however, so she said nothing.

'Matter of fact, I've done a bit of checking,' Peter went on. 'Seems that he worked in a tunnelling crew in the war, and one of the tunnels collapsed on top of him. When they pulled him out two days later, no one expected him to live. The fellow's a walking ghoul. Brings a chill wind wherever he treads.'

'I thought you didn't hold with superstition.'

'Ha.' With a grin, Peter lifted her hand and kissed it. 'Quite right, my darling. There is nothing to fear.'

The Kaiser trailed behind as they walked from the bandstand afterwards, across the gardens. Crisp red leaves scudded along the path, blown by the breeze. Ahead of them, an old woman was offering to tell passers-by their fortunes, and cupping her wizened hands to beg. Rejected by one person after another, she dismissed them with a rude gesture and shuffled off elsewhere. A moment later, a cry went up from a food kiosk near the park gates – and then Ute saw the fortune teller hurrying away from the kiosk towards them, thrusting something into her mouth.

A merchant from the kiosk shouted after her, 'Hey! Come back here!'

The old woman pushed between them, causing Peter to turn his head. Ute looked at him across the path, her earlier puzzlement replaced by a new suspicion. 'Peter,' she said. 'Are you celebrating?'

'What!' He laughed and frowned at the same time.

'Elias Frankel is in trouble,' Ute said, 'and you're . . .' – she searched for the right word, and then found it – 'alight.'

✠

Constable Theodore Hildebrandt watched from the doorstep as the mayor's automobile, and a second car containing his visitors, pulled up outside the police station. The mayor got out first and stood rubbing his hands. He was a small, rat-like figure of a man, with pockmarked skin and a narrow nose.

The morning's tour had gone very well, he declared, in response to the constable's greeting. His guests had already inspected several parcels of land within the locality as potential sites for the new fruit-packing factory and its associated buildings – engineering sheds, storage and so on. The mayor rattled on in this way, keeping his rodent eyes fixed on the second car. When the door handle began to shift, he sprang forward to help his guests from their vehicle.

Herr Dammertz, a bulky man with silver-tipped hair and a fur collar, stood to light a cigarette while his wife and two of their restless children toured the yard. 'But where are the horses?' one of the children whined, finding a mechanic inside the stable block, toiling at the battered motorcycle. Peering in at the cell door, the same child complained, 'Where are the prisoners?'

Returning his cigarette case to an inner pocket in the silk lining of his coat, Herr Dammertz threw the constable a glance and said, 'I expect you're the man to tell me who the good workers are around here, and who's likely to give me trouble?' He paused to exhale. 'Local Bolshies? Union men?'

The mayor stepped in to intercede. 'I'm sure the constable will help in any way he can. Perhaps you'd like to look inside? It's a modest station, as you can see. Very little criminal activity in the area, isn't that so, Constable?'

'As you say, sir,' Theodore answered, following them into the building.

Klaus stood at his desk to greet the visitors. In return, Herr Dammertz pointed his cigarette at the deputy constable's bruised cheekbone, and said, 'I see the locals don't like taking orders from a sapling.'

'This was an accident, sir,' Klaus said quickly. 'The motorcycle hit a patch of rough ground yesterday . . .'

The manufacturer cut him off with a nod. 'I saw the mechanic working on it out there. It seems to be the only motor vehicle in the place?'

Impressed by the man's swift observation, Theodore replied, 'At present it's the only vehicle of any sort, sir. When I was a young recruit, every station and substation, even the quiet ones like this, had horses as well as motorcycles.'

'You sound like an old man, Constable!' the mayor interrupted, attempting to conceal his irritation with a smile. 'Here we are, trying to bring you the benefits of modern civilisation, and you cling to a half-remembered notion of the past.'

Theodore ignored the mayor's warning, and continued, 'A motor car will only get so far, away from the main roads, and everyone will hear it coming. On a horse you can be fast or subtle. Thieves feared us because we knew the land as well as they did, all the places you could hide – and we could reach them too.'

'Herr Dammertz does not have time to hear this, Constable . . .'

But Herr Dammertz was interested. Speaking over the mayor, he said, 'So if a man were to buy land around here, he would need a good stable?'

Allowing a faint smile to rise to his face, Theodore replied, 'I know some people who could supply you with horses, if you were looking. Some call them gypsies, but they are skilled men, and they know how to train animals for this terrain.'

'Herr Dammertz,' the mayor said, stepping between them. 'If we're to get up into the hills and back before dark, we really must be on our way.'

⊹

Once the visitors had gone, Klaus stepped out to check progress on the motorcycle, leaving Theodore alone to brood. Friday afternoon. She would be with Peter Koenig now, in Angen, paying a visit to Professor von Brodnitz. 'A rising star in the profession,' as Theodore's friend Rudi Hoffmann had described him a few days ago, in response to the constable's question. 'Von Brodnitz has a strong voice in the eugenics movement, Theo,' Rudi had said, revealing his contempt with a smirk. 'Oh yes, it's a movement now. Plenty of improvers about, keen to meddle in the mating game. This one, yes, paired with this one – go forth and make children, you two, in the name of a strong Germany. As for you, and you and you . . .' Here Rudi had pointed at imaginary faces, and contorted his own in mock disgust. 'Not so much promise there. Have you considered the virtues of celibacy?'

Theodore had smiled at the performance, until Rudi turned to him with sudden seriousness and said, 'You know what it means, don't you, this business of improving the race?'

'No more cripples like me,' Theodore muttered to himself now, looking out of the window into the station yard. That was not quite true, he realised. Injured veterans were not the target of the healthy breeding campaign. The defects of soldiers, inflicted in the service of the nation, were considered noble, hard-won badges of courage. Theodore Hildebrandt's scars would not infect the Hildebrandt bloodline. All the same, he

110

shared Rudi Hoffmann's wariness about the convictions of von Brodnitz and his disciples. These enthusiasts for right living would teach people to pick and plan and breed with a view to the productivity of the next generation, and so on. So much design in it. So much *hygiene*. But what good was sex, thought Theodore, unless it was messy and startling and chaotic?

He raised his hands in front of him, and turned the palms upwards. If he closed his eyes, he could feel Ute's fingers curling around his, the heat of her hand . . .

The telephone rang.

He lifted the receiver with an inward sigh. 'Mittelbach Constabulary.'

'So you've found time to be at your post today,' said the caller. 'I'm honoured.' A male voice, but not the chief inspector's. Younger, with a sardonic edge.

'Zelinsky.'

'Found the runaway yet?'

*The runaway*, Theodore throught. He drew in a silent breath and replied, 'Why do I suspect that you set people running just so that you can chase them, Zelinsky?'

Zelinsky chuckled. 'Same old cynic, Hildebrandt. Always measuring people by your own failings. The chief's wondering why the hell you can't keep order in that little backwater of yours.'

'Someone messed up my little backwater yesterday,' Theodore replied. 'I'm waiting for the interfering wretch to admit it.'

'There you go again, Hildebrandt – waiting for someone else to take action. You might want to change that habit. I'll keep my fingers crossed for you.'

A hooting sound interrupted. Outside, a car horn beeped again, getting louder. Cutting Zelinsky off with a gruff goodbye, Theodore replaced the receiver and pulled himself up from the desk. He shuffled to the door and opened it to see the mayor's motor car turning into the station yard, less than an hour after it had departed. It came to a halt outside the stable block, where with a final hoot of the horn, the uniformed driver leaned from his window and called out, 'I'm to take this man to a doctor!'

# 13.

Theodore hobbled across the station yard, and Klaus emerged from the stable-turned-garage, both reaching the mayor's car at the same time. They frowned together into the back seat, where an elderly man, grey in the face, lay slumped and groaning. His thin frame was shrouded in the baggy working overalls of a road digger.

'Mayor's waiting for me to take the auto back,' the uniformed driver explained, showing his impatience in the speed and tone of his voice, and a fidgeting manner. 'The second car can't seat all of his guests. So, is there a doctor here or not?'

'What's his name?' Theodore asked.

The driver raised his eyebrows at the irrelevance of the question. 'He's a labourer, collapsed on the new road up there.'

'One of the crew,' Klaus confirmed, with a glimmer of recognition.

'Will you hurry up and tell me where to take him?' the driver demanded. 'I don't want any more filth oozing onto the upholstery back there.'

'I'll come with you,' Theodore decided, putting his hand on the car door. Helped by Klaus, he got in next to the driver. 'Left out of the gate.'

As he gave further directions, Theodore listened to the

groans of the man in the back seat, and asked what had happened. Had the car run into him?

No! The driver was offended by the suggestion. They had approached the roadworks to find a group of labourers crowding around this one – he jerked his head back – who was lying on the ground. Both vehicles stopped. Questions were asked. The mayor's driver couldn't hear all of it, but saw that Frau Dammertz, in the car behind, was upset by what the workers told her. He glanced sideways at the constable. 'Something about a prisoner of yours running off yesterday?'

Theodore's heart sank a little further. 'What about him?'

'Seems he hit this old fella before he ran.'

⁕

As soon as they stopped outside Doctor Hoffmann's house, on the edge of Mittelbach, the driver sprang out of his seat to rid the vehicle of its unfortunate cargo. Checking that his gloves were on securely, he took hold of the semi-conscious passenger under each of his feeble arms. 'He'd better not have spilled his guts in here,' he said, heaving the man out. 'I've got to drive the mayor back to Angen this evening – Oh!'

He recoiled, almost dropping the invalid as a wooden leg thumped onto the outboard. The loose-fitting trouser that covered it had caught on the underside of the car door. 'Ugh,' the driver exhaled. 'Holy Mother of God.'

Theodore picked up the wooden leg and made a silent guess that it weighed almost as much as its owner. 'Nice bit of chestnut,' he observed, tapping the prosthesis. The man's eyes were open but unfocused. He was in a bad way, no doubt about it; hands wrapped around his skinny middle, taking shallow breaths. 'What's your name?' the constable asked.

'Spiller,' he managed, with some effort. 'Gustav Spiller.'

'All right, Spiller,' Theodore answered. 'I'm Theodore Hildebrandt, the constable here at Mittelbach. We're at the house of my friend Rudi Hoffmann. Here he is now – the one who seems to have a crow's nest perched on his head. He's going to set you straight.'

The doctor came out of the house with wild hair and a distracted look, muttering to himself. He wore a velvet jacket, frayed at the collar, and above it was a face that had kept tally of every emotional contraction the man had suffered in the last fifty years. He and Theodore took hold of the invalid and carried him inside, allowing the mayor's driver to flee in relief. They settled Gustav Spiller on a couch, where Doctor Hoffmann opened the man's overalls to start an examination.

Theodore watched, trying to make sense of what he had learned from the driver. Elias Frankel *hit this old fella before he ran*. He ran yesterday afternoon. What connected that blow to Gustav Spiller's collapse now, twenty-four hours later? He leaned forward to ask. 'Herr Spiller, I need to understand what happened up there on the road. Did someone strike you?'

Spiller tried to answer, but coughed instead. Flecks of bloody mucus hit Doctor Hoffmann's hand. 'Hmm,' the doctor said at this sign. 'Let him rest, Theo.'

Moving away from the patient as requested, Theodore said, 'The driver claimed that someone hit him. Yesterday, not just now. Is there a bruise?'

'A bruise?' Rudi Hoffmann repeated, with a wry smile. He pulled back the man's overalls further to expose skin that was thin and blueish, with yellow patches, stretched parsimoniously over his ribs. Sure, the doctor agreed, the man had bruises. What labourer would cart mud and stones all day without getting knocked about? But bruises were the least of this patient's worries. Whatever had caused Gustav Spiller's collapse was the latest of a lifelong series of afflictions, the doctor explained. He was half-starved, probably tubercular, with a rotting liver and a missing leg.

Dropping his voice, Rudi added that the man was unlikely to

use his labourer's overalls again. 'The Reaper's been trying to cut this one down for a good while.' He placed a stethoscope to Spiller's chest, lifting it off again as a new coughing fit struck.

But if Spiller had merely reached the natural end of his own road today, the constable mused, then why all the fuss? What had caused the mayor to send this old man back in his own car for urgent attention? What had the other road workers said to the mayor's party, and to Frau Dammertz in particular, to rouse such concern?

He guessed that the men were still talking about the motorcycle accident they had witnessed yesterday, and in their excitement, as they had crowded around Spiller, various disparate strands of the story had become confused. Perhaps one of the men had seized on the opportunity to invent a struggle between Spiller and Elias Frankel, in order to divert attention from the fact that he himself had emptied Klaus Hildebrandt's pocket and let the key to the handcuffs fall out, thereby helping the prisoner to run?

'Ida,' the man croaked.

Theodore leaned forward, to encourage him. 'That your wife's name, Spiller? Would you like us to fetch her?'

Spiller frowned. 'Ida. Frankel's. Son,' he managed. 'Did they. Get him?'

'Not yet,' Theodore replied, watching him. 'You saw Elias Frankel run off, I suppose. Yesterday, when my deputy's motor-cycle overturned.'

'Hit me.' He moved a bony hand over his stomach.

'You're in the way, Constable,' the doctor said. He pulled at the sick man's eyelids and checked the pupils, then looked in his mouth and administered a clear liquid, droplet by droplet, onto his tongue.

Theodore watched the man's gaunt face sink under the effort of living. He asked, 'You mean Elias Frankel hit you? Yesterday? Why did he hit you?'

Spiller met Theodore's gaze, taking short breaths which filled his face with pain. His hand moved in a gesture of uncertainty.

'Were you trying to stop him? Did you see him looking for the key to the handcuffs?' the constable guessed. 'We know that one of your colleagues went through my deputy's pockets, so perhaps the key fell out then and you saw it. You saw Elias Frankel reaching into the grass for it and you approached him . . .?'

'Strong,' Spiller breathed. 'Like his – mother.'

'Theo,' the doctor warned.

✢

Obeying, Theodore left the man to rest, and moved to the window. He found it hard to imagine the motorcycle accident without getting stuck on his son's damaged, frantic face; and harder still to picture the actions of Elias Frankel, having never laid eyes on the man. So he concentrated instead on Spiller's words. *Strong, like his mother.* Had the old man's recognition of his attacker brought admiration, as that comment seemed to imply? Or something else – dread?

'Ida Frankel,' said Rudi Hoffmann, joining him at the window. 'That's a name I haven't heard in a while.'

'Friend of yours?'

The doctor shrugged. 'She was everybody's friend. Remarkable woman, Ida Frankel. No one ever knew where she'd come from, or why. She turned up about ten years ago, or it could have been earlier – some years before you arrived here, anyhow. Had a child with her, about so high,' he indicated the height by putting a hand level with his belt. 'He shot up into a beanpole, though – and that was another curious thing, because Ida Frankel was a small woman. Strong enough, and handsome in her own way – she had a long face, with big dark eyes – but not tall, not in the least. And this son of hers, you said his name just now . . .' He waved towards the patient.

'Elias,' Theodore reminded him.

'Hmm.' Rudi nodded, remembering. 'Must have reached six foot by the time Ida died. She died of the influenza,' he added, 'in 'eighteen.'

117

The constable knew this. He wanted more. 'But why did you notice her, Rudi? Didn't the Frankels settle out in Hindelheim?'

'Exactly!' the doctor roared, his eyes large with amusement. 'Jews in the countryside! My, that caused some excitement around here. The good people of Mittelbach are not used to Jews moving into cattle country. Would they know one end of a cow from another? How to grow turnips? Or would they come crawling down to the valley road, tails between their legs, and hurry back to the city?'

Rudi chuckled, and shook his head at the memory. 'Ida Frankel had a man with her, too,' he went on. 'Not the boy's father, I think. He never gave his name, so people called him "the Monsieur". He spoke Russian and Spanish, and French, of course – but what use were foreign words in Hindelheim? There was a sense of expectation about these people, you see, from the start; right from the moment they stopped here in Mittelbach to pick up some bits and pieces on their way up into the hills. Would the Frankels survive?'

He turned to the couch to check on Gustav Spiller, lifting the man's wrist to check his pulse. 'Still alive,' he concluded. 'For the moment.'

Theodore steered him back to the topic. 'When Ida Frankel and this unnamed companion opened their house as a store,' he said, 'did people go up there especially to take a look?'

'Possibly,' Rudi agreed. 'But we also saw her in the village here, quite often, when Ida brought her pony and trap into Mittelbach for supplies. I'd bump into her as she was buying hardware, or at the blacksmith's, getting the horse shod. The Frankels were doing well enough, clearly. I expect some people were privately disappointed, having predicted failure. But the naysayers could reassure themselves that it was only trading, you see, not working the land? They hadn't been proved wrong, exactly.'

Theodore nodded, and was about to ask another question when Rudi Hoffmann continued.

'Then a few years later, towards the end of the war, I was surprised by a visit from Friedrich Koenig, the physician in Hindelheim. My counterpart there, you might say.' He paused to remember. 'He would usually turn in the other direction if he saw me coming. Considered me something of a rogue.' A fleeting grin lightened his face, and then vanished. 'This was the only time Doctor Koenig had ever deigned to cross my doorstep.'

'Why did he?'

Frowning as if undecided whether to answer this, Rudi replied eventually, 'I suppose it's too late to matter now. This was in the summer of 'eighteen, and the Spanish Flu was picking off its victims. It got to Ida Frankel, and the doctor was desperate to cure her. Her in particular.' Glancing up, he explained, 'Of all the people who came under Ida Frankel's spell, Friedrich Koenig was the most severely smitten. His reputation began to suffer for it in the end. Spent more and more time at the Frankel store, in Ida's company. He was not the only one, mind. The store was always open in those days, with a fire going and some sort of brew on the stove. Ida's man-friend, the mysterious Monsieur, was turning into a drunk, a musical and gregarious drunk. He would sing songs in languages no one could understand. Very entertaining. And the boy-giant, Elias, was known for certain feral qualities which contributed to the . . . I don't know, the intoxicating atmosphere – where was I?'

'Doctor Koenig,' Theodore reminded him.

'Ah, yes. Smitten, as I say. I think it started when he delivered Ida's younger son.'

This opened a new door in the constable's mind. He asked, 'Was the boy his?'

Rudi pushed up his bottom lip in an uncertain gesture. 'Who knows? I don't think so. I had the impression, from what Koenig said, that he had become fond of Ida Frankel during the course of her pregnancy. They argued in an amicable way, he told me, about medical treatments. Ida made certain remedies of her own, you see.'

Here Rudi Hoffmann grew animated, turning to pace the room as the memories rushed back to him. 'Whenever I saw her, she would try to get me to tell her where the special mushrooms grow. Which I never did, by the way,' he added, with a conspiratorial smile. 'Old Rudi has to have his secrets too, yes? But I did take her a few, from time to time, and in return she'd give me a bottle of her tonic . . .'

There was a knock on the door, and Doctor Hoffmann's housekeeper stepped in. She was dressed in the same outfit – a coat and matching hat – in which she had delivered the miscreant children to Theodore two days ago. 'If there's nothing else, Doctor,' she said, 'I'll be going now?'

Rudi dismissed her, and the woman retreated slowly, taking a long look at the couch where Gustav Spiller lay, ashen-faced. Within ten minutes, Theodore guessed, a description of the patient would be circulated in Mittelbach.

'Go on,' he prompted. 'Doctor Koening wanted your help.'

'Because the flu virus had taken hold of his beloved Ida Frankel,' Rudi agreed, 'and the poor man could not accept it. He seemed determined to find some other explanation. Paced up and down this room, offering all sorts of wild theories.'

'Wild theories,' Theodore repeated. 'I thought they were your preserve.'

Rudi ignored this. 'He was willing to consider anything that I might suggest, other than influenza. It was pitiful.'

Theodore looked at him with surprise. 'So your rival came from Hindelheim to beg for some of your hocus-pocus?'

'Thank you, Constable.'

'Throwing his own reputation to the wind. Why would he do that?'

'Why do people do anything?' Rudi Hoffmann replied. 'Love or fear. In his case, certainly both.'

# 14.

The von Brodnitz residence stood in an elevated position to the west of town, with views along the river from its several balconies. At eight the dining room filled with guests: several medics, two attorneys, a woman who introduced herself as a poet, and an army colonel who boasted that he had spotted the genius of the prodigal Stefan von Brodnitz at a military research institute in the first months of the war, and was moreover responsible for introducing him to his charming wife. Wilma von Brodnitz elaborated on the story as she served her speciality, a glistening ham hock cooked in ginger wine.

Ute Koenig sat in preoccupied silence among the guests at dinner and afterwards, while the four von Brodnitz children sang to entertain their parents' guests. Peter watched her from the fireplace, where he stood with his host.

'I had a word with the police chief about your concerns.'

Stefan von Brodnitz swilled an inch of viscous spirit around the base of his glass to coax out the fumes, before drawing his nose down in supplication. He was a neat man with a sharp nose and wavy hair. A dark mole beside the upper lip gave his face a feminine quality. 'You shouldn't get any more trouble from the local constable,' he continued.

Peter acknowledged the favour. 'I didn't mean to put you out.'

'Not at all,' Stefan said. 'We can't have every chap in a uniform thinking that it qualifies him to question our professional opinions.'

With another glance at Ute, Peter turned towards the fire, so that she would not be able to read his lips from where she sat. He said, 'Another police officer came up from Angen yesterday to apologise for what he called a misunderstanding on the part of the Mittelbach constable. He assured me that the death certificate would be lodged without any further interference to my grieving family.'

Stefan took another sip, drinking through his teeth. 'Let's not talk about it more than we have to, Pedro. At least not the details.' He nodded towards the other guests, who were applauding at the end of his children's recital. 'We're among friends here,' he said, 'but until the law catches up with our advances in science and ethics, it's as well to be discreet about the—' he waved a hand, '*application* of one's convictions, hmm?'

At this Peter reddened slightly, and rocked on his heels. 'I hope you don't think I've been publicly advocating or admitting to an unlawful practice.'

'My dear fellow,' Stefan replied with a smile of reassurance. He seized Peter's glass, refilled it and gave it back to him. 'I hope *you* know that what the law calls murder, a true philosopher might call kindness or common sense. Where Nature grants the signs of a full and normal life, then by all means, let us follow her lead and do all we can to fulfil that promise. But where she lets go, allowing some physical or mental corruption to creep in, then we are justified in letting that poor, unformed life wither to nothing. It's another leaf falling in autumn. Your health.'

Peter lifted his glass, responding in kind. 'Health.'

'Now I need you to do something for me,' Stefan said, changing the subject. 'I'm giving a speech tomorrow at the retirement of an exceptionally tedious colleague. I've jotted the points down, but I have no patience for writing.' Digging in a pocket for a crumpled piece of paper, he held it out between two fingers. 'Pull it into sentences before you go, will you?'

Peter dutifully took the note, as the unspoken terms of this patronage required. Stefan asked if he had brought the corrected proofs with him, for the new issue. 'Wilma's impatient to see them. She's got some ideas to put to you.'

'Yes, although I also have a few questions—'

'Good, she'll enjoy that,' Stefan cut in, emptying his glass. 'She breakfasts with the children at around seven. Catch her then.'

'You won't be here?'

'Have to be elsewhere, I'm afraid.' He saw the seed of dismay or resentment on Peter's face, and said, 'I don't ask too much of you, do I, Pedro? Sometimes I forget that you only graduated this year. Perhaps with the journal . . . we're putting too much responsibility on your shoulders?'

Reddening again, Peter hurried to deny this. 'Not at all. I'm happy to—'

'Excellent,' Stefan said. 'Now I'm going upstairs to take care of the wife – and I suggest you do likewise.' He slapped the younger man's shoulder and turned away.

✠

In their assigned guestroom, Peter and Ute undressed. Sitting on the bed to remove his shoes, he noticed a book lying in her open suitcase. *'Principles of Pharmacology,'* he said, lifting it to check the spine. 'Eighth edition. From my study!'

'I hope you didn't miss it.'

He gave her a wary look. 'Are you spying on me?'

Was she? Ute paused to consider whether the accusation was true, and decided it was not – or not entirely. She said, 'Will I find your secrets in it?'

Peter laughed briefly at her answer. 'It's not a ladies' book,' he said, dropping it back into the suitcase. 'What are you doing with it, really?'

Ute sat down on the bed next to him, where she helped to remove his collar studs, and then his cufflinks. After an indulgent evening, Peter seemed glad to relinquish the task to her. 'You said that when the road comes,' she said, 'when there are more houses and patients, you might turn the breakfast room into a dispensary, and find a pharmacist to come in once a fortnight to run it.'

'What are you suggesting? That you could train yourself to do the work of a pharmacist, by reading a textbook or two?'

She objected to this with a glance.

'You've no idea how complex the discipline is, Ute. It would take any man – or woman – four years at least to master it. Ask Wilma if you don't believe me.'

'I did,' she replied. 'That is, I asked if she knew how I could be useful to you in the surgery – as an assistant of some kind, that's all.'

'And?'

Ute studied Peter's face, wondering if he would remember this conversation in the morning. The alcohol fumes were strong on his breath, and there was still a kind of excitement in him; directed, she sensed, elsewhere. She said, 'Wilma told me that since our men fought the war for us, the least we can do for them in return is to stop taking their jobs.'

Peter gave this an absent smile. 'Don't you think she might have a point?' Then he caught her hand and with a sudden switch of attention, leaned in to kiss her. His hand made a swift move up Ute's thigh, finding the responsive part of her skin. 'My darling,' he said, 'I hope you know that you're already useful to me.'

After a moment Ute drew up against him, finding that she wanted to be touched – and touched everywhere at once, so that no part of her body would be left untended. She pushed her breast into his hand. They lay down, Peter fighting his way out of the last barriers of his clothes. Ute pressed against the length of him, her belly and thighs flat on his. His voice came in hot breaths against her cheek. 'I'm not the only . . . one,' she heard, 'who is alight!'

✠

Some hours later, while Peter slept, Ute got out of bed and moved to the dressing table, where she turned on a lamp and cleared a space. All she had to write on were the pages of an exercise book – not ideal, but they would do. She began:

> Dear Herr Constable Hildebrandt,
> 'I have been puzzling all day over the purpose of your visit. You said that you had come to see me, and asked all sorts of questions about our lives in Hindelheim, but none about Elias Frankel. So why—

She paused with her pen in mid-air. Reading over the start of the letter, she saw that it struck a presumptuous note. Evidently the boldness of sitting in a café with the constable had given her a dangerous sense of licence. She must be careful, and make no assumptions. If Constable Hildebrandt had concealed from her his plans regarding Elias Frankel, it could only mean that he was suspicious of her.

Ripping up the letter, she swept the pieces into the wastebasket and sat for a while in silence. The only sound that intruded was an occasional creaking from the bed, as Peter rolled over. Ute realised that she did not know whether they were the only guests staying here overnight. Others who were at the dinner party might be sleeping in guestrooms on other floors, along other corridors, up other winding staircases, and she might never hear them.

She ought to go back to bed, and hope to sleep. But her mind was racing, and would not stop without some intervention. What if she were to start a new letter, putting down some of her thoughts, and then decide later whether to send it?

*'Dear Herr Constable Hildebrandt,'* she began again.

*There is more bad news from Hindelheim, I gather – Elias Frankel arrested, and your deputy's vehicle overturned. The road is not even built yet, and already it has proved unlucky. I can hear my Aunt Ernesta, muttering that misfortune has its own seasons like everything else, and we should study them to understand their pattern. The Night People are here, she would say, stirring up trouble.*

Here Ute paused for a moment, and then continued.

*But those superstitions belong to older times, and Aunt has been gone three years, as I keep telling her. I must try to pay her warnings less attention.*

She shifted on the chair, feeling the cold in her back and neck. Her toes, too, were starting to clamp together. Quickly, then.

*'Here I am, wondering what Elias has done; and there you are –*

Where was he? she wondered. Mittelbach, presumably – but asleep, alone? Did he have a wife? None of her business. Onwards –

*wondering, I imagine, where he is. Unless you have caught him already. This is an old story for us, Constable; everyone wondering about Elias Frankel. We have always wondered about the Frankels – him most of all. I myself can hardly say that I know Elias, even though I lived next door to him all my life until this summer.*

Enough, she told herself. The Constable has not asked for this. Go back to bed, soon. Just offer him one instance.

*I told you in the café that it was Elias Frankel who claimed to have seen a wolf in the hills overlooking the quarry. But I did not mention, I think, the coincidence in the timing of it – late in June of this year. It was in that same week that his stepfather, the Monsieur, fell from the steps at the back of the store, and plunged to his death.*

✠

Gustav Spiller died on Rudi Hoffmann's couch before daybreak on Sunday morning, and Constable Theodore Hildebrandt received the news ten minutes later, from a boy on a bicycle. He sat in the cold, grey light of the station office, feeling the grain of the chair through his nightshirt as he tried to dismiss a sense of doom.

Old man Spiller could have died at any time, from any one of a dozen causes – it just so happened that the end came now, here, in the wake of Elias Frankel's escape. There was nothing special or significant, Theodore told himself, in the timing.

But why did the old bastard have to die on a Sunday, when the population of Mittelbach and the surrounding farm country had nothing better to do than exchange and debate and magnify every tiny drop of news? If Spiller had held on for another day, then his fellow labourers would be at work on the road today, with little time or energy to spare for speculation, and the constable could have made arrangements for his disposal discreetly, while people went about their normal business.

As it was, the death coincided with a free day – and a fine one, by the look of it. Watching the sky lighten with the promise of sunshine, the constable groaned. Even worse. Now people would come out to enjoy this last, dry, day of October, and linger on their doorsteps to discuss the road worker's death. Sunday mornings drew people into Mittelbach for the purpose of refreshing their store of conversational topics. Some went straight to the inn, while others chose church, feeding at the fountain of godliness until they were bursting with eagerness to save souls, and crush evil.

As Theodore was wondering how he might delay or dilute the news, the telephone rang. Hoping, unreasonably, that it would be Ute Koenig on the line, he snatched up the receiver. 'Mittelbach Constabulary,' he said. 'Theodore Hildebrandt.'

The voice came after a pause. '. . . Hello?' Then more loudly, 'Who is that?'

Theodore exhaled. Another one of these. 'This is Constable Theodore HILDEBRANDT,' he shouted. 'Mittelbach—'

'Ah, Constable!' the other boomed. 'This is Chief Inspector—'

'Good morning, sir,' Theodore cut in, regretting it immediately.

'What's that? . . . Ah, you can hear me then?'

'Yes.' He did not dare add anything else.

The chief inspector's voice turned serious. 'The mayor came to see me last night, Constable. He cut short an evening at the theatre in order to tell me his concerns. That trip he made your way, with Herr Dammertz. What a bloody disaster, man. He tells me that he brought his visitor to the station, where you not only spoke out of turn, but failed to warn him about the runaway. That true?'

'What was I meant to warn him about, sir?'

There was a pause. 'Don't you even know what happened, Theodore? Good God, what's the matter with you? Are you sick?'

Theodore forced himself to make a reasonable reply. 'I gather that a man collapsed on the road crew, shortly before the mayor's car reached the works.'

'Not just any man, Constable. The same poor fellow who was

128

assaulted by your escaped ruffian the other day. Got punched in the stomach then collapsed a day later. In front of the mayor's guests! The mayor didn't even know that there was a violent runaway on the loose, and he is not happy that he had to learn about it in front of his visitors, from a digging crew! He thinks you made him look a fool.'

Theodore bit back a retort, and answered, 'Elias Frankel was not arrested at my instruction, sir.'

'And that's another point. I'd like to know why in God's name I had to send Officer Zelinsky up there to do your job for you. You'd better have good answers to give me first thing on Monday. You haven't forgotten the meeting, I hope?'

'No, sir,' he lied, thinking: *Monday. Tomorrow. Too late to find Ute again in town?*

'Get this Frankel boy in your cell before then, and we'll have a chance of pacifying the mayor. Put Klaus on the job too. Ask the farmers to search their barns. A local lad won't go far without someone recognising him. Bring me something I can tell the mayor, will you? Herr Dammertz and his wife are under the impression that the hills are filled with wild men.'

Theodore put down the receiver, and greeted the sabbath with a full-throated curse.

✠

The day progressed much as the constable had feared it would, with occasional questions following him across the village to the carpenter's house, where he ordered a coffin, and more persistent inquiries delaying his walk back. Several people claimed to know where 'that Frankel boy' or 'the runaway' was hiding, and many more had advice to speed the constable's search. He ought to look in this barn, or that shed, or follow a particular trail of muddy footprints along the riverbank, or speak to so-and-so; and he must keep a close eye on a certain other so-and-so, who might be helping the fugitive.

Theodore invited his conscientious neighbours to give their information to the deputy constable, Klaus Hildebrandt, who was sure to take note of it. Returning to the station, he found Klaus trying to turn away two men who claimed to be Gustav Spiller's friends and who wanted to know about 'this wretch who killed him'. But instead of agreeing with his deputy that the office was closed until tomorrow, Theodore irritated him by turning the sign to 'Open'. Francesca could make her own way to church, he said. Klaus was needed here. 'Write it all down,' he urged. 'Every bit of gossip and accusation. There might even be some truth in there. I want to go into the meeting tomorrow with a large pile of statements. Lots of ink on lots of sheets of paper. The chief inspector will like that. Looks like progress.'

'Why don't you do it?' Klaus muttered.

'Because I'm in the mood to beat someone over the head with my walking stick,' Theodore answered. 'And if you help me, I'll make sure it's not you.'

So they opened the office door, which did not close again for the rest of the day. The constable waved his steady trickle of visitors over to the other desk, where Deputy Constable Klaus Hildebrandt wrote down that a row of vegetables had been dug up from such-and-such a garden overnight by an unknown thief, and that a man with an unsteady gait had been seen lurching past the Valley Inn late in the night.

When he could no longer bear the twitching muscle in his neck, or the tone of concern with which the visitors mentioned poor Gustav and his 'nasty, needless death', Theodore seized a moment when Klaus was busy, and made his escape.

He went to the river, as usual, and watched the water flow. A breeze freshened the air and ruffled the weeds along the bank. There were plenty of people, he reminded himself, who took no interest whatsoever in the fate of Gustav Spiller or the absence of Elias Frankel. Tomorrow, when the church crowd found something better to do, the chattering would die down. And in the meantime, the power of debate would take its course. A sensible soul would ask his friends how a punch to the gut could cause Gustav Spiller's collapse a whole day later – and the gossipers would have no answer, surely?

'It's a rational world,' he said aloud, into the wind.

✠

On the street that led up from the valley junction through the centre of Mittelbach, he came across Peter Koenig's motor car. It was idling by the roadside with the engine running but no one at the wheel. Ute Koenig, waiting in the passenger seat, noticed the constable almost at the same moment as he saw her.

Her surprise gave him a fierce, mad hope. *She hasn't looked away! Surprised to see me – and glad? Or is it wariness? She must think I've been lurking here, waiting for her*, Theodore thought, *like a troll beneath a bridge*. As he approached the car, he wondered if she could hear the keening of his old-man lonely heart.

'Constable,' she said, looking up at him with a concentrated but elusive expression. She was in her town attire, as before, and there was a small travelling case strapped to the luggage rack. The Kaiser leaned out of the window, attracting the attention of a group of children playing ball nearby.

'Returning home, Frau Koenig?'

Ute nodded. 'Yes.' They watched each other, trying to find a way out of the silence. Eventually Ute glanced to one side, and remarked on the unusual number of people strolling about on an October day, in sleepy old Mittelbach. 'Is there a fair?'

'Ah, no.'

'I suppose they've come to look at the progress made on the new road?'

'Maybe,' he agreed, before falling silent again. What kind of conversation could they have, here, in public view? Looking down the street, Theodore saw that the cart that he had sent earlier to Angenberg had returned with Spiller's widow, and was making its way towards Rudi Hoffmann's house – watched, inevitably, by local residents from their garden gates.

Peter Koenig stood outside the hardware store, talking to someone – a patient, perhaps, who would no doubt be telling him the latest news. He had left the car engine running, evidently intending to return in a minute – and as the constable watched him, the young doctor turned his head to look back at the car, and frowned at what he saw.

'I heard about Elias Frankel,' Ute said, drawing Theodore's attention back to her. There was something beyond wariness in her expression now, he thought. Her eyes had taken on a look of urgency. She continued, somewhat hesitantly, 'But you didn't mention, when we met . . . You said nothing to me about arresting him.'

'No, I didn't—' he began, and then stopped himself. Although, in recent nights, Ute Koenig had become his private tormentor, the dream that deprived him of sleep, the constable could not allow her total control over him. A wall of caution, if not propriety, must stand between them. There was still a possibility, however reluctant Theodore was to consider it, that this woman took Johanna's baby from the cradle a week ago and carried it off somewhere private, perhaps simply to hold it – panicked – and brought it back, too late.

He changed his reply to a question. 'Why would you expect me to mention Elias Frankel to you, Frau Koenig?'

The question unsettled Ute, and she stumbled over her response. 'I thought . . . you seemed interested in all of our goings-on at Hindelheim.'

'Is he of particular interest to you?'

He watched her face – its contours and movements now familiar to him, yet endlessly surprising – as she prepared an answer.

'Constable Hildebrandt!' a voice called out, interrupting. Peter Koenig strode towards them. 'Fine day. May I ask what brings you out, besides the weather? Are you searching the motor car for any scoundrels we might have stowed away?'

Before Theodore could respond, he saw Ute's hand make a quick, furtive movement. Pulling something from her bag, she laid her gloved hand on the doorframe. Beneath it, he saw an envelope. He glanced at her. She was looking at him.

'Found one already,' he said, pointing behind Peter, at the dog in the back seat. 'If that's not a dangerous stowaway, I don't know who is. You'd have to produce a licence for it, if the law was up to me.'

'Ha,' Peter replied, without amusement, turning his head just far enough, for just long enough. 'Making a joke, Constable. You must be in better health.'

'Staying off the stimulants as you prescribed, Doctor Koenig.' He glanced again at Ute, who looked away. 'At least, I'm doing my best.'

✠

With the motor car behind him, the constable stuffed the envelope under his coat and walked on. At Doctor Hoffmann's house, he paid his respects to Gustav Spiller's widow and murmured to Rudi that his bill would be settled by the mayor's office.

Although his joints now ached from a day of traipsing around the village, Theodore pressed on up the slope towards the place where the new road forked off from Mittelbach, towards Hindelheim and the wooded hills. Ahead, he could see the join between the new road and the old track it was replacing. Trees and overgrowth had been slashed away on either side of the path, much as hairs are shaved from a wound to help the skin heal and grow. Up there was the ditch that had brought Klaus off his motorcycle, and the spot where Gustav Spiller keeled over; two accidents which, linked by the presence of Elias Frankel, were starting to combine into a single, supposed danger: a fugitive with a killer's touch.

The Koenigs' car had passed out of sight. As for Elias Frankel, where was he? Growing cold in a barn somewhere, watching for a chance to sneak home?

Theodore pulled his cap down to prevent the breeze from lifting it, and took out the envelope. This was hardly the ideal place in which to read a letter, but it had to be better than reading it at the kitchen table with his son and daughter-in-law looking on.

# 15.

Corporal Eckhardt Gröhlick lay on his narrow bed, staring at a dark suit of clothes that hung on the opposite wall. He had been given the suit at the end of the war, along with his food coupons and final pay. In the years since then, it had been hanging on the wall, unused. Now, though, after years of waiting, Eckhardt felt that he had been called to perform a new duty. It was not a call to war this time, but something at once more personal and more important. Something only he could do.

The summons had happened a few days previously, when Eckhardt had followed a noise across the school field to where a clutch of his neighbours stood watching two police vehicles outside the Frankel store. It was the second or third time in a week that the authorities had come to Hindelheim, but this time they had Elias Frankel in the sidecar of the motorcycle, with his wrists locked together.

'Hey, Eckhardt!' Elias had called to him. 'Look after the place, will you?'

At first it had seemed an ordinary request. Then, as the sidecar pulled away, Eckhardt saw the children staring at him, the ones who usually taunted him with oink-oink noises, screwing up their eyes to imitate his piggy face. They looked at him with surprise and new respect, because they had seen Elias beckon to him. Later that day, when news reached Hindelheim that Elias Frankel had broken out of his restraints on the ride to Mittelbach, the adults also began to wonder why Eckhardt, and no one else, had been hailed from the sidecar. At this point, the importance of the assignment dawned on him. He, Corporal Eckhardt Gröhlick, was being asked to keep order during a time of trouble. He was to stand guard over the Frankel store, at the heart of the village, and defend it from whatever dangers might arise until the storekeeper's return.

That first afternoon, Eckhardt had gone inside the store, secured the doors and come out again, to scowl at passers-by from the front steps. The next day, he made a tour of inspection, looking into the Frankels' rooms, the cupboards, the outside sheds.

Now, as he lay on the narrow bed in his father's house, thinking about everything that had happend in the last few days, the corporal saw that a new level of protection was required. He must be on watch night and day because Elias had killed a man, people said. They said that something of this kind was bound to happen, and that they had long suspected it, and that 'just wait until that brute comes back'.

Eckhardt Gröhlick did not think of Elias Frankel as a brute. Elias did not treat him the way many others in Hindelheim did. After the war, when Eckhardt came back but had no particular place to go, and no work to do, Elias would beckon Eckhardt down to the stream that ran below the paddock, at the back of the Frankel place, and show him something of interest wriggling in the water, or challenge him to a bottle-shooting contest in the wood. And now Elias Frankel had chosen him as his stand-in at the store; had beckoned to him – not to anyone else – from the sidecar of the motorcycle. The corporal could be trusted, that was why. Eckhardt Gröhlick was a man of honour, a man who had been given a suit by the officer in charge of decommissioning because he belonged to 'an honoured class of new citizens'; and as such, he intended to honour the agreement that he had struck with his friend Elias on Thursday afternoon. He would guard the Frankel place.

On the other side of the bedroom door, Eckhardt could hear the woman who was not his mother talking to her lodger, the new school teacher. The words were not clear – there was a kind of numbness sometimes in Eckhardt's left ear, which kept him from hearing things well – but he knew Frau Gröhlick's voice, and he knew that lying here listening to it would only worsen the pounding sensation in his head. He stood up.

There was no mirror in Eckhardt's room, so he could not see how the suit of clothes looked on him as he pulled them on. The wool was moth-eaten in places, and the legs were too short, but if he stood as the sergeant had taught him to do, he felt sure that he would make his authority known.

⛨

'Dear Herr Constable Hildebrandt,' the letter began. Theodore felt the thick, ruled sheaf between his fingers, rough at one edge where it seemed to have been torn from an exercise book.

> There is more bad news from Hindelheim, I gather – Elias Frankel arrested, and your deputy's vehicle overturned. The road is not even built yet, and already it has proved unlucky. I can hear my Aunt Ernesta, muttering that misfortune has its own seasons like everything else, and we should study them to understand their pattern. The Night People are here, she would say, stirring up trouble. But those superstitions belong to older times, and Aunt has been gone three years, as I keep telling her. I must try to pay her warnings less attention.

Theodore paused to draw up the collar of his coat, as a gust of cold air ran down the back of it. He stamped his feet, with some difficulty, to prevent them from cramping. *'Here I am,'* he read on,

*wondering what Elias has done; and there you are wondering, I imagine, where he is. Unless you have caught him already. This is an old story for us, Constable; everyone wondering about Elias Frankel. We have always wondered about the Frankels – him most of all. I myself can hardly say that I know Elias, even though I lived next door to him all my life until this summer.*

*I told you in the café that it was Elias Frankel who claimed to have seen a wolf in the hills overlooking the quarry. But I did not mention, I think, the coincidence in the timing of it – late in June of this year. It was in that same week that his stepfather, the Monsieur, fell from the steps at the back of the store, and plunged to his death.*

*The Monsieur was not a Frankel by blood, and of course 'the Monsieur' was not his real name – but no one ever knew what he was called. He came from somewhere else (another mystery) with Ida Frankel and her son Elias, some years ago, and they built a house, and opened the front room as a store, all the while avoiding questions about where they had come from. Or – not avoiding, but giving different answers each time. There was some mischief in Ida, and in the Monsieur, and there is certainly mischief in Elias.*

*When Ida's second son, little Otto, was born, everyone remarked that the two boys were different creatures. All of Ida Frankel's wildness had gone into Elias, while Otto had the Monsieur's milder disposition. (It was only later, after Ida died, that the Monsieur suffered from fits of violent anger.) But when the Monsieur fell from his steps this summer, it stirred up some old suspicions – for example, that Elias Frankel resented him, and had been looking for an opportunity to push him out of the nest; and that Elias had inherited a bad character from his own father, who was a convict or a freak of nature; and that Ida Frankel, escaping this first unknown husband, had brought her*

*freakish son to Hindelheim to hide him from the eyes of the
world.*

*Why did the Monsieur fall? Why did Elias see whatever it
was he saw? Such was the gossip that occupied us for a few
weeks this summer. There was even a rumour – spoken in jest,
I'm sure, but spoken all the same – that Elias Frankel was
raised by wolves, and that one of them came back looking for
him and calling to him in a secret language to kill his stepfather
and rejoin his old pack. You see what nonsense we talk to fill the
silence, Herr Constable. Even so, when you catch Elias, you
might ask him about the wolf. I for one would be interested to
learn how he explains it now.*

Here Theodore looked up and glanced around. It was getting
dark, almost too dark to read. The cows in the nearest field were
shadows, moving away from him as they were herded towards a
distant milking shed. He nodded at the farmer, but was not sure
if the man could see him. He read on.

*And now I am wondering again about why you came to see
me in Angenberg. If it was to ask about Elias, you should have
talked to Marlyse Pohlmann, who was in love with him for a
period in the spring. She spent many nights there at the Frankel
place, and became convinced that she had changed him. All the
other women who have shared Elias Frankel's favours failed to
understand the man, in Marlyse's judgement: she alone truly
knew Elias Frankel, and she alone would tame him. Well, I
wasn't so sure about that, but Marlyse can be stubborn.*

*They made a trip together to Marlyse's uncle, or a distant
cousin, I forget which (you must know some of the Pohlmanns?
They are everywhere!) at his porcelain factory. Marlyse came
back breathless with stories of Elias Frankel's genius. He had
shown her so many things. He had drawn her portait, in chalk,
on a wall. He had made love to her – forgive my bluntness – in*

*the open air, where anyone could have seen them, and carried her naked into a stream by moonlight.*

*But when they returned to Hindelheim, the affair soured. They had taken the trap and worn out the pony, so the Monsieur was cross when they returned. He yelled at Elias from the steps at the back of the store, and threw something at him. Elias shot the pony – it was lame – and withdrew from Marlyse, or simply turned his attention to another woman, as he has a reputation for doing. By the time of that wolf incident, he seemed to have forgotten her.*

*Marlyse never told me how they fell apart. She stopped talking about Elias, and has not mentioned his name to me since. Perhaps she was the one to forget him first, though somehow I doubt it. In any case, she would be the one to ask for information. As you can see, there is not much I can tell you that is not common knowledge in Hindelheim – or at least, common speculation. I've heard the same stories as everyone else. Marlyse may have others.*

*Yours,*

*Ute Koenig.'*

✠

By the time he got to the end of the letter, Theodore's fingers were numb with cold. Unable to fold the pages back into the envelope, he shoved them loose into a pocket and started for home.

For someone with no unusual knowledge of Elias Frankel, he thought, Ute Koenig certainly had a lot to say about him. She had written in a fast hand, by the look of it, and Theodore wondered whether it was furtive or anxious haste that drove her.

Expecting the office to be closed, the constable was surprised to find his deputy still at work, sticking pins in a map at the points where potential sightings of the runaway had been reported. Klaus thought it likely that Elias Frankel had made it to the railway line, or found a lift on the valley road, in which case he would by now be far away. If, on the other hand, he was still skulking in the area, as these local reports suggested, then surely it would not be long before someone spotted a six-foot Jew with a lazy eye, barely twenty years of age, sloping past in whatever place he was trying to hide.

'Have you heard what they're calling him?' he added.

Theodore had not.

'"The Wolf Man",' Klaus explained. 'I think it's something to do with his looks, or the way he ran off, crouching forward. What do you think of that?'

Sinking onto his chair, Theodore wished that he did not have to think or feel anything about it, but could plunge instead into a deep, oblivious sleep. But knowing that tomorrow he would have to face the chief inspector, and the rest of them, he forced his mind to sift through the fragments of description and legend that comprised his knowledge of Elias Frankel. He formed a picture of a long-legged, wild-eyed young man who was quick to anger, perhaps because he was prey to fears. What would happen when someone tried to pull him out of hiding? 'I think,' he replied eventually, 'that if he isn't already dangerous then he might soon become so.'

✛

Eckhardt Gröhlick began his inventory in the Frankels' back yard. In the largest outhouse, he made a mental count of empty crates, pieces of rusting metal, broken tools. There was a harness, but no horse; a workbench strewn with nails, straw, dust; and a grain-stuffed sack hanging from the highest point of the roof. This last item caused him to stop and remember. He and Elias had hung it up together one day a few years ago, to serve as a punching bag. Was it still good, he wondered?

He threw his fist into it.

The suspended grain sack turned only slightly in response. Eckhardt found a cloth and wound it around the knuckles of his right hand before punching again, and again, until the sweat seeped into the wool of his suit. Eventually his weight pulled the sack off the beam, and it hit the floor and burst. Dismayed at the damage he had caused, Eckhardt hurried to find a broom.

When he had finished in the yard, he climbed the back stairs, slowing towards the top, where the handrail had come loose and two steps were broken. Here Eckhardt paused to dismiss from his mind the talk he had heard about the Monsieur's fall from these stairs. It was not true, he told himself, that Ida Frankel's spirit or any other dead thing lived on in the coal bunker below. That angled lid he could see beneath him was not a door to the underworld – he was almost sure of it. When his hand was not so raw, he would fix the broken stairs, to prove that he did not mind the stories.

Inside, he called as a precaution, 'Elias?' and waited to see if there would be a response. There was no knowing when the rightful owner might return, and Eckhardt did not want to annoy him. He was here at Elias Frankel's request, but that did not mean he was to stay forever, necessarily. The kitchen table was covered with drawings and books and other items, including an unwashed copper pot, and a beaker of unfinished coffee. Eckhardt tipped the beaker and saw the liquid move at the bottom while a layer of film above it stayed level, dead but thickening, like a piece of Elias Frankel left behind.

Once, when Ida Frankel had been dead for a while, and the Monsieur was too drunk to look after little Otto, Eckhardt had sat here at this table, with Elias on the chair there, and between the two of them they had tried to feed the child. They chopped up one thing after another, and fed the pieces to baby Otto on a spoon, but he spat them all out again. The little titch could hardly reach the table, Eckhardt remembered. At one point a plate tipped over, and the knife fell from it blade first off the table, but Eckhardt caught it in mid-air before it could hurt Otto. The corporal was proud of that memory. It proved that he could be quick when he needed to be, despite what Frau Gröhlick said about him.

The keys that Eckhardt had found and tested over recent days now hung under his suit jacket, from a chain. Anyone who intended to break into the Frankels' place would have to contend with Corporal Gröhlick. He made himself familiar with every lock and latch, and unbolted and rebolted the front door several times to test its strength. The fly curtain at the back door puzzled him, and he spent some time moving the inch-wide, vertical belts of canvas this way and that, creating patterns of shade and light. He had seen something like it once, in a butcher's shop in Angen. Where was Elias now, he wondered; and what would happen when he came home?

✠

At eight o'clock in the morning, Eckhardt Gröhlick stood at the gate that connected the Frankels' property with the school field. There in the grey light he watched half a dozen small figures make their way to the schoolhouse on reluctant, Monday-morning feet. When his niece and nephew, Raine and Reinhold Gröhlick, appeared, he hollered. The girl came first, and Eckhardt opened the gate, saying, 'I've got something for you to do.'

Raine looked back across the field, where her brother watched for a moment before turning into the schoolhouse. 'I've got lessons,' she said.

'This is more important,' Eckhardt insisted. When that failed to impress her, he added, 'You'll like it.'

The girl considered. 'If it's work, you'll have to pay me for it.'

Eckhardt looked down at the small head, on which her hair had been neatly twisted into a plait. Thinking that the whole coil would probably fit into the palm of his hand, he lowered his hand onto it so gently that Raine did not notice for a moment. With his forefinger, Eckhardt searched for the end of the plait – and at this movement, the girl's head jerked up.

'What are you doing?' she demanded.

'Hold still,' Eckhardt pleaded, as a rope of hair began to lengthen in his hand. He held on, watching the golden coil loosen.

'Get off,' Raine commanded, pulling away. Discovering the damage done to her morning's handiwork, she threatened, 'Now you owe me already. You'd better pay up, or I'll tell Grandma Gröhlick you kept me from school.'

Eckhardt led the way inside, and told the girl what he wanted her to do. He brought boxes and tins from the shelves, emptying nails, buttons and the rest onto the counter. Raine listed each item in pencil, her erratic letters taking up all the pages of a book she found in the Monsieur's drawer. Battling tedium and weariness, she also itemised the SPIDERS (DEAD–12; ALIVE–3), WORMS (DEAD–1; ALIVE–2) and SNAILS (2 and a ½, ALIVE) that passed across the counter, and invented other items (6 x JARS OF EYEBALLS, etc.) to see if her uncle would notice. To her delight and contempt, Eckhardt held the list to his face and nodded, in imitation of a man who could read.

Raine's last task was to make a sign for the door: *STORE CLOSED PENDING OWNER'S RETURN. ENQUIRIES TO CORPORAL E. GRÖHLICK.*

✠

The police district headquarters, occupying the site of a medieval fortress, overlooked the oldest and busiest bridge in Angenberg. From one wall, the ground sloped steeply down towards the former moat, while the front gate opened onto the street. There, two guardsmen watched a tram offload its freight of clerks and shopkeepers at the start of the working day. It was the first day of November, and the weather had worsened overnight. Yesterday's bright sunshine was replaced with a severe, overcast sky.

Every month, the region's police officers and auxiliaries above a certain grade gathered around a vast walnut table at which Chief Inspector Lorentz Streicher presided. A polished surface stretched like a lake between the assembled men. In it, Constable Theodore Hildebrandt could see several heads turn to watch him as he took his seat. Lowering his weight onto one buttock, and allowing the weak right leg to flick out, as it must, he thought that if he turned his cap upside down and perhaps smiled or sang a little, then his colleagues might throw coins into it.

Chief Inspector Lorentz Streicher was a tall, thin man who did not like to sit still – or to sit at all, if he could avoid it. He spoke standing, at times leaning on the back of his chair, and at others springing from it, as if it were red hot. His thick eyebrows shot up in surprise at his own observations, and when someone else raised his hand to speak, he would look at the man as a deer in the forest might look at a gun-toting hunter. There were more points on today's agenda than usual, the chief inspector warned, and all of them to be treated as matters of some urgency.

First on the list were ministerial directives or notifications from Berlin: results of the programme for the redevelopment of former armaments factories; survey statistics showing a rise in the number of deaths from communicable diseases, and a fall in those from starvation, with implications for policing; new restrictions from the Agricultural Board on the use of chemical fertilisers, and consequent changes to licensing and monitoring procedures; progress of the federal road-building scheme, and the proposals of the Road & Transport Police Division for measures to combat crimes associated with road use, including unlicensed fuelling stations, wayside prostitution, and counterfeit travel papers.

Here the chief inspector paused to invite a response from Officer Zelinsky, liaison officer for the region's Transport Police. While Zelinsky spoke, Theodore studied him; his clean, white, indoor hands resting on the polished walnut, the fingers interlinked and unmoving. A sign of confidence, that stillness – the sort of thing that got a man promoted above his talent, Theodore thought.

As the discussion moved on, Officer Zelinsky looked over at the constable and smiled. The smile distracted Theodore as the chief moved on to local issues. Item one: a violent incident on the railway line the previous week, in which a woman had been stabbed. Chief Inspector Streicher was overseeing the inquiry. Item two: the threat of organised protest from a tenants' association in Angenberg, which was complaining about rents and conditions. The situation to be monitored by Angen officers. Finally, the chief inspector came to the matter of 'the Hindelheim outlaw'.

Looking down the table, he asked if Constable Hildebrandt had managed to find the rogue.

Pulling himself away from Zelinsky's hypnotic gaze, Theodore answered, 'Not yet, sir. But we have taken statements from a number of people who think they might have seen him. If they're all correct, he's slept in just about every barn in the district.' He pushed a stack of documents across the table, and saw a glint of white teeth as Zelinsky chuckled silently at the paper mountain. An old, cheap trick.

'Ah, good,' the chief said, sizing up the number of documents in Theodore's pile, and apparently reassured by the height of it. 'Well, I'll repeat to the room what I said to you on the telephone, Constable. It is most unfortunate that Herr Dammertz saw what he saw. This valued investor has been given reason to think that our police force is incapable of restraining even unarmed, solitary young men. Because of the importance of this issue, not least in the eyes of the mayor, I'm sending a team of mounted troopers up there to find Elias Frankel. Zelinsky.'

'Yes, sir.'

'I'd like you to lead the search in town, and along the north road. Look at Theodore's witness statements,' he slapped a hand on the stack of papers, 'and establish the fugitive's most likely route. Also try to locate anyone who's driven past Mittelbach in the last couple of days, and ask if they gave the man a ride.'

Officer Zelinsky inclined his head. 'Anything I can do, sir.'

It was the wrong answer. The chief inspector glared at him, repeating, 'Anything you can do. Indeed. It's generous of you to offer your help, officer, but I had rather taken it for granted, since Elias Frankel was your prisoner, arrested at your instruction, transported under your supervision, and lost from your motor convoy while you drove on ahead!'

A silence fell across the table. Blushing to the roots of his cologned hair, Officer Zelinsky said, 'With great respect, Chief Inspector, it was not my idea to ask the prisoner to step out of the sidecar and wait. Nor did I – or would I – allow the key to my handcuffs to get into the hands of a road worker. Those choices were made by Deputy Constable Klaus Hildebrandt, who was driving the motorcycle. Whilst I take full responsibility for—'

'You will take responsibility where I give it,' Lorentz raged. 'The deputy constable is no more to blame than your dog! I did not send you up there to make an arrest, or invite you to treat Constable Hildebrandt's deputy as your personal assistant. Now get out and find the rogue.' He waited for Zelinsky to get to his feet, and then dismissed the others. 'That goes for all of you. The meeting is over.' He glanced at Theodore. 'Constable, a word.'

From the door, Officer Zelinsky threw a look of venom at Theodore before turning out, ahead of the others.

✠

Once the room had cleared, Chief Inspector Lorentz Streicher shut the door and reached his desk in three long strides. Theodore stood before it, waiting.

'See what happens when you drop your toys, Theo?' Lorentz challenged. 'I give them to someone else, and he makes an even bigger mess than the one you created. What is it, man? You're glowering at me. Did no one teach you not to stare?'

'I was a poor student, sir.'

'And I fear you still are. The only reason we're in this mess is because you blundered into a sensitive situation and trod on everyone's toes.' He paused then went on, 'Zelinsky is no fool. He will do his utmost to beat you to the finishing line on this one. If I were you, I'd make sure that I found Elias Frankel before he does.'

Theodore thought for a moment that the chief was declaring a knockout contest with only one winner. But no – that was the way Zelinsky would think. Those blue eyes, beaming at him across the conference table, had somehow sent his brain into disarray. He replied, 'And if I manage that, what is the charge?'

'The charge?' Lorentz Streicher repeated in surprise. 'My understanding is that this Frankel boy left us with a wrecked police vehicle, injuries to your deputy, stolen handcuffs and a dead road worker. In addition to which—'

'The road worker was sick before Elias hit him,' Theodore interrupted. 'He collapsed a day later, sir. A full day. There is no connection—'

'Is. That. So?' the chief inspector intoned, silencing him. 'How kind of you to decide the law for us, Constable Hildebrandt. Here was I thinking that we would need magistrates and the rule of law! I imagined, in my simpleton's head, that in order to establish the truth of the matter we would make use of the institutions, methods and principles refined by our judicial system over the past several centuries – but no! All I needed to do was ask my old pal Theodore Hildebrandt for his opinion!'

Theodore lowered his gaze to the table as the chief continued. 'I know what this is, Theo. You're ashamed that you weren't there to catch this storekeeper brandishing his gun, or whatever it was he was doing. It was your area of responsibility and you overlooked it. Perhaps you're a little jealous of Zelinsky for doing what you failed to do? And naturally, you're pained by the mistakes Klaus made, and wish you could redeem them – any father would feel the same. But to close your eyes and pretend there is no problem, Constable: that is not the remedy.'

Turning away, he looked out of the window, which was was set deep within the old fortress wall, far above the moat. With his back to the constable, he said, 'The Department for Archaeology and Antiquities wants to excavate the ditch down there. Perhaps we'll find out how many medievals dropped to their deaths from these walls.'

Theodore followed his glance. 'If that's a warning, sir, you can rest assured that it will be no challenge disposing of me. A shove from the steps would probably do it.'

The chief inspector turned to face him again. 'Tell me this,' he said. 'Do you truly think we should assume that Elias Frankel is innocent of every conceivable wrongdoing, and leave him free to do as he likes, without even looking for him?'

After a moment, Theodore answered, 'No.'

'Then you agree that we should find and question him?'

'Yes.'

With a look of relief, the inspector returned to his desk. He turned over one or two of the statements that Klaus had prepared. 'So what's your best guess,' he said. 'The neighbours are talking. The man's not invisible. Where is he?'

Theodore thought for a moment, and then replied. 'He has a girlfriend. Marlyse Pohlmann. She rents a room in the factory district—'

'Good. Give Zelinsky the details. Tell him to put a watch on the place.' He looked up, and ran his gaze over the constable's face. 'I had quite a fight getting the Board to agree your current position, Theodore. If you want to be promoted to a role with investigative powers, you will need to learn some tact. Do you understand?'

He replied, 'I'll keep studying.'

# 16.

Dismissing Theodore with a sigh, Chief Inspector Lorentz Streicher called the next scheduled visitor into his office: one Werner Todt from the *Angenberg Gazette*.

A solid and humourless man with an impressive forehead, Herr Todt was preparing a report on the prospective land purchase near Mittelbach. He had already been to the Town Hall to gather remarks from the mayor and the developer, Herr Dammertz. He planned to begin the piece by detailing the industrialist's business interests and knowledge of exporting; his stated opinions on Germany's economic health and relations with its occupiers; and his wife's charitable ventures. Thereafter the piece would describe the couple's recent tour of the hill country, which had been interrupted when a road digger collapsed, following an attack by a local ruffian – and now fugitive – named Elias Frankel.

For this part of the report, Herr Todt would like to include a comment by Chief Inspector Streicher. Did he agree with Frau Dammertz's assessment of the incident – that it was worrying to hear of young men behaving with violence in a Christian country and escaping the clutches of local law enforcers?

'Violence is always worrying,' the chief inspector agreed. 'But your readers may be assured that this man has not escaped the law. He will be caught.'

Was there a problem with outlaws in the area? Herr Todt asked.

None at all.

Gypsies?

Certainly not, the chief inspector insisted. Leaning on his elbows, he added, 'Allow me to say, Herr Todt – and please be sure to print this exactly as I say it – that any one of the *Gazette*'s readers who wishes to travel to Mittelbach or the surrounding area can do so with peace of mind. There are no wild men in the hills. There is no curse on the new road. The recent events you're discussing involve a single, lone individual, and with the help of vigilant citizens, we will find him.'

✠

The service entrance of the Angenberg Jewish Boys' College was in constant use during the morning, as deliveries were carried in and kitchen staff came out to burn waste, or run errands. Shortly after ten, the school chef stepped out to enjoy a smoke, and noticed a figure standing on the far side of the road, in the entrance of an alleyway.

The man – or boy, it was hard to tell his age – seemed to be staring in this direction, towards the school. He wore a long dark coat, and his face was thrown into shadow by the angle of the sun. Something about him caught the chef's notice, causing his cigarette to burn unattended while he watched to see what the man would do. A bicycle passed, and then a bus, and then the man was gone. 'Just, gone,' the chef would say later, when telling the story. 'He didn't turn. He vanished.'

At the main entrance, moments later, the school porter opened the gates to a police automobile, and greeted the blue-eyed officer who stepped out of it. He directed the officer up the steps, and then turned back to close the gates. In his peripheral vision, a dark streak came and went, so fast that the porter did not look around but simply carried on with his business. In fact, it was only later, when he was listening to the chef's story, that the porter remembered this sensation he had felt of someone passing behind him, moving through the college gates without making a sound.

The headmaster met the police officer in the front hall and led him into the principal's study, closing the door. It was now five minutes before eleven, and the hall was busy with pupils and teachers moving between classes. Some of the boys noticed the policeman, and asked each other what he was doing here, but none of them paid attention to a tall figure in a dark coat who stood at a noticeboard, surveying the hall as it was reflected in the glass casing. A bell rang, speeding the pale-faced boys on their way up and down an ornate staircase, past pillars which reached from the floor to the carved wooden ceiling.

By the eleventh stroke of the clock, there was no one left in the school hall to watch the stranger as he stalked around it, looking at the paintings.

The school's art collection, diminished by the war, was dispersed over the walls with gaps between the paintings. Dark squares on the wallpaper indicated where other, more valuable works had hung. Those that were left, more modest in size, held gaudy hunting scenes, portraits of noble bores, and hymns in oil to the glories of the Ancient World. Selecting the thickest frame, the stranger took it down from the wall, wrapped it in a scholar's gown that was hanging on a hook nearby, and turned away.

According to the chronology constructed later, the sinister shadow-man was next seen on the other side of town, heading towards a pawnbroker's shop. Some hours after that, he appeared in the market square, where K., M. & L. Oberdorfer, Proprietors, Grocers & Provisioners, Export & Import, controlled several stalls in addition to the largest building in the square. Stacked outside the Oberdorfers' store were figs and walnuts, six kinds of local cabbage, Russian cranberries and heaps of root vegetables. Inside were dry goods and liquors, crates of soda and barrels of treacle. Everybody shopped at the Oberdorfers' place, including storekeepers from out of town, who would load up their carts in the yard behind, for a trade price, before riding back into the countryside.

It was therefore a surprise to shoppers and stallholders in the marketplace when, in the middle of Monday afternoon, an hour before their usual closing time, one of the three Oberdorfer siblings shut the door of the shop from inside, and pulled the blinds down. What was the problem? people wanted to know. Had one of the grocers died? Why, if the store was closing early, had the produce at the front not been cleared away?

As they discussed these mysteries, the door burst open again, and a young giant ran out. He must have been seven feet tall, as they judged it, with dark hair falling to his shoulders, and a look of menace in his eyes. The tail of his coat – or it could have been his heel, or knee – caught against one of the trays and knocked it over, spilling cranberries onto the ground. Startled bystanders stepped back as this unearthly figure of a man pushed past them, breathing fury, loping from one foot to the other.

Only when he had left the square did the onlookers feel safe to return to their tasks, some treading tentatively over scattered cranberries to the Oberdorfer store, in search of answers.

✛

Three mounted police officers sent from Angenberg dismounted in the back yard of the Frankel store and dispersed to search it. One sauntered over to the hen huts. Another climbed the back steps. The third poked around in the outhouses, with no particular aim beyond pocketing the odd bottle of liquor or box of tobacco. All he could find was a tin of sardines in an otherwise empty box – which he took, despite his hatred of fish. Turning to leave the shed, the trooper found a man watching him from the entrance. The man wore an ill-fitting, moth-eaten black suit, the shoulders of which reached to either side of the doorframe. It was hard to guess his age. The bulk of him suggested maturity – perhaps thirty years – but his skin was pink and chapped, like a boy's. He had small eyes and a snubbed nose on a broad, flat face.

'Good morning,' the trooper said, putting a hand over the pocket in which he had secreted the tin of fish. It seemed to him that the man was studying him with suspicion, and he wondered if he would have trouble getting past him, out of the shed. Straightening as far as he could under the low roof, he said, 'We're looking for this young blood who's got himself into trouble. Elias Frankel. Friend of yours, is he?'

The man watched him, scowling, and then said, 'What?'

The trooper shuffled closer, and spoke right into his face. 'Who are you?'

'Corporal Eckhardt Gröhlick,' the other replied, in a monotone. 'My name's on the front door. I'm keeping watch here.'

The trooper absorbed this, and said, 'Are you going to let me pass, Corporal?'

Eckhardt took a step back, but kept his eyes on the man. They stood together in the back yard of the store, while the trooper waited for his colleagues to finish their search. 'Has he been back yet?' he asked. When Eckhardt looked at him with the same uncomprehending frown, he raised his voice, 'Your friend, the runaway. Has he showed up here? For a change of clothes, maybe. Something to eat?'

Eckhardt's scowl deepened. He looked up the back stairs, and said, 'They're going through cupboards. They shouldn't do that. He asked me to look after the place.'

The trooper nodded. 'You know where he is, I'll bet. Some place you go to take him food, and to tell him who's come looking? Soon as our backs are turned, you'll scuttle off to give him a warning.' He grinned. 'I understand, son. It's loyalty. You should be commended for it. Any of us would help a friend if he asked. But the thing is, Corporal . . . You don't mind if I call you by your title?'

He saw the man blink at this, a stray dog in search of a master. He just needed to be fed right, and he would follow. 'There's two kinds of friends, see. There's your neighbours, like this Frankel lad, who just happen to live next door, and so you look out for each other because there's no one else, is there? You're lumped together, no choice about it. Childhood friends. You with me?'

Eckhardt was listening. He blinked again.

'Then there's what I'd call true friends,' the trooper continued. 'The friendship of equals, when a grown man such as yourself recognises the spirit and intelligence of another man who is like him. Who has lived the same hardships. Who respects the same principles. Soldiers like you and me, Corporal, we know what's behind a uniform. There's a kinship there. A man who's served his country recognises his true fellows. Whatever the job we're each doing now, it's the same thing we're working for, isn't it? Who else could claim to share our sense of duty?'

A silence fell as Eckhardt considered this. From the poultry yard, something squawked. In the first few days of his guardianship of the store, Corporal Gröhlick had forgotten about the poultry hut. When he did remember, it was too late to save the eggs from thieving hands, and all but two of the hens were dead. He would have to explain that mistake when Elias returned. 'I don't always hear them,' he said.

The trooper watched him. 'Don't hear what, soldier?'

'The hens. That's why I got to them too late.'

Seeing Eckhardt's face contract, the trooper said, 'Your friend is a wanted man, Corporal Gröhlick. I know you want to do the right thing, and in your place, I'd be wondering what the right thing was. "Do I protect Elias Frankel because he asked me to, and because I've known him since we were boys? Or do I think about the old man who died at the road, and the uniformed officers who are risking their own skins?"' He paused, and then went on, 'No reason why you should listen to my advice, Corporal. You don't know much about me, except that we have a sense of duty in common, and the ties of honour and brotherhood as fellows in uniform. But could I tell you something?'

He waited. One. Two. Eckhardt's broad, flat face turned towards him.

'I think you should carry on with what you're doing. Stay here, watch the place, make sure nothing gets stolen. The law's the law, and until Elias Frankel is brought to justice, none of us can say for sure what he has and hasn't done. So keep watching. And when the fugitive appears, you say nothing to him. But you let us know. Hmm? Will you do that?'

Eckhardt scratched his head, his ear. The smell of stale sweat came off his suit. 'I don't know . . . where . . .'

'I'm going to ask you a question now,' the trooper interrupted, 'to see if we understand each other. If you don't want to answer it, then I'll get the message, Corporal. I'll understand that you're on the other side, and that you don't want to cooperate with us. Me and my men, we'll leave you alone.' He glanced over at the second trooper, who emerged from another shed with something in his hand, which he fed to the horses. 'Who's Elias Frankel got, in the way of kin? Where are his people?'

One. Two. Three.

Eckhardt took a breath and let it out again. 'There's only Otto Frankel left. That's his half-brother. He's in Angen, at the Jewish school.'

'Anyone else? Girlfriend?'

Eckhardt answered this with a shrug. The trooper raised a hand to salute him. 'That's a good start, Corporal Gröhlick. We'll drop by and talk to you again.'

✠

Theodore picked up the ringing telephone, again. The Mittelbach Constabulary had never seen so much activity. There was a new police motor car parked outside, not for his use, but for two of Zelinsky's men who had been lurking outside the station all morning. Whenever the constable asked what their orders were, he would receive mumbled replies about coordination, lines of reporting and rapid response. He concluded that they had been told to watch him.

'Getting anywhere?' the voice demanded. As before, Officer Zelinsky did not bother to give his name.

'I've been to the doorstep this morning, if that's what you mean.'

'Very funny, Constable. I take it you're no closer to finding our mutual friend.'

Theodore forced himself to ask, 'Have you spoken to the girlfriend?'

'The Pohlmann girl? Yes, we wasted some time there. She's got nothing to say. I suppose you knew that when you gave me the so-called information. Getting cunning in your old age, Hildebrandt. But if you want to play dirty . . .'

'I didn't realise we were playing at anything,' Theodore replied.

The officer laughed. 'Then you should read more, Constable. Expand that provinicial mind of yours. The scientists say we're all in competition, all the time. Life is one big race. And guess who's predicted to win?'

❖

Marlyse Pohlmann's rise from dishwasher to hostess of the Bridge Street Beer Hall in Angenberg on Friday was followed, on the same night, by her descent into *get-your-picklehead out-of-here-and-don't-come-back* obscurity. It started when the proprietor learned that his usual bar girl was sick. Cursing his bad luck, the man pushed into the kitchen and came back with the new plate-scrubber in tow. 'Take that off,' he commanded, pointing at Marlyse's grubby apron. 'You're on the public side now, so straighten up and smile for the customers.'

One of the customers, watching from his regular seat, found the appearance of the new girl at the bar a welcome diversion from the earnest discussions of his friends. As the Cultural Affairs Correspondent of the *Angenberg Gazette*, Albert Dinter was obliged to see every performance at the theatre around the corner. The friends who had accompanied him there earlier in the evening were keen to know how he had found the play.

'Loud,' Albert replied, looking over his companions' heads at the new barmaid. 'I couldn't get to sleep until the second act, and then some clown woke me with a load of shouting and carrying-on. Here, however,' he pointed with his glass towards the bar, 'is a compelling scenario which I call "The Instruction of an Ingénue". The girl there, let's call her...' he paused to pick a name, 'Flat-Footed Frieda, was brought in from the kitchen a few minutes ago by the Prologue figure – we must take him to be the proprietor of this fine establishment. You know the man I mean; one sees him in the restaurant area, trying to sell wine to French businessmen. He gave our Frieda a cursory lesson in serving beer, and told her to remove the grubby apron in which she had been, I suppose, scrubbing carrots, or—'

'Taking a pounding from the chef?' suggested a member of the party.

Albert approved this intervention with a nod, agreeing, 'A crude coupling at the scullery sink, indeed; that fits the generic requirements nicely. Well, then, pressing down her skirt, Young Frieda is left by the proprietor to begin her new role. Which takes us to the present action. This must be the second or third tray of drinks she is serving now. Behold the bewildered expression, the unpractised hand at the keg...'

'Isn't the tap leaking?' one of the friends exclaimed, pointing at the floor behind Marlyse. 'She's left the keg untended and forgotten it. How exquisite. Shall I rescue her?'

They continued in this vein for a few moments, taking up the game that Albert had started, until two of the friends left, and those remaining at the table began a new conversation. Only Albert continued to watch as Marlyse moved in a haze of confusion between customers, barrels and glasses. Men smiled at her, vying for her attention. One of them pointed out the leaking tap. Albert found himself irked by the other customers' pursuit of her. She was his girl, his discovery, his creature.

At the close of business, the proprietor exploded at the havoc wreaked on his floor by the spilled beer. The girl was a moron, a cretin the like of which he had not seen in his life before. Single-handedly she had made a joke of his business and reputation!

Receiving her dismissal without a murmur, Marlyse turned from the bar towards the public door, her glance landing for a moment on Albert. Alone at his table he raised a glass and said 'Encore' under his breath. The proprietor, holding the door open to speed Marlyse's exit, took the opportunity to clip her on the ear as she passed. Albert caught up with her on the street, where he noticed with the affection of an old lover the heavy tread, as each foot landed flat on the paving stones. 'Good evening,' he said, falling into step beside her. 'Would you care for a drink?'

The eyes that looked up had nothing of the kitten in them, and no self-pity either. She was tired, outraged, sunk. The mass of brown hair that had charmed Albert from a distance smelled of smoke and chicken grease. 'Is that a joke?' she replied.

'No, actually, no. It wasn't meant to be.' He said that he was hungry and was going to find or make a sandwich, and would she like one?

Albert Dinter's home, until he could persuade the *Gazette*'s editor to raise his wages, was a room in the garret of a boarding house. Sweeping a pile of newspapers off the chair, he invited Marlyse to sit. Instead she stepped past the unmade bed to the window, and looked outside, at the rooftops opposite and down into the street below.

Watching her with some puzzlement, Albert wondered if there was a jealous farmer standing on the pavement with a shotgun, watching them at the window, or a church zealot ready to burst through the door to demand the return of his betrothed.

'We weren't followed, I hope?' he asked with a nervous smile. 'I mean, you're . . . not expecting someone?'

'What?' she scowled.

'Never mind.' Figuring that she was merely curious about a town that was still new to her, Albert asked where she came from.

'Hindelheim,' said Marlyse.

Albert recognised the name but took a moment to place it. 'In the hills near Mittelbach? Just up the north road?' It was not the distant place he had expected. 'I thought you'd journeyed to us from lands afar. You seem so new to everything.'

This struck Marlyse as an accusation, and she fell quiet. Albert strove to make amends with a tin of ham he found lurking at the back of a cupboard. This he presented on a saucer, the plate being in no fit state to eat from.

'Where's yours?' she asked.

'I'm not hungry.'

'You said you were.'

He looked at her, wondering if he could say that it was a standard first move in the game of getting a girl into bed. Instead he launched into a description of his work at the newspaper, where he wrote regular reports on whatever contrivance passed for art or culture south of Berlin. 'I play a game with myself,' he confided. 'If I can find the logical basis of a play, or the narrative thread of a painting, I dismiss it as crass. If, on the other hand, it resembles no object yet discovered on this planet, obeys no law of reason, and has no structure that I can discern,

160

I recommend it as a work of genius to our civilised readers. At the end of the week, I compare my reviews with the verdicts given in the city papers – Berlin, Köln, Munich; we have copies sent to the office – and more times than not, I get it right.' He pointed to a stack of national newspapers by Marlyse's feet.

When she did not look at them, he said, 'I'm boring you.'

Marlyse did not dispute this, but tilted the empty tin towards him and asked, 'Is there another?'

Albert returned to the cupboard to search again, and emerged with half a jar of apricots in syrup. 'All that I have I give to you,' he said, shuffling to her on his knees. He added, 'Though I must warn my esteemed customer that the greenish coating may be mould. Eat at your own risk, madam.'

'You talk like a book,' Marlyse observed, working around the mould with a spoon. She scooped out the fruits with sticky digits and chewed them while he watched on his knees, like a dog. Taking hold of her calf with one hand, he sought permission with a glance, and rolled down the stockings, one after the other.

Marlyse, looking at him, licked her fingers until Albert pulled her to the floor. He rode her on the pages of a newspaper that had fallen open, ripping the paper with his knees, smudging ink with his palms. Her eyes looked straight up at him, big and beautiful and unimpressed. He moved her hair, and saw that the skin of her earlobe was split where the bar owner's ring had caught it.

Afterwards she stood up and padded on bare feet to the communal washroom on the stairs. Then she came back and slumped without invitation on his bed, where she sniffed audibly at the stale pillow.

# 17.

In the morning, Albert Dinter took his coffee alone, standing at the window. Keeping his back to the bed, he lifted yesterday's shirt from the floor and checked the crisp parts with his nose before putting it on. 'What will you do?' he asked.

Marlyse replied with a sidelong glance at him, 'I thought I might stay with you for a while, until I find something.'

It was what Albert hoped to hear, and it spiked his pride, but at the same time he experienced an unease which came out as an accusation. 'Don't you have a boyfriend?'

A silence followed this, as Marlyse stared past him, at the wall. She sat up without haste, pulled on her drawers and asked, 'What about the *Gazette*? I could go to the office with you. Someone with your fancy title could find me some work.'

Before he could prevent it, Albert's surprise escaped as a burst of laughter. He glanced up and saw the hatred in her face. It was now Marlyse's turn to give him her back. She walked away from him to the table, pulling what looked like a huge dishcloth over her head to hold her breasts in place. 'Perhaps there's something,' Albert mumbled, admiring the bounce of her hair on her shoulders. 'I could ask; it's just that I'm not sure what . . . They normally require certain qualifications—'

'Forget it,' she cut in. 'I'll get a shift at the factory.'

Drinking her coffee at the table, Marlyse cast her eye over a copy of yesterday's newspaper which was lying open there. One article caught her attention, and she read it through in silence before asking, 'Did you write this?' She put her finger on the title of the piece: '*Incident On New Hill Road Mars Visit By Fruit Tycoon*'.

Albert looked over her shoulder, and then lifted the newspaper to scan the article, which was not his work. He muttered aloud: '"... Prospective land purchase for the construction of a bottling plant and fruit canning factory in the Mittelbach area ..."' Glancing down the column, he picked out another morsel and savoured it on his lips. '"In the words of Mayor Becker, 'The branches of a modern Germany will grow fruitfully from its ancient roots ...'"' He grinned and went on, 'I'll bet he was pleased with that. Let's see ... "Herr Dammertz agreed that, 'There is a marriage to be made between efficient industrial practice and the hardworking ethics of the common smallholder; between preservation and revitalisation, nature and technology ...'"' Interrupting himself again, this time with a chuckle, he skipped down to a passage near the end, and read: '"Last week's mayoral tour was interrupted by an incident on a section of the new road, involving the fatal collapse of a labourer which has been attributed to the man's encounter the previous day with a prisoner then being transported from Hindelheim" blah blah ... "raising questions about the maintenance of public order in remote communities" blah blah blah. Brilliant.'

He turned to Marlyse. 'Matchless pomposity. No one but Werner Todt could read this, let alone write it. But if you want to see what a reporter of some talent can do, let me show you my—'

'The police came to see me about it,' Marlyse said, interrupting.

'The police came to see you,' Albert echoed, his face tight with disbelief, 'about this?' He flicked a finger at Werner's article. 'The challenges of rural regeneration?'

'The runaway. Elias Frankel. They think I'm hiding him.' She bent down for her shoes, and added, 'Perhaps I am.'

Albert took a moment to register this. He read the rest of the article in silence, his scepticism warming to mild interest at the account of the runaway's flight and the chief inspector's response. 'What's he running from?'

Marlyse shrugged. 'Wouldn't interest you.'

'Try me.'

He caught the gleam in her eye as she answered, 'He's a brute.'

'Ah.' Albert turned away, ready to dismiss it. 'You have them there too.'

Considering while she drank her coffee, Marlyse said, 'No. He's not a brute the way you mean. Not like normal men. Elias Frankel is worse. There's nothing normal about him. I told you, the police came to talk to me about him. They're looking everywhere for him.' She put the mug down, empty. 'That should tell you,' she concluded. 'He's a bad one.'

Albert stood at the mirror straightening his tie. In the glass, he watched Marlyse's expression. She seemed to have something to say, and so he might as well listen. Turning back to her, he said: 'Bad how?'

✢

He found Werner Todt at his desk on Monday morning, on the first floor of the narrow building on the Radhausplatz from which the *Gazette* issued.

The Chief Reporter for Civic Affairs sat opposite the editor's office, his balding head bent low by the burden of responsibility and worsening myopia. Tapping a pencil on the bar of Werner's typewriter, Albert managed to irritate him into looking up. 'What's on the tip of your quill this morning, my friend?' he asked. 'You seem a little pale, if you don't mind me saying so. Let me guess. You had a sleepless night, worrying over how to sing the praises of whichever grandee dropped dead last week. Or, worse, no one of significance died, thereby leaving an embarrassing absence of ink on today's Obituaries page. You know I'm here to help, don't you? Just say, "Albert, I'm floundering. My Muse is flown . . . "'

'This from a tittle-tattle merchant with no tittle-tattle to sell,' Werner replied, pushing a finger under his spectacles to wipe the sweat that habitually gathered there.

Albert shoved the pencil into Werner's inkwell, and picked up a paperweight, asking while he examined it, 'Did they find that runaway from wherever it was—?'

Werner looked up with a distracted, and then wary, expression. 'Why do you ask?'

'To prove a point,' Albert replied. 'Despite the malicious accusation recently levelled against me, I do in fact read every single one of your pieces – all the way to their edifying conclusions. And though it pains me to admit it, I thought that was a particularly good report. How to instil discipline in farming communities without losing their essential spirit and decency – you've put your nib on a lively issue there. It agitates a lot of people.'

'You think so?' Werner blinked, flattered in spite of himself.

'Hmm,' Albert replied. 'Anything else planned, relating to this rogue . . . Frankel, or whatever his name is?'

Werner sighed at the mountain of papers before him, and said, 'We've had some letters. There was a disturbance in the Marktplatz, which may or may not be related.' He sat back, continuing, 'But as you say, it's the surrounding issues—'

'Quite,' Albert agreed, interrupting. 'Is that a visitor for you?' he asked, glancing past him at the open doorway. While Werner turned to look, he swept a handful of papers off the desk and held them behind his back. 'Someone walked past,' he explained, turning away. 'I'll go and see who it was.'

A few minutes later, when Werner was reabsorbed in his

work, Albert Dinter crossed the room again, unnoticed, and knocked on the editor's door.

⊹

A new life came screaming into the Hildebrandt household at three in the morning. Francesca had experienced the warning just in time for Klaus to fetch the midwife, on whose arrival the larger of the two upstairs rooms filled with a variety of cries, commands and coaxing sounds. The young father ran up and down the narrow stairs with jugs of water and every cloth in the house that might serve as a towel.

Theodore Hildebrandt evacuated his room, seeking refuge first by the fireplace, which was noisy, being directly under the birthing room; and then at the kitchen stove, where a kettle he could not lift without difficulty shrieked into his ear; and finally in the cold station office. When Klaus came into the office at eight to open the public door, Theodore sent him back into the house.

Alone, the constable lifted the telephone and dialled the operator.

'Good morning, sir. What number?'

'A Doctor Koenig, in Hindelheim.'

'Thank you. Please wait.'

He waited. He had been waiting since the Koenigs' motor car stopped in Mittelbach, granting him another brief moment in Ute's company. Her letter was in his hand now, smudged and creased from many readings.

The doctor's voice broke in. 'Peter Koenig.'

'Constable Hildebrandt. I'd like to speak to your wife.'

A pause. 'And why's that?'

Theodore remembered the chief inspector's warning, and forced himself to answer with tact. 'I understand that Frau Koenig taught at the *Volksschule*, until her marriage to you. I wish to ask her about a former pupil.'

'Ute's not available, I'm afraid, but if you tell me the name I might be able to help. It's a small place. Whoever it is, I'm bound to know the family.'

'I believe you do,' Theodore agreed. 'Otto Frankel.'

There was a brief silence, in which he imagined Peter Koenig pulling at his moustache. 'Hmm,' came the reply. 'I think our little Otto went off to the big boys' college, in Angen.'

'*Our* little Otto?' Theodore prompted. 'Interesting way to put it.'

A clicking sound indicated Peter's impatience. 'It's an expression, Constable.'

*Don't say it*, Theodore warned himself. *Thank him and hang up.* He said, 'I suppose you feel a sense of kinship . . . or rather, competition . . . with the Frankel brothers, because of your father's special interest, would you call it, in Ida Frankel?'

The pause was longer this time, more dangerous. 'You have an unhealthy interest in my family, Constable Hildebrandt. Last time I commented on it, the chief inspector of police in Angenberg was kind enough to take remedial action. I wonder what he will say when I tell him that you persist in offending—'

'It's not about your bloody family any more,' Theodore snapped, interrupting. 'The search for Elias Frankel is a regional matter, and an urgent one – in the eyes of the mayor, at least. All lines of inquiry are to be investigated, and all responsible citizens are expected to cooperate. If you're hiding something that relates to this search, then even your friend the police chief might lose interest in who or what is currently offending the delicate sensibilities of the Koenigs of Hindelheim . . . Hello?'

Nothing. He was speaking into an indifferent silence, like a condemned man as the hood is pulled over his head. He lowered the mouthpiece and was about to put the earpiece down when he heard a faint, female echo.

'Hello? . . . Constable?'

He lurched forward. 'Ute?'

'You . . . wanted to ask something about Otto Frankel.'

'Yes! Yes . . .' What had he wanted to ask? He scrabbled around in his mind, but the lights were out. 'I . . . What is the age gap between them?' As if he cared.

'Between Otto and Elias? About nine years, I think.' She sounded puzzled, as well she might be. Theodore had no idea what he was trying to establish.

'How do they get on?' he asked.

She made a sound in her throat, a brief laugh. Theodore conjured an image of her, sitting at the doctor's desk – or standing by it – holding the telephone close to her cheek. Peter Koenig was no doubt close behind her. 'Like a cat and a dog most of the time,' she replied. 'Otto's afraid of . . . or at least, he looks up to his stepbrother with some timidity. It's natural.'

She left a pause so that he could agree. He said, 'Tell me more.'

He thought he could hear her breath on the line, but it could be something else, such as her hand brushing over the mouthpiece. 'I don't know what to tell you, Constable. Otto Frankel is an ordinary boy. He would like Elias to notice him and play with him, and on the rare occasions when that happens, he's over the moon. When Elias taught him to box, for instance.'

'To box?'

'I think that's what it was. They used a grain sack, at the back of the store. Otto came into the schoolhouse one day with a glove that Elias bought for him. Is this . . . what you want to know?'

The constable considered, aware that Peter Koenig was probably standing at Ute's elbow. 'Thank you, Frau Koenig. Just one last question. Based on your observations of them, do you think that Elias Frankel, in his current . . . situation, will try to make contact with his stepbrother?'

'Yes,' she replied, without hesitation.

✠

Eckhardt Gröhlick was sitting in his now-habitual position on a stool behind the counter of the Frankel store, doing nothing much, when a young stranger came in.

The stranger was perhaps a decade younger than Eckhardt, and smaller in every respect apart from his eyes, which seemed to fill his whole face. Pale and wet and perpetually moving, the man's eyes seemed to pulse with curiosity, searching into the corners of the room as he entered it. His head, turning this way and that, was capped with hair so blond that it was almost white.

'You're Corporal Gröhlick, aren't you?' the young man said. 'You were with my brother. He told me about you, when he came home on leave.'

Eckhardt looked at him across the counter. 'Who are you?'

'Ulrich Reinisch.'

After thinking about it for a moment, Eckhardt remembered another man by the name of Reinisch, and recalled that the other one also had eyes that shone and quivered like these, and hair like down which earned him the nickname 'Gosling'. They had stood together on the railway platform one hot August day, along with seven others from the area, waiting for a train to take them to the war.

'What do you want?'

Ulrich Reinisch did not answer immediately. He looked up at the crowded shelves, where Eckhardt had inventoried and replaced each item, and past the counter into the Frankels' kitchen behind, where Eckhardt had been bolder, clearing the table and washing the pots. 'So this is where the Jewish boy lives,' Ulrich said. 'Must make you shiver, I'll bet, being in here?'

'I don't mind.'

'No? That's the soldier in you then. I suppose nothing makes you afraid.' He stepped closer to the shelf, and reached up towards a jar of liquorice sticks.

'You going to pay for those?' Eckhardt demanded. He pushed

himself off the stool, landing with a thump that made the stranger stop and turn.

Impressed by the bulk of Eckhardt's figure, and the sight of rattling keys chained to his suit, Ulrich swiftly drew back his hand. 'No thank you, sir. You won't catch me eating . . .' He nodded with bulging eyes towards the shelf, and then said, 'People do though, don't they? Folk in Hindelheim, they've been coming here for years. Buying their food from Jews.' After a brief pause, he rattled on. 'We heard about it, oh a while ago, about the foreigners settling here. Our farm's not so far away, but you probably know that. My brother probably told you where we lived, him and me?'

Eckhardt watched him with a concentrated frown, but said nothing. He had to keep his eyes on Ulrich's face in order to hear him, and to prevent any unexpected moves. If he were to relax his guard, Eckhardt had the impression that the young stranger might vault over the counter or pull down the shelves. So he shuffled in parallel with him, three steps this way, three steps that way, mirroring the other man like a courting swan.

'You're in the League, aren't you, Corporal?' Ulrich asked with a sudden, earnest frown. 'The German People's League?'

When Eckhardt said no, he looked disappointed. 'You don't go to the meetings? Or take the newsletter?'

Again Eckhardt shook his head, and Ulrich made a clicking sound with his tongue. 'That's a shame,' he said. 'My brother would be a captain in the League by now, or maybe even head of the Angen chapter, if he was still alive.'

He fell silent for a moment, and picked at the counter between them. For something to do, Eckhardt lifted a cloth and folded it, although it had not been used since the last time he folded it. Eventually he said, again, 'What do you want?'

This time Ulrich answered. 'They're looking for a new worker to dig the road down there, near Mittelbach, after they lost a man on the crew last week. You heard about that, did you?'

Two or three times a day, whenever a passing neighbour looked into the store to see what there was to see, Eckhardt heard about it, but he did not say so.

'Struck in the belly by the runaway,' Ulrich continued, not put out by the older man's silence. 'You know about that, I guess. After Elias Frankel hit him, he turned green in the face, the man did. Started burbling like one of God's accursed. Did you know he fell down exactly one day to the minute after he was struck? To the minute,' he repeated, delivering the revelation with a grin. 'What do you think about that?'

Eckhardt, breathing hard, did not reply. Every time someone questioned him about Elias Frankel, his confusion deepened. Had Elias done these things? Several people said so, and there were policemen, men in uniform, looking for him . . .

Ulrich kept talking, running his hand along the counter as he spoke. 'Not often you hear about a man getting put under a spell, in this day and age. If that's what it is. I'm not saying it is, but Franz thinks it's worth looking into. He says there must be something here to explain it. That's Franz Schmidt, I mean, at the League – he's our leader now.' He looked up, as if expecting Eckhardt to take an interest. 'He thought it would be a good idea to find out more about this Elias Frankel, and I was happy to volunteer, seeing as I'm from the area, as you know. No harm in being vigilant, Franz says. Because everyone assumes that Jews are city people, don't they, but every year there are more of them spreading into places like this, and no one's keeping count. So that's why I'm here, Corporal.' He thumped the table, and drew himself up with another grin. 'To investigate.'

Eckhardt frowned. 'How do you mean, investigate?'

'That's what we do at the League. We investigate things.'

'What things?'

'Things that everyone else ignores,' Ulrich said, with a shrug. 'Those things.'

They continued their mirror-dance on either side of the

counter. The visitor touched and peered at every object, while Eckhardt watched in growing agitation. At the end of the counter, Ulrich looked through the opening to the kitchen, but Eckhardt blocked his way. 'You can't go in there.' The other man's restless eyes moved over him, questioning. 'I'm looking after the place,' Eckhardt explained. 'Elias Frankel asked me.'

Ulrich took this in. 'That's all right,' he murmured.

'What?'

After a moment's consideration, Ulrich raised his voice and repeated, 'I said that's a good thing to do, Corporal. Keep an eye on the place – that's not a bad idea, as long as you're careful. Keep your wits about you. You know it was their fault, don't you, how the war ended?'

Struggling to follow, Eckhardt frowned. 'Who?'

'Exactly.' Ulrich nodded. 'Who's the real enemy? Who's behind the mask? You can never be sure. They've got people everywhere, haven't they? Not just in Germany. America too. Every bank in the world. If it's better for them to have our people defeated, then that's what happens. You should hear Franz talk about it. He explains it better than I can. And I know he'd like to meet you,' he added. 'Yes sir, Corporal Gröhlick.' Pausing momentarily, he continued, wide-eyed, 'I tell you, Corporal, I was pleased to see your name on the door here this morning. Pleased isn't the word for it. It was, boy that was something. Corporal Eckhardt Gröhlick! *Hello*, I thought. *I know that name.*' He pointed at his head, pantomiming the moment of recognition. 'It's like – like Fate sent me here to help you, Corporal!'

Eckhardt's head was pulsing with the first signs of a headache. He put a hand to the back of it and rubbed. 'I don't need help,' he said.

'Oh I know!' Ulrich's eyes trembled with intensity. 'I know that. I know. I don't mean help, as in . . . You know my brother loved you, Corporal Gröhlick?' He interrupted himself, unable to contain this new thought. 'Yes, sir. My brother thought the world of you. On his last trip home, he said, "If anything happens to me, then you go to my friend Eckhardt Gröhlick in Hindelheim, and he'll be a friend to you." So you see I'm on your side, Corporal. You don't need to worry about me. I'm Gosling's brother. That means we're practically friends already, aren't we? That would have been me in the unit with you, fighting with you, if I'd been old enough. It's only because I was younger than him, that's the only reason I'm here now, not him. See?'

There was a canvas bag slung over Ulrich's shoulder, which he now put down on the floor. Eckhardt wondered what that meant. 'It's a noble act, what you're doing,' the newcomer continued. 'Standing guard for someone who's been menacing his neighbours – not that we know how, exactly. Not yet. That's what we'll be investigating. But if you're going to defend Elias Frankel now, you need to be sure that he hasn't got some other plan for you. That's all I'm saying, Corporal. You need to be careful.' He nodded over Eckhardt's shoulder, and went on, 'You've checked everything, I suppose. What's back there? What have you found?'

'Nothing,' Eckhardt replied. He waited for Ulrich to start talking again, and was disconcerted when the other man fell silent for the first time since arriving. Ulrich's bright, busy eyes were all over him, sweeping his face from side to side, searching. To escape the scrutiny, Eckhardt turned to look into the kitchen. The fly curtain was blowing at the back door. 'The steps were broken,' he said, 'but I mended them.'

Ulrich's gaze flickered past him, and then back. 'What happened?'

Eckhardt's head throbbed. He cupped a hand over his left ear, the one that gave him most trouble. Frau Gröhlick said it was because the devil sat there, on Eckhardt's left shoulder, throwing sand into his ear to confuse him. She said it was

173

working, all right, because he was a muddle-headed fool. After a moment, he replied, 'It's where the Monsieur fell. But I fixed it. It's not broken any more.'

'He fell down the steps,' Ulrich repeated, alert to every new piece of information. 'Did he die?'

Eckhardt nodded, causing the younger man to let out a long whistle. With another glance towards the back door, Ulrich crossed himself. For a moment he was quiet, considering. Then he looked up into Eckhardt's face to ask, 'Reckon this Frankel person is a devil, do you?'

Not wanting to answer, Eckhardt returned to his position behind the counter.

This time, Ulrich followed him, moving in parallel on the other side of the counter and then stopping to lean across it, on his elbows. 'Confusing business,' he said. 'I don't know what to make of it myself. Tell you what, though.' His eyes locked onto Eckhardt's. 'If I get any information from the road crew, about what happened down there, why don't I come back and tell you?' Without waiting for an answer, he went on, 'Because it seems to me, you're not being told everything, Corporal.' He tapped a finger on the counter. 'First of all, Elias Frankel hasn't told you his plan. What's he doing, this Jew friend of yours? Hey? What's he got up his sleeve? Plus.' A second finger slapped onto the counter. 'Even your neighbours are keeping you in the dark. Am I right? I'm right, aren't I? No one's telling you the truth and what's what. So I'll be your lookout, while you command things here. How about that? It won't be any trouble. In any case, I'm glad to do it – with you being my brother's best friend.'

Eckhardt's reply was an uncertain frown, which Ulrich seemed to take as a certain answer. 'Right then,' the younger man said. 'That's what we'll do.'

# 18.

The telephone conversation with Ute Koenig replayed in a corner of Theodore's mind as he moved through the morning's duties. *I don't know what to tell you, Constable . . . Will Elias try to make contact with his stepbrother? Yes.*

Without Klaus to help him, the constable found himself talking until his throat was dry and writing until his good hand stiffened with cramp. In addition to advising and reporting efforts made by the mounted police to find the runaway, he had all the usual duties to attend to: filling forms, sorting mail, and listening to the complaints of his neighbours – this had been stolen, that person was suspected, and so on.

Local visitors to the station had been outnumbered in recent days by representatives or hirelings of Herr Dammertz, the manufacturer. These men, who were used to working at a city pace, expected Constable Hildebrandt to take care of every new bureaucratic obstacle in their path to wealth, and to do so now. How long would it take to get planning consent for the proposed fruit-bottling plant? Could the surveyors and engineers prepare the site? Would the constable help to settle a dispute with a farmer who refused to sell the new landowner a certain patch of woodland?

From time to time, as he shuffled papers on his desk,

Theodore would catch sight of last Friday's copy of the *Angenberg Gazette* which lay buried under everything else. He had still not been able to read to the end of the page which described how the Dammertz family's tour had been disturbed by the collapse of a road worker in suspicious circumstances. As his eyes swept over the article, they always seemed to land on the same words. *Renegade. Elias Frankel.* In his weary, fuddled brain, the words seemed to strike a rhythm, like the tolling of a bell.

He felt summoned to act, and resented the feeling. What else could he do, trapped in this office, at this desk? Supposing someone came in with real information instead of rumour, and supposing Theodore could find a way to act on it – to visit Otto Frankel, for instance, at the college in Angenberg – then what?

At two o'clock, having eaten nothing since six, the constable turned into the house to find Francesca in the kitchen, feeding the baby. She was smiling for once, a house-robed priestess drunk with satisfaction at her dribbling divinity, while Klaus and the midwife fussed around her. Theodore mumbled what he hoped were suitable comments, and left. Pursued by the howls of the infant usurper, he turned into the washroom, which in a matter of hours had become a shrine to the newborn.

Linen cloths dried on lines of string, dripping soapy residue into the basin and bathtub. Jars of ointment crowded the shelf, obscuring Theodore's shaving brush. And the tub was brimful of a murky, foul-smelling concoction in which yet more cloths were soaking. He wondered when, if ever, he would be helped into the bath again.

Relinquishing all hopes of a meal, he found a boy playing in the yard – apparently one of the midwife's own brood – and sent him off with a message for a certain woman in the village. If she was not at home, the boy was to take the same message to a second woman. Theodore returned to the office, hurried through the rest of his chores, and closed the public door behind him sharply at half past four.

Taking a walking stick to increase his speed, he crossed the yard and turned down the slope towards the valley junction.

As he walked, his eyes searched for hiding spots on the edge of the village, among trees that lined the riverbank. Upstream was Hindelheim; downstream, Angenberg. Between the two, Elias Frankel had slipped away from the angler's line, thereby making himself a just-missed opportunity; a prize as yet to be caught, whose dimensions expanded with every iteration of the story. *He was this big; no, bigger.*

✠

The largest of the Valley Inn's bedrooms was described on the tariff card as a 'suite', because it had its own bathroom and an alcove big enough to accommodate a small table. Dropping her coat over the chair, Theodore's companion, who was not Sabina, wanted to know why they were in here today, instead of the cheap room by the stairs. And why the big hurry? She sat down, and the flesh of her thighs flattened and extended into the corners of the chair. In some places, the floral print of her dress was stretched so tight that the roses distorted, becoming translucent.

Theodore told her that this would be the last time. He had not planned to say it, and indeed the decision came as news to him. Noticing the woman's silence, he added, 'Not just you, I mean . . . our friend too. I won't be coming here again.'

'Well, well,' she replied, undoing her buttons, neck to breast. 'So our comrade is deserting the cause. Which part does he want to say goodbye to first?'

The sight of her flesh, bared and boastful, dismayed Theodore. 'I want you to give me a bath,' he said, and turned to remove his own clothes.

After a moment, the woman fastened her buttons, accepting this change of plan. While the water fell, clunking and hissing from a green-rimmed mouth, she talked about her children, her problems at home and work, her sore feet.

Theodore held her arm and climbed into the tub, savouring the heat of the yellowed, gritty water. With a brush he scraped and flayed his grateful skin while the woman waited for direction. How should she help?

'Where would you go,' he said, 'if you were in trouble?'

She looked at him in mild surprise. 'To family.'

'But if you were being watched . . . If you wanted to disappear?'

'Then I'd find somewhere busy and stay in the crowd,' she replied. 'I'll be in the room. Call me when you want to get out.'

Theodore leaned back to shut his eyes. He could hear her in the bedroom, singing as she waited. He let his thoughts drift to where they always drifted when left to their own devices, these days. Ute Koenig had written him a letter which he had not yet acknowledged. How could he reply in a way that was true, and at the same time not absurd or presumptuous or humiliating? Theodore had never possessed the smooth man's gift for words, even when he was fit and free. Collecting his first girlfriend for the fair, where later that day they would conceive Klaus, the then-young Theo Hildebrandt had stood on her doorstep and said, 'Are you coming then?' 'Yes,' she replied. That was as far as his wooing went. The recollection brought a chuckle, and then a sudden, infuriating pooling of water in the corners of his eyes. *Damn you, Theo, you sentimental old clown.*

He wiped his eyes, and became aware of a definite silence in the other room. Holding himself still, he called twice.

When it was clear that the woman would not come to his aid, he put his weight on the good arm, rocked sideways, fell back with a splash and tried again. With a struggle, he was out. The pool of spilt water on the bathroom floor almost seized him again, but he reached the door and held fast. From here he could see his clothes on the bed, their pockets turned inside out after a thorough search. She had left him a crumpled handkerchief, and nothing else.

✛

Downstairs in the salon, the innkeeper's veined eyes studied him across the bar, assessing the evidence: clinging shirt with an open buttonhole, steam-red face and damp hair. 'You didn't say you wanted hot water,' he concluded. 'Hot's extra.'

As he negotiated with the innkeeper, who seemed unsurprised to learn that the woman had robbed him, Theodore became aware that the conversation at one of the tables was particularly animated. Half a dozen road workers sat there in a huddle. They were talking not in the way men usually do at the end of a day's hard labour, but with effort and excitement, straining to cap one another's stories.

The man they were seeking to impress sat at one end of the table, in a city suit, with a notebook balanced on his crossed knees. Beside him, staring through slow, owl eyes from a forest of copper-dark hair, was the only silent member of the group. Theodore recognised her as Ute's friend, Marlyse Pohlmann.

He waited, watching from a distance while he worked out in his mind what Marlyse was doing here, now, with this visitor from the city, in the company of the road crew. He listened as the men claimed that they had tried to stop Elias Frankel and but were overpowered by his unnatural strength. He watched the visitor write it all down with practised speed.

Catching Marlyse Pohlmann's eye, the constable stepped forward. 'You must be from the *Gazette*,' he said, stopping at the reporter's side.

The man taking notes looked up at Theodore's dishevelled figure. 'Albert Dinter,' he said. 'And you?'

'Constable Hildebrandt.'

'Ah,' Albert said. 'Then we are fellows-at-arms, are we not, Constable? Both searching for the elusive Elias Frankel – unless you've found him yet? Any chance of giving me a clue?' When Theodore did not answer, he went on. 'Never mind. I'm lucky to have these gentlemen providing me with information.'

'Information,' Theodore echoed. 'Is that what you call it?'

'Hey,' the crew boss with the purple nose protested. 'We put ourselves in danger up there. That Frankel boy was looking for a fight. And where were you, Constable? When Gustav Spiller took his deadly blow, God bless him, where was our local officer of the law? Upstairs, were you?' He raised his voice, enjoying himself. 'Mind if I tell this gentleman reporter your whore's name?'

Theodore felt the mood of the group harden against him. He looked again at Marlyse Pohlmann, who made an effort to return his gaze with a defiance that betrayed her apprehension. 'Fraulein,' he said. 'A word with you?'

Marlyse started to get up, but the reporter's hand landed on her knee. Stopping her with a look, Albert turned back to the constable. 'He's been seen in Angen, did you know? Harassing citizens. My readers. What do you say to that?'

Keeping his eyes on Marlyse, Theodore urged, 'Come to the station, and give your report there. Whatever you know—'

'Whatever she knows, Constable,' the reporter cut in, 'will be safe in my hands. I'm a newspaper man. My duty is to supply information that will protect, illuminate and improve the lives of the *Gazette's* readers. What's yours, sir? When you're not otherwise occupied, that is, with the ladies of the night.'

Theodore looked at him, feeling a bead of water running from his steam-dampened hair down his cheek and into the groove of his scar. As he brushed it away, Albert's eyes followed. 'The chief inspector of police reminded me two days ago,' he replied, 'to withhold judgement until the case against Elias Frankel has been proved one way or the other. I was in danger of drawing my own conclusions prematurely. That must be a risk in your profession too?'

Albert Dinter met his gaze and seemed to consider this. Then he dug in a pocket and held up a handkerchief. 'Allow me to lend you this, Constable. I fear the sweat of your recent labour is still upon your brow.'

Theodore ignored him, but saw that he would not win the battle for Marlyse Pohlmann's cooperation – at least not here, where the performer had already wooed his audience. With a departing look at Marlyse, the constable turned away, and heard the murmur of conversation start up again behind his back.

Outside the inn he stood alone for a while, shivering in the last of the afternoon's sunlight, looking out towards the hills. He made a tally of omens in his mind, stringing them together in a kind of silent incantation. *A wolf. A dead baby. A motorcycle fall. A dead road worker. A newsman heading up-country.* There was no inherent menace in any of these things. They were disparate and mundane. And having scorned the false reasoning of his neighbours, Theodore saw the hypocrisy of what he was doing, which was almost the same. He was seeking significance and connections where there were none.

But there it was. A chain of events, or warnings, was forming in his mind, if nowhere else. Although he did not know where the ill luck would fall next, or who might be hurt by it, the constable felt sure that there was worse to come.

✢

Shortly after the constable had left the inn, the reporter's hired car passed him. Albert Dinter waved, while Marlyse Pohlmann drove.

At the fork in the road they turned towards the hills, over the new paved surface and onwards on the rough, old track, where a series of ruts threw Albert time and again against the passenger door. 'Sweet Jesus,' he exclaimed. 'Will you listen to me? Slow. Down!'

'I thought you'd want to be there before dark,' Marlyse replied, clamping her hands to the steering wheel and her foot to the accelerator pedal. Until this morning, she had not driven a motor car, and being ignorant of its potential for harm, she had no fear of it.

Albert frowned at the path ahead; a long, curving incline that cut through fields and trees, with no human habitation in sight. It seemed to go on forever. 'Before dark?' he repeated. 'How far is this place?'

They shot forward, then rocked through a ditch, then shot forward again. After half an hour of this, Albert raised his hands in surrender. 'Stop. Just stop.'

He exhaled as they jerked to a halt. From the trees around them came a chatter of bird-call. It was almost six by Albert's watch, and the colour was draining from the sky. Ahead stretched the track: more stones, more mud. 'This is a waste of time,' he said. 'I can write up what I've got without getting my kidneys shaken out of me.'

'Coward,' Marlyse said. Then: 'Look!' She pointed, as an owl flew past them and dropped, in silence, into the trees.

Albert watched, impressed. He looked ahead, took a deep breath, and decided. 'All right, let's go. Kidneys be buggered. Take me into the lair of the beast.'

✠

Frau Koenig Senior preferred to eat with Helga in the kitchen, so the meal began with five people at the dining table. It should have been six, but Heinrich was late for supper, so his chair stood empty, with a knife and fork laid before it, unused. Glancing at the empty plate, Ute wished she had the nerve to lean over and place a lighted candle on it, using one of her aunt's incantations to dispel the bad luck.

The visitor, Albert Dinter, drank everything that was offered to him, brushing aside Peter's warning about the strength of the home-brewed potato wine. 'This could catch on,' he mused, peering into the murky liquid. 'Bacchus, beware. The grape has a rival.' Whenever the conversation stopped, he began to fidget, and in one such momentary silence, he asked, 'So what happens here? What do you people *do*?'

Peter answered in a tone of polite mockery that 'Even here,

Herr Dinter, life happens. You urbanites always think that the town or city is at the vanguard of modernity. But the inventors of any society are country people, creating lives in the wilderness. We're the moderns.' With a glance at Johanna, he launched into an account of their father's pioneering work in Hindelheim, explaining how the former Doctor Koenig had shocked colleagues by turning down a regular physician's wage to settle out here. 'Public health policies always favour the cities, you see. Migrants and slum-dwellers are pampered by civic officials until they can do nothing for themselves but breed and spread their diseases, while German families hard at work on the land . . .'

The newsman looked as if he had indigestion. Staring at Ute through bloodshot eyes, he asked, 'And you, Frau Koenig? Don't you find it quiet here?'

'Quieter now that Marlyse has gone,' she agreed, looking across the table at her friend. Marlyse caught her eye but did not hold the gaze, and Ute felt another pang of regret that their friendship had begun to cool. Living in the cottage, they used to be so easy with one another. Here under the Koenigs' roof, as in the shared apartment in town, they seemed unsure of each other, as if waiting to learn the new rules. Perhaps she could find a way to ask Marlyse, in private, what had prompted this visit. Ute had an uneasy suspicion that it had something to do with Marlyse's changed view of Elias Frankel.

'Why don't the two of you stay in Aunt's cottage tonight,' she said, 'if you'd like to? I went down there today, and aired it.'

Marlyse liked the idea, and even smiled. 'All right,' she agreed. In answer to Albert's questioning glance, she explained, 'Where I lived before. With Ute.'

'Excellent,' Albert said forcefully. 'Will Auntie mind?'

Ute exchanged a look of amusement with Marlyse. 'She might grumble at first,' she replied, 'but there are ways to pacify her. Marlyse will tell you.'

'They're teasing you, Herr Dinter,' Peter warned. 'The aunt's dead, and there's no need for you to sleep in her bed. We have a room here.'

Albert emptied yet another glass of potato wine. 'No, no, no,' he intoned. 'I'll take the haunted cottage, thank you. Fact, I'd be damned disappointed not to find something ghoulish here, after that s-spooky drive and Marlyse's . . . description of the place. I'm especially interested, as you might imagine, in the . . . in the mysterious Elias Frankel.'

At this a silence fell, and Johanna Koenig lifted her gaze from the table, for the first time that evening. She exchanged a look with Peter, who sat opposite her, as always, at the other end of the table. Taking a silent cue from his sister, Peter asked, 'What's the nature of your interest in him?'

Albert gave this a solemn frown. Finding his glass empty again, he reached for the carafe. Ute suspected that he was too drunk to notice the effect of the Frankel name on those around the table. 'Pro-professionally speaking,' he replied, 'I would like to eshtablish the source of this claim about a . . . Don't believe it was a wolf, you see. Checked.' He waved a hand in the air, for no apparent reason. 'Last of the wild wolves seen in eighteen ninety . . . No, in nineteen oh – oh, who the devil cares when. Long bloody time ago.'

'Perhaps it was a wild dog,' Peter suggested. 'Seen in a poor light, they can appear quite ferocious.'

Ute looked again at Marlyse, who was winding a strand of hair around her finger.

'Personally speaking,' Albert went on, deaf to all voices except his own, 'I would like to – I'd like to meet him. Yes I would. My Girl's Last Lover. My rival for this little bunny . . .' He squeezed Marlyse's thigh under the table, and was swatted away. 'Elias Frankel,' he continued, oblivious. 'The Wolf Man. Grrr. Very bloody frightening I must say. Show us your teeth, Mister Wolf. Ha ha ha.'

'His mother was a witch,' Johanna said. Sitting straight-backed in her chair, she directed her comment across the table, at no one in particular.

'Hmm?' Albert frowned, vaguely aware of a noise coming from somewhere else on the table.

'Ida Frankel bewitched our father,' Johanna continued.

'Johanna,' Peter warned.

'And within a year my son was born,' she went on. 'Mute. Full of noise and terror but hasn't spoken a word in his life. Would you call that a coincidence?'

No one answered, and for a moment no one ate. Finding an excuse to cross the room, Peter laid a hand on Johanna's shoulder and whispered something to her. She laid her hand on his, and gave it a squeeze before brushing him away. 'Let's all drink to witches,' she said then. 'To witches, and to the Frankels! I mean it, Peter. Why not? It's a sport. She won a round, that's all. Ida Frankel stole our papa. But we don't have to be defeated.'

Ute watched the changing emotions flit across Johanna's face, and saw how Peter's expression changed in tandem. He was the only person, Ute guessed, who understood what connected his sister's fluctuating moods.

After a moment, Johanna spoke again. 'Where is he now, does anyone know?' She looked around the table. 'Marlyse? Ute? Who is Elias Frankel charming these days?'

Heinrich arrived, creating a new distraction, which released Marlyse and Ute from the obligation of responding. To excuse his lateness, he muttered something about his dogs, and reached for the carving knife. With the noise of clashing cutlery and the activity of passing dishes down to the newcomer, an air of normality returned to the table. Peter changed the subject by asking Heinrich about domestic and wild dogs, and the difference between them.

'A witch!' Albert burst out, having just got what he assumed to be a joke, made several minutes earlier. He grinned blindly. 'Ha ha ha! Yes, I expect she is.'

# 19.

After dinner, in their bedroom, Peter was restless and irritable, seething at the newsman's patronising assumptions and upset by Johanna's lack of discretion. Ute tried to soothe him, but he twisted away from her touch, saying, 'I don't know why you had to send them down to your aunt's place. How is that going to help anything?'

A mournful cry woke them in the middle of the night.

'Friedrich! Where are you? Friedrich?'

'Christ,' Peter groaned. Heaving himself upright, he reached for his dressing gown. 'Mother's wandering again,' he said, pushing his feet into slippers. As he shuffled out of the room, the Kaiser rose from his basket to follow.

'Stay,' Ute told the dog, but he remained at the door, ears busy. From downstairs, Frau Koenig's voice rose above Peter's and Helga's attempts to quieten her. 'Help me find your father's . . . Not a *book* . . .'

Ute, listening, thought: *this is what witchcraft is – not stirring frogs in a cauldron, but doing things that cannot be forgotten, and remembering what cannot be forgotten, and so keeping the old resentments and fears and desires bubbling forever.* She had seen Johanna's fingers interlinked with Peter's for a moment, at the dinner table, and wondered now why it had not disturbed her.

Because it was no surprise, she decided. The siblings' alliance, fuelled by envy of the Frankels, would never be affected by their ties to other people. Ute was Peter's distraction, and he desired her, sometimes fiercely, for his own reasons; but she would never alter the course of his primary passions. It was a dizzying, and somehow liberating, realisation.

The dog circled excitedly as Ute swung out of bed, and then ran ahead of her down the stairs. In the kitchen, she heated milk on the stove. The air was cold, the floor colder. Perhaps it would snow soon. Clutching the mug with both hands, Ute turned into the sitting room in search of heat. The remains of the evening's fire burned low in the grate, its cedar-sap smell so sweet that it was almost cloying.

Moving to the fireplace, she did not at first notice the two shadows on the sofa. A sucking sound startled her, and she looked around to discover that she was not alone. Heinrich sat in his vest and leggings, in the near-darkness, eating something from a knife. Competing for space with the dish of food on his lap was Dirk, who lay across his father's knees, staring sleepily into the room. Ute saw what looked like a piece of bread in the boy's fingers. He was shredding it, and burying the crumbs deep in the sofa. They looked settled, as if they had been here for some while and were at peace with each other and with the midnight gloom.

'This is exciting,' Heinrich said, in a voice that sounded far from excited. 'Everyone awake at the same time, raving or supping on filthy, steaming brews. In another age, we'd be in the centre of an orgy. Or in an opera, full of female tragedy.'

'I hope I didn't disturb you,' Ute replied.

Heinrich let out a laugh, in several loud bursts. Then he fell quiet. 'What disturbs me,' he said after a pause, 'is to be living in a madhouse. What disturbs me is to be woken up by my son's hand, slapping against my arm for reasons he cannot or will not tell me, and then to find – oh, marvellous.' He broke off to listen to a new sound, this one from outside.

The dogs were barking: first one, then two, then all in the enclosure, their gruff notes joined by higher and weaker yelps from further off. Trotting to the window, the Kaiser tilted his head to add a fulsome, ascending whine to the chorus.

'It must be a cat, or a fox,' Ute said. At the window she knelt beside the dog and raked her fingertips through its coat, head to tail, until it began to quieten.

Or a wolf, she thought, but did not say. Or Elias Frankel, lurking in the darkness on his way home, or on his way somewhere.

'This is how the ancient plagues began,' Heinrich was saying, on the sofa behind her. 'Dogs howling, babies wailing, mothers babbling. Madness perpetuates, don't they say? It's a contagion, carried in the air, and in the blood, one generation to the next.'

After a while, Peter came in and turned on a lamp. He noted the presence of Heinrich, Dirk and Ute with some surprise, and then went to fetch his mother. 'Come and sit with us,' he urged, leading her into the room. 'You could play the piano.'

Frau Koenig entered, stately in a black housecoat with her white hair piled above it. Her smile, vague at first, snatching at its target, soon found a focus on the piano, where Peter cleared the stool for her and lifted the lid. 'I'm not sure,' she said.

'Go on,' he urged. 'Just like the old days. It'll do you good.'

As Wilhemina Koenig played, on keys that had not been tuned for a decade, Helga stood at the doorway, arms crossed over an old brown dressing gown. After some minutes, the sound of fluid but discordant music drew Johanna into the room. She shuffled in past Helga, tousled and heavy-lidded, just as Heinrich leaned over the sofa to lift Dirk. The boy was almost asleep, and made no protest. Johanna's surprise mellowed to something else as she watched. She caught her husband's eye and held onto it, extending the moment.

Frau Koenig's hands, moving easily over the piano keys, slowed before coming to a rest. She stared at the keyboard, bereft of the memory that had allowed her to play only seconds earlier. 'Very good,' Peter said, kissing her head.

✠

Guided back to the room she shared with Helga, Frau Koenig got into bed. Her fingers found, by habit, an old notebook kept under her pillow. Pulling it out, she turned to a page that had been consulted so often, it almost came away from the binding in her hand. For the umpteenth time, her finger ran over the worn handwriting. A hastily inked paragraph was punctuated by several question marks towards the end. Here her finger stopped.

'What does it say here?' she asked, not for the first time. 'I can't make out Friedrich's writing. Can you?'

Helga settled herself beside her companion, and took the book to read the last, scrawled line of the doctor's notes. 'Something cough,' she offered. 'Consistent influenza. TB question. In brackets, rabies question, question.' Glancing at the patient's name at the top of the page, she closed the notebook and said, 'Ida Frankel's been gone a long time, Wilhemina.'

Frau Koenig nodded agreement. 'He couldn't let it rest,' she said. 'I daresay she had the same as all the rest, but that wasn't good enough for him. It had to be something special. A special condition for his special woman.' Falling silent for a moment, while Helga turned out the light, she added, 'When is Johanna having her baby? It must be any day soon.'

'That one's come and gone,' Helga said into the dark. Turning her head towards Wilhemina, she added, 'but they were looking at each other kindly while you played the piano just now, so perhaps there'll be another soon. Sleep now, dear.'

✠

They settled the boy into his bed, Heinrich carrying, Johanna folding the sheet under his chin, and returned to their room. There, while Heinrich splashed water on his head and neck from a china bowl, Johanna hunted in a box until she found a perfume bottle that was not quite empty. The lid was stiff from lack of use, but she prised it off and shook a few drops of liquid onto her fingertips, and then onto her wrist. With a glance at Heinrich, she lifted her hair with one hand while applying perfume to the exposed skin.

'How do you like it?' she asked, as Heinrich climbed into bed beside her.

He turned his head to smell the proffered wrist. 'Not bad,' he said.

Johanna put her hand on his chest and waited, like a new bride, comparing the thud of his heart with her own. As Heinrich continued to watch the ceiling, not moving, she let her hand slide off him onto the sheet between them. Not yet, then.

'I think he's improving,' she said. 'Don't you? He hasn't had a fit for days.' Following this optimistic thought with another, she said, 'Tomorrow I'm going to burn the baby's clothes, and get Dirk to help me in the kitchen. It's time to stop moping about. I've been making myself miserable to everyone.'

Heinrich turned his head to look at her, not unkindly. 'Bit of a waste to burn them, don't you think? Plenty of local girls expecting. You could give the clothes to one of them.' After a pause, he added, 'Gretchen Pohlmann's large now.'

'Gretchen Pohlmann,' Johanna repeated, surprised not so much by the name as by the fact that Heinrich, usually so indifferent to his neighbours, had taken notice of an individual among them. A young farm girl. 'I didn't know that you . . . knew her,' she said, and watched.

Heinrich held her gaze, letting the realisation sink in.

After a time, Johanna said, 'Oh.'

The relief of shedding his secret brought a tear to Heinrich's sunken eyes. His grey-flecked folds of skin puckered into an approximation of a smile as he said, 'You thought I was all dried up, didn't you? All these years. Pitying yourself, and letting your

190

brother console you for the impotent, fat slug that was your husband.' Johanna was unable to reply, but he went on, 'You convinced me too, I'll admit it. Who could imagine that the Koenig line might be anything less than abundantly fertile? Impossible!' He laughed, desperate, as the tears spilled. 'And then I poked that girl a few times – against a tree, in a cowshed. That was it: she swelled up like a ripe peach. That was all it took. Easiest thing I've ever done.'

When he had said what he wanted to say, Heinrich rolled away to wipe his cheek on the pillow, leaving Johanna to stare at his back, while the world slid away from her.

✠

Dawn saw Constable Theodore Hildebrandt at his desk, reading the newspaper. It was the same newspaper that had been buried there for almost a week, and he had now read the whole of it, every column, twice. What had started, late last night, as an attempt to get himself to sleep had become, some hours later, a vague but absorbing exercise.

He was trying to move closer to Elias Frankel by looking through this window onto the mundane and exceptional affairs of the region's population, and imagining how the runaway might respond to them. Did he know any of the people mentioned in this particular edition of the newspaper? How many of the places mentioned here had Elias Frankel visited? Was he in one of those places now? Had he read this report by Werner Todt, about Herr Dammertz's visit to Mittelbach, in which he himself was mentioned? Could he read? Did someone read it to him? Where? Did he buy the paper, or find it? What had he eaten since he ran away? Who were his friends?

He stared at a piece about the renovation of public monuments, but no thoughts came. Turning back a page, to something that had delayed his eye there, he read, under the general title of 'Sport Meetings & Fixtures', an announcement headed: '*Boxing Club Prepares to Welcome Max Schmeling in Much-Awaited Contest with Local Hero*'.

He had taught Otto to box, Ute had said. Something about a boxing glove in the schoolhouse. *If I were young and fit*, the constable thought, *nothing would keep me away from a boxing match of this stature. And if I were moving about from place to place, trying not to attract notice, and I heard about a fight . . .*

He looked at the advertised date and venue. The match was to be held in Angenberg on Saturday, the thirteenth of November. The day after tomorrow.

✠

'Reckon you've got the strength for it, do you?'

The chief of the road crew scowled at the blond chick of a boy who stood before him, asking for work. Ulrich Reinisch had youth on his side, though he hardly seemed to carry more muscle than old Gustav Spiller, whose place he would be taking. Still, he was here, and he was keen.

'Strong enough,' Ulrich insisted. 'And I've got the will for it too. You can see that for yourself.'

It was true: the youth had demonstrated his determination by waiting at the roadworks in his own overalls, ready to start work, when the truck had arrived at six in the morning to disgorge the older, bleary-eyed labourers and their equipment into the biting wind. With shining eyes, this self-appointed newcomer said that he was ready to replace the dead man, no matter what the task required.

An icy wind blew over them, making the chief's eyes water. His head and throat hurt, after a long evening at the inn. With a nod, he hired the new boy and gave him his orders.

Ulrich's eagerness lasted throughout his first day's labour on the road. He seized every opportunity to question his new colleagues. Where had Elias Frankel been standing when the police motorcycle spun out of control? Who had been watching him at that moment, and what did they see? Where was old man Spiller, and how did the runaway get from over here to over there, to strike him? Did he leap?

He took it all in through shimmering eyes, ready to relay the details to his new friend, Corporal Eckhardt Gröhlick, when he returned to Hindelheim later.

✠

There had been a hard frost in Hindelheim overnight, and it was slow to clear. A white skin clung to the garden path, while in some dark corners around the guttering, and under the shed roofs, patches of water had frozen to form icicles. But the boy's routine did not bend to the weather. On this, as on every morning after breakfast, Dirk Müller made the same, slow circuit around the Koenig property, while his mother followed.

A piece of loose and rusting pipe scraped against the kitchen wall as Dirk brushed against it, prompting him to stop and glare at the sound. He stopped again at a windowsill, where frozen droplets had gathered. With a grunting 'uh-uh-uh', the boy twisted his head under the sill to gather an icicle onto his outstretched tongue.

Ute watched from the orchard as the two slow figures approached, wrapped in thick layers of clothing. They shuffled down the path from the kitchen garden as the constable had done nearly three weeks ago, though it now seemed a distance of years. Had he gripped her hand, and turned it over to inspect her palm, or was that a false memory? Ute remembered the look on his face with more certainty: she had seen it again, more recently, in Mittelbach, when he stopped for a few minutes beside the car. On both occasions the constable's attention unsettled her, causing this constant re-examination.

By questioning Helga one morning as they cooked together, Ute had learned that there were two women who met Constable Hildebrandt each week in the Valley Inn. Did he look

193

at them with that same close attention that he had given her? Ute wondered. She supposed so. Adjusting the scarf around her neck, she forced herself to dismiss the thought.

When Johanna was close enough to hear her greeting, Ute explained that she was waiting to go down to her aunt's cottage and make breakfast for the guests, but guessed that it was still too early.

Johanna looked past her and said, 'You've been to the grave.'

A trail of footprints, pressed into the frosted grass, showed where Ute had stood, at one edge of the orchard, beside the small wooden marker. She replied with an apology. 'I hope you don't mind, Johanna.'

Expecting a sharp reply or none at all, she was surprised when Johanna linked arms with her and drew close, replying with sudden warmth, 'You'll get your turn, Ute. But you may wish you hadn't.'

Dirk edged along the fence, flicking frost from the bramble bushes as the two women watched. His gloved hands scrabbled for a stick, which he used, ineptly, as a kind of weapon, trying with frantic yelps and thrashings of the air to strike the Kaiser's nose. Ute watched, ready to intervene at the first pained whimper, but the dog bore his treatment without protest.

'Heinrich's dogs would never have put up with that,' Johanna observed.

Ute noted the past tense, and looked over at the kennels, which stood empty within the enclosure. Heinrich could have taken his dogs out for their usual morning run, but Ute had the feeling that today was different, the emptiness more final.

She said, 'Did you mean what you said last night, about Ida Frankel?'

Johanna took in a breath. 'No. Maybe, in the moment – but now it seems . . . it was a foolish thing to say. You know, I sometimes wonder if my mother's condition is already affecting me. At moments, I am out of my mind.' Withdrawing her arm from Ute's, she covered her face with both hands – to hide or suppress tears, Ute imagined.

But then Johanna pulled her hands away to reveal a faint, amused smile. 'Did Peter ever tell you,' she said, 'about the promise we made once, on our birthday?'

Ute shook her head. She knew that Johanna and Peter had been born on the same day, several years apart. The coincidence was one of the many sinews that bound them together.

'It was his fifteenth, I think,' Johanna continued. 'Or perhaps sixteenth. I was pregnant with this one.' She nodded at Dirk, and kept her eyes on him as she retrieved the memory. 'I'd made a cake – a horrible, flat little thing. There was only a handful of flour, and no sugar. Peter couldn't find anyone to come and eat it with us. Mother was already in a state by then, so Helga was with her. Heinrich was in town, working. We asked Papa to join us for a celebration, and he said he would. But then he forgot, of course, and went down to the Frankel place, because Ida was ill.' She frowned, uncertain. 'Or was it that day he'd caught a butterfly, and was taking it down for Elias to put in his collection? In any case, Peter and I were alone with the nasty birthday cake, and we decided that the world could go to hell, as long as we had each other for company. Peter promised to come back here after university, and I promised to stay – not knowing how the boy would turn out . . .'

Her voice trailed off for a moment. Then she turned to Ute and, making one of her habitual, and inscrutable, leaps to a new subject, she said, 'I treasured Heinrich, in my way. It was not enough to keep him, evidently. I hope . . . I do hope Peter does a better job of showing you that he needs you.'

Ute sensed that she, as well as Peter, was meant to rise to this challenge. Not knowing how to respond, she called the dog, and buried her hand in its warm fur. After a moment, Johanna walked on, and Ute called after her, 'Elias Frankel is on the run, Johanna. Some people think he hurt your baby.'

Johanna stopped beside the grave, with her back to Ute. She answered without turning. 'No one would think any such thing if he hadn't pursued me as he did, would they?' After a silence, she let out a quick exclamation. 'Wolf Man! I think that myth is one of Elias Frankel's inventions, don't you?'

She looked around, but Ute gave no response.

✛

Returning to her room, Johanna peeled the woollen hat from Dirk's head, watching his mouth bite at the air between them. He continued to do this as she sat on the edge of the bed and looked at him. The remoteness of his gaze was made severe by a protruding forehead. 'What am I going to do with you,' she asked him, 'for the rest of my life?'

The bed was neatly made, with a single glass of water beside it, on Johanna's side. She lay down and stared at the hollowing on the other side of the mattress, the only visible evidence that a man had also lain here beside her for a decade, until this morning. She wondered if anyone would ever sleep beside her again.

'Come here,' she urged, coaxing the boy up onto the bed. 'Lie with me.' She drew him to her, so that his head was beside hers on the pillow. 'We'll take off on our own adventure,' she told him, looking at the ceiling. 'Where would you like to go – Algiers? Alicante? The Black Sea. The Red Sea.'

Dirk did not like lying beside his mother, with his wrist clamped to her side. He used his free hand to thump her belly. When Johanna rolled to face him, he bit her hand, but she kept it pressed to his cheek and forced him down, moving her body over his. Using her weight as a press, she was able to free her hands for the pillow.

Hooking one foot under the bars at the end of the bed, to prevent her son's flailing legs from escaping the pressure of her thighs, she lay across his struggling body and drove her weight into the pillow. The sound that came through it, losing clarity as it travelled through ten thousand goose feathers, was a tuneless monotone.

Johanna held her breath as she might do in order to dive deep into the ocean; and although she had never swum in an ocean, or in any deep water, she seemed to be pushing herself far down below the light of the world and the colours of living and moving things, into weeds, darkness, a floor. The boy's small boots scraped her calves, unnoticed. Only when his fingers wriggled free and found her nipple did the cry escape her, exploding from her lungs as a bellowing sob.

Throwing aside the pillow, she rolled off the boy and used both trembling hands to wipe the mucus and sweat from his face, and to lever him, coughing, into a sitting position. While he coughed, he allowed her to sit behind him and offer her body as a chair, a brace, an extra spine. Her breasts were soft against his back, her fingertips tentative on his forearm, the apology whispered from wet lips into his ear, over and over.

# 20.

Theodore considered a number of potential excuses before deciding to tell his deputy the truth – or part of it. He was going to Angen tomorrow to watch a fight.

'A fight?' Klaus repeated, standing in front of the constable's desk. Having allowed himself a short paternity leave, he was back in the station office, on duty.

'A boxing match. Thought I might pick up some tips,' Theodore added, unable to resist a chance to provoke him. 'Improve my technique.'

Before Klaus could question him, a visitor stepped in, stamping her feet on the doormat to shake off the weather. They both recognised her instantly, and silently, as Johanna Koenig – though her appearance was subtly altered, somehow, since that first visit to Hindelheim. *Lipstick*, thought Theodore, as the woman drew back the hood of her cloak. *A hairclip to hold her curls in place. She has dressed for this outing.*

Johanna's gaze swept over the two men, and their desks, before settling on the constable. She said, 'I'm here about Elias Frankel. Have you caught him yet?'

'No,' he answered, and waited.

Johanna Koenig looked down for a moment, preparing herself. 'Will he be brought here,' she asked, 'or to the station at Angenberg?'

'Probably both,' Theodore guessed. He watched her reach into her bag and pull out a thick envelope.

'When he's found, I'd like you to give him this,' Johanna said. 'My husband was late paying our store credit last month. The rest Elias may need for . . . eventualities.'

Theodore took the envelope and knew from its weight that it contained more money than the Hindelheim storekeeper would take from all his customers together in a month. Watching him, Johanna explained, 'It's the last of Heinrich's salary. We've been making plans, on and off, for some years, to move to town and hire a nurse for Dirk. But now, well. One ought to pay one's debts.'

Accepting this with a nod, Theodore replied, 'But I'm afraid I can't guarantee that I will see him. Unless, perhaps, you could tell me where he's hiding?'

At this Johanna's pale eyes, accentuated by lines of kohl, skipped over him in surprise. She said, 'I wonder why you suspect me of collaborating with a runaway, Constable?'

'Someone knows,' he answered. 'People don't disappear.'

'I hope you're wrong,' Johanna replied. She snapped the clasp of her handbag shut and made a half-turn away from the constable's desk. Then she paused to add, 'Though it would be better for everyone if Elias never comes back to Hindelheim.'

Theodore, watching her leave, lurched after her. 'Wait. A moment. Please.' He caught her at the door. The effort of moving quickly made his breathing uneven, and he swallowed before asking, 'What do you mean by that? Elias Frankel is not even twenty years old. From what I gather, he's an oddity. Aloof. A . . . braggart, who keeps to himself. But he's just a young man. Why should he be a danger to anyone?'

Johanna frowned in the direction she was about to take, out into the windswept yard. She answered after a moment, 'Some people bring out the worst in others, don't they? Elias Frankel has his mother's . . . charm.' There was a pause. Returning her gaze to the constable, she continued, 'Ida Frankel used to make a concoction she called her health tonic. It was very popular in Hindelheim. Everyone drank it. Sometimes I wonder if Ida put something in that potion to drive us all mad.'

'In what way, mad?' Theodore persisted. He followed her out onto the doorstep, where he caught a blast of cold air.

Lifting her hood, Johanna thought for a moment before answering. 'Mad for what we don't have, Constable. Filled with impossible desires.'

❖

Leaving the police station, Johanna walked down to the valley junction and stood by the roadside, trying to remember when she had last left Dirk at home with Helga for a whole day. In early September, almost three months ago, she went with Heinrich to Angen to have the baby – but that was different; she was not alone then. Or rather, she could still convince herself, at that time, that she had a husband. Now that he was gone and the baby too, Johanna could do whatever she wanted with her day in town.

She watched a distant vehicle approach from the north, a motor car making its way past rye fields in the direction of Angenberg. It was moving slowly towards her, weighed down by a cargo of boxes or planks tied to the roof. The sky behind it matched the road's surface: a dark, uniform grey. In a moment, when the driver was close enough to see, she would raise her hand to beg a lift.

Helga was expecting Johanna home the following day, on the Pohlmanns' wagon. But supposing she were to stay away for longer? Or forever?

Hearing the engine of a second vehicle close behind her, Johanna turned to look, and caught a smattering of raindrops on her face. Freedom, she thought, adjusting her hood with trembling hands. Hadn't she once been known for her free spirit – condemned, even, for an excess of it? She watched as a truck pulled out of the entrance of the Valley Inn and drew level with her at the junction. There it paused, and the truck driver looked out to ask where Johanna was going. It was clear from the position of the wheels that he was about to turn northwards onto the highway, heading towards the approaching motor car, in the opposite direction.

*Choose*, she told herself. *Angen or elsewhere. Hold on or let go. Choose!*

✜

In the *Gazette*'s printing room, Albert seized the new edition with enthusiasm. His article occupied half a page, below Werner Todt's report on the overcrowding of the town's cemeteries. Although he would have preferred to have the page to himself, it was a definite improvement on the placement of his theatre reviews.

'Next time,' he told Marlyse, who stood beside him, trying to read over his shoulder. 'When Elias Frankel is arrested, I'll push Werner off the front page.'

He turned to push a stack of handwritten notes into her arms. 'Now I need you to do some things for me. Marlyse, are you listening?' She was trying to read the article. 'Type these up and take them to the post,' he said. 'Quick as you can. But before you do that, go to the library and borrow this book . . . hold on . . . can you read that?' He scribbled the title on the uppermost piece of paper. 'The chief witch there will tell you that I've lost my borrowing rights,' he continued, 'because of unreturned loans, unpaid fees, et cetera. All lies. Fight her. With sharpened fingernails if you have to. I need to read this book by tonight – oh, better idea.' He saw her attention wavering, and used a finger to lift her chin. 'Why don't you look through it while you're there? Jot a summary for me, main points of the play, shouldn't take you long.' Experiencing a stab of doubt, he added, 'Darling, you can read and write, can't you?'

Marlyse, staring, nodded once.

'Just checking.' He sent her off with a smack on the buttocks. 'Good girl.'

Marlyse walked around the corner from the print works, found an unoccupied doorstep, and sat between a sleeping dog and a stack of crates to read.

### ANGENBERG CITIZENS WARNED TO BEWARE OF HILL-COUNTRY 'WOLF MAN'

*Alarm is growing at the continued disappearance of a local renegade from the hamlet of Hindelheim, district of Mittelbach, following his violent escape from a police vehicle two weeks ago. The nineteen-year-old runaway, Elias Frankel, who is known to his neighbours as 'Wolf Man' following his improbable yet highly significant claim to have found and killed a wolf in nearby woods, overpowered a crew of road workers, as reported in this newspaper on 5th November. That incident left the arresting police officer with an injury to the eye, and one of the road crew, Gustav Spiller, with a fatal injury to the stomach. Victim Spiller collapsed the day after the shocking attack, in the presence of Mayor Becker and the Dammertz family, falling into a coma from which he did not recover. Fellow members of the road crew, who witnessed the attack, have told this reporter of the 'unnatural strength' with which the Wolf Man struck their colleague, and of the 'impossible speed' with which he outran his pursuers – moving, they say, in an inhuman fashion, crouched, as if on four legs instead of two. With what neighbours call an 'eerie power', Elias Frankel managed not only to vanish under the eyes of the pursuing police officer and road diggers, but to remain hidden during a region-wide search. Although sightings have been reported in Mittelbach and from several places along the highway, there is overwhelming evidence that the outlaw has been living among us here in*

*Angenberg since his escape. A grocer with premises on the market square was menaced in broad daylight by the wild man, who once again evaded capture, this time merging into the noontime market crowd. One witness from that incident wrote subsequently to the newspaper describing a tall, loping figure with an expression of the deepest malice and fresh blood on his hands.*

*Chief Inspector Lorentz Streicher of the Angenberg Regional Police Division states that: 'Elias Frankel is sought in connection with the theft of an item of police property, but is not considered a threat to public order.' Neighbours of the runaway are not so sanguine, however. Many asked this reporter: if he is guilty of nothing worse than a minor disturbance, why did he beat a road worker to death in an attempt to escape police questioning? One resident of Hindelheim, who prefers not to be named, suggests that the parents of a previously missing, and now dead, child are afraid to accuse 'Wolf Man' Frankel of the abduction despite local knowledge that implicates him. A storekeeper and tool-worker in the remote hill village, Elias Frankel recently alarmed neighbours by his erratic behaviour at the burial of his stepfather, who died in a sudden and unexplained fall from the back steps of the property. One of the few pieces of common knowledge about this mysterious young fugitive is his strange nocturnal habits. He is said by all who have had more than a passing acquaintance with him to have kept unusual hours, often wandering outside through the night.*

*Some doubt that the Hindelheim runaway poses an immediate threat to citizens of this town, arguing that every region has its wild men who live outside social institutions, often defying the virtues of work and marriage in favour of a renegade life. There is no reason to suppose, argue the sceptics, that the individual dubbed 'Wolf Man' by his neighbours is responsible for anything other than the particular crimes he is known to have committed: aggressive conduct and intimidation, theft of* police property, and avoiding arrest. In the interests of maintaining a balanced argument, we put these views to a retired neurological specialist and former director of the Angenberg General Hospital, Professor Masloff, and asked him to comment on those few facts of the case which are beyond dispute – the existence of a nickname, Wolf Man, and the unusual nocturnal habits that gave rise to it; the blow that was delivered to road worker Spiller's stomach with lethal force, resulting after an uncanny delay in the man's death; the lurching manner of Elias Frankel's disappearance, and his continued ability to evade notice. In a considered response, Professor Masloff emphasised that there is no such thing as a werewolf. The notion of the 'undead' or 'walking dead' is not a scientific category, and consequently such terms have no place in the discourse of medical science, he insisted. Yet, the professor went on to say, there have been some interesting cases of symptoms which mirror the zombie state; cases of extreme insomnia combined with a propensity to aggression, charted in almost every decade of German history stretching back to the notorious Peter Stubbe. The term implies a spectrum of possibilities, according to this expert in the field: it is therefore not inconceivable that the Wolf Man, Elias Frankel, is affected by some as yet unidentified condition.

Until the fugitive is found and brought to justice, the author of this report, together with his editor and colleagues at the Gazette, would advise readers to be vigilant, and to present any matters of concern to the Angenberg police, or to this newspaper. ALBERT DINTER.

Marlyse continued to grip the newspaper for several minutes after she had finished reading. Despite the cold air, her hands were clammy. She had believed in Elias Frankel's passion, and suffered in silent shame when he turned away from her, without any explanation, in the summer. He deserved to suffer for that neglect, if for nothing else, she reasoned. The careless wretch ought to listen to what people said about him – and if this new notoriety hurt him, then so be it.

But her eyes jumped back to the exaggerations in Albert's report: *killed a wolf, lethal force, zombie state*. Marlyse had never expected that her hints about Elias would lead to this level of public warning. The sense of triumph that had shot through her in the *Gazette*'s printing room, on seeing the fresh ink – *I did this!* – was now mutating, second by second, into sickening, leaden misery. *I did this. God help me, I did this.*

Getting to her feet, she continued blindly along the street for a while and then, struggling for breath, stopped to lean on a railing. The wall of the old fort that housed the police station towered before her, and below it was a watery ditch, once a moat. There Marlyse hurled the newspaper into the mud, and sent the other papers flying after it. She did not care who stopped to laugh and point at her strange behaviour, as long as she never saw Albert Dinter, or Elias Frankel, or Ute, or for that matter anyone from the old life, again.

✠

Theodore travelled to Angenberg in a brewery truck, which was returning to the plant after making deliveries out of town. It would take him close to the former meeting hall in the factory district where the fight was to be held. 'Which side?' he asked.

'Which side?' the truck driver repeated, with a sideways glance.

'Is your money on?' Theodore explained. Noting the man's look of distaste, he added, 'Or your prayers, if you're not a betting man.'

The driver's nostrils flared as he drew in breath. He replied, 'Our boy is going up against their Goliath, and you ask me which side? That's not the kind of thing you choose. It's how it is. Matter of faith. Matter of loyalty.'

The constable let this pass, as he had no money to bet with in any case. He bounced forward on the broken springs of the passenger seat, as they came to an abrupt halt. While the barrels were rolled off the back of the truck, and fumes rolled in at the front, Theodore let himself down into the five o'clock gloom.

He found himself amid a sizeable crowd of men who shuffled, talking and smoking, into a low, windowless shack of a building. Chalked in large letters above the doorway were the names of the two fighters.

As a boy, Theodore Hildebrandt had pounded someone's nose into a new shape and thereby earned the name of 'Boxer' for a week or two. In the village where he met Klaus's mother, the cry of 'Fight!' would go up now and then, and everyone would run towards it, to be blessed with the awesome sight of pain given and received. Around that time, scuffling gangs in alleyways began to practise their moves, and the wrestling pit at a local fair began to attract crowds of sufficient size to interest the local bookmakers. It was now an organised sport, he knew, but the queues and tickets and announcement in the newspaper: all of that surprised him.

Shunted forward between two men whose higher shoulders concealed his own, Theodore was thumped in the chest by a doorman demanding his ticket. In reply he glared until the man noticed his uniform. 'Constable Hildebrandt,' he said. 'You've got one of mine in there, a jail dodger. Will you let me through, or shall I assume you're hiding him?'

Once inside, he stopped to adjust his eyes to the dim fug of the hall, which was athrong with shoulders, elbows, heavy feet. Before he could decide where to look, or what to look for, a voice hailed him.

'Hildebrandt!'

Stepping out of one of Theodore's recurring bad dreams into the sweat of the boxing hall, Officer Zelinsky took shape before him. 'I didn't take you for a sporting man,' he said. 'Come to learn a few tricks? Never too late, old man.' He bounced a light punch off Theodore's chest, his grin tooth-white in the gloom.

Theodore glanced over the officer's shoulder and saw that two junior policemen had accompanied him. One was talking to the doorman. 'I'm looking for someone,' he replied. 'A crook from my district.'

A light glimmered in Officer Zelinsky's blue eyes. 'Elias Frankel's here?'

'I don't know about that,' Theodore replied. 'Possibly, but I'll leave him to you, since you were the one to lose him. I know how badly you want to crawl back into the chief inspector's favour. Mine's a pimp. One of his girls robbed me as she was . . . let's say, answering my questions in the Valley Inn. I've reason to believe that the prick is here,' he glanced round, 'and if I can get hold of him, I fully expect to leave with a profit. '

'Oh yes?' Zelinsky watched him, looking for a crack. 'Not been the best month for you, has it, Hildebrandt? The Mittelbach station ledger must make for painful reading. *Criminals apprehended: nil. Outstanding crimes . . .?*' He let this hang for a second, before continuing, 'Still, maybe you'll be lucky tonight. All the scum floats to the surface in a place like this.' His eyes bounced over the gathering spectators, as if to summon a lightning rod to strike them down. 'Here they all come. Flies to a turd, Hildebrandt. Flies. To. A. Turd.'

Theodore found himself ushered onto a bench in front of the standing spectators, where he was required to sit with his uniformed fellows. There was no hope of edging quietly around the back of the hall during the match, as he had planned to do. Instead he looked across the ring, between the boxers, at the faces watching in semi-darkness on the far side of the arena. Although he had had a list of the now-famous features in his mind – long legs; pale, hirsute face; an uneven squint – he had never met Elias Frankel, and might well miss him, if indeed he was here.

When for the second time the local champion went down, causing a rumble of frustration in the crowd, an argument seemed to break out some way behind the policemen's bench. Officer Zelinsky turned to look, and Theodore did likewise, though this involved twisting his whole body and rocking the bench.

The commotion involved a handful of men standing towards the back, where their view had been momentarily blocked by someone lifting a boy onto his shoulders. It could be any child, of course: there were plenty in the hall, and all Theodore could see from this distance was a tall shadow separating itself from a shorter one. Even so, it was worth a try.

'What is it?' Zelinsky demanded, as Theodore struggled to his feet. 'You've seen him – your pimp?'

'No.' He put a hand on his stomach, glad for once of his ready talent for nausea. If necessary, he could cough a little phlegm onto the officer's boots. 'I'm prone to . . . Let me out, will you?'

Needing no further invitation, his three colleagues shrank back to avoid a spray of vomit, as Theodore stumbled from the bench and through the rows of men standing behind.

# 21.

Shadows turned into faces as he approached, but none revealed the features he was seeking, and none glanced at Theodore with anything more than the usual irritation of spectators forced to make way for a tottering invalid.

Reaching the back of the hall, he turned into a corridor and looked both ways. No one in sight. The steamy air of fighting sweat gave way, as Theodore turned down the passage, to a stench of urine. An outer door at the end of the corridor stood open, abandoned no doubt by a guard who had left his post to watch the fight. Beyond it was an unlit yard, open to the sky and enclosed by a broken wall. The whole of it was a toilet, without a drain or running water, its use recognisable from the underfoot stickiness and fierce smell.

A hand seized him from the darkness, clamping his mouth and drawing him back against the wall. 'I know who you are,' said the assailant's voice, close to his ear. 'Klaus Hildebrandt's papa. Who's with you? How many?'

Theodore groped for a hold on the wall behind him, which seemed to be covered in some kind of malodorous slime. 'Six. Indoors,' he hissed between his teeth. 'If I don't go back in, they'll follow me out here. Let go.'

After a moment, the pressure on his jaw eased, and the man

moved sideways to check the entrance to the passageway, allowing Theodore to look up at him. Though the light was dim, he could see that Elias Frankel's face carried a new growth of stubble and a patina of grease. His infamous squint was hidden beneath a frown and a curtain of dark, unkempt hair. Despite his restricted view, the constable could find a haunted, even savage quality in the angles of the young man's face that would, he guessed, be capable of provoking – how had Johanna put it? – *impossible desires*.

The sudden proximity of the man stunned Theodore for an instant, making him forget whatever it was he had planned to say. Nothing in this moment was in his control. He should feel triumphant, invigorated yet wary; but instead he was aware only of a sense of heaviness that pinned him to the wall, and slowed his brain.

Elias stepped back and brought his face down close to the constable's, glaring at him. He pressed one arm against the wall where it formed a barrier, preventing Theodore from moving aside. This position, against the cold and stinking wall, would have to do. 'I didn't mean to kill that man,' he said. His breath was sour, and when he blinked, one eye closed more tightly than the other. 'The road worker.'

'Spiller,' Theodore replied. 'His name was Gustav Spiller, and he knew you. Or your mother, at least.' Surprised by the other man's confusion, he went on, 'Didn't you speak, before you thumped him?'

Elias frowned. 'He had the key,' he said. 'I saw him, standing apart from the others. He had the deputy's coat in his hand and he was going through the pocket. I moved up to him and said give me that, but he just looked up and stared . . .'

'He would have helped you,' Theodore said, then regretted it. What use was that comment now? 'It wasn't your fault,' he added. 'The death, I mean. He would have died anyway.'

With an impatient snort, Elias pushed himself off the wall.

Theodore watched him, his natural wariness returning. 'What about the rest of it? Tell me.'

With a sidelong glance, Elias seemed to size him up. Then he answered, 'The Oberdorfers . . . in the market . . . I paid them what we owed but they wouldn't accept it. Said I'd inconvenienced them and the price had doubled. There was – an argument.'

'You seem prone to arguments.'

'Three of them against me.'

'And before that?'

He blinked.

'On the day Johanna Koenig's baby went missing,' Theodore continued, 'you went to the house and caused a scene. Got yourself that limp.'

At the reminder, Elias shifted his weight from one leg to the other. 'I may have said some things,' he said. 'To Heinrich. He owes us and never does anything about it. Spends his days screwing Gretchen Pohlmann. I said . . . I asked when was he going to start working for his tobacco like an honest man. Lazy slug – can't even do his duty by his own wife. I called him a useless cretin. It was out of my mouth before I remembered. Their boy, you know?'

Theodore nodded. The envelope from Johanna Koenig was in his pocket, but he didn't want to get it out, not yet. Not while Elias Frankel was talking freely like this. There might not be another opportunity. 'That's when he hit you?'

'Whipped me,' Elias corrected. 'With the chain he used on his dogs. I wasn't expecting it, and I slipped getting off the doorstep.'

'You didn't fight back?'

From the passageway came a roar from the crowd, as the boxing match continued inside. The constable kept his eyes on Elias, who glared back at him.

'What are you saying?'

211

'I'm saying that you could easily knock out a "useless cretin" like Heinrich Müller, and take the chain from him. Why didn't you?'

The question seemed to throw him, and he blinked for a moment before admitting, 'I don't know. Like I say, I wasn't expecting it. He just exploded. It seemed like . . . the rage was already there, and I got in the way.' His eyes roamed the constable's face, as if it would help him to remember. 'Peter Koenig was right behind him with a spade. I guess I thought they might—'

'A spade?' Theodore interrupted. It was his turn to be surprised. 'Why?'

Elias shrugged. 'He was digging in the orchard when I arrived. When me and Heinrich started arguing, he looked over . . .'

Someone stepped out into the yard, cutting him off. They stood together in the darkness, watching, as a man sent a sulphurous spray of urine against the far wall. Theodore was conscious that he ought to turn back inside. There was not enough time to ask all of his questions. He would have to take what he could and think about it later. 'This is for you,' he murmured, as soon as the man had gone.

Elias looked at him in puzzlement, and then took the envelope.

'From Johanna Koenig,' the constable explained, watching him tear into it.

Surprised anew at the quantity of notes inside, Elias froze. 'Is this a trick?' he demanded. 'Are you trying to trap me?' His eyes darted into the shadows.

'If it's a trick, it's not of my doing,' Theodore replied. 'Johanna said it was to cover their debt. Do you believe that?'

Elias held the envelope on his palm, touching the notes as if they were the feathers of an injured bird. 'I don't understand.'

'I imagine it has something to do with the baby.'

The confusion in his face took a moment to clear. 'Johanna's?

The one that died? Why – what does that have to do with this?'

'You tell me,' Theodore said, and kept watching.

'I never even saw it!' he exclaimed. 'I gave the – the lace to the housekeeper because she said Johanna was sleeping.'

'Did you come back for it?'

'What?'

'After Heinrich drove you off, did you come back to take the baby, to punish him?'

'No. No,' Elias repeated, apparently exasperated. 'Why won't you believe me?'

Theodore remembered now what he had planned to say. A theory that had formed when Johanna Koenig had stepped into his office. 'Because I think it was your child, Elias Frankel. I think your humiliation of Heinrich Müller started long before that day, months before, when you started screwing his wife. I think she heard you at the back door, and let you take a beating, because by then you had neglected her and switched your affection to Marlyse Pohlmann—'

'No.'

'But when she saw what happened afterwards. All this,' he continued, gesturing to the mouldering, confined environment of the pissoir. 'I think Johanna regretted that she'd not stood up for you. That money is her way of apologising.'

Alarm and confusion seemed to contort Elias Frankel's face. He gave a faltering answer, searching for the words as he spoke them. 'She's . . . Johanna is a troubled woman, Constable. What she believes . . . is not always the same as what actually happens. It's true that I saw her sometimes. She would call me up from the store to deliver something, or to explain some particular thing she wanted to buy, and I . . . never believed that was the real reason I was there. She would make a point of telling me that Dirk was asleep.'

'Go on.'

He scowled into the darkness, then turned back to face the

constable. With a long finger, he jabbed Theodore in the chest. 'What's so special about you? Show me, show me! What's your magic, Elias Frankel?' He gave a nervous laugh, and Theodore realised that the jabbing motion was an imitation of Johanna. 'Once, I kissed her,' Elias went on. 'She was so determined to find a secret, I just grabbed her and kissed her and said: "There, see? Normal." It was the only time. Maybe in her mind there was something more. She seemed to . . . enjoy aggravating me.'

Theodore shifted. His leg was numb, and the stench underfoot was bringing genuine nausea to his throat. One more question, and then he must decide whether to raise the alarm or let the man go. Part of him had already decided, but that part could be deluded. Self-deception was not the preserve of lonely women with rotten husbands. Lonely police constables could be stricken by it too. 'Did you get her pregnant?' he asked.

'Johanna? No.'

Something about this answer called for more scrutiny, but there was no time for it now. Elias turned his head to let out a sharp whistle. Another, higher whistle answered from the darkness beyond the wall: Otto Frankel, Theodore guessed, keeping watch somewhere nearby, on his stepbrother's orders. 'Use it,' he said.

'What?'

'The money. Get out of the district and stay there, for as long as you can.'

Elias Frankel searched the constable's face, and then pushed the envelope into the pocket of his long, dark coat. 'How will I know when it's safe to go back?'

'It might never be,' Theodore admitted. 'You chose a bad moment to run off. It inconvenienced the mayor. If you are caught, act penitent. The mayor will like that; his cronies too. Be confused. Let Officer Zelinsky crow over you. He'll enjoy the victory so much, it might distract him from lining up any decent evidence.'

Elias scratched at his stubble. 'Why do you care what I do?'

'Who said I cared?' Theodore replied. 'I'm here for the fight.'

✠

A high, warning whistle interrupted. Elias looked in alarm at the doorway, through which footsteps could be heard marching down the passageway. Their eyes met again, briefly, before Elias turned to scale the wall.

Unbuttoning himself, Theodore chose a position in the middle of the yard, where the policemen would have to pass him to go after Elias. He let the two junior officers pass, shouting – 'There! The wall!' – and then turned in mid-flow to face Officer Zelinsky, showering him on the knee and boots.

'Holy Christ,' Zelinsky exclaimed in disgust, stepping back.

'You surprised me,' Theodore replied, with feigned concern. 'Did I catch you?'

Zelinsky looked at his feet, and then at the two junior policemen clambering over slime-covered bricks in the darkness. Eventually he returned his gaze and said, 'No, Hildebrandt. *I* caught *you*. I'm arresting you for aiding and abetting a wanted outlaw.'

Theodore watched him reach for his handcuffs, and told him not to bother. 'Do you think I'm going to run, imbecile?'

✠

'Pissing on a senior officer?' Chief Inspector Lorentz Streicher glared from the armchair in which he had been disturbed while enjoying a light supper. 'Like an animal. Like a dog!'

The remnants of the meal stood on a tray beside him, apart from a few flecks which had fallen onto his housecoat, and one which clung to his shadowed chin. He had not been expecting company this evening, and the arrival of Officer Zelinsky and his charge at this late hour turned what might otherwise have been a surprised response into one of outrage.

Standing before him, Theodore replied, 'I've always suspected that the field surgeon forgot one or two details when he stuffed the various bits and pieces of me back into this skin, sir. The waterworks division has been operating erratically ever since.' With a glance at Zelinsky, who stood to one side of the chief inspector's armchair, he added, 'It was unfortunate that I misfired just as my esteemed colleague stepped into the pissing alley.'

'He didn't *join* you, Theo. He was following you. On my orders.' Catching Theodore's surprise, the chief inspector turned to tell Zelinsky to wait outside. With a glance of triumph, the officer obeyed. Lorentz turned back. 'Sit down,' he offered, pointing at a chair in which a small, hairless dog lay curled, foetal and rat-like.

Theodore remained standing. 'If you're going to give me my notice, it would probably suit us both to be brief,' he replied.

The chief inspector smiled. 'Do you think I'm going to fire you for giving that grease merchant a dose of Mother Nature's own acid? I hope I'm not so petty, Theo. One has standards.' He paused, and went on, 'I'm firing you for conspiring with a fugitive.'

'Conspiring,' Theodore echoed. 'Fugitive. Big words for a small . . .' he hesitated, keeping his eyes on Lorentz, '. . . town, like this one.'

'I see you ignored my advice to learn some tact.' He rose to his feet, crushing a napkin in his hand. 'So I won't expect you to develop gratitude or humility.'

'The odds would seem to be against it,' Theodore agreed.

Lorentz Streicher shook his head. 'You've got a grandson now, Zelinsky tells me. Good for you. Good for Klaus. Perhaps the newborn child will have an influence on you, where the rest of us have failed. Old men have been known to regain their innocence at the very end. Even you could hope for some . . . lightening of the spirit.'

Theodore started to answer, but found to his dismay that his throat had seized up. He cleared it noisily, causing the inspector to grimace, and then forced out his plea. 'Don't punish Klaus for my actions, Lorentz. If he'd known why I came to town today, he would have done everything in his power to stop me. You see that, don't you? Klaus Hildebrandt is the man for you. He'd follow your orders if they were to—' Stopping himself before he could sabotage his own argument, he began again. 'I think that Zelinsky has spoken to him, and made promises he has no intention of fulfilling. Klaus won't be expecting petty vengeance from him, but I do.'

'Yes, you would.'

'He's a grease merchant, Lorentz. Your words. Put Zelinsky in charge at Mittelbach, and he'll kick Klaus into the gutter just to spite me.'

The chief inspector waved this away and turned to pour himself a drink. 'I'm not a nanny, Theo. You're all grown men. Sort out your own squabbles.'

Theodore watched the rat-like dog uncurl and shake itself. He said, 'Do you remember the doctor at Hindelheim who complained about my interference? Peter Koenig?' When the chief gave a suspicious frown, he went on. 'He's a convert to the science of eugenics. Pull out the weeds so the flowers can grow tall and strong. Improve the species by selection. Well as it happens, young Koenig's sister has a defective child, born just after the war, a mute boy who needs watching day and night. The mother can hardly leave the house, even now.' He saw, and ignored, the signs of impatience in the chief inspector's movements. 'Suppose,' he continued, 'that this woman gave birth in the autumn, after years of waiting, to a second handicapped child.'

'Why should I *suppose* anything of the sort?' Lorentz drained his glass. 'It's late, and believe it or not, I have more pressing matters to concern me . . .'

But Theodore kept talking. 'She is, to say the least, disappointed. Her husband likewise. The doctor – a friend of Stefan von Brodnitz, the famous eugenics man – has the means to end this child's life quietly and painlessly, under his own roof, with an extra spoonful of cough medicine. Suppose it is agreed among the three of them, one quiet afternoon, and then – an opportunity arises to cover their tracks.'

Lorentz Streicher sighed. 'Did I forget to mention that you're sacked? As of . . .' he checked his watch ' . . . ten after midnight. Constable Hildebrandt is no more. Your carriage has turned back into a pumpkin. It's over, man.'

'The Jewish storekeeper arrives at the back door,' Theodore continued, ignoring him. 'Or perhaps they summon him especially – this lad is an irritation to them, for other reasons. They decide to fake the dead child's abduction and call in the local constabulary, knowing that somehow, with a gentle hint or two, suspicion will fall on Elias Frankel. The doctor directs this . . . play, if you like, making sure that he is never at any point seen to lay the blame at Elias Frankel's door . . .'

Slamming his glass down, Lorentz performed a loud yawn. 'Ayaya . . .'

'Suppose this happened,' Theodore urged. 'Or something like it, and you took a call from the doctor, Peter Koenig. Or you were cornered at your gentlemen's club by Koenig's friend von Brodnitz – a man of science, respected by the town elders – who reminded you, in the presence of your mutual associates, that the maintenance of social harmony in these times of change relies on a mutual understanding between his profession and yours—'

'For God's sake!' the chief inspector roared, turning on him.

'You danced to their tune, Lorentz! You were their puppet – Koenig's, and then the mayor's, and perhaps now you'll let Zelinsky pull at the strings!' Theodore could see fury blazing in the chief inspector's eyes, and knew that he was burnt beyond redemption. So be it. He continued, 'You've allowed yourself to be led by suggestion and brandy-smooth logic. And even if no one – not even that coward of a doctor – planned to whip up a region-wide storm of hatred against Elias Frankel, it has all contributed. Everything that's been said and not said and not done has led to this manhunt. Which means you carry some of the guilt, and so do I.'

The other man seemed on the verge of responding to this, but changed his mind, as if spotting a crack through which doubt or hesitation might creep in. He said, 'You know the way out. Leave your uniform with Officer Zelinsky.'

## 22.

He followed a stray cat down a street in which nothing else moved. It was still dark when he found a bakery and stood outside it in his shirtsleeves, waiting for dawn, his nostrils flaring in anticipation of the smell of sweet, warm bread. An hour passed and he remembered it was Sunday. There would be no bread today, at least not in this part of town. He shuffled onwards, letting his feet take him across Angenberg without yet having a clear purpose in mind.

His clash with the chief inspector had left Theodore oddly unmoved. It struck him that he should be perturbed by the end of their friendship, if not by the end of his respectability as a man with a uniform, a man with a reason to be alive. He had shed the exoskeleton of authority – peaked cap and stiffened shoulders – and though it left him shivering with cold, and aching for nourishment and sleep after another night without either, he was relieved to be carrying a lighter load. No doubt he would mourn his losses later, when he allowed himself to think about the implications for Klaus and the new baby, but for the moment Theodore felt unencumbered in his soul.

So it was not the row with Lorentz that occupied him as he walked, but his encounter with Elias Frankel in the piss-stinking yard. One part of it in particular repeated in his ears. *Did you get her pregnant?* The answer: *Johanna? No.*

The fugitive had not fathered Johanna's child. Theodore believed him. He had watched and listened as best he could, in the filthy darkness behind the boxing hall, and the answer seemed to him sincere. *Johanna? No.*

Not hers, but perhaps someone else's? Could Marlyse Pohlmann be pregnant? It might explain her disloyalty to Elias Frankel, if the man had cast her aside in that condition . . .

'No,' Theodore said aloud, forcing himself to reconsider. He had heard what, exactly? *Johanna? No.* The briefest of hesitations, and a request for clarity. *Johanna?* It meant: 'Are we still talking about Johanna?' Elias Frankel was nervous, distracted, bewildered in that moment. He was a man on the run, clutching an envelope that could be a trap, and bombarded with questions from his uniformed pursuer. While the constable asked about Johanna, Elias was thinking of a dozen other things – and Johanna Koenig was not one of them. That initial uncertainty – *Johanna? No* – merely indicated that Elias was not preoccupied with guilt or worry about her.

Theodore stopped a woman on a bicycle and asked a few questions, to which she pointed and nodded in reply. In exchange for the coins in his pocket, she gave him half of a plum cake from her bicycle basket. He found a water pump, and persuaded another woman to operate the handle while he held his hands underneath. The water was so cold that he spilled most of it by shaking, and had to wait for his fingers to thaw before he could manage to eat the cake. Finding a stone to sit on near the pump, he dug in his pocket and pulled out the letter he kept there.

During his years as a constable, Theodore had only once or twice received a piece of personal correspondence, and as far as he could recall, during his two brief but contented years as a husband, before his bereavement, he had never received a letter from Klaus's mother; which meant that Ute Koenig's letter was his first from a woman in all of the forty-five years of his life. It gave him a sharp, unnerving pleasure to smooth out its creased pages, and to consider again how – or if – he should reply.

He bit into the cake, and read, his eyes lingering where the crumbs fell. *I myself can hardly say that I know Elias, even though I lived next door to him all my life until this summer.* All her life, he thought. He read the sentence again. So conscious of her proximity, and her ignorance. Would that explain the perplexed look on Ute Koenig's face that first day, at the bonfire? And later, listening to her in the café, Theodore had gained the impression of someone trying to solve a private, intransigent puzzle. Was this it? Had she been watching Elias Frankel over the hedge week after week, year after year, *all my life*, developing a simple but intense curiosity towards this particular neighbour?

He turned the page, took another bite of the plum cake, and read about Marlyse Pohlmann's involvement with Elias Frankel – how the girl had gone off with him on a romantic excursion in the springtime, returning some days later to boast of their adventures to her watchful, pensive room-mate.

Theodore folded the letter away, sensing that he was in danger of prying. He ought not to peek into gaps between the words he had been given. But, a reply? Yes, he would surely be justified in sending one. It was a question of finding the words to invite Ute Koenig – or beg, or trick her – to share more of her puzzle with him. The prospect of setting pen to paper was strangely daunting, however. If Theodore had been awkward in his constable's uniform, he was a blushing boy without it, shy and tongue-tied, shuffling in a wide circle around the girl of his dreams.

Time to get some air to the brain, he decided, and force courage into his feeble limbs and lungs. This was not a plan so much as an urge or need for physical exertion of some vigorous kind. Since first encountering Ute at the bonfire, Theodore had felt propelled by an excess of energy, despite a string of short nights and wearing days. His desire, rebelling against the limitations of his body, needed an outlet.

✛

He arrived in the early afternoon at a waste tip on the outskirts of Angenberg, as directed by the woman on the bicycle. Behind a scattering of sheds and rusting junk, the gypsies' makeshift paddock came into view. A pair of chestnut horses nosed each other, while another three ran loose in the frosty sunshine, their hooves landing on a mixed terrain of mud and scrubby grass. Theodore stopped to watch, his mind running alongside the creatures. So many horses died in the war. Hundreds of thousands of sleek and powerful animals reduced to rubble, food for flies and soldiers. But here were five horses who would never – would they? – hear the sound of machine guns or exploding mortar bombs.

A pot was steaming on the fire in Pavel's camp, as usual, but this time Theodore declined his friend's offer of food. The plum cake had done its job, and the new hunger creeping over him was an ache for something else. Sitting while the others ate, he made his bid to a committee of three men and four women, plus assorted children. In exchange for his labour on any tasks they might be willing to entrust to him, Theodore asked to be lifted onto one of their horses, for an hour or two. He wanted, he explained, to remember what it felt like to be strong. If he could be released momentarily from the prison of his body, it would be easier afterwards to return to Mittelbach and tell Klaus that he had lost his position, and their home.

'You want to ride?'

Pavel's stare asked all the obvious questions, and Theodore's silence was taken as an answer. The proposal was weighed up, but not for long. In this community, every man had a right to decide for himself how to spend the force of his madness. The risk to Theodore's diminished body was his own business. Pavel lit his pipe and agreed the deal with a warning: 'Steal it and we'll cut off your testicles.'

An hour later, he was sitting on the saddle of a chestnut mare, with a wooden board tied to his back to hold his withered frame upright. Pavel's wife, Natascha, offered to climb on the horse with him – Theodore could hold onto her – but he declined the offer, saying that he feared her nerves would not withstand the speed.

The gypsy children thought the sight of him on horseback was a great joke, and so it was. Theodore would have laughed with them if he had not been trying so hard to stay in the saddle. Lifting the reins for the first time in almost a decade, he forced himself to go slowly, concentrating on the movement beneath him, making the base of his spine sink as if melting into the creature.

Completing a first tentative circuit of the field, he let out a breath that was part-exhilaration, part-frustration. Why had he let himself be incapacitated for so long? Riding was a collaboration in which the horse took the greater share of responsibility. All Theodore had to do was convey his respect and gratitude. That he could hardly do at walking pace, however. He needed to ride at speed; to feel the wind on his face and let the animal flex and stretch beneath him.

With a sideways glance, he saw that Pavel's crowd had dispersed. Seizing the unobserved moment, he broke into a gallop, tricking his ghost of a body into life. This was fine. He was moving. He was alive. Ahead, in the distance, he could see the faint outline of the hills beyond Mittelbach. Keep this up, and he would be able to ride all the way to Hindelheim and stop his princely steed below the gates of the Koenig fortress, ready to whisk the fair lady away.

But the fantasy was interrupted by a painful shortness of breath. The cold air made Theodore cough, and the coughing motion exacerbated every other discomfort. Feeling the supporting board shift behind him, and worrying that it would slip and dig into the horse's back, he turned back towards the camp. In his frustration, he made the move too sharply, and the horse reared up, causing Theodore to release the reins. An invisible hand, as Natascha would later describe it, pushed him to the ground, where his face smacked against the earth. He remained conscious for a moment, listening to a rattling sound. Some part of his supporting contraption had broken loose in the fall and was chiming against a stone, he thought, or perhaps against a shivering limb.

It was even cooler on the ground than Theodore would have imagined when looking at it from above. Was that ice on the horizon, just past his nose? The question dimmed, as something in the darkness of his brain flashed white.

✢

The newspaper revelations about Hindelheim's 'Wolf Man' passed from hand to hand, and from mouth to ear, until they reached the Frankel store, where Corporal Eckhardt Gröhlick kept guard, night and day, in his black suit. Everyone with an opinion on the subject came to deliver it to Eckhardt, and everyone took his scowling silence as surprise, imagining that he – or she – had been the first to tell him the news.

In fact, Eckhardt had heard the words of Albert Dinter quoted so many times that he knew some of them by heart. *Unusual nocturnal habits . . . uncanny delay . . . lurching manner . . . no such thing as a werewolf . . . undead . . . walking dead.* Eckhardt's young niece, Raine Gröhlick, read the whole article to him over the gate that connected the Frankels' yard to the school field, and then returned with a group of friends who wanted to know what Eckhardt was doing in the house of a half-man, half-beast. Why did he sleep there, and what did he see? Did the Monsieur's ghost roam in the dead of night? Had Eckhardt noticed a pair of flashing amber eyes, or similar signs of the person once known as Elias Frankel, appearing as a wolf?

'Oh!' Raine gasped suddenly, pointing over her uncle's shoulder. 'Look! The Beast!'

On the lid of the coal bin, the impression of two monstrous animal paws drew Eckhardt's concerned attention. To the astonishment of the watching children, he moved closer and peered at the gigantic prints, and then looked around for more, trying to discover the creature's route across the yard. With his good ear turned away from the girls, he did not hear their laughter until it had grown into a collective fit of breathless, squealing hilarity. Realising at last that he was being mocked with false prints, he stormed up the back stairs.

Retreating to the darkness of the Frankels' kitchen, Eckhardt Gröhlick stood in the back doorway, concealed from view behind the fly curtain, watching through the gaps between the canvas strips as his young tormentors tired of their game and left. The trooper had been right, he thought. These neighbours were not his true friends. They did not see the things that he did, the images that disturbed his nights and forced him awake in dry-eyed terror. They did not know the effort it took him to get up every morning and climb back into his suit and stand, arms straight, shoulders back, the way the sergeant had taught him.

The troopers looking for Elias Frankel had not been back since that first search, so Eckhardt had not seen the man again, the one who spoke about two kinds of friends. But soon after his visit, Gosling's brother had appeared, Ulrich Reinisch, with his shimmering eyes and eager loyalty. Could he be the true kind of friend?

Eckardt was not sure what to make of this strange little scrap of a man who had turned up one day and declared his allegiance. But in the days since then, he had grown used to the sight of Ulrich's white-blond hair at the kitchen table, and even looked forward to his company in the evenings, as the November nights closed in.

Since getting a job on the road crew, Ulrich Reinisch had

returned to Hindelheim every night, walking all the way, in the dark, until he reached the Frankel store. They had agreed upon a code, a series of knocks – quick, quick, slow, slow – to let Eckhardt know that it was Ulrich at the door, and no one else. This system only worked if Eckhardt was in the front room where he could hear the knocking. Once he was in the bedroom, looking at the dead insects and maps of the stars and other things that Elias kept there, so that he did not hear the sequence of knocks. Ulrich had come to the bedroom window instead and startled him. Now Eckhardt stayed in the kitchen every evening after lock-up, so that he would be ready.

They ate at the Frankels' kitchen table, working through a broth that Eckhardt had made out of the last two hens. Eggs had done them well enough for a few days, but both men agreed that the meat of the chicken was better. As they ate, Ulrich usually asked for stories about Elias Frankel. There must be something Eckhardt had forgotten to tell him! And if not, then Ulrich was happy to hear the old stories again – about the two of them feeding baby Otto, and shooting a rifle together at tin cans, and how Elias would always let Eckhardt sit on the back stairs if he had nowhere else to go.

Eckhardt liked to remember these times, although Ulrich looked at them differently, and often found aspects of the Frankels' history that 'concerned' him – that was the word he used. When Eckhardt showed him some designs the storekeeper had made, of tools or contraptions he meant to build, Ulrich said that here was evidence of a cunning mind, and they would have to watch out for traps and suchlike around the house. Also, when Ulrich examined Elias Frankel's collection of dead butterflies, and his drawings of insects and birds' nests and spiders' webs, he concluded that the man evidently had an unusual understanding of the wild. Had Eckhardt ever noticed animals behaving strangely around the Frankel brothers?

Suspecting mockery, Eckhardt met this question with a wary frown; but Ulrich seemed sincere in everything he said, and even though Eckhardt had no first-hand stories to relate about Elias Frankel's dealings with animals, Ulrich returned to the question from time to time.

✠

In exchange for what Eckhardt taught him about the Frankels, Ulrich described, with great animation and enthusiasm, some of the events and discussions that took place at the local branch of the German People's League. One of the issues that interested Franz Schmidt, the League's regional leader, as Ulrich explained to Eckhardt, concerned the special qualities of the Jewish people. Because they had roamed the earth for centuries, Franz believed that some Jews – only a few, Ulrich thought – had developed skills that were not quite human, or something more than human. In these obscure and, for the moment, unfathomed cases, the individuals were able to conceal or transform themselves with almost miraculous subtlety. If it was true that some Jews could do this, Ulrich said, then it would help to explain how they managed to influence and organise so many things without being detected.

Risking Ulrich's irritation, Eckhardt asked what things were being secretly organised in this way; and, as he anticipated, Ulrich answered with a sharp sigh, aggravated at having to explain the obvious. 'Deals between nations,' he said. 'Same thing with business affairs. They decide who wins and loses, and where all the money goes.'

Once their plates were clean, they would clear the table so that Ulrich could work on his journal. The journal was a book with bulging covers and well-thumbed edges, which Ulrich entrusted to Eckhardt's safekeeping during the daytime, when he was working. Each evening, he opened it out on the table to review the previous entries, and to add whatever new fact or question or theory he had gathered during the day. Franz Schmidt of the German People's League had encouraged Ulrich to collect information about Elias Frankel, not because there was substance to all the rumours, necessarily, but because no one else would. 'Collect and analyse,' Ulrich liked to say, quoting Franz. 'First we collect the evidence and then we decide what it means.'

Some of the facts were gleaned from other members of the road digging team, although the older men in the crew had tired of telling their story, so Ulrich had to look elsewhere for information. He spoke to everyone he passed on the hill path about what they knew of the so-called Wolf Man, and visited the Valley Inn whenever he could, to renew his stock of reported sightings. So far, he had the following key points:

1. Otto Frankel, aged 9 yrs, boasted that his stepbrother had fought off a wolf in the hills near Hindelheim. This was in June, just before Otto went to register at a Jewish school in Angen.

2. Elias Frankel, aged 19 yrs, did not deny or explain the wolf claim.

3. No one else in the area has seen a wolf but there have been other, unrelated incidents that are consistent with a wolf attack — see notes and clippings elsewhere in this journal.

4. Elias Frankel's own conduct resembles a wolf — see report by A. Dinter, enclosed. Additional interviews reveal that the subject (hereafter E.F.) lives like a wild man and copulates like a beast, with animal promiscuity.

5. Did E. F. invent the supposed wolf-sighting in order to conceal his own transformation? Note: this question is met with sullen and hostile responses from local people, which could mean that they are afraid.

6. Ida Frankel, deceased, and her illegitimate husband, alias 'The Monsieur', also deceased, refused (out of fear?) to say where E.F. was born. Without this information, it is impossible to know if he has any German blood.

In addition to the notes he made by hand, Ulrich collected and glued into the journal other material, such as: readers' letters published in the *Gazette*, in response to Albert Dinter's article; copies of Ulrich's own, as yet unpublished, letters, which had been sent in duplicate to the editor of the newspaper and to Albert Dinter, neither of whom had yet replied; a column of newsprint detailing the funeral of Gustav Spiller and the charitable donations sent to his widow; and reports published in the *Gazette* or other newspapers of any local acts of destruction, theft or violence where the guilty party had not yet been discovered.

Often Ulrich would comment aloud as he cut pieces from the newspaper: 'Six pigs killed or taken in one night, from different parts of the district, and no one has seen a connection.' Or: 'Frau Berger claimed that she saw the figure rise up – are you listening, Eckhardt? – from four legs to two.' Or: 'Listen to this part: "The robber took off over neighbouring rooftops, scrambling so fast from one high perch to the next that the pursuing police officers were eventually forced to abandon their search." He was too quick for them, Eckhardt!'

Crimes that took place at night interested Ulrich in particular, and especially so if they involved animals. Eckhardt wondered sometimes why a dog's escape from a kennel, or the poisoning of cats, or a sickness affecting a herd of cows should have anything to do with Elias Frankel. But when he asked about this, Ulrich made an impatient clicking sound with his tongue, and looked at him with eyes so wide and trembling, it seemed the whole eyeball might come loose. 'It's all valuable information, Corporal,' he would say. 'Something here could turn out to be important, and how would you feel later, if we had the clue in our hands and threw it away?'

✠

What troubled Eckhardt privately, more than Ulrich's endless talk, was the fact that Elias Frankel had never spoken to him about these things. Elias was supposed to be his friend, but almost every day Eckhardt discovered something new about him.

He thought back to the summer, when Elias and the Monsieur were getting Otto ready for school. There was a lot of shouting and activity at the Frankel place at that time, and so Eckhardt had stayed away for several weeks. Elias did not come to tell him about the wolf, or where and why he was taking Otto, or anything else. At the time, Eckhardt did not suspect that he was being kept out of a secret; but now?

Yes, now he could see that Elias was excluding him. Eckhardt did not even know that the Monsieur had died, for example, until Frau Gröhlick told Eckhardt's father that Elias was up in the burial field, putting the man into the ground between Ida Frankel and the wood. *'Like beasts they lived . . .'* she had said, with a raised eyebrow. Eckhardt did not know what she meant, or why people thought that Elias had killed his stepfather. The Monsieur was drinking heavily because little Otto was going away to school. That was why he fell – wasn't it?

There were other things making him uneasy too; moments when Eckhardt felt that some part of Elias Frankel was still here at the store, watching him. It happened just the other day, when he was wringing the neck of the last chicken, and something made him turn around expecting to see Elias Frankel behind him, even though he knew he was alone. It also happened one night, when he woke with the idea that both of the Frankel boys were there in the bedroom with him, about to throw a sack or a fishing net over his head. Wavering between good memories and bad thoughts, Eckhardt wondered if it was right, after all, for Elias to put him in charge of the store. Why hadn't Elias sent a message of any sort to his old friend?

According to Ulrich, Eckhardt would never know the truth from Elias Frankel himself, because some people have secrecy and cunning in their blood.

To comfort himself, Eckhardt decided to look through a pack of cards that he had found among Elias's things. They were fortune-telling cards, according to Ulrich, and they could tell a man his destiny if he looked at them the right way. Eckhardt did not know the way to look at them, but he liked the colours, and the feel of the cards in his hands, and so while Ulrich worked on his journal, he studied each card in turn.

'What will we do if he comes back?' he asked.

Ulrich lifted his head to reply. 'We've been over this, Corporal. That's your side of things. You've got to be ready, and move fast if you have to.'

A moth hit the lamp, and dropped onto the heap of dead insects beneath.

# 23.

At eleven-thirty on a Monday morning at the end of November, a fortnight after Constable Theodore Hildebrandt had left his desk at the Mittelbach police station for the last time, three men walked into the public room of the Valley Inn. As there were no other guests in the room at that hour, the innkeeper had an uninterrupted view of his customers. One was more than six feet tall, he guessed – could be seven. One was four feet tall; and the other somewhere in between. Or, as the innkeeper would later tell it – in walked Big Bear, Little Bear and a shit-for-brains businessman who had stopped on the highway as he motored north, to give two strangers a ride.

The innkeeper stared as the mismatched trio took their seats, stared again as he took their order for soup, steaks with mustard, beer and coffee, and kept staring as he retreated, one foot behind the other, back to his observation post behind the bar. It couldn't be, could it? That wasn't . . .? He wouldn't . . .?

'Trying to catch flies in there?' the innkeeper's wife sneered, with a nod at his open jaw. He could manage only a whispered reply.

'It's him. Look!'

They looked together. The innkeeper calculated aloud, in a low voice, that the Mittelbach police station could be reached from here in, say, twenty minutes by foot, or ten if they sent the kitchen boy on his bicycle. 'We'll have to play this carefully,' he murmured. 'Keep him talking, don't let him get nervous. Then when they snatch him, we'll be at the front of the line for a reward.'

'What reward?' his wife said, refusing to whisper.

The innkeeper glared. Did she know nothing? Had she not heard of the infamous fugitive of Hindelheim, a man-beast descended from a race of giants in the East, with a taste for Christian blood? Look how pale the youth was, and how thin!

His wife replied that her husband was a moron if he believed a word of it, but instead of taking offence, the innkeeper gave her a cunning smile. Who said anything about believing it? He had merely heard comments of this kind spoken here in the bar; and if he knew the rumours, then so did other, more trusting and anxious souls. Think of the Mittelbach mothers who whispered Elias Frankel's name as a warning, commanding their children not to approach the young man if they saw him: would these parents not thank the innkeeper for removing a potential danger – however remote the threat might be?

And, he added, excited by a new thought: what about the policeman who had recently come up from town to replace the disgraced Constable Hildebrandt? Here was a perfect opportunity to lodge an early favour with this zealous new officer – what was his name now – Zelinsky, that was it! Officer Zelinsky.

'All right,' his wife finally agreed, pulling off her apron. 'I'll go up to the station. You talk to the customers, put that great gob of yours to good use.'

When the steaks were ready, the innkeeper carried them over and put one in front of each of the three guests. He made idle conversation, and found other excuses to loiter near the table while the businessman and the Frankel boys ate. His gaze returned again and again to the elder brother, who worked at his food with a bristled jaw. Only the businessman replied to the innkeeper's questions, explaining in a placid tone the nature of his business, and the length and frequency of his road trips. It was clear that the man did not live in the area, and that he had no idea about the dangerous identity of the passenger he had brought with him.

Then Elias Frankel spoke. 'When will Herr Dammertz be back?'

The innkeeper's eyes shot across the table. He could hardly believe that the runaway had asked this normal-seeming question, in words that could be understood. First ordering steaks in broad daylight, and now talking as if he were an ordinary citizen – the daring of it! But what was he trying to do, by asking such a thing?

'What makes you think he's staying here?' the innkeeper asked in return, talking to the crown of his head. Elias Frankel's black hair hung forward as he leaned over his plate, sawing, forking, chewing.

In reply the man looked up, straight up into the innkeeper's face – although straight was not the word for it, as one of his eyes looked askew – and without saying anything for a moment, he pointed to the centre of the room, where the inn's biggest dining table was set for a party of eight.

The table was indeed set for Herr Dammertz and his entourage, who had taken over the inn for the past week while the manufacturer negotiated with local farmers, landowners and suppliers. They were, as it happened, expected to return for an early lunch. But how did Elias Frankel know this? 'Either he's got people keeping him informed,' the innkeeper would later say, 'or the boy can see into a room from a distance, and know what's happening.'

✠

When the businessman finished his meal and left, with a polite bow to his companions, the innkeeper cleared the plates away and took a moment to recover his breath in the kitchen. Returning to the dining area, he found the two Frankel brothers sitting in silence over their empty plates. They seemed in no hurry to leave.

The small boy, Otto Frankel, pushed a stack of coins towards the innkeeper, who picked one up and bit into it, testing the metal with his teeth. Meeting Otto's solemn stare, he said, 'Excuse me if it seems like I don't trust you. It's not every morning we get a kid in here on a school day, eating lunch with a . . .' he waited until Elias raised his head, and then said it: 'a fugitive from the law.'

The fugitive and his stepbrother continued to stare. Their silence unnerved and provoked the innkeeper, who decided that he was not going to be intimidated. Not on his own premises. Not by a pair of young Jews. Dropping into a seat at the end of the table, he said, 'So now that you've crawled out from wherever it is you've been hiding, you might as well tell me what happened up there on the road, Elias Frankel.'

He paused to see if Elias would deny his name, and then continued. 'I heard it a dozen different ways from the men on the crew. There's one fellow swears you never even touched old Spiller: you just pointed that long finger at him and put a spell on the poor bugger so he'd drop down dead when you were gone, just as he did. So which was it, then? A lethal punch, or some kind of magic, a slow-working curse?'

Elias looked at him and replied, 'Are you sure you want to know?'

In a moment of hesitation, it occurred to the innkeeper that the worst rumours might, after all, be closest to the truth. 'I'm not saying you shouldn't have hit him, if that's what you did,' he said, 'or that you meant to kill him. That's not what I'm saying. I'm just giving you a chance to set the rumours straight.'

'Introduce me.'

'What?'

The fugitive's chin jerked upwards to the door, which slammed open as the three Dammertz children raced inside. Frau Dammertz swept in after them, tugging off a pair of gloves as she issued instructions to her young brood. The innkeeper rose to greet her, hoping that Madam's morning had passed well. As Frau Dammertz rattled off a reply – they had been to see a glass manufacturer about the supply of bottles to the new plant – the innkeeper glanced back at the table to find that Elias Frankel was still there, watching.

This was not good. Now the Dammertz family would want lunch – here was the manufacturer now, stepping in with his foreman – and they would see the police arrive. Herr Dammertz would not react well to such a disturbance. It was possible he would fly into a rage and take his family to stay elsewhere, in an inn that did not cater for violent renegades. The innkeeper would lose the best-paying guests he'd had in years, all thanks to this wretched runaway. If only the police officer had already come and gone, removing Elias Frankel from the dining room before Herr Dammertz came. If only that tardy wife of his had run up to Mittelbach instead of dawdling, damn her!

He scuttled off to serve the meal, moving to and fro with trays of soup. Every time he passed the Frankel boys' table, Elias would be staring at him as if to reissue his request. *Introduce me.* The innkeeper strove to ignore him. What kind of fool would take instruction from a criminal? *Introduce me.*

Herr Dammertz, seated in silver-haired dignity at the head of his party's table, was now the most powerful man in the district, following his purchase of parcels of land on either side of the valley road. Within the space of a few weeks, the manufacturer's holdings had grown to include vineyards, woodland, fields, barns and even a sawmill. In this quiet corner of the world, Herr Dammertz could make a man's fortune by bestowing his patronage, or break it by withdrawing his custom. Was the innkeeper going to risk offending him, merely to rid himself of the creeping unease that impinged on him with Elias Frankel's stare? *Introduce me*. No chance!

Elias Frankel stood up and crossed to the central table, causing a lull in the family's various conversations. Father, mother, sons, daughter and foreman looked up at the strange figure towering over them. In alarm, the innkeeper intervened.

'Excuse me, Herr Dammertz, but this young man from Hindelheim would like to pay his respects—'

'My name is Elias Frankel,' the other interrupted, moving his gaze around the table. 'But you would know me by my popular name. I'm the Wolf Man.'

✠

'Mama?' breathed the youngest of the Dammertz children, gazing up at the pale and hirsute face. Frau Dammertz took her hand.

Herr Dammertz, glaring under his silver-tipped eyebrows, said, 'We're hungry, Herr Frankel. Long morning. Why don't you say whatever it is you've got to say to my foreman here?' He indicated the man beside him.

'Because this is a matter for you,' Elias Frankel replied. He pulled out a chair and sat down, causing the innkeeper's pulse to race. 'Won't take more than a few minutes,' he continued. 'The innkeeper has sent his wife to inform the police that I'm here, which means they'll arrive at any moment to arrest me. I expect you know why?' He glanced at Frau Dammertz, who did her best not to flinch. 'Folk have got the impression that I killed a man on the road up there.'

The innkeeper, watching from behind the manufacturer's chair, thought he might have a heart attack. What to do? This was a disaster. Would that damned wife of his ever return with the policeman, as he'd asked her to?

'We've read the newspaper, if that's what you mean.' Herr

Dammertz looked his uninvited guest up and down. 'And what do you suppose I can do about your . . . situation?'

There was a pause before Elias Frankel replied, 'Anything you choose to. You have the mayor's ear. The mayor can control the rest of it, one way or another – whether to have me charged, and what for.'

Herr Dammertz smiled. 'Only children believe in Santa Claus, young man.' He turned to look over his shoulder, and with a frown of irritation, told the innkeeper to stop buzzing around like a fly, and leave them alone.

Retreating with an apology, the innkeeper tried unsuccessfully to hear the rest of the exchange between the manufacturer and the Wolf Man. At one point Elias Frankel drew a rolled-up document from inside his coat. The foreman looked at it, while Herr Dammertz tucked a napkin into his waistcoat and started on his soup.

What was happening? the innkeeper was burning to know. How was he going to relay the conversation to his other customers later? Herr Dammertz tore into a piece of bread, and said something that made his children laugh. Elias Frankel remained at the central table while across the room, his stepbrother waited.

After a few minutes, the door burst open and Officer Zelinsky marched into the room, with Deputy Constable Klaus Hildebrandt following behind. At last!

The new policeman seemed to possess everything that Theo Hildebrandt had lacked, the innkeeper thought, greeting Officer Zelinsky with relief. Here at last was a man of strength, an officer with a proper respect for the law he represented. It was gratifying to see him stride up to the table and pull Elias Frankel from his chair.

Neither the renegade himself nor any of the diners at the central table objected as Officer Zelinsky announced that Elias Frankel was under arrest. Locking the prisoner's arms together, the officer warned that there were four other men waiting outside to take him to the cell – so that this time, there would be no escape.

Herr Dammertz leaned to say something to his wife. Only Otto Frankel, at the far table, called out in protest, 'I'm his brother! I told him to steal the painting from the college. That was me! Take me with him!'

✠

Deputy Constable Klaus Hildebrandt put Elias Frankel in the holding cell, directing him to take a seat on the narrow plank of a bed. It was the first time in many months that anyone had been held here, other than the time when the former constable had led a group of children inside for a jest. The room was dark, damp and cold – but it was, now, secure. Klaus Hildebrandt had been preparing for some time to catch this particular prisoner. With the approval of his new supervisor, Officer Zelinsky, he had reinforced the door and changed the locks. But even without Zelinsky's oversight, Klaus would have approached the task of securing Elias Frankel with this same, solemn urgency. Now more than ever, following Theodore's sacking, the deputy needed to prove his worth. He must not, under any circumstances, repeat the mistake he had made with Elias Frankel on that fateful journey from Hindelheim.

This time, Klaus was not lying when he warned Elias that he had a gun. There was a pistol holstered to his belt, and the same was true of the two colleagues standing guard outside the cell. Bending to unlock the prisoner's handcuffs, the deputy issued his warning in a firm, quiet voice. 'Do not run. Do not move without prior permission or instruction.' He did not look into Elias Frankel's face as he spoke, but their heads were so close that Klaus could not avoid smelling the coffee on his breath and the smokiness of his coat. Beneath these smells of the civilised world, there was also a faint animal scent rising from the man;

but Klaus refused to find anything sinister in it. Anyone living a furtive life, on the run, would struggle to stay clean. For the same reason, Klaus did not let his eyes linger on Elias Frankel's fingernails, which had grown long and ragged; or on the stubble that covered his chin and throat.

He knew that the man would not attack him, or try to break from the cell, unless he was too dim to realise that the game had changed now: there were new and more aggressive hunters, all around, determined to bring this chase to an end.

Elias raised a freed hand to his neck, and pulled back the collar of his coat, which made a scratching sound against the stubble. 'This is yours,' he said.

With a start, Klaus saw the scarf that he had dropped into his prisoner's lap during that cold afternoon on the motorcycle, somewhere in the woods between Hindelheim and Mittelbach. He stared at it, recoiling from the thoughts it provoked.

From the yard came the sounds of hammering and voices, as building work progressed on the old stables, under Officer Zelinsky's direction. The Mittelbach substation was to be transformed, as Klaus had lately learned, into a central operating point for the region's transport police. An architect had arrived from Angenberg with one of Officer Zelinsky's assistants, bringing plans for the newly extended building. Klaus did not know when these plans had been drawn up, or whether his father had known of them, and it came as a surprise to the deputy and his wife when they were asked to move into lodgings in the village while the station house was redesigned.

Alarmed at the prospect of Officer Zelinsky finding out how his scarf came to be in Elias Frankel's possession, Klaus shook his head. 'Keep it.'

'That's it? You've got nothing better to say to me?'

Catching the man's look of defiance, Klaus thought fleetingly of his father, bringing his chin up at a challenge. Constable Theodore Hildebrandt would relish the question. He always had something to say, and it was never what the other person wanted to hear. But it was easy for him to court confrontation. The constable had no one's affection left to lose, whereas Klaus had a wife and infant son to guard.

He answered, 'You'll be taken to Angen tomorrow, to await your trial.'

'Wait,' Elias demanded, delaying him at the door. 'Herr Dammertz agreed to look after my brother. He's taking the store in exchange. Will you see that he keeps the bargain?'

Klaus felt a new resentment surge through him as he heard the implication behind this request. *I can ask you, because you're weak. I tell you to wait, and you obey. You'll do what I want.* No, he decided. Not any more. Without a backward glance, he turned out of the cell and heard one of the guards turn the lock behind him.

# 24.

Ute Koenig started feeling unwell as soon as she heard that Constable Hildebrandt had fallen from a horse and, according to the rumours, might not recover. Her own symptoms – shooting pains in her legs, a dull bellyache, dizziness and shortness of breath – came on so suddenly after hearing the news, that she could almost believe there was an unseen communication of some kind between her body and Theodore's.

Determined to ignore her relatively minor discomfort, Ute found an excuse to go to Mittelbach on the Pohlmann farm wagon. It was a bitterly cold, slow ride. Rain showers had alternated, in recent days, with the first snows; and on this morning, all the forces of winter seemed to combine in a gale of relentless, hurtling sleet which smacked into Ute's face whichever way she turned it. To open her eyes in the icy wind was a struggle, and when she did so – blinking off the moisture as more blew in – she noticed that Matthias Pohlmann, at the reins, wore no gloves, and his fingers were turning purple.

Not wanting Matthias to know where she was going, Ute got off in the centre of Mittelbach village and walked from there. With each numb and sodden footstep, memories of the place returned, increasing her urge to shiver. Five years ago, Ute had fainted in the post office here one afternoon, spilling coins all over the floor and prompting a flurry of whispered concern. She was helped by bystanders to the house of Doctor Rudolf, or 'Rudi', Hoffmann, an eccentric known to all in Mittelbach for his unsound views and unsavoury habit of offering treatment, and even friendship, to prostitutes.

Approaching the doctor's house again now, Ute hesitated. Would the constable recognise and welcome her, if he was conscious? How would she explain her visit, if there were others present?

Before Ute could answer her own questions, Rudi Hoffmann's housekeeper opened the door and stared.

'I understand that Constable Hildebrandt is here,' Ute said, 'under Doctor Hoffmann's care. I'd like to see him, if possible.'

The housekeeper replied without moving or shifting her gaze. 'Theodore Hildebrandt is no longer a police constable, Frau Koenig. And he's not well enough to receive visitors.' She paused. 'Unless they're members of his own family.'

Ute felt the colour deepen in her wind-chapped cheeks. Her first instinct was to stride over the doorstep and push inside, refusing to accept the woman's implicit judgement of her as an interloper. But while this response might soothe her own pride, it was no solution to the greater problem: Theodore Hildebrandt was injured, and Ute was powerless to help him. She might, at best, provide a few minutes of distraction from his pain; but what would be the lasting benefit? On the other hand, Ute felt – no, she *knew* – that there was something unspoken between them. Surely he would be glad to see her, no matter what the local observers thought?

Rudi Hoffmann's housekeeper, watching Ute's indecision, said, 'I'm going to shut the door now.'

'Wait.' She took a step forward. It was too soon to be sent away. That look on the constable's face when she had taken hold of his arm at the bonfire: if she could only provoke that look again, it would cheer him. 'Is he . . . Is Herr Hildebrandt recovering?'

The woman gave a measured nod. 'Yes.' She glanced over Ute's bedraggled figure, and then said, 'You should go home now.'

At this suggestion Ute pictured her dog, the Kaiser, waiting for her; and from there her skittish mind jumped to the kennels that had been vacated one morning two weeks ago, when Heinrich had left his wife and son, and moved into the Pohlmann farm.

A parallel between these situations nagged at Ute, calling for attention. Had anyone told Heinrich to go home, she wondered, when he started his affair with the fifteen-year old Gretchen Pohlmann? If so, Heinrich had ignored the advice, and seized what he wanted. Now he would be a kind of husband to the girl, which suited him; but if Gretchen changed her mind after the baby, that would be too bad for her, because she would not find another match. Here was the similarity: Ute suspected that she, like Heinrich, was doing what she wanted without regard for the effects of her actions on other people. If she insisted on seeing the constable, it would damage the reputation of two men, one of whom had already suffered many kinds of fall.

Looking again at the housekeeper, Ute saw that the woman was not, in fact, forbidding her, but warning her against the likely outcome of this visit. Perhaps in a few days or weeks, Ute thought, when her head was clearer, she would write a second and final letter to Herr Hildebrandt – briefer this time, wishing him well.

Eventually reaching a decision, she thanked the housekeeper for her help – *no, no message* – and turned away.

✢

Returning from Mittelbach with a sore throat and worse shivering, Ute crawled into bed on Peter's instruction. It was a seasonal cold, he said, which would pass with a few days' rest. He challenged her to prescribe her own remedy, using the pharmacology book she had borrowed; but the book had lost its appeal to Ute weeks ago, as soon as Peter said she was welcome to read it. This was often the way between the two of them, she recognised: they had a tendency to resist one another, each of them finding more pleasure in the push-and-pull than in the static interludes.

Minutes after sending Ute to bed, at four o'clock that afternoon, Peter decided to follow. He climbed into the bed, fully dressed, and made fierce, brisk love to his wife's aching body, before returning to his work downstairs.

The next morning Ute lay alone, staring up from the bed at a square of grey-white light in the window. The days were getting shorter, and above the trees, the sky was burdened with snow. Despite an intermittent fever, Ute's body heat failed to rid the sheets of their stubborn, damp chill, and so in the early afternoon she headed downstairs, intending to fill a warming pan with hot coals and bring it up again.

Halfway down the stairs she heard excited voices in the hall below. Two people, out of sight, were telling someone – presumably Helga – that Elias Frankel had been arrested. *They got him, yesterday afternoon! We heard it from—*

But Ute did not stay to hear how they heard it. Running back up the stairs, she threw on an assortment of clothes, and then tumbled out of the house by the back door, followed by the Kaiser. There was no clear purpose in her mind beyond a wish to mark – more than that; to feel – Elias Frankel's absence and changed prospects.

Approaching the Frankel place from the lane, she saw Frau Gröhlick knocking on the front door and calling to her stepson. 'Eckhardt? Let me in!'

Swerving to avoid the woman's gaze – there was something owl-like about Frau Gröhlick's ability to see behind her – Ute ducked into the school field, where the new schoolmaster was teaching his pupils to play football, disregarding the field's recent, and still fairly light, covering of snow. Returning the man's greeting with a raised hand, Ute tried the gate into the Frankels' yard. It was locked, so she climbed it, warning the dog to follow her quietly behind the empty hen huts and over the snow-dusted paddock.

As she turned to glance back at the building, Eckhardt Gröhlick stepped out from behind a scrawny winter hedge.

'Oh,' she said. 'Eckhardt. Your stepmother's at the door.'

'What?' A frown drew up his cheeks and buried his eyes.

'Frau. Gröhlick,' Ute repeated, trying to speak clearly. She pointed over his shoulder. 'She's looking for you. Are you hiding?'

He nodded at this, and Ute answered with a look of understanding. The woman had married his father Hans Gröhlick during the war. Swiftly establishing herself as the dominant member of the local School Board, Frau Gröhlick had taught Ute in Hindelheim's schoolhouse from the age of twelve to eighteen, and thereafter trained and supervised her as a junior teacher. The experience of being at Frau Gröhlick's command had given Ute a sense of kinship with Eckhardt, even though they rarely spoke. She knew that Frau Gröhlick had made her stepson sleep outside for the night of his twenty-seventh birthday because he had broken a vase.

'Eckhardt,' she said, waiting for him to look at her before giving him the news. 'Elias Frankel has been arrested.'

Eckhardt's mouth fell open a little, and he breathed hard, thinking about this. He pressed his palm into the back of his head, as if to rub away a thought. 'What will happen?' he asked.

'I don't know. They're holding him at Mittelbach, I think. Perhaps there will be a trial.'

'A trial. When?'

Ute shook her head. 'I don't know.' After a while, she turned

247

away from him and continued down the paddock until it ended at the stream. There the Kaiser nosed along the bank, watching for fish, barking as bubbles came and went over the stones. The water ran fast and cold between a scattering of trees.

Finding that Eckhardt had followed her, she pointed to a spot where the branches of two beech trees, one on either side of the stream, stretched towards each other, almost meeting. 'Do you remember when we used to fix a rope-bridge here, in the summertime?' she asked.

Eckhardt did not reply, and perhaps had not heard her. But he turned his head towards her a moment later, and said, 'Is it because of the Monsieur?'

Ute's drowsy mind took a moment to follow this change of topic. 'The Monsieur. You mean . . . how he died? That was a heart attack, Eckhardt. Nothing to do with Elias. Is that what you heard? That Elias pushed the Monsieur down those stairs?'

He shrugged, without meeting her gaze. Ute turned to look back at the building, where in Ida Frankel's day there would have been a constant flow of voices and baking smells drifting out through the fly curtain at the back door. After Ida's death, the noises changed. From her aunt's cottage, and sometimes from the schoolhouse, Ute would hear the Monsieur's solitary singing, and increasingly, his drunken shouts. Then one June day he collapsed on the top step, and crashed down the rest of the staircase, and an eerie silence fell over the Frankel place. No one except Elias had witnessed the fall, but Ute remembered every minute of the days leading up to it: that was the week when Elias had maybe, or maybe not, encountered a wolf.

'It's just not possible,' Ute insisted. 'Elias Frankel wasn't here when the Monsieur fell,' she lied. 'He'd gone to Angen to register Otto at his new school.' In fact, Elias had returned on the Thursday night, and the Monsieur died the next day, on Friday; but Ute doubted that Eckhardt's memory of events would be as clear as hers. With so many people – Marlyse, apparently, included – willing to invent or exaggerate Elias Frankel's faults, it seemed no crime to add one lie in his favour.

Eckhardt said nothing, but kicked something into the stream. Ute, standing with him, felt her fever return – and with it, a vague, new sense of disquiet.

⊹

In Theodore's dream, Ute Koenig's face came and went and merged with other faces, from other periods of his life. He opened his eyes to find Francesca, his son's wife, standing over him, complaining about his recklessness and the cost – she meant also, the inconvenience – of keeping such a foolhardy old man alive. It was like having a second baby to feed and watch, she said. Theodore heard a child wailing and thought, *Klaus, my son*.

When he came round again, Rudi Hoffmann was sitting beside the bed, ignoring his patient as he told someone a story. Theodore could not see who was listening. Though he tried to concentrate, he found that his brain or ears would not connect the pieces into a coherent whole. The doctor seemed to be saying, ' . . . rumour that he died in the earth . . . one of the . . . shell of a man trapped between worlds . . .'

He coughed himself awake, and the cough turned into a heave. Something bitter flooded his throat and burst its banks, jerking him forward in an explosion of nausea.

'Dried blood,' the doctor said, turning at last to look at him. His bloodshot eyes loomed. 'You broke your nose as well as your collar bone, so there'll be some debris to clear out if you decide to stay with us. I'm not making any assumptions on that front, by the way. The gypsy who delivered you here said you've been trying to get yourself killed. It would be unlucky for them, I gather, if you were to succeed on one of their horses, which is why they decided to transfer you elsewhere. My couch is rather more neutral, so if you want to die on it, I won't interfere.'

249

He followed this with a brief burst of laughter. Klaus Hildebrandt stepped to the bed and looked down at his father, but said nothing.

'The horse?' Theodore asked.

Klaus nodded. 'Unharmed, as far as I know. No thanks to—'

'I know,' he cut in. 'No thanks. Bloody horse. Never get a word out of them.'

Rudi Hoffmann obliged him by chuckling at this. Klaus did not.

'Elias Frankel's in the jail at headquarters,' Klaus said. 'Officer Zelinsky drove him down there yesterday. I suppose you know that Zelinsky's now . . .?'

'Mm,' Theodore agreed, not wanting to hear it. 'How's he treating you?'

After a brief hesitation, which Theodore noticed, Klaus said, 'Well. Everything's in order.'

'Uh-oh.'

Another spasm in his chest interrupted. Doctor Hoffmann moved in, pressing a hand against his patient's ribs, and then through a region of pain beneath. 'That hurt?'

When Theodore could breathe, he answered, 'Hellfire.'

'Good,' said Rudi.

Whenever the doctor moved out of the way, Theodore looked at Klaus and saw, each time, a different shade of emotion on his son's face.

'What fascinates me,' Rudi mused, 'is the relationship between a man's face and his . . . I don't much care for the term "soul" . . . his view of the world. The pattern he sees in the universe, do you follow? This scar of yours, Theo, wandering as it does from the outer corner of the eyelid to let-us-not-speculate-where: ugly as sin, to most people.'

'I have to go,' Klaus said, and turned away.

'Most people look in the mirror and see symmetry – one side of the oval matching the other. And so they look to the world expecting balance. A proportionate distribution of justice or anything else. Whereas you, my friend, are blessed . . . or crippled . . . with extreme asymmetry. Now does that cause or follow from your stubbornness, I wonder?'

Theodore's gaze followed Klaus to the door and stayed there. He did not reply.

✛

Peter drew back the curtain, and sat down on the edge of their bed. Watching him from the pillows, Ute thought that he moved with a preoccupied, expectant air. As he felt her forehead to check her temperature, he was humming a tune.

'What day is it?' she asked, in a hoarse voice.

'The last day of this bug, I trust. Drink,' he said, removing the spoon from a glass and passing the glass to her. A few grains of powder remained undissolved on the surface of an otherwise clear solution. 'Right to the end,' he urged quietly.

When she had emptied the glass, Peter rearranged her pillows and said that he expected her to be in rosy health when he returned from town.

'Stefan's?' Ute said. She vaguely remembered, but her fever had taken a delirious turn, confusing the boundary between sleep and waking. Everything seemed distant, in space and time.

Peter nodded. He would stay with Stefan for the next three nights, until Sunday, in order to fetch the journal from the printer's and discuss the next one. 'I've told Wilma not to expect you this time,' he said. 'Is that right?'

Ute replied with a slow smile, 'Best to hide me away while you advance the nation's health.' Intending it as an offhand reference to her cold, she was surprised by Peter's reaction.

Looking at her, he said seriously, 'I've always defended you, old girl. You know that, don't you?'

A protest started to form, silently, in Ute's mind. Perversely, she did not want to be defended. The resistance again.

'I'll look in on the trial while I'm in town,' Peter said, standing. 'See how this sorry business with Elias Frankel ends.'

*Trial.* As the word penetrated the sludge of her mind, Ute lurched forward. 'Oh then I'll come.' But the movement made her dizzy, and she allowed herself to sink back down. 'So that's why,' she said. 'That's why you were humming just now.'

'Was I?' Peter paused at the foot of the bed.

Ute looked at him and asked, 'Will this end it for you?'

'Hmm?'

'The Frankels never set out to hurt you, Peter.'

He returned a quick, bright glance. 'Are you his advocate?'

'No,' Ute said. 'Elias barely knows I exist.'

'And yet you leap to defend him, attend to him, adore him – you and everyone else!' Peter gesticulated with sudden indignation, from the end of the bed. 'That squint of his – from looking at the sun, do they say? No. It's everyone else who is blinded. Dazzled by the wonder of the Frankels, until they can no longer see anything straight!'

'You most of all,' Ute agreed.

Peter heard her accusation but did not respond to it. After a short silence he turned away, without saying goodbye. By the time the door closed behind him, Ute was asleep.

# 25.

He had been expecting a visit from Zelinsky. It came one evening when he was sitting up for the first time, alone on Rudi Hoffmann's couch, pulling his clothes with slow and painful movements onto his ever-more-clownish body. His naked torso, reflected in the dark window, almost formed a question mark, hollowed under the ribs on one side. It seemed to ask, *What now?*

Theodore played along with the officer's pretence that this was a courtesy call. He endured Zelinsky's taunts about the riding accident, his humiliating dismissal, and the ruinous state of his reputation and prospects. He nodded when Zelinsky praised the zeal with which Klaus Hildebrandt had locked Elias Frankel in the holding cell, and even managed to agree that 'the boy' – as Zelinsky now referred to Klaus – would do better, and learn more, under the direction of his new supervising officer.

Only when Zelinsky started to gloat about tomorrow's trial of Elias Frankel, and the severity of the punishment that would follow, did Theodore cut him short.

'So tell me,' he said. 'Now that you've won the race to net the rascal, what exactly do you think you've got in the bag? I didn't get much of a look at him back there at the boxing hall. What kind of creature is he?'

The officer leaned forward in his chair, hands interlinked, and replied with a grin, 'One careless young man, who at this moment is wishing he had never tried to run from me.'

Theodore considered this. 'Not a wolf-child?'

Zelinsky scoffed. 'Come on.'

'No demonic powers? No wildness in him?'

Suspecting a trap, the officer said, 'What are you up to, Hildebrandt?'

In reply, Theodore moved the arm that was not in a sling away from his chest, to reveal his pathetic physique. After an hour of fumbling, he had struggled into a vest and cotton leggings. 'I'm unarmed, Officer. No weapons. I haven't set a trap under your chair. I've just been lying there, with my back to the fiery pit,' he said, 'thinking about what we've been doing, what we've been fighting. What's our real enemy – the Wolf Man of Hindelheim, half man, half beast? That's peasant logic – otherwise known as lunacy.'

He earned a quick smile from Zelinsky, and continued. 'But it's not lunatics or peasants who put this stuff into circulation. There are grown men out there talking about a wolf man. Men with better breeding than you or I, Zelinsky. They don't believe it. But they listen. Behind the knowing smile there's a tinge of, let's say, curiosity. Walking home from the bar, or the office, they see a shadow across the pavement, hear footsteps, feel a chill down the spine. Think: "Who . . . what was that?"'

Zelinsky waited then spread his hands. 'One or two drunken clots, maybe. I have more faith in the good sense of our townsmen than you do, Hildebrandt. The ordinary man wants the law enforced. That's all. He's indignant, as he should be.'

Theodore nodded agreement. 'So there he is in the Angenberg Courthouse, your ordinary man, to see justice done, truth revealed, harm punished and prevented. He wants some explanations.' Using the fingers of his unbandaged hand, Theodore itemised. 'Elias Frankel pays a visit one Sunday to a

254

house with a newborn child. Three days later, the child is dead. Elias Frankel is arrested by Klaus Hildebrandt. Within hours, Klaus Hildebrandt is thrown off his motorcycle. A road worker tries to stop Elias Frankel, who hits him. Two days later, the road worker is dead.' He paused to frown. 'But will Elias be questioned about these . . . I don't know what to call them. Effects?'

'I damn well hope so.'

'Because he caused them? How?'

Zelinsky's eyes narrowed as he replied, 'You're trying to get me to say that the man's some sort of a witch, but it won't happen, Hildebrandt. Unlike you, I know my limits. I'm a police officer. I arrested him. The rest is for the judge to decide.'

'You mean, the judge will decide what kind of harm he's caused to his victim or victims, if any, and by what means?'

Officer Zelinsky met his glance but did not answer it.

'Are you afraid he'll harm you?' Theodore asked. He saw a slight twitch of the eyebrow – surprise? concern? – and pressed on. 'You arrested him, Zelinsky. You're trying to get him locked away! If you succeed, well, good luck to you. Surely you've noticed what happens to people who cross the path of our Wolf Man.'

The officer replied, 'You're full of shit, Hildebrandt,' and stood to leave.

Theodore moved to the window, which was almost in darkness. He heard the door slam, and the crunch of the officer's boots on the day's new fall of snow. Pressing his fingernails to the windowpane, he dragged them down the glass with a high, jarring sound that made Zelinsky stop in his tracks and look around.

❖

On the morning of the trial, the tramcar that passed in front of the Angenberg Courthouse deposited a greater load of passengers there than usual. The snow underfoot was soon dirtied and flattened, while the nearest café ran out of cake before nine o'clock. Waiting for the doors to open, people blinked snowflakes from their eyelashes and repeated to each other what they had heard from someone else.

Among them were several individuals with no knowledge or interest in the activities of Elias Frankel. These passers-by had stopped to see why others were waiting, or had spied a public building with the lights on, and come to spend a few hours in the warmth. There was also a middle-aged couple who attended every trial, funeral, rally or public ceremony in the town, regardless of who or what was being commemorated. The man wore a ceremonial sword, and his wife carried a tapestry cushion, in order to be ready for any length or style of occasion.

A placard bobbed above and through the waiting crowd. In hand-painted letters that became smudged in places as the snow melted on it, the card warned, 'BEWARE AND GUARD YOUR CHILDREN. THE WOLF MAN IS COMING!'

When the placard reached the edge of the crowd at the foot of the courthouse steps, it was smacked to the ground by one of six young people who stood together there, glowering in opposition. Another member of the group shoved the sign-bearer in the back, causing heads to turn as he fell. The six sign-smashers were supporters of Elias Frankel – fellow highwaymen, ruffians and underdogs, as they saw it. Lovers of freedom and enemies of convention. One of the young men in the group had previously tangled with the law himself, and was loud with sympathy for the misunderstood Wolf Man. The female supporters each carried a single red rose, which they planned to throw at the feet of the prisoner as he was escorted from the jail.

As the doors of the courthouse opened, the six supporters saw that they were being kept apart from their chained and maligned fellow-in-arms. Either the accused was already inside, or he was to be led there by an underground passage, concealed from public view, in order to prevent his allies from calling encouragement. The authorities were trying to break his spirit. They were going to kill him twice – once with hatred, and then with their so-called justice, which was nothing but a charade.

✠

Ute woke alone, feeling nauseous but rested. Sitting up, she found her hand resting on a piece of paper. Or rather, several small scraps of paper, torn from an exercise book. Some of them bore her handwriting: . . . *puzzling* . . . *you said* . . . *sorts of questions* . . .

Sifting through the scraps, she recognised them as fragments of the first letter she had started to compose to Constable Hildebrandt, some weeks ago, in the guestroom of Stefan and Wilma's house, before tearing it up and starting a second. She had brushed the rejected scraps into the wastebasket – hadn't she? Or had they somehow got folded up with her nightdress and other things in her suitcase, and from there spilled unnoticed into this bed, here by Peter's pillow?

With a knock on the door, Helga came into the room with a tray of coffee and dry toast. As she set it down and opened the curtains, Ute asked if she knew anything about this old letter she'd been lying on. When Helga said that she did not, Ute ran through all the possibilities she could think of, and then settled on the first one that had sprung into her mind.

She took the toast with an unsteady hand, and found that she was hungry for it. Ravenous, in fact. Unable to wait for Helga to pour the coffee, she crunched and gulped, forcing the dry bread down her dry throat. Seizing the cup when it was offered, she gulped that too.

Hovering beside her, Helga said, 'Will you have a little tonic?' Her aged hand gestured at a bottle that stood on the tray. Brown glass, with an old, stained cork.

Ute looked from the bottle to Helga, and asked, 'Did Peter suggest it?'

The housekeeper hesitated, her expression closed as always. The woman's lips formed a single line, slightly thicker and slightly darker than the other lines of her face. Eventually she replied, 'No, dear. But I don't think it will do you any harm. It's only a cordial, made with sugar, and cherries, and I think a little brandy . . .'

'With a touch of Ida Frankel's magic,' Ute said, reaching for the bottle. Under Helga's gaze, she pulled the cork and smelled it, remembering. 'Aunt Ernesta used to keep her supply under the bed, so that she could reach out and clobber any would-be thief who approached during the night.' She turned the bottle in her hands, feeling a slight stickiness around the neck. The liquid reached two thirds of the way up the bottle. It moved sluggishly when tilted. 'Whenever she drank it,' Ute continued, 'or "tasted" it, as she would say, her nose turned red, and the world became a better place.'

'Yes,' Helga agreed. 'It has that effect. Perhaps there is a fair dose of brandy.'

'Was that Ida Frankel's secret, do you think?' Ute asked. 'Was it the brandy that made people feel good in her company?'

Helga, as expected, did not want to answer. 'I wouldn't like to say.'

Turning to the tray, Ute found a clean glass on it. 'You have this one,' she said, 'and I'll use the cup. Have you ever been drunk before noon, Helga?'

'Yes, dear,' the woman replied, with the first hint of a smile. 'But not for many years.'

✠

Theodore Hildebrandt accepted a lift to town in the back of Officer Zelinsky's motor car. Following Klaus Hildebrandt and two other former colleagues into the courthouse, he turned towards the public benches, while the policemen turned the other way into the courtroom, to take their seats behind the court officials.

Scanning the four rows of public spectators, Theodore was disappointed not to see Ute Koenig's face among them. Nor were any members of her husband's family here. There was no sign of the mayor, of course – or of Herr Dammertz, or Chief Inspector Lorentz Streicher. Albert Dinter, the reporter, stood to one side, at the end of a row, poised to slip out once the proceedings became tiresome. He seemed restless already. Marlyse Pohlmann was not with him, Theodore noted. A small mercy.

Gustav Spiller's widow was already seated when they arrived. Officer Zelinsky had made a point of striding over to her and leaning down to shake the widow's hand, further cementing the connection between her private grief and this public swell of anger – if it was anger, and not something more mundane, like despair.

Theodore's sweep of the crowd ended on his son, seated at the far side of the room between Zelinsky and another policeman. Studying his withdrawn expression, Theodore thought: *This is Klaus Hildebrandt's trial too – and my own.*

A latecomer sat down in front of him, causing several others on that bench to shuffle along, to make room. Theodore studied the back of his head – ginger-brown hair, trimmed above a slightly frayed collar – and silently urged himself to leave it. Not your business. *Tact, Theo.* Leave it alone. The murmuring around him was constant but muted, as everyone waited for the trial to start.

Leaning forward, Theodore said, 'Here alone, Koenig?'

The neck straightened, and then twisted to allow the doctor's colourless eyes to fall briefly on him. 'Ute's unwell,' he replied, then turned back.

Theodore felt a pang of disappointment. Then a second, of suspicion. 'Just a winter cold, I hope?'

There was no reply.

'If I were to ask you to send my regards to her,' he continued, 'would they make it all the way to Hindelheim? Or might they vanish mysteriously into the wind, or into a hole in the ground, as things do up there?'

The conversation beside him stopped, and one or two spectators in the row ahead turned to see who was talking, before falling silent to listen. Clearing his throat, Peter Koenig turned again, this time twisting his shoulder in order to look directly at Theodore. He replied, 'Just this once, Hildebrandt, I will make an exception to my usually high standards of behaviour, sufficient to say that I'm glad I see the world through my eyes, and not through yours. You are a rude, sour man. Neither my wife nor I want any further dealings with you. Is that understood?'

Now everyone was listening. From the far side of the courtroom, Klaus Hildebrandt noticed the sudden, tense silence on the public benches, and looked over at his father. The other policemen looked too, spotting Theodore without difficulty, since he sat on the end of the row, with his arm in a sling and a walking stick jutting into the aisle. Officer Zelinsky murmured to a colleague, and grinned at his old enemy's new humiliation.

✠

Ute took another slug of the syrupy liquid, licked her lips, and offered her hand to the Kaiser. It was ten o'clock in the morning, and the three of them sat close together on the bed, enjoying the intoxicating effects of Ida Frankel's tonic; Ute slumped against the pillows, Helga sitting on the edge of the bed, and the dog lying in between.

'When we've finished the bottle,' Ute said, 'will you help me to pack up my things?'

Helga looked at her with apprehension. 'Which . . . ?'

'All of them,' Ute replied, casting her gaze around the room. One side of the wardrobe, and the lowest of three drawers in Peter's chest, held what she had brought with her from the cottage, which was all she needed. Her coat, hat and winter boots were downstairs, along with a faded tennis ball belonging to the Kaiser.

'Will you be away for long?' the housekeeper asked. Receiving a nod, she went on, 'And you're going today, before Peter gets back?'

'Yes,' Ute said. She lifted the bottle to see what was left, and poured half of it into her cup, and the rest into Helga's glass, ignoring the woman's brief resistance.

Helga took a sip, her eyes busy with concern. She said, 'Will you leave him a note?'

Ute looked again at the torn fragments of the letter which Peter must have kept hoarded all this time. It was evidence of a sort, and by leaving it on the pillow before he left, he had made a kind of accusation. But it was not only that, she thought. She could see something gentler in the gesture too – an invitation, a plea, even an admission of defeat. 'In actual fact, he left me a note,' she replied. 'Peter and I have . . . taken what we needed from each other. I wonder if that makes any sense to you?'

Helga studied her carefully, and gave a slight nod.

They fell into another silence, until the housekeeper finished her glass and replaced it on the tray. She turned her mild face towards the window and said, 'Another fall of snow last night. You'll find it sharp outside, dear.'

'Then I'll wear socks over my stockings,' Ute decided. She wondered how it was possible to feel so elated, and so bereft, in a single moment.

⁜

'Look!'

A young girl, sitting on her mother's knee in the centre of the public seating area, pointed up at the domed cupola of the courthouse, where a decorative detail in the plasterwork had caught her eye. In the row behind her, several adults followed her gaze with an intake of breath, as if expecting to see the shape-shifting Wolf Man suspended in the air above them, or drifting in from a high window as a gust of demonic smoke. While they were looking for him in the heights of the courthouse ceiling, Elias Frankel entered from a side door, in a suit, and took his seat as directed by a court officer.

The judge's introductory remarks made clear to all present that the day's proceedings against Elias Frankel would involve nothing more serious than a charge of disruptive conduct, and would be confined in space and time to the defendant's journey in a motorcycle sidecar from Hindelheim to the roadworks near Mittelbach, where he was accused of having ignored the request of a local deputy constable to wait at the side of the road, and from whence he removed, without prior consent, two items of police equipment, viz. one pair of handcuffs, and the key to those handcuffs.

Having thus outlined the charge, the judge proceeded to read from a stack of police reports and other documents, in a monotone, with head bowed.

A murmur of discontent rippled across the benches, becoming audible in the seats around Gustav Spiller's widow. Friends of the dead road worker were aghast that Elias Frankel's assault on poor Spiller – clearly a murder, albeit of an indirect and sinister kind – was not even mentioned. Not even a charge of accidental killing! Was it a mistake? Where were the charges of violent menace? What about all the other unexplained and deviant acts that had left victims trembling across the region?

The onlookers' dissatisfaction took various forms. Some grumbled at the wasted trip, and stood to leave. Others leaned forward, frowning, as if to urge on a sprinter who had fallen behind, and then gradually, minute by minute, grew tired and left too. Both supporters and accusers of Elias Frankel felt cheated. Where was the scandal they had been led to expect?

The judge was either dim-witted or corrupt, many agreed. Mumbling in that dull voice of his about the most minor infractions, while ignoring all of the runaway's worst crimes – what was wrong with him? Had Elias Frankel put a charm on him? Had Jewish lawyers been working behind the scenes to turn the judge into this tame, toothless thing?

For showing insufficient respect to members of the regional

police force, and for failing to respond promptly to the summons put out for him, Elias Frankel would spend three weeks in the Angenberg jail, the judge declared to a diminished audience shortly before one o'clock in the afternoon. During this period of internment, the young ward, Otto Frankel, would be cared for by a charitable institution at the personal expense of a benefactor who preferred not to be named in court.

Hearing the sentence, Theodore Hildebrandt glanced across the room to see if Klaus Hildebrandt would share his relief. But the deputy was already on his feet and turning away, following the intemperate commands of his new boss, Officer Zelinsky.

✠

Ute and Helga worked quietly, side by side, deciding what would be worn and what carried. In order to save room in the suitcase, and as protection against the cold, Ute pulled socks over her stockings, and wore two vests, her aunt's over her own. Next, a shirt, buttoned to the neck. A woollen waistcoat which had belonged to her cousin Jurgen before the war, and which was still loose, even after several attempts at alteration. Over it, a jacket which almost matched the skirt, darned in only two places.

In the mirror, she saw her cheeks blazing with fever and exhilaration. Apart from washing the sleep from her eyes, she had done nothing to improve her face. The hair, all out of place, would be contained by a hat. That would have to do.

Shutting the case, Helga said, 'I'll fetch you something from the kitchen to take. Is there anything in particular . . .?'

'One thing,' Ute agreed, turning to face her. 'But not from the kitchen. I'd like to ask you something, Helga. Will you stay for a little while longer?'

Apprehension returned to the housekeeper's face. She threw a glance at the door. 'I ought to check on Wilhemina. She's been alone for the past hour.'

Unable to object to this, Ute nodded. 'Of course. Thank you, Helga.'

Helga lingered. 'What were you going to ask?'

She wants to hear it, Ute thought. *She wants to tell somebody.* 'I was going to ask what happened that afternoon,' she replied. 'When I went out with the Kaiser and came back to find you at the scullery sink, scrubbing mud from their boots. Do you remember?' After a pause, she went on. 'There was one boot in your hand and several others lined up on the washboard. I guess three pairs. Heinrich's and Peter's and Johanna's.'

At this Helga lowered herself in silence onto a straight-backed wooden chair, where she sat with hands together, knees together, feet together; providing, as she always did, a point of stillness in the room.

Ute took a seat opposite her, on the end of the bed. She continued. 'All three of them were outside that afternoon, getting mud on their boots. Johanna would normally be resting with Dirk. Heinrich would normally take the dogs out, alone. Peter . . .' She shook her head. 'I hardly remember him going into the garden at any time since I've lived here. But on that day, that . . . dry, crisp October Sunday, Peter decided to help Heinrich – Heinrich, the gardener! – clear fallen branches and other debris to make a bonfire. To *make* a fire, not to light it. Whose idea was that, I wonder? Did they go outside, all three of them, with that purpose – to build a bonfire?'

'No,' Helga answered. 'That came later. They went outside to bury her.'

Ute took this in. 'So Maria-Theresa was already dead when I left the house,' she said. It was only partly a question. 'Or else soon after.'

'I wouldn't know when, exactly,' Helga replied. She touched her face and added, 'Peter said the child died naturally, in her sleep.'

Ute left a silence, to show that she doubted this. Then she

prompted Helga again. 'Why the hasty burial?'

Helga shook her head. 'They disagreed about it. Johanna wanted to be alone with Heinrich, just the two of them. Peter told them to wait until the notifications were done and so on, but Heinrich wouldn't wait another minute. He snatched up a spade, and the other two followed. Peter looked nervous going out. I suppose he was thinking about whether any questions might be asked later.'

'Yes,' Ute said. She remembered his agitation that evening, so severe that it convinced her, for those first few hours, that the baby had gone missing.

'I was in the kitchen, watching Dirk,' Helga went on. 'Johanna came back half an hour later, on her own, white in the face. Exhausted. Almost before she'd got her coat off, there was a knock at the back door. Johanna stood close by, at the window there, listening while I opened it. It was Elias Frankel, with a parcel of brown paper in his hand, asking for Johanna. I – I didn't know what to say.'

Breaking off, she dropped her gaze and twisted a narrow band of gold that was buried in her swollen, weathered left hand.

'I said, "She's resting, with the baby",' Helga resumed. 'It was out of my mouth before I could think of anything better. It wasn't meant to make things worse for them.' Here she looked up with an expression of startled appeal, almost panic. It was the first time Ute had seen Helga's self-possession threatened by strong emotion. 'I only thought,' she explained, 'I thought they wouldn't want anyone knowing that they were . . . out there, burying her. It was private. A private burial.'

Ute, watching the woman, quietly steered her back. 'What did Elias say?'

Helga's eyes moved from side to side, retrieving the moment. 'Nothing to me. I gave the parcel to Johanna. We heard their voices outside – Elias, and then Heinrich, arguing. Harsh voices, close to the house. I expect Elias saw them digging as he turned away from the door, and Heinrich came over . . .'

'To distract him,' Ute agreed. She took a moment to picture it, and then added, 'He wouldn't have welcomed Elias at the grave. Neither would Peter. How did Johanna react?'

'She went back outside, as soon as Elias had gone – when Heinrich had chased him off. I don't know what she said or what they . . . agreed. I was still in the kitchen, you see, busy with Dirk and Wilhemina, and worrying I'd said the wrong thing to Elias. Now he would think the baby was still alive. But maybe that wouldn't matter, I thought. I didn't see that it would matter so much what Elias Frankel knew, since he's alone at the store – he *was* alone there, at that time, I mean – with only customers to talk to, and why would any of them ask him about Johanna's baby?' She looked up.

Ute started to search for an answer to that question, and then decided not to. If there was something between Johanna and Elias, she preferred not to know.

'But then Peter came in,' Helga went on, pausing to catch her breath as her distress grew. 'He came to the kitchen, and told me it was very . . . very unfortunate that I'd said what I said.' She brushed a hand over her face. 'Because now there might be questions. A neighbour might ask . . .' She glanced at Ute. 'Or you might hear one thing at home, and another at the store. And so Peter said we would have to find a way to – to delay the burial, even though it had already happened.'

'To delay the burial,' Ute repeated, 'for a day or two, while they . . . you . . . made it seem that the baby was still alive.'

'To put things in the right order,' Helga agreed, with a sigh. 'That's what Peter wanted.'

# 26.

*What Peter wanted.* Ute considered this once Helga had left the room. Remaining seated at the end of her husband's bed, beside the packed suitcase, Ute knew that she needed a few more minutes here, to solve it in her mind. Then she could go.

What did he want? She guessed that what Peter wanted, at that moment, on the day of Maria-Theresa's death, when Elias Frankel had arrived unexpectedly and walked dangerously close to the baby's open grave, was a complex assortment of desires – only some of which he would have recognised in that moment.

Certainly he wanted to 'put things in the right order', as Helga said. Peter liked order. He wanted to be in the right. It must have made him squirm, Ute thought, to write a lie on the death certificate – not only about the cause of death, but about the date. That administrative impropriety would upset him. He wanted to be a good doctor; to be better than his father, in deed and reputation. And although he would be sure of his right to kill a handicapped baby for the sake of purifying the bloodline, using the reasoning of Stefan von Brodnitz to ward off any qualms, Peter would not carelessly flaunt his crime. He would want to be safe from suspicion in the eyes of the law.

But he also wanted not to be safe, Ute thought. She had felt this before, on several occasions, catching a reckless look in

Peter's eye, or hearing him make an aggressive remark. In bed, too, there were often times when Ute was surprised by his desire to be brought to the edge of pain or danger. It was as if Peter was always looking for a fight and, at the same time, afraid to lose it. *He is still competing*, she thought. *Peter is still competing with Elias for his father's attention.*

She moved to the window. Beneath her, the garden lay sheathed in snow, fringed by the broken white-and-shadowed expanse of the wood beyond. There, somewhere between the house and the gate at the far end of the orchard – she looked for a likely spot, beyond the kitchen garden but within sight of the house – Maria-Theresa had been given the first of her two burials that Sunday afternoon, six weeks ago, at the end of October. Ute tried to imagine Peter's state of mind that day.

Of course Peter had not acted alone, she realised; he was not even the father – here Ute blinked, forcing her thoughts onwards – he was not, surely, the father of Johanna's baby. But since the death of the elder Doctor Koenig, and possibly for some time before it, Peter had been the prime mover in this household. He was used to making the decisions here, and being obeyed. Moreover, there was something theatrical and perverse, even gleeful, in the claim of a missing-then-discovered baby that suggested to Ute it was of Peter Koenig's designing. The plan, or rather the unplanned fabrication, had an absurd quality that seemed to issue from his mind, and no one else's. Peter, she thought, had concocted a drama that was only just credible, to see if he would be caught in the lie.

So, how had it happened? Ute looked down, her eyes following the snowy path from the kitchen garden past the sheds and towards the orchard. There, she thought, settling on the first patch of clear ground, where a few piles of rubble and a tin bucket protruded from the snow: there, or thereabouts, was where they dug the grave. It was a natural disposal area, near the house and relatively free of tree roots. While Peter watched and Heinrich laboured – or perhaps on this occasion, both men worked together – they noticed Elias Frankel at the back door, with a parcel for Johanna.

Had they seen him approach? Ute wondered. She looked down to the end of the orchard, where a gate – now scarcely visible in the snow – led into the garden from the wood. Had Elias sauntered past the two men while they were digging? Or had he come around the side of the house from the front, and not noticed them? Either way, the storekeeper appeared, with typical stealth and bravura, at the back door, normally used only by members of the family. From Helga's account, it seemed that Heinrich had gone over to confront Elias – *what do you want?* – while Peter stayed at the open grave, listening. Ute pictured him shovelling earth onto the tiny box of a coffin, or leaning on a spade to listen while Heinrich raged at Elias Frankel.

All the accusations and questions that Peter had nursed in silence, year after year, must have replayed in his head while he watched the row. It was almost a proxy fight, with Heinrich standing in for Peter; a rehearsal for the tirade that Peter dreamed of unleashing on Elias. How was it that Friedrich Koenig – *Papa* – had been lured to the Frankel place, again and again, to dance with Ida and her boys, while his own wife, here at home, was quietly losing her mind? Why was it that Doctor Koenig would mark pages in a book that might be of interest to the brilliant young Elias, or trap a butterfly for Elias Frankel's collection, while his own son struggled through the medical textbooks, without companionship or encouragement? Why were Peter and Johanna left to eat their birthday cake in their father's study, alone, while a mile away, the doctor paced beside Ida Frankel's sickbed, oblivious to the rest of the world?

But despite his age-old resentments, which Ute had caught in fragments – some spat out by Peter, in angry moments; some gathered indirectly, elsewhere – Peter did not seize this moment to release his fury by joining Heinrich's outburst against Elias

Frankel. He left them to argue and kept out of it because, Ute guessed, he had spied a better opportunity in the timing of the storekeeper's visit. Peter decided, watching the row on the doorstep, that he would have Elias blamed for the death of Johanna's baby.

Did he smile as the idea occurred to him? Did he pull on his moustache?

Ute pressed closer to the window, as if it might help to transport her into Peter Koenig's mind on that day in the garden. The glass was cold against her arm, despite her layers of clothing. A crow hopped across a fallen tree stump and brought its beak down, hard, to crack open a nut or a snail – it was too far to see which, from up here.

✢

While Heinrich chased off Elias Frankel, Ute thought, Peter formed his new plan. He learned that Helga had, in her nervous surprise, told Elias that the baby was sleeping; and this mild, apparently inconsequential lie gave Peter the perfect excuse to rouse the others into a state of alarm. 'Don't you see?' he was able to tell Johanna, Heinrich, and even Helga herself. 'If Elias or anyone else raises a question about Maria-Theresa; if even a hint of possible infanticide reaches the authorities tomorrow, when I send off her death certificate, then we are all in dire trouble. Is that what you want – to be arrested for murdering your child?' Or, an even better threat, guaranteed to spur Heinrich into new, desperate action: *Do you want our neighbours to know that you produced a child so inadequate that the only solution was to let it die?*

Having persuaded the broken couple to protect themselves by his scheme, under his direction, Peter finished heaping earth into the grave, spadeful by spadeful, until it was level with the ground. Then he hid the square of fresh earth by placing, Ute guessed, the old oil drum over it, to conceal the grave from a casual glance. No one would notice anything out of place, or step closer to look . . . except, perhaps, Ute.

Peter knew that his wife was always in the garden. Did he worry about that? Yes, she thought. He had an idea. He decided to give her a distraction, something else to catch and absorb her interest, to prevent her from nosing around the area and finding the fresh grave. So he gathered a pile of twigs, ready to be lit. It was a dry day, and it would be a dry night. Peter knew she would not be able to resist.

Ute did not resist. She puzzled over the bonfire next morning, from this window, but accepted – or at least, did not challenge – Peter's explanation: that he and Heinrich were about to light the fire when the baby's crib was discovered empty, with its little blanket cast aside. While the police were summoned, she went downstairs and set fire to the twigs, unaware that the baby was dead in the ground beneath her feet.

Was Peter enjoying himself by this time? Ute wondered. He was having an adventure. He had tricked his wife. He had assigned dramatic roles to the rest of the household, no doubt instructing them how to mention Elias Frankel's name – *quietly; wait for the question about visitors and then drop it in*. He had bullied Helga into supporting a lie which hurt and disgusted her, because it shamed his mother.

And then Constable Hildebrandt arrived. Ute took a deep breath, to calm the agitation she felt at remembering that joyful encounter in the light of this new understanding. Or had the understanding always been there, in the back of her mind?

Peter went out of the house that morning, Ute remembered, just as the police motorcycle was heard chugging up the lane. Was it to size up his adversary from a safe distance? She suspected that he did not go far – into the wood, perhaps, or the clutch of trees opposite the front of the house, where he could watch the constable clambering out of the sidecar. Or perhaps Peter made himself absent because he did not yet trust himself to play his own role well? He was too nervous. Too excited.

The constable did not stay in the nursery and listen to Johanna lie, as he was expected to do. He came into the orchard, to join Ute at the bonfire. He looked around with those wary eyes of his; and his scrutiny must have thrilled and unnerved Peter, Ute thought. Here was a shrewd opponent – a little too shrewd, even. As soon as Constable Hildebrandt left on that Monday morning, Peter returned to the house and stood at the back door, Ute remembered, frowning across the garden. Was he wondering if the constable would return with a team of men to dig it up? Did he decide to hurry to the next stage of his plan – to disinter the corpse and move it to the log pile?

She stared down at the snow-covered spot where she had stood with Constable Hildebrandt that day, by the fire; where he had stumbled. She crossed her arms, remembering how his hand felt against hers.

After a moment, once she was satisfied with her own imagined reconstruction of events, Ute turned away from the window. It was done now. Time to go.

Leaning over the bed, she gathered up the fragments of her letter which were scattered on the sheet, finding the salutation on one of them: *Dear Herr Constable.* Peter must have retrieved the letter from the wastebasket hours after she wrote it. He knew from the start, then, that Ute had met the constable and was still thinking about him in lonely moments, in the night. Why had Peter kept the letter until now, she wondered, unless it had given him some pleasure to do so? Did he want her to betray him, so that he could reject her, if and when it suited him, without compunction?

Tucking the scraps of paper carefully into the pocket of her coat, Ute picked up her suitcase and called to the dog.

✠

Johanna Koenig was waiting for her on the landing, right outside Peter's bedroom. Ute almost bumped into her and stopped with a gasp of surprise, frozen under the woman's direct, unblinking gaze. Johanna's arms were crossed over an apron she had taken to wearing in recent weeks. It bore streaks of the blue paint she was using to redecorate the nursery. When Ute had last looked into the room, from the parlour, a few days ago, she had found Johanna painting stars and snowflakes, among other symbols, on the wall. From downstairs, Ute could hear Dirk's wordless cries: he was in the nursery now, contributing, perhaps, to his mother's artistic project.

'Helga tells me you're leaving,' Johanna said, assessing the evidence with a swift movement of the head, which made the curls of her hair bounce on her shoulders. 'Are you coming back?'

Ute did not know how to answer.

'I hope so,' Johanna continued. 'You're doing something brave – good for you. But come back, afterwards.'

Ute glanced at the Kaiser, who was waiting, and then back at Johanna. 'What about you?' she asked. 'Have you considered moving away?'

After a silence Johanna answered, with a brisk smile, 'Don't be silly. Where else would I have so much fun?' A harsh, mute cry rose up the stairs, but she made no sign of hearing it. 'I've invited the new schoolmaster to have coffee with me this afternoon,' she went on. 'He was pulling a toboggan up the lane there yesterday, and I went to talk to him. Fresh from the seminary, apparently. I don't know what we'll talk about.' She returned her attention to Ute and paused. 'I suppose we should . . .' she began, hesitating again. The act of saying goodbye seemed to flummox her, as if Ute's departure posed a new challenge to the precarious stability of Johanna's world.

With awkward suddenness she held out her hand, and then noticed it was streaked with fresh paint. 'Oh, wait.' Withdrawing it, she began to wipe off the paint with her apron.

Ute, interrupting, clasped the woman's arms and reached up to kiss her cheek instead. 'Goodbye, Johanna,' she said.

# 27.

Theodore Hildebrandt spent the period of Elias Frankel's incarceration trying to find Ute Koenig, and at the same time, to forget her. He succeeded in neither task. He also tried to convince himself that the crisis surrounding Elias Frankel was over, following the trial; that the knot of problems involving the Hindelheim storekeeper and his neighbours had finally come loose. There too, Theodore failed.

From a telephone booth in Angenberg's central telegraph office, he learned from the Koenigs' housekeeper that Ute had gone away for a while – some weeks at least – for the sake of her health. Theodore expressed his surprise that a lifelong resident of Hindelheim should suddenly find the climate there hard to endure, and asked if she was staying with a relative or friend, and where; but the housekeeper repeated that she had nothing more to tell him, and put down the phone.

Searching through registers at the Town Hall, he found the details of Ute's marriage to Peter Koenig, and traced the few individuals who shared her maiden name, Prinz, to their deaths. *Ernesta Prinz, d. 5 April 1923, aged 68 yrs. Jurgen Prinz, d. 4 April 1918, aged 20 yrs.* There was no record of a parent, and Theodore suspected that the so-called Aunt Ernesta of Ute's letter had raised an orphan, and given the girl her own name.

He started to look for relatives living further away, but stopped when he found a familiar queasiness creeping up on him. He was prying. If Ute had wanted him to know where she was, she would have told him, somehow.

Trespassing one last time, Theodore returned to the apartment in the factory district where he had first found her – so long ago, as it now seemed – staying with Marlyse Pohlmann. But Marlyse was no longer living there, and the current tenants – shift workers at the factory and other, itinerant labourers who moved from place to place, sleeping four to a room – did not even recognise the name.

The search ended at the café two streets down, where Theodore drank his only meal of the day, and ordered himself to leave Ute Koenig alone. She was a young, married woman who, despite his wish that it were otherwise, was still a stranger to him. What had he been to her? He mused for a few seconds, and then withdrew the question before his fantasies could take hold.

All the same, when the door of the café opened, his gaze leaped to it. *Hope*, he thought, *is the last organ to die*.

There was no obvious reason for Theodore to stay in Angen, now that his latest injuries had almost healed, and he had no wish to return to Mittelbach. He had found a room at a boarding house, which he could leave at any time. Where to go, then? A veterans' charity would keep him alive; but Theodore was not ready to spend his days arguing, singing and weeping with other old soldiers. Sitting on the horse had reminded him how hungry he was for life, and falling from it had not dented his appetite. All that had changed in the last few weeks was a shift of position, from inside the walls of respectable society to without. From here it might even be easier to keep watch, as he felt he must do – but over what? What was he watching for, now?

In order to do something, Theodore collected his savings from the bank, such as they were, and divided the paltry amount into two envelopes: one for Pavel, by way of apology for the clumsy use of his horse; the other for Klaus. Father and son met in town one day, when Klaus was in Angen to run an errand for Officer Zelinsky. They ordered cups of soup in a shop near the train station. The place was small, steamy, and cheap. From his skittish manner, Theodore could see that Klaus was agitated, and took it as a sign that Zelinsky was finding new ways to exercise his old grudge against the former constable, through the younger Hildebrandt. But he did not say so.

They talked briefly about Elias Frankel's trial, and Theodore asked if there had been any response to it in Mittelbach, among the road workers or at the Valley Inn?

Klaus shook his head. Nothing. No unusual incidents, fights or rows. Talk about the Wolf Man had died down. The road crew had dispersed for a while, and the farmers had other things on their mind. The Frankel property in Hindelheim, like many in the area, had passed into the ownership of the Dammertz Fruit Packing & Preservation Company.

'So it's over?'

Klaus gave him a wary look. 'Of course.'

Theodore nodded, as if by signalling his acceptance he could make the assessment true. He hoped it was over. He understood that there was no evidence to suggest otherwise. So why was that worm of doubt still wriggling?

Towards the end of their conversation, Klaus admitted that he was being moved out of Mittelbach, to a post as an assistant record-keeper in the police archives here in Angenberg. As of next week, he would be filing documents all day in the basement of the regional headquarters, four stories underneath the chief inspector's office. He did not need to say that it was a demotion, and that he would have to move his protesting wife and child again, into worse lodgings in town.

Theodore had once visited the gloomy, airless basement, and knew exactly why Klaus was being sent there: it was in every sense the lowest job that Zelinsky could have arranged for him. Attempting to make light of it, he said, 'I know the place. Handy for the sewers. The chief archivist has a friendly rat he keeps under the desk.'

'Don't.'

'Don't what? I'm just glad you're finally joining the family business. I spent a lot of time burrowing underground in the war. If you ask me, daylight's overrated.'

'Father,' Klaus warned, silencing him with a forlorn gaze. 'I don't want your sympathy. I have work to do. Don't worry about me.' He pushed the envelope back across the table, leaving the money untouched. Searching Theodore's face, he seemed to form a question but did not ask it. Instead he said, in a tone of quiet finality, 'Worry about yourself.'

✠

The Angenberg branch of the German People's League met in a room above a brewery, on the third Sunday of every month. At the December session, newcomer Eckhardt Gröhlick from Hindelheim was initiated and welcomed by his fellow members. Then branch leader Franz Schmidt asked Ulrich Reinisch to come to the front of the room and present his report on the pressing matter of the so-called Wolf Man, Elias Frankel, who would shortly be released from Angen jail and loosed once again upon the unsuspecting world.

Ulrich began by explaining how he had been able to gain a special vantage point for his investigations thanks to his good friend here, Corporal Eckhardt Gröhlick. It was the Corporal's idea, he said, to take up residence in the subject's own home and pretend to guard it, in order to study the man in his natural, or rather unnatural, environment.

The sharp sound of hand-clapping startled Eckhardt, causing him to swing round in his chair. All the other members were smiling at him, he discovered, as if to congratulate him for what

Ulrich said he had done. Eckhardt fidgeted, and as Ulrich's talk continued, he retreated into his own thoughts.

During the trial, Eckhardt had watched the distant figure of Elias Frankel at the far end of the courtroom, never once taking his eyes off him. Yet Elias had not turned to look into the public benches even once, to acknowledge his old friend. What did that mean? Had Elias forgotten all about him? Or was it, as the others said – Ulrich and the other men who sat on the bench with them – a trick? Could it be that the figure standing before the judge was not even the real Elias Frankel, but only a shadow-form sent to confuse everyone, while the real Elias was out there, free, laughing at them? That was one of the questions that made Eckhardt fidget.

The other problem worrying him was the Frankel store. People said that another man owned it now, and that a new family would move into it, or even knock it down and put a new house in its place. It was Elias Frankel's own idea to sell it, they claimed. The rascal had gone up to Herr Dammertz, bold as brass, in the Valley Inn, and offered him the building and the plot of land, right down to the stream.

But how could that be, Eckhardt thought, when Elias had asked him to *look after the place, will you*? Eckhardt Gröhlick's name was on the door. He had a key to the Frankel store in his pocket. He had mended the back steps, and cleaned the outhouses, and kept the Monsieur's register of goods. He slept in Elias Frankel's bed.

Before coming to town for the trial, Eckhardt had told Frau Gröhlick that the reason he stayed at the store was because Elias had asked him to look after the place.

'Eckhardt Gröhlick,' his stepmother had answered. 'It's time you got this into that thick skull of yours. Elias Frankel has been playing you for a fool.'

✠

Another burst of applause roused Eckhardt, and he saw that Ulrich had at last finished talking. The others were standing, some of them crowding around a table at the front of the room to look at the journal that Ulrich had put out on display.

Eckhardt sprang up on numb feet and staggered towards a tray bearing flasks of coffee and the remains of a cake. But just as he reached it, the others returned to their seats, and a second speaker took the floor. It was one of the men who had come to the trial with them. The man said that the authorities' failure to investigate the more disturbing aspects of this Frankel character demonstrated, once again, that certain kinds of menace were allowed to continue undisturbed in the regions overlooked by Berlin; and that this failure left the League with no choice but to take the initiative in asking the hard questions, and considering the most perplexing, even outlandish, possibilities. To that end, the man had decided to compare the rumoured capabilities of Elias Frankel with those of other suspected wolf men in Germany, past and present.

The man showed them a map covered with pins, which made little sense to Eckhardt. In each of the places marked with a pin, the speaker said, a shape-shifting individual had been found attempting to live undetected among his – or sometimes her – ordinary neighbours. All cases dating from the twelfth to eighteenth centuries could be discounted, however – and here the man pulled out all the blue pins – because they occurred before the development of scientific reasoning and legal proof. These were simply rumours. Those that remained – he gestured at a scattering of red pins across the map of Germany – were worthy of more serious consideration, because they were cases in the modern age which had not yet been satisfactorily explained. 'And by the way,' the man added, turning to look at his audience, 'a disproportionate number of these suspected shape-shifters are, or were, Jewish, which perhaps should not surprise us given what we know of the unstable and mercurial nature of Jewish blood. Now . . .'

He passed around a number of photographs, which interested Eckhardt more than the red and blue pins. The photographs were taken recently, and showed ordinary men, in starched collars and city hats. These were men that 'move through our civilised society as if they were as normal as you or I', as the speaker put it. 'But look closely,' he warned, and Eckhardt did. Looking closely, he could see that the men's shadows were strangely elongated, or absent altogether. There were other, darker photographs which, the speaker explained, had been obtained with some considerable difficulty. These were not to be shown or discussed outside this room, he urged. They bore evidence of violent acts committed, in all likelihood, by demons disguised as men.

At first Eckhardt could see nothing in these photographs except dark, blurred shapes. But as he studied them, the white areas between the shadows became recognisable as body parts, the flesh of animals and women, cut open and leaking blood. 'No one knows,' the speaker explained, 'what tool made these cuts, but they do not appear to be the work of any man-made, manufactured implement.'

The picture that interested Eckhardt most of all was not a photograph but a drawing, cut into a woodblock many centuries ago, according to the speaker. Thick black curves joined the figure of a man to the head and feet of a wolf. 'A man-wolf,' said the speaker. 'One of the earliest European depictions.' The creature seemed to be looking out of the picture, grinning at Eckhardt. Droplets of blood dripped from its teeth and from its claws, which stretched out across the whiteness of the page towards a smaller figure, of a baby. There was a halo over the baby's head, and a cross on its front. Eckhardt wanted to take the picture home, so that he could look at it whenever he wanted. But the woman sitting next to him leaned across and started to tug at the page, so he let go.

✠

Still the meeting was not over. After the man with the photographs came the branch leader, clearing his throat to give a concluding speech. Eckhardt knew that this man Franz Schmidt, a bearded enthusiast with a short squat body, was Ulrich's hero. Franz was a founding member of the League, and a true patriot, so Ulrich had told him. Ulrich's eyes shimmered with admiration as Franz spoke.

'Fact!' Franz Schmidt bellowed. 'Elias Frankel of Hindelheim duped the court by unknown means into rewarding his wickedness with a sentence that insults the honour and memory of his victims. His sentence was, by common consent, a travesty of justice.

'Fact! The beast's young stepbrother, Otto Frankel, is living like a prince under the misplaced benevolence of Herr Dammertz, the industrialist.

'Fact! The authorities have hitherto failed to protect our community from this menace, and are making no plans – I repeat, no plans – to maintain their surveillance of the Wolf Man once he is set loose.

'The question, my friends, is not whether it falls to us to organise a watch. The question is *how*. How do we follow the trail of such a man, when there is a possibility – only a possibility, at this point – that he has the ability to change shape, or even to take two forms at once, appearing in this town and another, in this room and another, or, God forbid, in this world and in another world at one and the same time?'

When the murmurs had died down, Franz asked his gathered friends for their continued commitment to the values of the League, and warned of the need for especial vigilance at the approach of the holy season.

✠

Ulrich tried to persuade Eckhardt to stay on with him in town, while work on the new road was suspended for the winter. He had enough money to keep them both fed for a few days, and he knew a place where they could sleep, and where they had a chance of getting paid to chop firewood and do other kinds of work. Members of the League would help them too.

But Eckhardt wanted to get back to Hindelheim, to the Frankel place, and judge for himself whether it was true that Elias would not be coming home. So he took a lift up the highway to the valley junction, and waited in Mittelbach for two days, lying on straw in a loft, where he looked at his fortune-telling cards and blew on his hands for warmth, until early on the third morning the Pohlmanns' winter sled appeared, pulled by two horses down from the hills through ice-encrusted mud.

When Katharina Pohlmann had made her deliveries, and taken on new provisions, Eckhardt Gröhlick rode beside her on the homeward journey. Katharina told him that right after Elias Frankel's trial, the factory man had come with his agent to look at the store. They stood in the paddock for a while, talking and pointing, and then went away. Two days later another man rode up, and nailed a board across the front door. No one was sure what was going to happen, although there was talk that Elias had got himself a fortune through the sale. Since the new road would pass right by the Frankel place, perhaps Herr Dammertz was going to turn it into a roadside inn, or a weekend cottage for his own family.

Eckhardt found that he could hear the woman's voice only if he kept his head close to hers and faced forward. If she turned aside as she was speaking, or if he looked the other way, her voice vanished. After a while he tired of the effort of listening and turned away from Katharina, choosing silence, and the wind.

In the short while that he had been away from Hindelheim, snow had buried the ground and the surfaces of things, while ice clamped the edges of streams and water pumps and buckets. Ponds froze, and then disappeared. Farms retreated into the sky. Periodic melts had turned the lane, soon to be the new road, into several types of mud, interspersed with half-frozen puddles and dirty, trodden snow. The front steps of the Frankel store had been recently disturbed, Eckhardt saw; trampled flat by the movement of several feet. A board was nailed across the door, shutting him out, just as Katharina Pohlmann had warned.

The sign with Eckhardt's name on it was gone. He hunted around for it on the ground, and amongst a pile of rotting timber, until his palms were full of splinters. There was no message for him that he could see, and no one around to ask. The schoolhouse on the far side of the field was closed.

Eckhardt rubbed his face, wondering what to do. He still had the key to the back door hanging from a chain under his coat, and so he walked around the side of the building, where the policemen had brought Elias out that day, two months ago.

Crossing the yard towards the back stairs, he noticed that someone had cleared snow off the coal bunker too. The lid, slick with a thin layer of ice, gaped like a big black mouth. Who had looked in there, he wondered, and what had they found?

He climbed up the back steps, knocking off a slab of snow with each tread. There was no need to hold the stair-rail, but he did. His breath was coming fast and shallow, and his heart was racing. The top steps were firm where he had mended them, but even so Eckhardt felt that his legs might buckle. Perhaps he would drop down dead, right here where the Monsieur did. The more he thought about this, the more likely it seemed. Something beneath him was waiting.

It was a trap. The entrance to the store was blocked at the front, and so they – or he, Elias in all his shadowy forms, and his demonic family – knew that Eckhardt would come around here, to the back. As soon as he turned the key in the door – wham, he would fall to his death. Elias Frankel had planned it all along. *Look after the place, will you?* As Eckhardt remembered it now, there was a smirk on the storekeeper's face as he made that request. The false friend, the man of many masks had planned to lure Eckhardt to his death here . . .

'Why?' he said aloud.

Nothing answered. The silence was strange to Eckhardt after so much time in the company of the chattering little Ulrich Reinisch. He knew what Ulrich would say. 'Devils don't need a reason, Corporal. Making fun of us is their game.'

Returning the keys to his suit pocket, Eckhardt pressed his face to the icy glass and peered in at the darkness. He could not be sure that anything had been moved, but at the same time everything seemed different. The building that had once been left in his charge now seemed to jeer at him. He retreated carefully, one step at a time.

# 28.

Theodore arrived at the prison gate at seven on the morning of 23rd December, an hour before Elias Frankel was due to be released. It was still dark, and a fresh fall of snow overnight made for cold, difficult walking. He found a place to wait, standing hunched in a doorway while the town woke. In front of him, across the street, the wall of the prison turned gradually from black to brown to grey, and the gate appeared, though the sign identifying it as 'Angenberg Prison: This Entrance for Wardens Only' was fringed by snow and partially obscured. His promptness would surprise Klaus, he thought. Constable Hildebrandt had rarely been early for an appointment. But this was not an appointment, and he was not following an order from the chief inspector, or a complaint from a nervy resident. It was a different kind of summons that had woken Theodore several hours before dawn this morning, tapping him on the shoulder and drawing him from his lodgings with an unseen but powerful hand. The same force had kept him in Angen since the trial, wandering, musing, waiting. He could not shake off the feeling that something was going to happen.

A rifleman will sometimes wake in the night and prepare for an assault that only he knows is coming. A stalker will take up position in a certain hollow, to await the stag he has not yet seen. And so Theodore Hildebrandt stood ready, opposite the gate, watching his breath move through the cold air.

The street was quiet under its winter coating. Two delivery men passed, one with a sack over his shoulder, the other dragging cabbages behind him on a sledge. Another man knocked on the door of a shop that was opening, said something, and was turned away. He approached each of the delivery men in turn, presumably with the same question – *work? food?* Twice rebuffed, he started to approach Theodore. Looking him up and down, and concluding that here was someone in a worse state than his own, the man changed his mind and turned away. Theodore chuckled.

Only one other person besides him seemed to be waiting for the prison gate to open. A young man with white-blond hair paced nearby, hands in his pockets, testing the iced crust of a puddle with his boot.

He might have some other business, Theodore thought, at the prison or elsewhere. He might be a reporter waiting to question Elias Frankel, or an evangelical Christian wanting to blast hallelujahs at the chastened man. If he was here to sustain his curiosity about the Wolf Man, then it looked as if he was the last believer left in town.

There was no crowd of protesters or fanatics to greet Elias, as Theodore had feared there might be. The snow seemed to have dampened tempers, as well as keeping people indoors. *Perhaps curiosity has a short lifespan*, he thought, *like a fly that buzzes for a season and then falls on its back*. The change was so abrupt, it was amusing: a month ago, everyone in Angenberg was looking for the Wolf Man. Now he was about to emerge from behind that wall, and go about his business in the town like any other citizen, and there were only two people taking an interest.

The gate opened. Elias Frankel stepped out and looked both ways down the street. This was Theodore's third sight of the man, and he found himself staring in fascination. Even here, in sober daylight, with the fever of suggestion and speculation long since ended, there was something about Elias Frankel that caught the eye.

He was tall, no question, with a thin frame and narrow shoulders which accentuated his height. Three weeks in jail had deepened the shadows of the long white face, beneath the long black hair. The suit that Elias had worn in court was gone – returned to its owner, Theodore guessed; and instead, he wore a coat that did not fit him in any direction: it hung off the shoulders, sagged in the front, and ended halfway down his forearms, leaving several inches of white shirt protruding from the black coat sleeves. But it was somehow evident from the way Elias held himself, gazing down the street with a preoccupied frown, that he had no regard for his appearance. *Here is a man*, Theodore thought, *who picks up resources – clothes, food, women – as he needs them, and drops them without thinking when the need is sated.*

Elias chose his direction, and stepped away from the gate. Not wanting to intrude on a meeting between friends, Theodore turned to see if the young blond-haired man would call out or hurry after Elias; but the man did neither – he only stood with a bowed head, kicking the snow, showing no interest in anyone. So Theodore stepped out of his shelter, and started across the road towards Elias.

✠

'Remember me?'

Elias looked up at him, then past him, stopping on the edge of the pavement, where the snow, as yet undisturbed, was deep enough to bury his shoes. The wariness in his face suggested that he was ready to flee at the first sign of danger.

'I'm alone,' Theodore assured him, indicating the near-emptiness of the street. There were several individual pedestrians navigating their separate ways along the pavement, and a carthorse approaching slowly down the road, but no groups or vehicles or uniforms in sight. 'No police officers on my heels this time,' he said, 'as far as I know. You're a free man again, Herr Frankel. Congratulations.'

Elias turned up his collar, but did not answer. At this close distance, his face appeared as asymmetrical as Theodore's own, but in a different way: the eyelids opened at different speeds. It made Theodore feel that he was being assessed twice over, from a short and long distance, at the same time. These were the famous Frankel eyes, one direct and demanding, the other slower, sly, shrewd.

'Will you go back to Hindelheim?'

'No need,' Elias replied, with the beginning of a smile. Pleased with himself, almost smug. Theodore could see how this self-satisfaction might both attract and repel people, perhaps the same people, perhaps at the same time. 'What are you doing here, Constable?' he asked, apparently unaware that the title was no longer his.

Theodore wondered whether Elias did not know, or simply did not care, how things had changed in Mittelbach, in his wake. 'Something I meant to ask you, when we met before,' he said. 'The wolf you claimed to have seen, up there towards the quarry. What was it?'

The smile stretched a little wider. 'A wolf,' he replied.

'That can't be.'

'Big feet,' Elias said. 'Wolf eyes. I watched it . . .' He was silent for a moment, looking over Theodore's shoulder into the distance. 'I watched it,' he repeated. 'I know what it was. I can't explain it. But it was a wolf.'

Theodore studied him for a moment, and then nodded his thanks and wished him well. Elias moved on, and Theodore shuffled slowly in the same direction, trying to make use of the furrows ploughed through the snow by the younger man's long strides. Someone overtook him, understandably, and Theodore would have paid the overtaking figure no attention if he had not sensed the man turning to look at him in passing.

It was the blond-haired young man who had been waiting by the prison wall. The man's face turned sideways to appraise him with frank inquisitiveness through a pair of prominent, busy eyes. Feeling a pang of unease, but unable to find a reason for it, Theodore watched as the man continued on ahead of him, into the white winter morning.

✠

'How about this?'

A tiny sound chimed far behind him. He nodded.

'And this?'

The sound started up again, more clearly a bell this time, rung as it seemed close behind his chair. He wanted to turn and snatch the thing, but forced himself to continue watching a dark spot on the wallpaper. He could hear the creak of the floorboards as the doctor moved. A man should not creep up on another man, in Eckhardt Gröhlick's opinion, unless he wanted to have his neck broken.

'Now this time,' Peter Koenig's voice called from a distance, 'I won't say anything. I just want you to raise your hand when – no, don't look.'

Forgetting his instructions, Eckhardt had twisted his head to hear better, only to find the doctor standing in a corner of the surgery signalling him to turn away. He did so, returning to face the wall as a school dunce would, or a prisoner waiting to be shot. Blood pulsed through his head while the rest fell silent. He listened. Nothing. Kept listening. Still nothing. Then a sweet, smoky breath of air on his neck.

Eckhardt spun round, causing Peter Koenig to shrink back. 'I'd like to take a look in your ears,' the doctor explained. There was an instrument of some kind in his hand. 'Will you let me do that? This one first. Try to stay still . . . Does it ache?'

'No.'

Moving to face him, Peter enunciated, 'Does either ear ache at any time?'

'I told you no.' This was a stupid business. He should never have let Frau Gröhlick pester him into it. 'Only the skull.'

'Your skull aches?' Peter repeated, watching him. 'Which part exactly?'

Frowning at the stupidity of the question, Eckhardt lifted his hand and slapped it, palm down, fingers spread, on the top of his head. What the wide palm did not cover, the digits did. Peter returned to his desk and wrote for a while, then replaced his ink pen in its holder and ran his fingertips across the fine ginger hairs of his moustache.

From a cupboard behind his desk, the doctor found and extracted an ear horn, which he placed on the desk. 'I can let you borrow this,' he said, taking care to pronounce the words clearly and to keep his eyes on Eckhardt as he spoke. 'And if you want to keep it, I'll help you apply to the Ministry for an injured veteran grant.'

Eckhardt stared at the contraption. 'I don't need that,' he said. 'I'm not deaf.'

Peter Koenig brought his hands together but did not answer.

Eckhardt felt the ache starting up again, at the base of his skull. He almost got up and left, but knew if he did that, he would never find out the answer to his question. There was no one else to ask. So he drew in a breath, and said, 'Is it a curse?'

The doctor's eyebrows lifted. 'Say that again?'

'A curse! Is. It. A. Curse—'

'All right, Eckhardt. I understand.' He raised a hand and made a pressing motion with it, signalling Eckhardt to sit still in his chair, which he tried to do. Peter watched him. 'Why do you think someone might have put a curse on you?'

Eckhardt shrugged. 'I thought you'd be able to tell. If it is or not.'

'Does this have something to do with the Frankels?' the doctor asked. 'I gather you stayed there for a while, in the empty house. That was brave.'

'Why? Doctor. Why was it brave?'

He watched as Peter Koenig waved a hand in the air, replying, 'One hears reports. I don't know that they're true.' After a pause, the doctor went on, 'It's most likely that your hearing was damaged in the war, Eckhardt. Deafness is a common result of exposure to loud artillery of any sort. A shell exploding near you—'

'What about the ache?'

Peter nodded. 'That too. It could be a nervous condition brought on by the experience.' He paused then went on. 'Or the cause could be, as you suggest, something more . . . intangible.'

Eckhardt waited for an answer that made sense.

Leaning forward, the doctor continued, 'Modern secular science does not recognise the categories of good and evil, or the power of prayers and spells. Curses. I cannot tell you whether witchcraft exists, Eckhardt. And I'm afraid there's no way that I can establish whether it has been used in this case, to rob you of your hearing and cause you pain.' He paused to meet his patient's gaze. 'But nor can I rule it out.'

⁕

*A wolf.* Theodore shut his eyes, remembering the confidence of Elias Frankel's answer, the slanting smile that crept up his long jaw to his eyes. *Big feet. Wolf eyes. I watched it . . .* And so did Theodore, at this moment, in his mind. He could see the mythical creature. He would go on seeing it, like this, whenever he shut his eyes, until he found out exactly what was behind that confidence. *I can't explain it. But it was a wolf.*

He started with Pavel. If anyone had come across wild dogs, or an escaped circus animal, or stories of the same, it would be the gypsies – so Theodore thought. Returning to the camp early in the New Year, he asked and asked again, and was passed from one person, who did not know, to the next, who might know something . . . but who did not.

Returning to the Public Library, he asked the librarian for help. She brought out zoological studies and works on natural history, in heavy leather bindings; newspapers, regional and national, with an index volume running from the last century to the present day; a dozen types of encyclopaedia, and on and on. It was a game of hunt-the-needle, but with a hundred haystacks to search instead of one. The librarian seemed determined to rig the game against him, making this simple question impossible to answer. Theodore left the library with blurred vision and a new suspicion regarding the sanity of keepers of books.

He tried to persuade Klaus to search the police archives for permits granted to circus troops within the last year, or for reports of sheep-stealing and maimed cattle that could indicate the presence of a wild or escaped wolf. But Klaus met the request with a sorrowful plea that his father find some new occupation.

For the sake of maintaining this fragile bond with his son, Theodore looked for employment that would keep him in Angenberg and pay for his room at the boarding house. In February, with a sum total of five marks left in his possession – two in his pocket, three under the mattress in his rented room – he found a job in a tailor's shop. There he was given general duties, such as sweeping the floor and rolling up fabric after the cutting work was done. He liked the quietness at the back of the shop, where the tailor and his assistant worked in near-silence, and the drama of the front room, where townsfolk came in to clothe themselves for life's various performances.

One day, when he was clearing up scraps of thread, Theodore paused to remember Ute Koenig, standing by the bonfire, referring to a children's tale about invisible elves that helped a shoemaker at night, cutting and preparing his last pieces of leather to be sewn the next day. As always, he tried to put the memory from his mind, knowing that it would return, in another form, a few hours later.

Whenever Hindelheim was mentioned in a conversation, Theodore would stop to listen. When Professor Stefan von Brodnitz addressed an invited audience at the Town Hall one evening in early March, Theodore stood in the darkness of the square to watch as the guests emerged afterwards. Peter Koenig appeared on the steps, helping a woman into her coat. The woman took his arm, and the two of them turned, smiling, to join von Brodnitz and his wife. The woman was not Ute.

Did Peter Koenig have a new wife? Theodore's mind galloped as he watched the two couples walk together towards a nightspot. What – what had the doctor done with Ute? Had something terrible happened to her, which Theodore had failed to notice or prevent? Did the housekeeper lie, when she told him that Ute had gone away? What if she never made it out of the Koenig house, but was even now stiffening on a wood pile, or mouldering in the garden, having been cast aside like Johanna's and Heinrich's unfortunate baby?

☩

At the first opportunity, a fortnight after spotting Peter Koenig and his ladyfriend in Angen, Theodore asked the tailor for two days' leave, and found a lift to Mittelbach.

An early spell of warm weather had allowed work to resume on the road, and so the workmen were back, felling trees and widening the old track so that the new world could motor along it. Preparations for the Dammertz fruit-canning factory were in evidence too. Behind a length of new fencing, a group of builders stood pointing at the derelict old mill, with a pile of bricks on the ground beside them.

Staying the night with his friend Rudi Hoffmann, Theodore learned that there had been disputes between Herr Dammertz and the farmers and the Transport Ministry over issues of responsibility for drainage and water supply, electrical lines, the fencing of grazing lands, and so on. Unassuaged livestock owners had seized the road diggers' tools one day, causing Officer Zelinsky to request assistance from officials in Angen.

As Rudi told these stories, Theodore looked at his ageing face, and at the velvet coat that belonged to another century. He wondered which of his former neighbours would change their ways along with the new road, and which would simply get out of its way. What makes some people eager shape-shifters, and others the sworn enemies of change? Would Elias Frankel, the man who broke from police custody and snapped off his own chains, be hailed as a hero in another era, or another place, rather than a villain? Perhaps a secret admiration did explain the legend of the Wolf Man, Theodore mused. If we were all free to invent our parentage, who would not wish to be descended from a giant, or raised by wolves?

✠

He rode from Mittelbach to Hindelheim in a motorised truck for part of the way, and then in a horse-drawn wagon. Spring flowers and fresh green grass carpeted the base of the valley and some of the banks. Looking into the spruce trees that edged the road as they climbed, Theodore wondered if the animal that Elias Frankel claimed to have seen was still there in the wood, or on lower ground elsewhere in the region, keeping to the last patches of wild scrubland or marshland, looking for its next meal.

If he had more time and mobility, Theodore thought he would like to visit some of the local farmers he knew and put to them the private theory that he was developing about the wolf – though if anyone were to ask why it mattered, he would not be able to give a reason. He did not understand his own compunction to dwell on rumours that had run their course and died down months ago.

Asking to be set down in Hindelheim outside the Frankel store, Theodore made a slow tour around the property, from the boarded front door to the back yard, where a small paddock or field led down to the stream.

There was nothing to see, except for a few footprints in the last, late-melting patches of snow. No customers to animate the building, and no storekeeper to serve them. Theodore guessed that the new owner, Herr Dammertz, would knock it down later in the springtime, when the road finally arrived here, in order to replace it with a bigger shop or house or inn.

A side gate connected the yard to a larger field, where half a dozen children, just then emerging from the schoolhouse beyond, balled up a few handfuls of snow to fling at each other. The thaw was slower up here in the hills, and the final traces of winter would not disappear from Hindelheim for some time yet.

All was quiet here, he told himself. All was well. The tiny hamlet, ruffled briefly, long ago, by an autumnal breeze, had settled back down to sleep.

And yet. And yet.

# 29.

The closest building to the Frankel house was a small timber cottage, behind a hedge. There was no light inside, but a patch of dark timber roofing around the chimney, exposed by melting snow, indicated that it was inhabited.

Theodore shuffled around to the entrance and knocked on the door. No one answered, but as he was turning away, a man approached, in a hat and coat, from the direction of the school field. He was young, with pale, freckled skin and a pleasant smile.

'May I help you?' he asked, meeting Theodore at the gate.

'I was looking for Ute Koenig. This is – was – her aunt's cottage, I think?'

'Ah, yes.' The man hesitated for an instant, and Theodore could not tell if the pause was due to uncertainty or caution. 'I haven't seen Frau Koenig for some months,' the man continued, sounding apologetic. 'In fact I only met her a few times, soon after I arrived here. I'm the new schoolteacher, you see. Doctor Koenig was kind enough to suggest I use the cottage, as it was standing empty.'

Theodore acknowledged this with a nod, adding, 'Could you give me an address for Frau Koenig? I suppose you send rent . . .?'

'I'm afraid not,' the man replied. 'My arrangement is with Doctor Koenig.'

There was no avoiding it, then. Theodore braced himself for the visit he had hoped to avoid.

✠

It took him half an hour of walking to reach the Koenig house, and when he did, the place seemed subtly changed. A notice at the front door invited patients to ring the bell and enter, which he did. Finding himself alone in the hall, he looked down the corridor towards the back door, where he had first seen Ute, calling – as he had mistakenly imagined, for an instant – to him. From the parlour came the sound of another, louder woman's voice, and then Peter Koenig appeared in the doorway, looking down the corridor with a cup and saucer in his hand.

The doctor saw Theodore, finished whatever was in his cup, and strode along the passageway towards him. 'Well, well,' he said. 'I never expected to see Theodore Hildebrandt again, least of all here. Have you brought a message from my wife?'

'Your wife?' Theodore repeated, bewildered.

Peter looked at him, and replied as he led the way into his study. 'I thought you would have stayed in contact. Aren't you the best of friends?'

Theodore followed him into the room, and sat down opposite the desk as invited. Near the inkwell a stack of letters, perhaps three or four of them, caught his eye. The handwriting was hers. He said, 'I haven't heard from your wife for many months, but evidently you have. I'd like to know that she's well?'

Peter studied him for a moment, then reached for his pen and scribbled on a piece of paper. 'Porcelain factory,' he explained, passing it across the desk. 'Owned by a relative of Marlyse Pohlmann. Ute's working there, so she tells me.' He smiled. 'You look disappointed. Were you hoping for a great scandal? Country doctor poisons wife – that sort of thing?'

Theodore caught the challenge behind the smile. He looked

again at the piece of paper in his hand, replying with a question. 'Why are you giving me her address?'

Stroking his moustache, Peter considered. He said, 'You and I had a tug-of-war, Hildebrandt. I think I won, didn't I?' When Theodore did not contradict him, he gestured at the piece of paper. 'Call it a . . .'

'Booby prize?' Theodore supplied. 'A consolation?'

'If you wish.'

'You're giving me permission to seek out your wife,' he observed, 'after telling me more than once to stay away from her. What's changed?'

Peter threw himself back against his chair. 'You really are finished here, aren't you? They must have sent you into distant exile, if you no longer hear the local gossip. My wife left me, months ago. Walked out.'

Theodore considered this, and looked again at the letters on the desk. The address in his hand seemed precious and poisonous at the same time. If only Ute had given it to him, and not her husband. He said, 'But she still writes to you.'

The doctor shrugged. 'Women can never make a decision without endlessly revisiting the reasons afterwards, over and over, wondering if they've done the right thing, dragging everyone else into the mire to help them out. I wish she'd stop. It's over. Finished. Done.' He gave the ginger hairs above his lip another tug. 'I won't take her back, if that's what you're asking. Imagine how that would seem.'

'How it would *seem*? Is that the issue?'

Peter Koenig looked at him as he replied, 'Reputation is not vanity, Hildebrandt. It's currency. The modern man has a responsibility to manage the connections he has with other people. To give the best account of himself. The new road is almost here, and if one intends to participate in what's coming . . . Well, it's time to give up the notion that one can live in eccentric, pig-headed solitude.'

Theodore responded with a smile. 'It's interesting you should say so. Just last night I was listening to . . .' he paused, deciding not to mention Rudi Hoffmann's name, '. . . a friend talk about the changes up here. He was bemoaning this and that, the loss of isolation, and I thought, what an old dodo. But from what you're saying . . . I'm the dodo, if I don't like the sound of this new way?'

Peter nodded agreement. A new thought struck Theodore, and he swept another gaze across the desk. Not finding what he was looking for, he levered himself up and hobbled to the shelf, which held not one but a whole row of editions of *The Foundations of National Health*, dated on the spines, one for each month.

'I see the eugenics campaign is progressing,' he said.

'It's a science, not a campaign,' Peter corrected. 'But yes, we're moving in a very positive direction. Lots of healthy new babies born to well-suited parents.'

'And you advise the unsuited ones to . . .?'

'Refrain.'

'Or put their sickly offspring on the log pile.' He turned. 'Are you busy in the garden these days, doctor?'

Peter leaned back in his chair with a grin 'I don't know why I once let you disturb me, Hildebrandt.'

'Perhaps you were twitchy about something,' Theodore replied. 'Nerves can make people see a giant when there's only a mouse.'

He shook his head. 'I let you irritate me for a while, that's all.'

'Whereas you continue to intrigue me, Doctor Koenig,' Theodore said. He stayed on his feet, making a slow tour of the room. 'I'd have to admit that the mysteries of Peter Koenig's mind are more obscure to me than the supposed enigma of Elias Frankel. Elias, in the light of day, is no great puzzle. A man who does what he pleases, and does it alone, thereby infuriating everyone. But who do *you* please, I wonder?'

He turned to glance at Peter, who watched him from the desk, silent but attentive.

'I can't decide why you killed the baby, you see,' Theodore continued. 'Pragmatism? The poor wretch would die anyway, in a few months or years. Might as well shorten the wait. Frustration? You'd grown impatient with various things, and here was yet another problem, a defective baby in the house. Something you could do about that, at least. Or was it shame that prompted you?'

'This is entertaining,' Peter remarked. 'Am I meant to respond?'

'Shame,' Theodore repeated, ignoring him, 'at having this failure in the family? Or were you acting on principle?' He gestured at the row of journals. 'You advocate interference, or selection or discrimination – however you put it – over whose bloodline should be continued, and whose cut short. To be consistent, you ought to apply the policy to those nearest to you. That was my first assumption – that you persuaded your sister to sacrifice her child to preserve the health of the race, the nation. But . . .' He paused. 'Tell me, is Dirk still here – Johanna's boy?'

Peter kicked back from the desk and stood up, demonstrating his annoyance with a sigh. 'Shall I bring him in, to prove it?'

'No.' Theodore moved back towards him, reaching his conclusion with quiet sincerity. 'I believe you. Your sister is attached to that child, and you wouldn't dream of touching him unless she begged you to. And she did beg you, I think, when she came back from Angen with a second problematic baby. She asked you to release her, and so you did. Johanna's life before the new baby was constrained enough, but to have a double burden . . . You responded out of compassion, I think?'

Peter returned the gaze, the colour high in his cheeks, but did not answer.

'Which means that at the heart of my mystery, the puzzle of

Peter Koenig, is a beating heart.' Theodore stopped at the desk and faced him across it. 'You should watch out for that, Doctor,' he warned. 'A capacity for pity could be inconvenient, I guess, for a man in your position, if you continue to follow von Brodnitz along that path to progress . . .' He made an inconclusive gesture, at an unknown future.

After a moment, Peter said, 'Goodbye, Hildebrandt.'

Theodore looked down at the piece of paper in his hand, with Ute's address scribbled on it in Peter Koenig's handwriting. He folded it, twice, and turned away.

✠

As planned, the four of them stood ready on the railway platform at Angenberg an hour before the train's departure. Franz Schmidt, branch leader of the German People's League, carried the picnic. Beside Franz was his son, a boy of thirteen whose dimpled, passive face made him look younger. Ulrich Reinisch, his blond hair haloed in the sunshine, carried a large canvas bag containing the equipment they would need.

Eckhardt Gröhlick, the fourth member of the group, took no luggage apart from a pack of fortune-telling cards in one pocket of his suit, and an ear horn sticking out of the other. He did not intend to use the horn unless he had to. On the one occasion he had put it to his ear back in Hindelheim, his niece Raine Gröhlick had screamed at him down the trumpet, and poured milk into his ear.

It was a holiday, and the train was packed, as Franz Schmidt had predicted, with travellers eager to fill their lungs with the first breath of spring. Thanks to their planning and promptness, the four Leaguers were able to find seats together, where they spread napkins over their knees to enjoy a feast of sliced sausage and pickled eggs, while around them the compartment filled with jostling newcomers in hiking boots, carrying cake boxes and mewing pets.

Watching the bearded lips of the expedition leader sucking and smacking as he talked, Eckhardt tried for a time to make out the man's words, but then gave up. Ulrich was listening for them both, in any case, leaning forward with those shining eyes of his to soak up whatever Franz said. From time to time, Ulrich would tap Eckhardt on the arm and repeat prize nuggets of the leader's wisdom. At one point he dug an elbow into Eckhardt's ribs with such force that Eckhardt almost smacked him. 'What?'

Ulrich frowned and repeated whatever it was, and then pointed at the ear horn. Grudgingly, Eckhardt took the trumpet from his pocket and drew it up to his ear with as little movement as he could manage, but it was no good: Franz Schmidt Junior ogled from the opposite seat, and another boy, among the standing passengers, tapped his mother's hand and pointed. Eckhardt flinched as a confusion of sounds wailed down the amplifying tube into his ear – laughter and shouting, rattling, squealing brakes.

'I said you ought not to be ASHAMED,' Ulrich yelled. 'Franz says that's a PATRIOTIC INJURY you've got there.'

✠

They arrived at the town, where they had reserved two neighbouring rooms at a guest house, and where a delegate from the local branch of the League came to meet them. Once the introductions had been made, the man led his visitors through the marketplace, which was occupied by a fair at this time of year. From there, they continued down narrow streets through the old medieval centre, along a residential avenue to the edge of town, where the lanes gave way to fields beyond.

Their destination was the distribution yard of an agro-chemical plant which made a type of fertiliser used widely in the region. This being a Sunday, the factory was closed, but through the fence they could see the locked gates of a garage that housed the delivery trucks. Their guide, helped by other local members of the League, had drawn up a schedule from observations recorded daily over the past three weeks. According to this schedule, the gates of the factory would open at seven the next morning, and soon thereafter Elias Frankel would arrive for work.

From the moment of his release from Angenberg prison, where Ulrich Reinisch had begun to follow him, to his first day of employment at the fertiliser plant, the Wolf Man had been under constant surveillance by a network of observers who met regularly to share notes and discuss tactics.

It was the first time that the League had mounted such an operation, and Franz Schmidt was delighted with its success. The diligence of his associates would bring this outrage to a just conclusion, but that was only the start. Their methods could also be applied, in future, to some of the more routine instances of civic threat which the authorities failed to control. A creature with Elias Frankel's dangerous potential must clearly be stopped – but so too must the less exotic, less famous monsters; men who hid their origins and intentions so well that ordinary Germans married them, and employed them, and trusted their most private thoughts and possessions to them without realising how these parasites would drain away their own identity and power.

✠

The four visitors and their local host spent the evening in the corner of a tavern, discussing their plan for the next day. Starting in the morning, they would take turns to watch from the perimeter fence as Elias came and went, making his deliveries. The last watcher on duty would follow him home at the end of the day, along the riverbank, where the others would be waiting at the place agreed. There they would all gather to stop him, and talk to him, and make their proposal: leave the region, go to Berlin to be with people of your kind, and never come back here again.

'What if he says no?' It was the boy, Franz's son, who asked it, but Eckhardt had been wondering the same thing. He thought he knew, but wanted to hear it.

'That's why we've brought the tools,' Franz answered. 'To show him we're sincere. Once he sees what's in the bag, I think he'll agree.'

'But if he doesn't,' the boy persisted. 'Will you hit him?'

Franz wiped foam from his beard, and said, 'We're just going to warn him.'

'Just a warning,' Ulrich repeated, with a wink at Eckhardt.

Eckhardt shifted in his seat, feeling the familiar pain claw its way up from the base of his neck across his skull. His chest felt strange too, tight and fluttery, as if he'd swallowed a bird and it was still alive, beating against his ribs. He wanted the day to be over, and tomorrow too – but there were so many hours still to get through, with Ulrich watching him and winking at him and telling him what to think.

The waiting and sitting, with no clear idea of what would happen or when, was no better than being back in the trenches, Eckhardt thought. After so many hours of it, the situation began to merge with the war in his mind. In the inn, and again outside in the half-light of the evening, Eckhardt felt that someone was creeping up behind him. He wanted to shout, 'Who's there?' The hidden enemy was watching them from somewhere; he was sure of it. A sniper – behind those shutters? Up in that tower?

'What's wrong?' Ulrich demanded, as Eckhardt turned to look behind them.

He grunted. 'This way.' They took a side street, walking around the back of the guest house. Better, thought Eckhardt. An unexpected approach. Confuse him. Confuse them. Did Elias Frankel have his own company of men, he wondered, as

Franz said? Men he trusted, not from Hindelheim. Men who were not men. A secret network of Elias Frankel's friends, uniting – to do what? Eckhardt was unsure. The more the Leaguers told him, the less he understood. But he knew that if a man was trying to hide, he would not want to be found like this, forced from his hiding-hole. Suppose Elias and his crew had seen them coming and were watching, right now?

A tap on his shoulder. He spun around to find Ulrich looking at him with those wet, incessant eyes. 'Seen something? Someone following us?'

They were at the door of the guest house, lingering in the twilight before turning inside. There were fair-goers all around them, couples and groups of people in a holiday mood, making a slow retreat from the market square, where the stalls had closed for the day. Franz Schmidt Junior implored his father to go with him to the fair tomorrow.

Eckhardt replied to Ulrich with a shake of the head, but he was lying. He felt sure that Elias Frankel was among this crowd somewhere, concealed but aware of their presence. It was the one hope Eckhardt had left. He hoped that Elias would find him at the guest house, or slip a message to him – the message that Eckhardt had been waiting for so long to receive. 'Join us,' it would say. 'You alone. Tell no one else. We need you, Corporal Eckhardt Gröhlick.' Then Eckhardt would join Elias Frankel and his band of wild brigands, and all the rest of it – those questions he wanted to put to Elias – that would all be forgotten, because none of it would matter any more.

✠

Franz Schmidt came into the second room of the guest house late in the evening, when his son was asleep next door. Making sure that the curtains were closed and the door locked, Ulrich knelt on the floor over the bag and took out each item in turn, to check and clean it. There was a rifle, a pistol, a hunting knife, and lastly, bigger and heavier than all the rest, the head of a garden fork. Its handle had broken off, or been sawn off for the sake of transportation, leaving four long metal prongs.

'You remember the rule about this one, don't you?' Ulrich urged, looking up at Eckhardt, who was sitting on the top bunk bed.

He knew the rule. He had been told a dozen times. He said, 'No,' causing Ulrich to rise up with an impatient click of the tongue, and reprimand him.

'Keep it down, Ulrich,' Franz urged. 'Be patient. We're a family now. Eckhardt's our brother, and we don't scold our brothers.'

Having quietened Ulrich, Franz crossed to Eckhardt's bunk and leaned his arm against it. 'I have my doubts about this old-woman folklore, just as you do,' he confided. 'Why should it be with a fork, and not some other way? How do we know if the rules work? That's what you're thinking, Eckhardt, and I agree with you.'

He paused, frowning at the pillow behind Eckhardt's head, and occasionally glancing directly at him. 'We're men of reason, you and I,' he went on. 'We need to be convinced. And I'll tell you something else.' He lifted a hand into the air, where Eckhardt's gaze followed it. 'Until I see Elias Frankel turn from man to wolf, with my own eyes, I won't be sure of it. A scoundrel, yes. Slippery, no question. And cunning – oh, boy, is he cunning! But a werewolf? Let's see. Let's wait and see.'

'But the journal,' Ulrich put in, his eyes wide with alarm. 'All the things he's done. People have seen it – seen him move on four legs and – Eckhardt, tell Franz about how he killed his stepfather and put a curse on you, and the other things.'

Eckhardt looked from Ulrich to Franz, and saw that both men were waiting for his answer. After all this talk, they knew nothing. All this moving about, and writing in books, and sitting in dark rooms with other ignorant cowards and bores – and these so-called experts were leaving it to him to tell them what to do. He breathed out through his nose. His mouth was dry. 'How should I know?' he growled.

'Exactly,' Franz agreed. 'We can't know for sure, until we see it at first hand. That's why we're going to take it in stages, and proceed with caution. First we stop the man and say what we've come to say to him. Then we watch his reaction, and make sure we're ready. If he runs, we strike. If we see him shifting shape—'

'We'll have to be quick,' Ulrich interrupted, stepping across the bag of weapons to join them at the bunk bed. 'The change will happen fast.'

'If it happens,' Franz qualified, nodding slowly. 'Yes, we'll move fast. Each of us will have a weapon, and the fork comes last. That one's my responsibility. We use it at the end, if we use it at all.'

# 30.

Out of the pack of fortune-telling cards that he had found in Elias Frankel's bedroom, the one that most fascinated Eckhardt had an orange circle in the centre, against a blue sky, with winged creatures at each corner. On the circle were small shapes, perhaps letters. He held it above him as he lay in the bunk bed, and waited for the contours to take shape in the grey, pre-dawn light. The curtains were closed, but Eckhardt had lain awake all night, and his eyes were growing used to the dark.

As Ulrich snored on the bed beneath his, Eckhardt thought about the elder Reinisch boy, the one they called Gosling, who had travelled with him and others from the farm country around Mittelbach to the recruiting base. Given a rifle with bayonet, each man was to master the weapon by sundown. At one point in the exercise, the sergeant sent them to lie on their stomachs behind an earth rise that encircled the training dummies. 'I wish they'd get on and tell us to charge,' Gosling had grumbled, smacking at the insects that were biting his legs. The sergeant, overhearing this, jabbed his finger in the direction of the straw men and said, 'That's your enemy. He's coming to kill you, boy. Why are you waiting?'

When he was sure that Elias Frankel was not going to come for him, or send a message to him, Eckhardt placed the cards and his ear horn together on the bed, and left them there. Then he swung down from the bunk, and picked up the bag. He left the room without waking Ulrich, and trod carefully past the the expedition leader's door.

As the sky cleared, he made his way through town following the route they had been shown, turning past a row of houses onto a path thick with weeds that ran beside a sluggish stretch of water. Skirting the fence around the distribution yard, he settled on a position in a ditch filled with rubble. A patch of tall weeds fringed the ditch. Looking out through them, Eckhardt could see the doors of the storage and transportation sheds.

At six-thirty, a mechanical noise started up in one of the sheds. Towards seven, the caretaker crossed the yard, muttering to his dog, and opened the gate. Not long after that, the first worker arrived, and then another two or three. Each man nodded to the caretaker before disappearing into one or other of the sheds.

Elias Frankel arrived next, or someone who looked like him. The slope of the shoulders, and the angles and shadows of his face were the same, but the long hair was gone, cropped short. Eckhardt gave some thought to why he had changed his hair like that, and whether this was the real Elias Frankel, not a shadow version.

He moved with ease through his new workplace, swinging his arms, taking long strides, flicking a cigarette butt onto the ground. Nothing disturbed him. It seemed to Eckhardt that the man was not thinking about the store or the people he had left behind – not a thought for them. Did Elias Frankel even remember his old home in Hindelheim? Eckhardt wondered. Or was he born with new memories every day, after a sleep that was not the usual, human sleep – but more like a short death?

He turned to a passing worker and said something that caused both men to smile. He had friends here, Eckhardt saw as he watched through the weeds, through the fence. That was how it was for Elias Frankel – he slipped without effort through the world, picking up what interested him and dropping what did not, changing appearance or changing form as he chose.

The caretaker's dog ran up to him, and Elias bent down to pet it.

'Here you are!'

Ulrich dropped beside Eckhardt with hissed triumph. 'Franz said we'd find you at the ambush, but I knew you'd be here. He was pretty furious that you took the bag.' He looked at the bag, which lay open on the ground by Eckhardt's feet. 'Hey, why have you— What are you going to do?'

Without replying, Eckhardt positioned the rifle and searched for his target, which had suddenly disappeared. Then the long Frankel face came into view, framed in the doorway of the nearest shed. He was lifting a metal drum.

'But,' Ulrich protested. 'We're not supposed—'

*Click – BAM.*

'Oh,' Ulrich sighed.

❖

He caught the bullet as he was turning, and his hand jerked up into the air as if to wave. The metal drum he was holding clattered to the ground, and the noise of it sent the caretaker's dog into a frenzy of wild yapping. He looked down at his bloodied hand, and then moved his gaze around the yard in bafflement, searching without focus.

Eckhardt readied the rifle a second time.

'Is he dead?' Ulrich bleated. 'I can't see. Let me see.' He scrambled up the side of the ditch beside Eckhardt, jolting his elbow.

Perhaps hearing the noise, the wounded man looked in their direction, standing for an instant with the dog yapping at his feet. Then he lurched to one side and ran. Losing sight of him, Eckhardt aimed at the next moving thing.

He fired, and the dog fell.

'Don't!' Ulrich told him with rising excitement. 'Forget the dog, come on, we have to go after him. We have to finish it now! Oh my. I bet he's behind that wall. Give me that. He can't move far, not like that. Eckhardt, come on. I see him.'

Eckhardt had the caretaker in his sights, as the man moved at a hurried shuffle, wailing, towards his dead dog. But Ulrich was tugging at his sleeve, making it impossible to keep a steady aim. Sitting back on his haunches, drawing fast breaths through his teeth, Eckhardt said, 'Give me the fork.'

'What?' Ulrich was on his feet. 'Oh, right, yes.' He bent and rummaged in the bag for it. 'We'll go and finish him off. Franz won't mind, as long as we do it properly and don't leave anything. Between the eyes, remember? You remember the rule, Eckhardt? That's the way it has to be done.'

Eckhardt dropped the rifle and replaced it with the colder, heavier fork. 'I remember,' he said. 'So the human part dies, while the wolf part keeps on living.'

'No, it's the other—' Ulrich began, his lips opening and closing on the word, as the fork's two central prongs speared his forehead, one above each eyebrow. The blue eyes quavered for the last time before filling with blood.

There was a single moan, almost a sigh, and then Ulrich's jaw dropped, his bloodied face hanging like a puppet from the tool in Eckhardt Gröhlick's hand.

Turning with his arm still flexed, Eckhardt dragged his burden into the ditch and let go. There Ulrich's feet mopped the rubble, while the rest of him slumped in silence onto a bed of rusting metal, red eyeballs turned skyward. What remained of the fork's handle protruded outwards from his skull like a truncated horn.

'Leave me alone,' Eckhardt told the dead man, breathing heavily, the buzzing now strong in his head. 'I did what you want, now leave me alone!' He glared around the ditch, the trench, confused for a moment about where he was. Where were the others? Should he sit for a while? No, there would be an attack. From where?

Everywhere, soldier! On your guard!

He looked up, eyes darting one way then the other. The birds above him were hammering out their excitement with mechanical agitation, like the wind-up toys Eckhardt had seen at the fair. A few squat trees fringed the ditch. Would the next attack come from there? He must be ready. Onwards, march!

But march where? Not to Hindelheim. Nothing left for Eckhardt Gröhlick to do there. The Frankel store was gone, taken over by strangers. Secret deal. Deals between nations. *It was their fault, how the war ended.*

Eckhardt stepped over the blond-haired corpse and stumbled out of the ditch, then remembered something and turned back. From the bag he snatched up the pistol.

Two more workers arrived for work, turning in at the factory gate in their usual, unhurried fashion. In the yard ahead, they saw the caretaker kneeling on the ground, his shoulders heaving as he sobbed. Cradled in his arms were the bloodied remnants of his dog. As they quickened their pace towards him, the men heard a pistol shot fired, somewhere beyond the fence.

✠

Theodore saw his train pull into the platform, and hurried from the ticket counter towards it. He was moving without a walking stick now, and had persuaded his employer to lend him a new suit of clothes for the day, although he would not – and could not – say what the occasion was. There might not be an occasion. She might no longer be at the address Peter Koenig had given him. She might be unwilling to meet him.

But the tailor would not be deterred. 'Think I don't know when the nesting season has started? This is your spring plumage, Herr Hildebrandt,' he had said. 'Borrowed or not, it's

312

as fine a suit as the lady will ever see. Guaranteed to impress.'

In his hurry to reach the train, Theodore did not at first pay attention to the news-seller calling down the platform, 'Wolf Man strikes again! Jewish Wolf Man!'

Then he did.

Slowing, he saw that a queue was forming at the news kiosk. He dug a coin from his pocket and took his turn. Over the shoulder of the woman in front of him, he read the headline: *'Jewish Wolf Man Suspected of Two Further Human Slayings!'*

A carriage door slammed shut, and then another. The whistle blew as he paid for his newspaper, and the train pulled out as he stood reading it, blind to everything else. Turning back out of the station, he rode the tramcar to police headquarters, where he used a plea, then a lie, then a threat to get inside. The tailored suit, having missed its intended outing, was at least of some use to Theodore here, helping him to pass unnoticed through the building.

In the windowless basement that served as the Angenberg Police District Records Office, he found Klaus Hildebrandt wheeling a trolley from shelf to shelf, replacing files. The tedium of the work showed in his face and listless movements, causing Theodore to pause in the doorway and watch him while a spasm of guilt passed.

'Have you heard?' he asked, falling in step with the trolley.

Klaus looked at him, and then paused to take the folded newspaper that Theodore held towards him. Before he had finished reading the article, Theodore interrupted to say, 'We need to find out who's investigating. Thank God it won't be Zelinsky, up there.'

'No.'

'Can you get away?'

'*No*,' Klaus repeated, raising an incredulous gaze to meet his father's.

Theodore saw it, and continued with his hushed entreaty. 'I

want you with me, Klaus. I need my deputy – I know, I know.' He anticipated the objection. 'In spirit, I mean.'

'It's nothing to do with us,' Klaus replied, returning the newspaper.

Theodore gripped his arm, forcing Klaus to wait. 'I kept my thoughts secret from you before, and you were right to resent it. Now I'm telling you. This.' He released his grip and snatched the newspaper. 'I'm thinking about this. I'm giving you the chance to come with me and find out what happened here.'

Klaus replied by turning back to the trolley.

'Don't you want to take a look, for your own peace of mind?' Theodore persisted, struggling to keep up with him as he pushed the trolley down another aisle. 'The tyranny of ignorance, Klaus! Surely we've stomached enough of it lately.'

The trolley creaked between them.

Theodore tried to soften his plea. 'For your own sake, Klaus. I know you've always wondered about Elias Frankel. Come and judge for yourself.'

Pausing midway down the aisle to select a shelf, Klaus gave him a mirthless smile. 'Is that what you think you're doing – reserving judgement, maintaining neutrality? So that you, with your superior wisdom, will be able to divine the truth of the matter. You alone will see what everyone else has missed – is that it?' Without waiting for an answer, he pushed a set of steps against the shelf.

Silenced for a moment, Theodore watched Klaus climb. He passed up a stack of files, which Klaus shelved. 'I don't know any more than you do,' he said.

'But you've already made up your mind. Nothing could persuade you that Elias Frankel is a culprit of any crime, whatever the facts might be.'

'That's not—'

'Yes it is.' Klaus pushed the files into place on the shelf, and looked down. 'It is true. Your only satisfaction is in pushing against things, taking the contrary view. You pushed yourself out, and now you want to stand in judgement over those of us who continue inside, within the system, under the law. We give our best efforts to the police service, and you despise us for it. You think you can do better. It's arrogance, Father. I won't come with you. I don't have the luxury of being an outsider, as you do.'

Theodore dropped his head to consider this, and after a while turned away without another word.

Klaus came down the ladder and held onto it for a moment, finding that his legs were unsteady. At the issuing desk, the chief archivist was pretending not to listen.

✛

That afternoon, Theodore Hildebrandt stepped out of a bus in the town named in the newspaper. He asked directions to the fertiliser plant, and on arriving there, found the gate open. It took him a few minutes to locate the caretaker, who was standing just outside the property on the far side of the fence, telling his story to a young woman.

The woman who had been listening to the caretaker became distracted as Theodore approached. Looking over the caretaker's shoulder, she said, 'Constable.' It was not the correct title, and she took a breath to correct herself, but did not.

Too astonished to speak, Theodore kept his eyes on her, not noticing the weeds he crushed underfoot, or the ditch he passed, or the patches of dried blood among the rubble. He joined them to become the third point of a triangle. Finally, he managed to say her name. 'Frau Koenig.' Then, after a tentative pause, 'Ute.'

Becoming aware of the unusual intensity of their greeting, the caretaker looked from one stranger to the other, from him to her, and back again.

# 31.

Ute Koenig was dressed in an outfit of sturdy green and brown clothes – working clothes, he guessed – and a felt hat that came down over her ears. Looking at her reminded Theodore of things he had forgotten, even though he thought about her every day. The way she smiled without moving her lips. The way she looked at him, without disgust or embarrassment. The way that everything she did and said affected him.

But he could not say any of this yet. They were not alone. The caretaker's eyes drilled into them, and there were other men working in the yard, behind the fence. 'I suppose that we, we're . . .' he began, clumsily, 'here for the same reason.'

'Eckhardt Gröhlick,' Ute offered. 'This is where—'

'Is this where—'

They spoke at the same time, and broke off at the same time, causing the caretaker to stare open-mouthed. Ute turned with some relief to acknowledge him. 'This man was in the yard when it happened,' she said. 'When Eckhardt died, and the other man—'

'And my dog,' the caretaker put in.

'And his dog,' Ute echoed, returning her gaze to Theodore. 'He's been kind enough to describe to me—'

'I'd like to hear it,' Theodore cut in. Anything to win a few more minutes of observation, so that he could stand here watching her and nothing else.

The caretaker did not immediately comply. Running a wary gaze over the newcomer, he said, 'Constable, is it? That's three visits from the police now. Plus a gentleman from the news-paper. I've told them all the same thing. What else do you want to hear? The facts don't change just by telling them over again. Those two dead men that lay here with blood all over them won't get up and walk. My dog . . .'

'I'm sorry about your dog,' Theodore said, and saw the caretaker's hostility melt instantly. *I'm learning*, he thought. Ute nodded, probably in sympathy for the caretaker – but also, perhaps, recognising Theodore's improved manner?

'Died right at my feet,' the caretaker murmured, his voice dropping to a whisper. 'Blood all over her. Her insides coming out. Heart beating like a – like it was going to pop. Why'd he have to do that? You tell me. Why did that crazy monster have to go and kill my dog?'

Before either of his listeners could respond, the man turned sharply to point at a gap in the fence which led from the yard out onto the river path, and to the place where they were standing. 'Saw him run out there from the sheds with the blood still on his hands, towards the trees there,' he said. 'I couldn't see him after that because of the weeds here, and the slope, see? But I heard another shot, and afterwards my men came out from the yard and went running after him.' He gazed along the river path, and shook his head. 'No use. He was long gone. Long gone.'

'You're talking about Elias Frankel?' Theodore asked, to be sure. 'He was the one who ran?' Getting no response, he looked at Ute, who nodded.

The caretaker spoke away from them, into the distance. 'There was a trail of blood going right along the path there, but that's gone now too . . .'

Theodore saw Ute's eyes follow the caretaker's along the path, and knew why she had come. Her arms were crossed around her waist, and the fingers nearest to him were turning white at the tips as she pressed them into her arm. She needed to see where Elias Frankel had disappeared, he thought, in order to accept that he would not come back.

'Devil's work, it was,' the caretaker concluded, brushing a hand across his face. 'To kill a dog for no reason. What kind of a person would do that?'

'I bet she was a good dog,' Theodore said. 'Loyal.'

The man nodded, unable to speak.

Theodore kept watching him. 'And you were loyal to her.'

'What?' The caretaker turned to face him. 'What are you talking about?'

With a glance at Ute, who was now frowning at him, Theodore continued. 'You protected your dog, that's all I'm saying. You kept her in the yard, within your sight. You never let her go lonely or hungry, I bet.'

'You bet right,' the man answered quickly, his chin lifting.

'The men, the workers, they knew her name, did they? Treated her right. You made sure of that.' He waited for the nod, and went on, 'And the new man, Elias Frankel – how was he with the dog? Same as the other men, I expect?'

'Well I – I'm not sure. No, I'm not—'

'Must have been,' Theodore interrupted, 'because otherwise you would have known about it. You'd have known if the dog was afraid of him, and you would have done something. But that didn't happen, did it? Because Elias Frankel was new in the job. He wanted the job – came from a way off, to start a new life in this town and make new friends here. He wanted the wage. He wanted to get on. And you were happy to open the gate to him every morning for the past few weeks, since he started working here. You would see him come and go through the yard. I expect he gave the dog a pat now and again. Threw it a stick.'

'*Her*,' the caretaker corrected. His eyes were cold. 'And I don't know what you're trying to say . . .'

'Did Elias Frankel usually bring a gun to work?'

'What is this?'

'Did they find the gun, by the way? That morning, when the police officers arrived, and the two bodies were lying here.' He looked down, moving his heel across the ground, and casting his eye over the ditch. One of the dead men, according to the newspaper report Theodore had seen, was killed with a fork. The reporter's hypothesis, attributed to the local police, was that Elias had done the stabbing and shot the second man before running off. Theodore drew the caretaker's attention to a stained patch by his foot. He said, 'Was there a pistol here, by any chance, lying in the grass by Eckhardt Gröhlick's feet, or maybe in his hand?'

The caretaker scowled. 'I don't remember.'

Theodore nodded, and looked away. 'No, well, the officers probably took it along with the corpses. Or threw it in the river. Did you hear a splash?'

'You're not a police constable,' the man realised, backing away from him. 'You're not even wearing a uniform. You're an . . . You're a liar, and I'm going to send word to the station right this minute,' he warned, raising a finger as he stepped away.

'If you loved your dog,' Theodore said, to the caretaker's back, 'you would tell the truth about her death! There's no respect in a lie!'

The man hurried away, through the gap in the fence, and Theodore returned his gaze to Ute, who was watching him.

'Picking scabs,' she observed.

'Yes,' he agreed. 'Same old bad habits.' Then tentatively: 'But I'm trying to change?'

✠

They walked down a path that ran past the lazy stream. Ahead of them, a small footbridge led into a cluster of aspen trees on the other side of the water.

Ute said, 'Is that what happened – Eckhardt shot at Elias, and then killed the other man, and then himself?'

'I don't know,' Theodore replied. 'I don't know.'

'But he's alive,' Ute said. She was silent for a moment, her eyes fixed ahead on the horizon, as they walked. After a while, she spoke again. 'It's the same pattern, isn't it? Elias Frankel gets into trouble, or Elias Frankel stands in the path of trouble, and runs from it. And so it begins again.'

Theodore had nothing to say to this. They turned onto the bridge in silence and, without discussing it, stopped at the centre of the arch. There, side by side, they looked down at the brown, sleepy water. A patch of sawdust and grime circled on the water's surface before being dragged with sudden speed into an eddy.

'I saw Eckhardt,' Ute said, 'in December, before the trial. I went to the Frankel store, while he was looking after it. I don't know why – why I went. For no particular reason.' She paused, and resumed, 'I wish I'd said something to him.'

'What?' Theodore frowned into the stream. 'What would you have said?'

'I don't know. Something . . .'

'No one could have prevented this,' Theodore said. He heard his voice, sounding sharp and defensive. It made him think of Klaus.

Ute was speaking, he realised after a moment. She had changed the subject, and was comparing this stretch of water below them with the stream in Hindelheim. 'There's a wide part,' she said, 'where it runs behind the school field and the Frankels' place. It's cold, of course, even in summer – but that never stopped us. We used to play a game on the rope-bridge, a kind of race between two opposing teams. The bridge is gone now, I don't know why.'

After a pause, she said, 'Something happened there, in the

summer before I turned sixteen. It's the reason I'm here, in a roundabout way.'

Theodore did not respond or move, in case it distracted her.

'This game,' she continued. 'It's something we invented. One team on the near bank, one team on the other side. Each player takes a turn to climb up onto the ropes to meet an opposing player from the other side. You try to throw him off the bridge,' she explained, making a gesture with her hand, 'or you dodge past and get quickly to the other side. There's an umpire and – all sorts of penalties and points.'

'Hmm.' He nodded, waiting.

'I was fifteen,' Ute reiterated. 'I'd outgrown the game several years previously, and so had Marlyse and her cousin Matthias, and a few others who were sitting on the bank. We were there to jeer at the younger children. Peter Koenig was there too for once, taking a break from his studies. Everyone knew he was going to be a doctor, like his father. As we "grown-ups" all sat there, thinking how adult we were, Elias Frankel leaped up on the bridge from the other side, and yanked the ropes. That was the signal that you were ready to play. Everyone laughed and called out to him: lunatic! What are you doing? You'll break it! Because he was too tall, you see. Elias was fourteen, but he looked much, much older. Older than the rest of us.'

She turned to face away from the water, leaning her back against the stone wall of the bridge. In that position, she looked past Theodore at the copse of aspen trees where, according to the caretaker, Elias had disappeared. 'But he didn't care what anyone thought,' she went on. 'Elias never seemed to need anyone's approval. It made us wary of him.'

'And curious?' Theodore put in.

Ute met his glance. 'And curious, certainly,' she agreed. 'I went up against him. I climbed onto the rope-bridge to race against Elias Frankel. Pushing in to take some poor child's place, I expect. I was showing off, but not to Elias – not at first.

321

I wanted to impress Peter Koenig, the eldest of the spectators. I remember listening for Peter's laughter as I jumped onto the ropes, and thinking, *He's watching me now.* This is not to my credit,' she added.

Theodore smiled. 'I'd like to think you can talk to me without apologising,' he said. 'Even after this space of time, I feel that we are . . . friends?'

Ute met this with puzzled concern. 'Did you get my letter?'

'Of course.' He was surprised. 'You put it in my hand, as you were sitting in the motor car. I opened it as soon as—'

'Not that one,' she broke in. 'At the start of the year, this year, I sent a letter to the station at Mittelbach, to be forwarded to you. Your son would pass it to you, I hoped.'

'Ah,' Theodore said. 'Klaus – moved, and I'm afraid the officer in charge there wouldn't have, have known my whereabouts.' He looked away before Ute could see what he was thinking; that Officer Zelinsky probably tore open the letter, read it, mocked it – *Hildebrandt, that old dog* – and passed it around.

'Then I'm sorry,' Ute said. She looked as if she wanted to say more, but was held back by doubts.

Theodore steered her back to the story. 'Tell me who won the race on the bridge.'

'Oh.' She smiled. 'Elias did, in about three seconds. He pulled the ropes and threw me off balance straight away. I floundered, trying to disentangle my foot and pull myself upright while he sauntered forward. Then he jumped up and down to make the bridge rock even more. As soon as I could, I – my fist shot out, balled tight. I drove it into his thigh, and – I'll never forget the look on his face, this terrible grimace. Maybe it wasn't the thigh I struck. Maybe I was stronger than I thought. He limped off in agony . . . so it seemed . . . and dropped into the grass with a howl of pain.'

She paused, and Theodore took a breath, anticipating.

'Soon everyone on the bank grew tired of watching and turned to leave,' Ute went on. 'They'd all forgotten about the punch by then, except for me. Elias seemed to have vanished in the long grass on the bank, and I was afraid I'd hurt him badly. He might die. I might have killed him. Peter was walking away, with the others. I wanted to go after him, to hear Peter congratulate me for my bravery or something. For defeating the village giant. I started after them . . . and then changed my mind.'

In the water below them, a heron which had until that point stood motionless suddenly drove its beak into the water and brought up a fish, which it swallowed.

'I found Elias kneeling there, not moving,' Ute went on. 'His head was bent down and that long hair of his was hanging forward. I flung myself down beside him and begged. "Sit up. Elias. Please. Sit up, forgive me, sit up won't you!" Eventually he did, and I saw a wide, tight smile on his face, as if he was laughing inside and couldn't wait to let out his breath.'

Theodore had a vision of the smile widening on Elias Frankel's face, towards his ears. *It was a wolf.*

'I was furious. I hit him, on the arm. He hit me back. We were laughing. Fighting and not fighting.' Ute picked at something on the stone of the bridge, and went on, 'Elias took my hand and moved it over his body, to show me the injury I was supposed to have caused. We lay down in the grass, where we were, not moving out of sight of the others – not even thinking of them, until later.' Looking up, she said, 'I expect you've guessed that I was pregnant with his child.'

Theodore turned to reply, but could only manage a nod.

'Not that I knew then, of course,' Ute explained. 'For a few weeks I persuaded myself that I was in love with him. We were going to run away. We made wild plans and stole a map from the schoolhouse. I waited in a barn one day, three miles out of Hindelheim, but Elias never came. He'd never intended to, I realised afterwards. To him, it was another game, I suppose, and he'd grown tired of it. Of me.

'The next time I saw him, in the store, talking to someone else, I decided never to mention it, and never to think about him again.'

Theodore glanced sideways, and she acknowledged with a smile, 'Of course I did think about him, all the time. But we barely spoke, from that point on.'

⁘

They had been standing on the bridge for a while, and Theodore suggested that they move on. He indicated the cluster of aspen trees, guessing that Ute would want to continue to the spot where Elias Frankel had last been seen.

'And the child?' he asked, as they walked.

Ute answered, after a moment, 'For a while, my aunt seemed to be looking forward to it. It would brighten our lives in that dark little cottage, where she was forever mourning my cousin Jurgen. We made preparations. She made sure I had plenty to eat. Then something changed her mind. Perhaps she saw a sign. One of her bad omens. Or someone said something to her.' She paused. 'In fact, I'm sure they did. Our neighbours could see that I was expecting, and most of them knew whose it was. An orphan girl having a Jewish boy's baby – what damned little wretch would we produce?'

Theodore said, 'Is that why you once told me that no one besides Peter would marry you? Because they knew about you and Elias Frankel?'

Ute nodded. 'As Aunt predicted,' she said. 'It's the only time I saw her cry. She talked until she'd talked me round, and then we went to the doctor in Mittelbach.'

'Rudi Hoffmann?' Theodore felt stupid for asking. Of course it was Rudi. Doctor Koenig had died in the last year of the war. Hindelheim had no doctor until Peter returned home, a graduate, some years later. So Ute Prinz, aged fifteen or sixteen, had lain in Rudi's front room just as Theodore himself did, just a few months ago. The connection made him feel him awkward, and humble. He glanced again at Ute. She was beside him, but far away.

'It seemed to be – effective,' she continued, hesitating on the word. 'I walked out of the doctor's house that same day. But a few days afterwards I collapsed, with no warning, in the post office of all places. There was more blood, and cramping pain. I was taken back to Doctor Hoffmann's, so now everyone in Mittelbach knew about it, as well as Hindelheim. Though by then I was past caring.

'Some of the rumours I heard later, from Marlyse. People said my unborn Jewish baby had grown to an unnatural size in the womb, and could not be removed by normal means. That it tore up my insides, out of malice, to prevent any German seed taking root. I had been taught a lesson.' She turned towards him but did not seem to see him.

Theodore looked away.

✠

They stopped under the aspen trees, in dappled sunshine. There was a scattering of litter in the grass – it was not far out of town – but nothing to indicate whether Elias Frankel had, in fact, passed through here, or where he had gone next. Looking towards the town, Theodore could see an old clock tower rising above the rooftops in the centre, and on the outskirts, part of the railway line.

'I heard that you found him,' Ute said, moving to his side, 'in Angenberg, and helped him. Is that why you lost your position?'

He shook his head. 'I barely saw him. It was a chance meeting. We exchanged a few words. I suggested that he get out of the region. He did the opposite.'

'Of course he did,' Ute replied. Turning to face him, she said,

'I wonder if you would accompany me, Herr Hildebrandt. To the station. Or further, if you can spare the time?'

Theodore looked at her and wondered if he would ever tell her about the ticket that was in his pocket. He said, 'If you're ready to go?'

Looking around once more, Ute nodded. 'Elias Frankel is far gone by now,' she said, 'if he's still alive. This time, I expect, he will keep on running.'

# 32.

They took a bus to the rail station. Ute noticed a squat, bearded man and a boy who was probably his son staring at them on the bus, and whispering. She noticed them again, briefly, on the train. Theodore had insisted on a private compartment in the first-class carriage, hinting that he had a profitable new form of employment and was accustomed to travelling in comfort. There, as they settled into their seats, the boy from the bus reappeared, poking his head around their carriage door until his father called to him from the corridor beyond, 'That's for first-class passengers, son.'

Ute saw how the boy looked at Theodore, and suppressed a pang of unease. She was trying to break the habit of seeing everything around her as a portent for the future. *Don't look for the good luck to break*, she told herself. *This is perfect. This is enough*. The constable – not the constable; Theodore, her friend – had accepted her invitation, and found the train with her, and bought the tickets, she realised, all without asking where they were going. As if he already knew.

When she pointed this out, Theodore hesitated for a moment in the seat opposite, and said, 'I ran into your husband. He mentioned where you were working.'

Ute thought about this, and looked at his suit of clothes, and wondered. She looked out of the window. The journey was to take an hour, and the first part of it took them through flat, agricultural land. 'What else did Peter say?' she asked.

'I think we spoke about the new road,' he replied.

She smiled at the false indifference in his voice. 'I thought we were friends,' she said, quietly rebuking him. 'Tell me what you're leaving out.'

Theodore gave this a lopsided smile, and replied, 'For a long time I couldn't see why you'd married him. But what you told me this afternoon makes some sense of it. If Peter Koenig knew what everyone else did, and didn't judge you – the only one – then I understand your choice a little better.'

Ute nodded, slowly. There was more to it. 'Peter has never much liked Elias Frankel,' she said. 'To pick me up when Elias had dropped me – it was a chance for him to show that he was the better, more decent man. He wanted a heroic project, I think, and I was ready to be rescued. But it's become harder over time, for Peter to accept the choice he made.' She paused. 'I've never been pregnant again,' she went on, 'and perhaps it won't be possible. That doesn't sit so well with Peter's views about the importance of good breeding.'

'Are they really his views,' Theodore asked, 'or notions that he's borrowed from Stefan von Brodnitz, and is trying on for size?'

Ute shook her head to indicate that she did not know. She said, 'I think Stefan has advised him to look elsewhere for a mate.' Here she paused again, wondering if she could tell him the rest; that several times since Peter's return last summer, she had fallen prey to a sudden sickness which was exacerbated, not alleviated, by the drugs Peter administered; that she had sometimes harboured dark suspicions about the cause of the illness, and the intentions of her husband-doctor.

Studying Theodore's face, Ute decided: *Yes, I could admit my suspicion to this unflinching man, and he would not despise me for it.*

328

But because she could tell him, she did not need to – not yet, anyway. Some other time.

The view outside the carriage window darkened, as fields were replaced by tall industrial buildings and warehouses. Ute pointed out the porcelain factory among them, and said, 'We're almost there. I'm . . . glad you're with me.'

Theodore took a breath, preparing to say something, but did not. From his throat, he replied briskly, 'Hmm.' But when the train pulled to a stop, and Ute stood to offer him her hand, he took it. With his palm in hers, he stood to face her, and neither of them looked away.

⊹

It was growing dark when they reached the Pohlmann Porcelain Works, and the factory had closed for the day. The main entrance was a door set into the wall, next to a pair of iron gates wide enough for a lorry to pass through. While Ute found her keys, Theodore looked at a printed advertisement pasted onto a board beside them. '*Warehouse Sale of Fine China. Many items reduced to half of their original price! Choose from Traditional German Pattern, Ottoman Style or New Oriental.*'

The sound of footsteps on cobblestones caused him to turn and look back down the street. A man strode past, clutching a briefcase and folded newspaper, presumably hurrying home after a late appointment. There was no one following or watching them, and Theodore chided himself for suspecting that something bad might happen even now, even here. He had no reason to think that the boy who had stared at him in the bus, and then again on the train, was anything other than the usual curious observer, intrigued by his scar or hunched posture – or, today, by his companion. Ute's invitation had turned Theodore into an over-excited schoolboy, jumping at noises, waiting for someone to tell him: no, *verboten*. He must not waste a moment of this extraordinary evening, he decided, by peering nervously over his shoulder to see if anyone was looking at them. Let them look.

Once inside the gate, they crossed the first, large courtyard between warehouses into a second, smaller yard. There Ute turned into a low building, which was in darkness. As she unlocked the door, a dog barked within.

'Still alive,' Theodore noted, following her inside. 'My luck had to run out sometime.'

The Kaiser did not stop barking until Ute had hung their coats on a hook behind the door, and turned on the lights and drawn the curtains, and told the dog a dozen times to be quiet. She explained that the factory's proprietor, a second cousin to Marlyse Pohlmann, was often away for long stretches of time. Before setting off for his current expedition, Herr Pohlmann had widened Ute's duties from bookkeeping to general supervision, and had invited her to use his accommodation.

'I'd like to think that it was a mark of his trust in me,' she said, 'but I think he's more interested in having a dog here night and day, to deter intruders.'

They were in the first of the three small, adjoining rooms which comprised the manager's on-site accommodation. It was a plain kitchen, with two wooden chairs at the table, and an armchair beside the stove. On the shelf was a selection of china, presumably from Herr Pohlmann's own collection. As he moved closer, Theodore noticed that all the pieces were broken or misshapen. There was a cup with a handle slanting at an angle, and a bowl which wobbled on the shelf.

'Misfits,' he observed.

Ute replied, 'Even misfits deserve a new chance. Don't we?'

Warning that it would be a simple meal, as she had not expected visitors, Ute gathered assorted items at the stove. Onions. A block of butter. A knife, which she tested against her thumb. Theodore lit the fire, and Ute dropped butter into a pan. When it began to darken and bubble, she added thin strips of onion, filling the room with strong, sweet smoke.

✛

The smoke drifted over the courtyard to a path behind it, where Franz Schmidt and his son stood in the semi-darkness of this April evening, peering over the factory wall. The boy had found a pile of broken bricks to stand on, to give him the necessary height. He had a notebook with him, which he laid open on the top of the wall.

'A quarter after seven,' Franz said, checking and then closing his pocket watch. The boy wrote this down, leaning in close to the page. In front of them, on the far side of the courtyard, pale light leaked from behind the curtains of the window. It was the only occupied room among the factory buildings. 'And make a note that there's a dog,' Franz added. 'In case we need to come back at any time, and pay the young lady a visit.'

His son frowned. 'Aren't we going in?'

'We're just collecting information.'

'What if the Wolf Man's inside?' the boy urged. 'Or if they've got him hidden nearby? We should at least wait and see if Hildebrandt leads us to him.'

'Don't get ahead of yourself, son,' Franz warned. 'Ulrich – God bless him – only said that the man could be in Elias Frankel's circle. Only could be, d'you hear? We can't be sure of it. We're just going to keep an eye on him, that's all.'

The boy frowned, trying to fit it all together in his mind. 'But he's not a Jew,' he said. 'What is he, then? What's wrong with him?'

Franz thought about this. 'Well, maybe nothing,' he said, obeying his private rule to be moderate and reasonable at all times. 'Constable Hildebrandt fought a war, son. He's a German veteran, and we respect him for that. But there's a subversive streak in some people. You know what I mean by that, do you?'

331

The boy blinked, and then nodded vigorously.

'Subversives have a fault here,' Franz continued, tapping his head, 'and a weakness, here.' He laid a hand on his chest. 'In the heart. That weakness makes them susceptible to the wrong sort of influence, and so their principles get all mixed up. Now Hildebrandt's found this lady . . .' he nodded towards the lighted window, 'and she's got some bad in her too, so that could spell trouble for the future. Might not, but could do.' He looked at his son, and smiled. 'We're on lookout duty, aren't we?'

They stood for another moment, looking through the darkness of the courtyard towards the light. The cooking smoke that drifted towards them caused the older man's stomach to gurgle, and his son to snigger. 'Come on,' Franz said. 'Let's go home.'

Turning after him, the boy asked, 'How long?'

'What's that?'

'How long are we going to keep an eye on the subversives?'

Franz led the way around the side of the factory, back onto the cobbled street. 'As long as we need to,' he replied. 'Now that Hildebrandt's in the book, the League will always know where he is. We'll keep two dozen pairs of eyes on him. Right?'

'Right,' the boy agreed, hugging the record book to his chest.

✠

When they had eaten, and washed up the plates, they turned into the second room, which held a bed and little else. A door in the end wall led to the washroom, Ute explained. She stood by the bed and looked at him, and began to take off her clothes.

There was no mirror in the washroom, and so when he had stripped naked and scrubbed off the day's various sweats, Theodore stood under a light bulb and looked down at the body that he was about to present to his lover. It reminded him of a younger man who had inhabited this skin – or an earlier version of it – a long time ago, in the farmhouse where Klaus was born. It also reminded him of the man who had worn a police constable's uniform until shedding it some months ago. But it was also quite a different thing; a newcomer to the world, greedy for sensation. He towelled the scar, allowing himself to wonder whether Ute would linger on it or pass over it in search of a smoother place, unbranded, without history.

Turning to the door, he waited for a moment longer, thinking of the woman on the other side of it, and of what would happen when he stepped back into the room.

✜

One night three weeks later, when Theodore was still sleeping and waking with Ute in the same bed, having exchanged letters with the tailor in Angenberg, Ute said, 'I didn't tell you everything about Elias Frankel and me. There was another night, last summer, when we were – together, in a way. Not in this way.'

Theodore lay watching her, as she continued. 'Elias was going around with Marlyse Pohlmann at the time. They had just returned from a trip – to the factory here, as a matter of fact, to visit her cousin. Marlyse gave me all the details. I don't think she was trying to make me envious. I think she was trying to make sense of Elias, by talking about him. In any case, after she'd told me about the fun they'd had, and finally gone to sleep – this was when she was still living with me in Aunt's cottage, just before I moved up to Peter's – a noise woke me in the middle of the night. I heard stones scattering against the wall and a shout: "Wake up. Hey. Marlyse!"

'I waited for her to move in the other bed, and when she did not, I went over to wake her. She pushed my hand away and burrowed back into the pillow, so I went to the door. I knew who it would be, of course, but when I opened it he looked at me with some surprise, as if I were a stranger. Perhaps he'd forgotten that I lived there. Or forgotten me altogether. We had barely spoken in the last five years.'

Theodore thought, but did not say, how strange Ute's existence must have been during those years, when she lived next door to Elias Frankel, watching his lovers come and go, and listening to everything people said about him.

'I said, "It's late, Elias. Or early. Either way, Marlyse's asleep."

'"Then wake her, will you?" he said. "I want to show her something." He held the top of the door, angling his head under the lintel to peer inside. I turned back inside to do what he asked, but when I stepped into the other room, I changed my mind.'

She paused. Theodore watched her across the pillow, feeling that he was in that room, on that night, and that if he listened carefully he would hear, under Marlyse's slow breathing, Ute's heart racing.

'After a minute or two,' she continued, 'long enough for him to think I had been and talked to Marlyse, I returned to the door, where Elias was on his haunches petting the dog. I told him, "Marlyse said to tell you to go to hell."'

'Did he believe you?'

Ute considered, resting her hand on her cheek. By silent agreement, neither of them distracted the other by touching as she spoke. 'Maybe not,' she replied. 'I think he saw that something was amiss. There was a curious look on his face, and he asked me, "What would you say if I told you that I saw a wolf tonight?" I told him he'd be lying, because there were no wolves left in Germany, and hadn't been for many years, but as I was saying so, he just said, "Come with me."

'And so I did. I snatched up my boots and followed. It took us at least an hour, maybe two, to find our way through the dark to the place where he had seen it, whatever it was. I stumbled trying to find my footing, but Elias had no difficulty. We followed the ridge round and then walked down the slope a little way to a clearing. I knew the place. There are no trees there, just a few scrubby bushes and hollows. On a clear day you can see across to the face of the old stone quarry. But this was night-time, and there was not much of a moon. The sky was grey, and I could just about see a scattering of bones on the ground, around a half-eaten carcass.

'Elias said that's where the wolf had been when he came across it. The noise, crunching on bone, is what he noticed first. Then the wolf saw him and moved away. But he was sure, for some reason, that it would come back to that same spot and finish its meal if we only waited. I asked him all the obvious questions, but he wasn't interested in talking. So we sat down on a patch of scrubby grass and waited.'

Again, Elias Frankel's face came into Theodore's mind. He asked, 'Did you believe him?'

'Oh,' Ute said, frowning at the inadequate question, 'I could hardly believe any of it – that I was there, with him, after all that time. In Marlyse's place.'

She paused at the thought, and Theodore realised that this was the answer to another question that had once puzzled him: why did Marlyse Pohlmann gossip to a stranger about the lover who had jilted her? Because of this, he thought – because of the ease with which Elias had shifted his attention to Ute that night, and because it was Ute who saw the wolf. Betrayed in a single moment by her man and by her friend, Marlyse had probably never stopped wondering what she had missed.

'Elias had a pocketknife with him,' Ute went on. 'A small blade, the kind any of us might use for cutting apples. He sat fiddling with it, cleaning it on his sock. There was not much else to do. I hugged my knees, and watched the sky lighten, little by little. At one point, I stood up because my foot was numb. Elias said, "Watch out!" – making me jump. But I turned to find him grinning at me.

'Soon after that, the birds woke, and I told him again that the wolf would not come. Eventually, he seemed to accept it, and we turned to leave. Only neither of us felt like going home straight away, so we agreed to visit Luther's shack in the woods.'

'Luther . . .?'

'A trapper,' Ute explained. 'He comes and goes. Some years we never see him. No one knows where he spends the rest of the time. And I can't tell you whether he was in the shack that day, because we never got there. We'd just stepped over a small gully – I was walking ahead – and there it was, ahead of us, moving between trees. Near enough that I could see the size of it. The length of it. The jaw.

'I stopped dead. Elias moved beside me, and we watched. We watched it watching us. Tilting its head to test the air, the smell of us. I wish I could tell you how it felt to be looked at . . . to be examined by a wolf.'

Theodore met her gaze and said, 'You're sure it was a wolf?'

Ute smiled. 'An impossibility, I know, but there it was.'

✢

Theodore lay awake, thinking about Ute's history with Elias Frankel. It was possible that every part of it was invented, a fantasy she had come to believe. He could see why she might sustain herself on such a fantasy, just as Theodore had sustained himself with thoughts of Ute in recent months. Other people would always doubt the sincerity of Ute's affection for him, and they might be right. So be it. He would keep his fantasy alive, by an act of will, and leave Ute to maintain hers.

They dressed before dawn, as was their new habit. Theodore enjoyed touring the porcelain works before anyone else arrived, opening gates and doors, switching on the machinery, easing his body into the day. As he fastened a hook on the back of Ute's blouse, he told her, 'I was in the barber's chair in Angen, a few weeks ago. There was a man in the chair next to mine talking about an aristocrat he used to work for, by the name of von Lahr, who died in the war.' He paused to ask if Ute recognised the name, but she did not.

'His old estate, or what's left of it, is on the other side of the hills beyond Hindelheim,' he went on. 'The new road will pass close to it. Anyhow, according to this man at the barber's shop, von Lahr was an oddball. He wanted to turn the clock back five centuries, and recreate a lost, ancient wilderness, starting on his estate. So he imported half a dozen wolf cubs from the East – from Russia, this man thought. Smuggled them in without alerting the authorities or his neighbouring landowners.'

Ute turned to face him, brightening in anticipation.

'The estate fell apart within the first year of the war,' he continued. 'All the fencing collapsed. The women who were left behind had barely enough to feed themselves, without sacrificing the last of their livestock or game, so they shot the wolves that hadn't already starved. But it could be that some had already gone.'

'So it could have been von Lahr's wolf that we saw? Or an offspring.'

'It seems possible,' Theodore agreed. He was about to add a qualification, but changed his mind when he saw that Ute had already decided to believe it.

Taking his face between both of her hands, she kissed him.

# 33.

*South-west German Railway, Twenty Miles from the Swiss Border. October, 1933.*

Ticket inspector Klaus Hildebrandt, of the Reich Transport Police, moved with practised balance through the second-class compartment of the Munich–Basel Express, his gloved palm extended to take the travel papers of the next passenger.

Afterwards he would wonder what made him look up from this particular passport, the moment he opened it, to compare the identification photograph with its owner. Which came first: the pulse of recognition; or the suspicion of a discrepancy between the seated figure and his written name?

Too tall to make himself inconspicuous, the passenger had chosen a persona of flamboyant eccentricity. His hair was slicked to one side with oil. A silk handkerchief protruded from the upper pocket of a striped suit, the trousers of which extended some way into the aisle, even though the man's legs were crossed. The hand that rested on the uppermost knee was missing the last finger, and part of the fourth. But rather than hide this maimed hand, the man had chosen to draw attention to it with an onyx ring, worn on the long middle finger. It invited a question to which he undoubtedly had an elaborate answer at the ready.

Klaus stared at the man's papers, and through them, to a dark little room in which a storekeeper glared back at him across the counter; and then to a cold autumn day, on which the same face looked up at him from the sidecar of a motorcycle, jaw clenching, teeth chattering. He saw the sky turning black as his motorcycle tipped over, in the first of a series of falls precipitated by this same man – then his passenger, now his passenger once again. Gripping the passport with both hands, Klaus looked back at the man, focusing this time on his face.

'You're an inventor, Herr Baum,' he said, studying the mismatched eyes, impressed by the barrier they had thrown up. It was almost possible for him to believe from this gaze that Elias Frankel did not recognise him. Almost.

A flicker of nerves was chased away by a bright, amused smile. 'I would prefer the term *gentleman-scientist*, if your people would allow it.'

Klaus kept watching. The man before him was still a fugitive from the law, wanted for the murder of two men at a chemical factory six years ago. Although his father had complained about the findings of that inquest, Klaus Hildebrandt was still inclined to believe that Elias Frankel had a guilty hand in the men's deaths. If they had attacked him, then he must have provoked them. Otherwise, what? Did bad luck simply follow this individual, causing one accident after another?

Keeping his eyes on the passenger, Klaus decided to test him. He said, 'If our list of recognised professional categories were extended to include gentlemen-scientists, would you still be travelling out of Germany?'

He saw the bejewelled, maimed hand move over the man's throat – to hide the movement there as he swallowed. But if he was guilty, he was also brave. The eyes, though regarding him at different angles, were steady.

'Temporarily,' the passenger agreed. 'I have a patent to lodge at Geneva, with my collaborator there.' Leaning forward with exaggerated mischief and conspiracy, he murmured, 'Should I tell you what the invention is, officer? May I trust you?' He put the three and a half digits of his right hand to the side of his face and confided in a whisper, 'A mechanical bird-scarer!'

'Is that so?' Klaus replied, noticing that his voice sounded cold, even as his temperature seemed to soar. He was alarming the other man, forcing him into this strenuous, theatrical performance. He, Klaus Hildebrandt, the lifelong junior destined to work out his days in the pettiest corner of officialdom, was causing his passenger to tremble. The other passengers were quiet, pretending not to listen whilst their lungs breathed in the tension in the air, and their hearts pumped a little faster. Klaus shared their nervous excitement and knew he was the cause of it. He had the power at this moment to decide whether Elias Frankel lived or died; and the knowledge of it sent his blood racing red-hot around his veins.

The passenger who called himself Herr Baum, Gentleman Scientist, glanced at his fellow travellers, and went on, 'If you'll allow me to speak freely, officer; I don't much mind who knows the purpose of the mechanism, but I would rather not take the designs out of my case in the company of strangers. It's the particular features that make it, if I may be so bold, a uniquely valuable invention.'

Elias Frankel's ability to hide whatever rage or fear he was feeling behind this performance made Klaus feel inept. He was being outdone by a better, quicker actor. In frustration, he drew himself back to the choice that he was required to make: accept the runaway's disguise, and risk the wrath of his superiors if he were later to be discovered as having shielded an enemy of the new Reich?

Or seize the showman's passport, causing everyone in the carriage to watch while Klaus fetched the senior conductor and made his accusation: 'I suspect this man of possessing forged identification papers and of trying to flee the country while certain criminal charges against him remained unanswered'?

The nearest passengers were now watching, alert to every movement of the ticket inspector's hands and face and shoulders, noting the length of time he was taking over this particular passenger. Conversations fell to a murmur, and then stopped. Coughing, scraping and creaking sounds jarred in the near-silence.

As the heat prickled under Klaus Hildebrandt's gloves, he closed the passport and handed it back, with a clipped: 'Next!'

The woman in the next seat offered up her papers for inspection. Klaus checked and returned them. As he did so, he noticed a tin of sweets tucked between the woman's thigh and the striped trouser of her neighbour. The tin was open – for their mutual convenience, evidently. 'Are you are Herr Baum's secretary?' he asked, catching her by surprise.

The answers came simultaneously. 'Yes,' said the woman.

'No,' said Herr Baum. Touching her hand, he added, 'She is so much more.'

Klaus looked from one to the other. He had the impression that Elias Frankel almost wanted to go on with this game – to be tested again, to lie again – so that Klaus would be forced to expose their connection in front of the other passengers. There would be a great scene. The runaway, never shy of drawing attention, would tell this ad hoc audience, with a mocking grin, what an idiot young Deputy Constable Hildebrandt had been the first time they were in this situation – releasing his prisoner from the police vehicle and so allowing him to run away. 'Careful now, Deputy!' Elias would warn, with a wink, holding his arms out to be arrested. 'Better not let me go this time!'

Perhaps the accusations would go further. In each of his brief encounters with Elias Frankel, Klaus had sensed the shrewdness under his careless manner – and here it was again, the penetrating scrutiny behind Herr Baum's smile. This man knew his failures. Under the fugitive's gaze, Klaus felt suddenly that he himself was the one fleeing and hiding.

'I always thought—' he began. Stalling, he paused and then began again. 'I always that the best bird-scarer was a man with a gun.'

'Quite so,' Elias agreed. 'But a man cannot be everywhere at once.'

Klaus held his gaze, not to challenge him, but to let the other read his expression. If Elias Frankel knew the worst about him, as he suspected, then there was nothing to hide. It came as a relief to acknowledge this. Eventually he replied, 'I'll look out for your mechanism, Herr Baum. Have a good journey.'

✠

As the ticket officer moved away from them down the compartment, the passengers identified as Herr Baum and his assistant remained as they were without speaking.

He slid his hand from hers, and from the tin between them plucked a candy between his thumb and index finger. Cracking it with his teeth, he swallowed the sweet and took another, and then another – until, gradually, his heartbeat slowed.

From nearby seats, other travellers continued to watch him. He saw their reflections in the window. Letting the last fragment of fruit-flavoured sugar dissolve on his tongue, Elias Frankel looked further out, beyond the white faces reflected in the glass, into the distance, where the fields moved towards him.

# Acknowledgements

Warmest thanks to my editor, Emma Mitchell; my agent, Louise Lamont; Jocasta Hamilton and everyone at Hutchinson; Dr Ben Anderson, who answered my questions with great patience and generosity; Antonia Logue; English department staff at MMU; Neel Mukherjee; Julie Barr and Andrew Macdonald; Matthew Haynes, who supplied the dog without realising it; and above all, my husband, John.

PAULA LICHTAROWICZ

# The First Book of Calamity Leek

Lying in her hospital bed, broken, burned and scared, Calamity still believes that Aunty loved her. For as long as she can remember, Calamity, along with her sixteen sisters, lived in a Garden behind the Wall of Safekeeping. Like it said in Aunty's Appendix on the first page of the Ps: 'Everything has a purpose', and they were being trained for a very special one. In the Ns the Appendix said, 'Nosiness leads to nonsense.' As Calamity sees it, this is what led to their Garden's downfall, because when the sisters started questioning what was outside the Wall, they started questioning what was happening inside it too.

But doubt is contagious. Watching your world crumble is frightening. And people who are frightened can be dangerous.

# JEDEDIAH BERRY

# The Manual of Detection

'Jedediah Berry has an ear well-tuned to the styles of the detective story from
Holmes to Spade and can reproduce atmosphere with loving skill'
MICHAEL MOORCOCK

In this mind-expanding debut novel, an unlikely detective,
armed with only an umbrella and a singular handbook, must
untangle a string of crimes committed in and through
people's dreams.

Charles Unwin is a humble file clerk working for a huge and
imperious detective agency. All he knows about solving
mysteries comes from filing reports for the illustrious
investigator Travis Sivart. When Sivart goes missing, and his
supervisor turns up murdered, Unwin is suddenly promoted
to detective, a rank for which he lacks both the skills and the
stomach. His only guidance comes from his new assistant,
who would be perfect if she weren't so sleepy, and from the
pithy yet profound Manual of Detection.

*The Manual of Detection* is a brilliantly conceived, meticulously
realised novel that will change what you think about how
you think.

'Imaginative, fantastical, sometimes inexplicable, labyrinthine and ingenious
. . . Great fun and very clever. My comparison? Flann O'Brien's The Third
Policeman – which is about as good as it gets'
OBSERVER

'The plot's bursting with as many twists and surprises as you could hope
for . . . It steams along the smooth rails of Berry's neatly constructed
sentences, barrelling round each well-cambered turn with barely a judder'
LONDON REVIEW OF BOOKS